# BEACH HUT
# SURPRISE

*Who's There?*
*Lovers, Vampires... A Body?*

Libertà Books Anthology

# BEACH HUT SURPRISE

*Who's There?*
*Lovers, Vampires... A Body?*

Louise Allen
Lesley Cookman
Liz Fielding
Joanna Maitland
Sarah Mallory
Sophie Weston

Libertà Books Anthology

Published by Libertà Books, 2025

BEACH HUT SURPRISE
Anthology originally published by Libertà Books in 2020
First print edition 2025
libertabooks.com

Paperback ISBN: 978-0-9957046-7-1

Cover Design: jdsmith-design.com and Joanna Maitland
Cover Image: stock.adobe.com/Pictulandra
Clipart: stock.adobe.com/barbulat
Interior Formatting: Joanna Maitland

# Dedication

One of the six authors of *Beach Hut Surprise* was
Lesley Cookman, a much-loved friend of all of us.
Very sadly, Lesley died on 29th June, 2025.
Creating this anthology back in 2020 gave all six
of us loads of fun and laughter. And inspiration, too.
This first print edition is
dedicated to Lesley's memory with all our love.

# TABLE OF CONTENTS

**GRAND DESIGNS FOR LITTLE PIDDLING**
An Edwardian Entertainment *by Sarah Mallory*          **1**

    About Sarah Mallory          47

**GOING HOME?** *by Sophie Weston*          **49**

    About Sophie Weston          111

**THE BODY AT SATIS HOUSE** *by Lesley Cookman*          **113**

    About Lesley Cookman          175

**PAST ECHOES** *by Liz Fielding*          **177**

    About Liz Fielding          227

**I, VAMPIRE**
Romance with Bite *by Joanna Maitland*          **229**

    About Joanna Maitland          285

**GRAPES AND ALE** *by Louise Allen*          **287**

    About Louise Allen          335

**Dear Reader from Libertà Books**          **337**

# GRAND DESIGNS FOR LITTLE PIDDLING
## An Edwardian Entertainment
### *by Sarah Mallory*

# Chapter One

Sir Hereward stood in the bay window of Wakeleigh Towers and gazed out at the vista. It was not an unpleasant one—the Towers' elevated position commanded a view of Little Piddling's beach and the promenade—but on this bright March afternoon it brought no pleasure to Sir Hereward. A heavy frown had settled on his brow and his bushy eyebrows were drawn together. He had a Weighty Matter preying on his mind.

In a chair beside the fire, his wife was reading the latest copy of the *Piddling Post* and, once again, all the articles on the first few pages concerned Little Piddling's larger neighbour, Much Piddling. It was insufferable. It was not to be borne. Sir Hereward did not begrudge Much Piddling its market, nor its larger population, but its position inland was far inferior to the salubrious sea air they enjoyed in Little Piddling. And yet, its name hinted at superiority.

"Dora, something must be done!"

Lady Wakeleigh looked up from her perusal of the society page and blinked myopically at him.

"Must it, dear? About what?"

"As Mayor of Little Piddling, it is up to me not only to defend our noble town and its environs, but to improve them."

"How right you are, dear." She gave him a vague smile and turned her attention back to the newspaper, wondering if she should try the new Spirella corset which, the advertisement boasted, had been a revelation to millions of women.

"I have considered carefully, and I must act." He strode to the door. "I am going out."

"Out?" Dora looked up again. "Will you be back for dinner? It is your favourite; I had Betty pick up some cod cheeks."

"Yes, yes, of course I shall be back. This should not take long."

He collected his coat, hat and cane and set off down the hill.

His destination was on the far side of Jubilee Gardens, a neat little villa in Cosmo Terrace. An equally neat little maid opened the door and showed him into the drawing room, where Mrs Alice Spendlove was waiting. She had been a widow for the past ten years, but a casual remark that she looked very well in deep mourning had encouraged her to wear black ever since, and she looked very much like a blackbird against the yellow chintz furnishings of the room. She came forward, one hand held out, eyelashes fluttering.

"Sir Hereward. How kind of you to call. To what do we owe the pleasure? Shall I ring for tea, or perhaps you would like a small sherry? I do not myself indulge at this hour, but it is nearly dinner time and I know how you gentleman like a glass of wine."

Sir Hereward touched her hand briefly and muttered that he would not trouble her for refreshments. Her effusion unnerved him. One could never be too careful with widows.

"I came to see young Spendlove," he barked, declining the invitation to sit down. "I thought I had left it too late to catch him at the office."

"Rudolph? Why, yes. He came home a few moments ago and is upstairs changing his coat. I am sure he will not be very long."

As if on cue, the door opened.

"Did I hear my name, Mother?" A tall, thin young man entered. He had his mother's dark hair but his eyes were a paler blue, and they peered anxiously at the world through his round spectacles.

"Why yes, my love. Sir Hereward has come to see you." She smiled at her son, but at the same time her eyes went questioningly towards her visitor. However, when Sir Hereward said nothing, she gave a little laugh. "Well, well, I shall leave you gentlemen alone. I am sure you will want to talk business, and I should be of no help at all."

She fluttered her eyes again at Sir Hereward, waiting for him to contradict her, but he remained obstinately silent and, finally, she made her way towards the door.

"Thank you, Mother." Rudolph smiled as she passed him and closed the door carefully behind her. Then he looked back at Sir Hereward. "What can I do for you, sir?"

"I do not like to trouble you at home, but the matter is rather...delicate."

The blue eyes widened in alarm. "Delicate?"

"I would rather the other council members did not know anything of this until I have the thing secure. You see, Spendlove, we need to put Little Piddling on the map. To make its name famous throughout the country. I would like Little Piddling to become the country's premier seaside resort, but for that I need to find some noteworthy occurrence from our past. That is why I have

4

come to you. As our Town Archivist, you will have such information at your fingertips."

"Well, not quite all of it," came the modest reply.

"But you are the best person to find something appropriate," Sir Hereward continued, his tone coaxing. "The visit of an important historical figure, perhaps."

The young man rubbed his nose. "Well, there is the connection with royalty…"

Sir Hereward gave a howl of outrage. "If you are referring to the scandalous liaison of His Majesty with that soprano from the Piddling Pierrots when he was Prince of Wales, then that is precisely the sort of thing I do not want. No. I need a grand design, Spendlove. Something with gravitas. Good God, man, there must be *some* event in the town's past that deserves publicity."

"There is a great deal of material in the archives," Rudolph said, warily. "This could take months."

"We have only weeks," snapped Sir Hereward. "I want you to find me something I can put to the council at the next meeting. But it must be convincing. I do not want to find myself on the losing side of a vote."

Not that it was very likely, he conceded silently. The Council generally fell in line with his ideas, with a little persuasion.

Rudolph Spendlove nodded. "I will see what I can do, Sir Hereward."

"Good. I want regular reports of your progress, but do not come to my office. Remember, I want this matter kept secret."

"Very well. I can call at the Towers…"

"No, that will not work. Lady Wakeleigh is very thick with Ada Arbuttle and would be bound to mention the matter to her."

"Hmm. Mrs Arbuttle is a friend of my mother's, too, so it would be no better your calling here." Rudolph gave a deprecatory cough. "Perhaps I might suggest we meet at my mother's beach hut. She doesn't use it at this time of the year. In fact, very few people go along that way out of season. Hers is in the middle of the row. Rassendyll Lodge." His thin face twisted in a grimace. "You cannot miss it."

"An excellent idea. Well done, Spendlove. No one will comment upon my taking an airing along the promenade." He nodded. "Very well. I shall meet you there a week from today. Same time."

When Sir Hereward had left, Rudolph stood at the window and watched him stride away. An unfamiliar and unexpected elation possessed him. This was his opportunity to make a name for himself. The Spendloves had been archivists in Little Piddling for generations. Their filing system was unique to themselves, passed down from father to son. Uncharitable townsfolk had been known to say that it was a ruse to prevent anyone else taking over the post, but Rudolph knew differently. It was an excellent system. Very secure. While Sir Arthur Conan Doyle's detective might be an expert at solving crimes, this would test the powers of even the great Sherlock Holmes. Rudolph was confident the Spendlove filing system would baffle the most ingenious villain. Although he had to admit it was unlikely any arch criminal would want to break into the archives of Little Piddling, but one could never be too careful.

Tomorrow he would set to work seeking out something that would make Little Piddling stand out from other seaside resorts. An idea so spectacular it would win him the praise and gratitude of his fellow Little Piddlers. Then perhaps his mother would be proud of him. In her eyes he might even rival his famous namesake.

Rudolph was well aware that he had been named after the hero of a novel. When he was a boy, Mother had read *The Prisoner of Zenda* to him frequently and he had seen himself as Rudolph Rassendyll, the noble Englishman, saving his cousin the king and falling in love with Princess Flavia, the king's betrothed. However, *he* would not have stood aside while the Princess did her duty and married a man she did not love. No, he would have carried her off, back to England.

Very much as he would like to run off with Millicent Simister who lived next door, if only she would fall in love with him.

The feeling of elation increased. Perhaps, once he had earned the gratitude and respect of the council, and Sir Hereward had sung his praises, Millicent might do more than wish him a good day whenever they met. She might even agree to be his sweetheart.

It was a heady prospect, and Rudolph could not wait to get into the office and begin his search.

A week later, Rudolph had come up with an idea and he paced up and down in the beach hut, waiting impatiently for Sir Hereward's arrival. When he heard a firm tread on the boards outside, he threw open the door and found the Mayor staring at the hut in open-mouthed horror.

Rudolph could not blame him. With its ornate wooden shutters and the abundance of decorative carving that positively dripped from the eaves and the front gable, Rassendyll Lodge was far more in keeping with an Alpine village than an English seaside town on the south coast.

"Mother designed it herself," he explained. "She is very keen on Mr Hope's novels. She wanted it to look like the hunting lodge." He held the door wider and stepped back. "Do come in."

After a furtive look about him, the Mayor stepped into the beach hut and Rudolph lost no time in explaining his idea for the elevation of Little Piddling's standing.

To Rudolph's delight, Sir Hereward thought it an excellent plan and ordered him to continue his researches. At that, Rudolph found himself bouncing out of bed each morning, eager to reach the Town Hall and shut himself away in the dusty archives.

On a blustery April evening, Rudolph hurried to the beach hut for his final tryst with Sir Hereward before the council meeting. After shaking hands, he held out a thick wad of papers.

"Here you are, sir. I have included all the evidence that might be required to counter any resistance to my idea." He added, trying not to sound boastful, "It is quite comprehensive. I typed it all myself, in the archives, so you may be quite sure no one else knows anything at all about it."

He waited anxiously as the Mayor quickly flicked through the first few pages.

"Good, good. And the historical evidence is accurate?"

"It is, Sir Hereward. I have documented every reference."

"Excellent. Very well. I shall put this to the council on Thursday."

The council meeting was as long and tedious as ever. Sir Hereward did his duty, agreeing the alterations to the public conveniences being built on the promenade, whilst rejecting Frederick Bethrong's suggestion that they should improve the drains at the same time. Good heavens, did everyone think the council was made of money? He gave his benevolent support to the inclusion of a dog show in the summer festival but vehemently opposed a request by the National Union of Women's Suffrage to use the Town Hall for their rally.

At length Edward Simister, the clerk, asked if there was any other business. This was traditionally the moment when everyone began packing away their papers.

"As a matter of fact, there is." To a man, they paused as the Mayor rose to his feet. "I think it is time we considered a few changes to this town."

Silence. He had their attention now. Sir Hereward drew himself up, one hand grasping the lapel of his coat. He gazed solemnly around the table before he launched into his speech.

"For too long we have languished in the shadow of our near neighbour, Much Piddling. That must change. It is time we put Little Piddling on the map. We have an excellent beach for sea bathing; we have the pier. We have the beach huts and the finest promenade on the south coast. Good heavens, we even have a public convenience on the sea front, which will soon include a section exclusively for the use of the ladies." He frowned. "And at great expense, too, I might add."

"And none of these things would have been accomplished in quite so fine a fashion without the generosity of persons such as yourself, Sir Hereward," put in Mr Arbuttle, a colourless little man whose aim in life was to placate his betters.

"There is no doubt that these amenities are all excellent," said Percy Flint, the local builder, "but with the exception of the new lavatories, the rest are so well established that the *Piddling Post* no longer considers them newsworthy. Of course, there is the Little Piddling Festival each summer, but apart from that, I cannot see what else we can do to attract attention to our town."

"Well, I do, Mr Flint. I *do* see what we can do." Sir Hereward paused, then said grandly, "We can amend the name!"

The announcement brought a murmur of surprise from the councillors, and not a little consternation.

"But Little Piddling goes back to the Doomsday Book," cried Mr Bretherson. "It would be sacrilege to change it."

"There is no intention of changing it," retorted Sir Hereward, testily.

"But you said—"

"I mean we should *expand* it. I have been looking into the matter. History shows us that we have a great maritime legacy—"

"That's news to me," muttered Percy Flint.

"A great maritime legacy," the Mayor repeated, glaring at the builder from under his bushy brows. "In the Middle Ages it was a thriving sea port, did you know that? Galleons sailed to the docks along the River Piddling. Ships were built here that carried our brave troops to Agincourt. At least," he temporized, seeing that Mr Flint was about to object, "they carried them across the Channel."

"But the river has silted up," objected Edward Simister. "The port hasn't been used for two hundred years. That's why the Anchor Inn is now five miles inland."

"Thank you for pointing that out, Mr Simister. Although if you read my report, you will see that the fact *is* noted. Nevertheless, I think we can use the information to our advantage. We should look to the sea." He paused to let the words sink in. "Weston has its Super Mare. Lyme and Salcombe have their Regis." Sir Hereward cast a fierce gaze around the table. "I propose that we should call our great seafaring town *Little Piddling sur Mer*!"

There was a stunned silence.

"It's not Latin," murmured a timid voice.

"I am well aware of that, Mr Arbuttle. Using the French name makes a great deal more sense to me. We are on the south coast and almost in sight of France. My researches show that large numbers of *émigrés* landed in Little Piddling during the French Revolution and many stayed. Why, you only have to look about the town to see their legacy. Laporte's bakery and Dumaine's Wines, to give you just two examples."

They were, in fact, the only examples Sir Hereward had found in Spendlove's report, but it was enough. He glared around the table, daring anyone to argue with him. No one did.

"Very well. Can we have a show of hands? All those in favour? Against? Thank you. Mr Simister, will you please note that the motion was carried unanimously."

The clerk hesitated, pen poised. "Actually, Mr Mayor, not everyone raised their hands in favour."

"True," put in Mr Flint. "Now, while no one is against the idea, Mr Mayor, I think we need time to consider it. Changing the name of the town is a major decision. It is not something we can take lightly."

Mr Arbuttle slowly raised his hand. "If I might suggest, we should minute the proposal for discussion at the next meeting."

"Very well, but we must decide, and soon." Sir Hereward sat down heavily in his chair and began to gather up his papers. "I want to announce the new name at the Summer Festival in July. We must have new signs, too, on each of the roads into the town. They will need to be in place ready to be unveiled at the Festival. And we need a suitable memorial to this great occasion. A stone monument, I think, at the western end of the promenade, near the entrance to Jubilee Gardens."

"But that site has been set aside for a statue of Sir Copson Bosomworth," objected Mr Bretherson.

"Aye," agreed Percy Flint. "Sir Copson is Little Piddling's finest son. You know we have spoken about erecting a memorial to our intrepid explorer."

"It has been discussed, yes, but are we *sure*?" Sir Hereward turned to him, brows raised. "Do we really want to celebrate a man who got *lost*?"

"He never returned from the Amazon," replied Mr Bretherson. "That is hardly the same as losing your way when coming back from Much Piddling."

The Mayor dismissed this with the wave of a hand. "Nevertheless, it must be thirty years since Sir Copson went missing. That is history, my friends. History! We should be looking to the future. I believe we should have a monument on that spot, where the majority of our visitors will see it, and it should be emblazoned with the town name."

"It will need to be the size of an omnibus for a name that long," remarked Percy Flint, grinning.

"It will be as large as required," declared Sir Hereward grandly. He stemmed a sudden murmur of consternation by putting up one imperious hand. "And I shall pay for the whole."

As he had foreseen, his munificence silenced most of the objections.

"But what about Sir Copson?" demanded Mr Bretherson, battling on gamely. "Lady Bosomworth will be most disappointed."

"Ah, Lady Bosomworth." Sir Hereward shook his head sadly. "An estimable lady, but, ah, not very free with the purse strings, shall we say?"

"She made a very generous donation towards the public conveniences."

"The original ones, I grant you, Bretherson, but she was not so forthcoming for the refurbishments, was she? Neither did she contribute towards the new heating system for the Town Hall, nor the new wing of the Cottage Hospital."

"Perhaps if we'd told her she'd have her name on a brass plaque outside each of those buildings, she would have been more inclined to stump up," suggested Percy Flint.

Sir Hereward ignored this.

"I have already approached Mr Lamb, the stone mason, and he has agreed to start work on finding a suitable design."

"And no doubt he will make sure that has your name is on it, too."

"As the major sponsor, I believe that is entirely appropriate," retorted the Mayor, glaring at the builder. "But to avoid any doubt, we will ask everyone for their thoughts." He cast a hard stare around the table. "All those in favour?"

A majority of hands crept up and Sir Hereward bent his unwavering stare upon Mr Arbuttle, who reluctantly raised his arm.

"Carried! You will minute that, Mr Clerk."

Edward Simister gave an apologetic cough.

"We can do nothing more now until the proposal has been fully discussed and we have a formal vote, Mr Mayor," Edward Simister reminded him. "I have added it to the agenda for the next meeting, at the beginning of May, which should give us plenty of time to get in quotations for the monument and road signage. Now, is that everything?"

Sir Hereward walked back to Wakeleigh Towers in good spirits. He would have liked to decide the matter of the name change immediately, but another few weeks would not make much difference and he was confident he would get his way. Percy Flint was the councillor most opposed to the idea, but he was about to put in a planning application for more houses on the edge of the town and would need Sir Hereward's support to push that through. A quiet word to Percy before the next meeting should do the trick.

Rudolph Spendlove could not settle to his work. It was over a week since the council meeting and he had heard nothing. He had expected Sir Hereward to seek him out and tell him how his grand idea had been received, but the Mayor had made no attempt to contact him. A casual enquiry of his neighbour gave him no clue as to what had happened at the meeting. Edward Simister had been clerk of the council for many years, and was not in the habit of divulging council business to anyone.

As he was preparing to set off for the regular Saturday bicycle club, Rudolph toyed with the idea of stopping at Wakeleigh Towers, but decided against it, mindful of Sir Hereward's instructions. And perhaps it would not be wise to call upon Sir Hereward today. What if he was shown into the drawing room and Lady Wakeleigh should see him? The sight of a man so scantily clad in his racing attire might well cause her to faint. He would have to wait until the Mayor made one of his infrequent appearances at the Town Hall and find an excuse to speak to him then. It was unsatisfactory, but it would have to do.

His opportunity came two days later, when he learned from Edward Simister that the Mayor was expected at the Town Hall that day. Rudolph armed himself with a sheaf of papers, in case anyone should ask him why he was not poring over old texts in the fusty atmosphere of his basement archives, and spent the morning prowling the corridors.

Fortune favoured him and he came upon his quarry making his way towards the Mayoral office along an empty corridor.

"Good morning, Sir Hereward." Rudolph positioned himself in such a way that the Mayor had no option but to stop. Rudolph lowered his voice. "I wanted to ask you what the council thought about my proposal?"

"What?"

"To change the name of the town."

"Oh, yes. It went down very well."

"Ah, that's good. The evidence in my report convinced them it was viable?"

"Your—" Sir Hereward looked blank for a moment. "Oh, that. Yes, yes, everything is going forward." He gave a hearty laugh and clapped Rudolph on the shoulder. "Couldn't have done it without your advice, my boy."

"Then they have already approved it?" Rudolph felt a sudden rush of pleasure.

"There is no decision yet. That will be made at the next meeting, but I have no doubt we shall push it through." The Mayor dragged his pocket watch out by its chain. "Goodness, is that the time? I must get on, Spendlove. If you will excuse me?"

It took all his courage, but Rudolph did not move. "You will keep me informed?"

"Oh yes. Of course, of course."

The Mayor hurried away and Rudolph made his way back down the stairs to his basement stronghold, elation filling his soul. He was no longer merely Town Archivist. He was Little Piddling's historical advisor. In future he would be consulted upon all manner of matters. Perhaps he might even write a book. *The History of Little Piddling.* It was likely that, after this, he would be asked by Much Piddling to research their past and produce a similar tome. After all, everyone knew they had lost their archivist years ago and now all Much Piddling's papers were locked away, unloved and disregarded.

Rudolph went back to his desk, but little work was achieved for the rest of the day. Instead he found himself drifting off into a beatific dream of fame and fortune.

The prospect of change wrought a transformation in Rudolph. It gave him confidence. He no longer blushed and looked the other way when he saw Millicent Simister. Instead he smiled and wished her good morning. They even, occasionally, managed a little conversation and, on the Sunday before the council's May meeting, he plucked up the courage to accompany her back from church.

It was all very circumspect, Mrs Spendlove following close behind with Millicent's parents while the two young people chattered away in front. When they reached their adjoining houses in Cosmo Terrace, Rudolph was encouraged to risk a further step.

He said, "It is such a lovely day, Miss Simister, I wondered— that is, perhaps you would like to take a stroll along the promenade with me?"

"What, now? Oh goodness, Mr Spendlove, I am not sure if my mother can spare me."

However, Mrs Simister was only too pleased to see such a steady young man as Rudolph Spendlove taking an interest in her daughter. If she was honest, she would have been pleased to see *any* man taking an interest in Millicent. At twenty-two, she was already past her prime and her fond mama had begun to despair of marrying her off.

"I can spare you very well, Millicent, my love," she said. "Off you go now and enjoy the sunshine."

For Rudolph, walking off with Millicent on his arm, the prospects had never looked brighter. They were getting along quite famously.

They walked almost the whole length of the promenade and when Rudolph looked up, he saw the row of beach huts standing sentinel in the distance.

"My mother owns one of the beach huts, did you know?"

"No, really? How absolutely wonderful. I have always thought they looked so pretty. I should dearly like to see inside it."

Her words delighted him and he beamed. "Then you shall." He escorted her to the beach huts and stopped halfway along the boardwalk. "Here we are. This is my mother's hut."

The brown paint stood out in stark contrast to the pale pinks, blues and yellows around it. Glancing at his companion, Rudolph saw a shadow flicker across her face.

"Oh. It is…it is very different."

"My parents visited the Isle of Wight for their honeymoon," he said by way of explanation. "Mother was inspired by the cottage Prince Albert built for Queen Victoria and had the hut—" he drew in a breath, taking in the false support beams, the fancy glazing bars and elaborate carving on the eaves and the balustrade "—transformed."

"Oh." Her gaze travelled over the hut and came to rest on the carved nameplate over the door. "Rassendyll Lodge. That is from *The Prisoner of Zenda*." She clapped her hands together and turned to him, her pansy brown eyes shining. "That explains everything. That is quite my favourite novel."

"It is?" Rudolph looked at her eagerly. "I was named after Rudolph."

For one dreadful moment he thought Millicent was going to laugh. Certainly, her eyes twinkled and there was a distinct tremor in her voice when she responded. "How…how fascinating." She waved towards the door. "May I see inside?"

"Of course." He unlocked the door. "After you, Miss Simister."

Following Millicent into the beach hut, Rudolph was glad his mother had kept the interior plain. There were just a couple of comfortable chairs where one might shelter from a chill wind, a little table and a small cupboard.

"Do you use this place to change into your bathing suit?" Millicent asked him.

"Yes." Rudolph felt a blush heating his cheeks. "Although I do not bathe in the sea very often."

She sighed. "I can swim, but only a little, and I haven't been in the water for years. If I had a hut like this, I think I should bathe in the sea every day, when the weather was fine enough."

He was tempted to tell her she could use the beach hut at any time she wanted, but he refrained. Mother might object.

She took a step back, towards the open door. "Thank you for showing me your beach hut, Mr Spendlove."

"Please, call me Rudolph."

"Rudolph, then."

"May I call you Millicent?"

"If you would like to."

She blushed adorably and he felt a strong and rather frightening desire to kiss her. That, of course, was quite out of the question, but he was emboldened to take her hands and risk a question.

"And...and will you be my sweetheart, Millicent?"

Her eyes widened. She looked startled and snatched her hands out of his grasp.

He said quickly, "I beg your pardon. I should not have presumed, upon so slight an acquaintance." He turned away, mortified. "I did not mean to offend you."

She touched his arm.

"I am not offended," she said gently. "It is merely that—" She stopped and he thought he heard a sigh. "I should be very happy to be friends with you, Rudolph, but I am not...not looking for a beau. At least, not one from Little Piddling. You see, I want more from life," she told him. "I want adventure. I so want to see the world. I have no wish to settle down yet."

"You think I am boring."

"No. Well, yes." She flushed. "A little. You have told me all about your work, remember, so I know that you are cooped up all day in the archives, poring over dusty papers. You must admit that it is very dull work."

"No, no, you are quite wrong about that. It is fascinating, I am never happier than when I am working."

She gave him a pitying look and said gently, "I think that rather proves my point. I am so sorry to disappoint you, Rudolph. I hope— I hope very much we can forget what has happened here and we can still be friends?"

If only he could explain to her how much he enjoyed his work and the thrill of discovering a little-known fact in some obscure document. He especially wished he could tell her about his report for Sir Hereward and how he had been instrumental in improving the fortunes of Little Piddling, but he had been sworn to secrecy. However, when it became public knowledge that he was behind the grand plan to change the name of the town, he would be able to explain it all in detail to her. Perhaps even take her to the archives. She could not fail to be impressed when he showed her the shelves full of rolls, ledgers and boxes of papers that he had scoured to seek out and document the little details that had been required to support his argument.

But that was for the future. Now he had to rescue this very delicate situation. He straightened his shoulders and gave her a smile.

"Of course we can be friends, Millicent. Will you allow me to escort you back to Cosmo Terrace?"

Once again, the day of the council meeting arrived and passed and Rudolph heard nothing from Sir Hereward. However, this time, he was not kept wondering for long. A few days after the meeting, Rudolph came down for breakfast to find his mother already seated at the table, the latest copy of the *Piddling Post* in her hands.

"Good Heavens," she said, by way of greeting. "Have you seen this?"

She held the newspaper towards him and he read the headline emblazoned across the front page. *"Grand Plans for Little Piddling."*

At last. He schooled his face into a look of polite interest and asked her as calmly as he could what it meant.

"Sir Hereward has proposed that the town should in future be called Little Piddling sur Mer. Apparently he prepared and presented a full and comprehensive report, outlining the town's close ties with the Continent."

"*He* prepared a report?" It was as much as Rudolph could do not to snatch the paper from his mother's hands. "May I look?"

"Of course. Dear me. A change of name. We shall need new visiting cards, of course, and headed notepaper. But Little Piddling sur Mer has a certain…*cachet*, don't you think?"

Rudolph was not listening. His eyes ran down the page and with every sentence his anger and chagrin increased. Sir Hereward had claimed the idea for his own. His fellow councillors praised his diligent endeavours on behalf of the town. Mr Sydney Arbuttle was even quoted as saying the move was a stroke of genius. Rudolph read the report over a second time before accepting the unpalatable truth.

He was not mentioned.

Injustice burning in his breast, Rudolph left the house, but instead of making his way to the archives, he strode up the hill to Wakeleigh Towers. Sir Hereward, he was informed, had not yet left his room. When the maid would have closed the door, Rudolph put his foot in the gap.

"Then ask him to come down. If you please."

Shaking at his own daring, he followed the maid into the drawing room and paced anxiously while she scurried away to find her master.

"Well, Spendlove?" Sir Hereward came in and closed the door behind him with a snap. "Is there an emergency? Has something happened at the Town Hall?"

"This has happened." Rudolph pulled the folded newspaper from inside his coat and thrust it at Sir Hereward.

The Mayor looked at the paper but made no attempt to take it from him.

"What of it?"

"The name change," said Rudolph. "This report says it was entirely your initiative. That the idea, the research, was all your own."

"But of course. What else should it say?"

"The name change was my idea." Rudolph spluttered. "I suggested we add 'sur mer', that we use French instead of Latin. It was *I* who sought out the historical evidence and compiled all the arguments in favour. I spent days, weeks, producing that report. All forty pages of it."

"And I appreciate your effort, Spendlove, but really, do you think anyone would have taken any notice if I had put this forward as your idea? If I had told them this was the brainchild of a mere office boy?"

*Office boy!* Rudolph flushed to the roots of his hair.

"But it was my idea."

"Ah, but would you have thought of it, if I had not asked you to look into the matter? That is where we differ, Spendlove. Mine is the creative mind, the intelligence that comes up with the grand design. Your role is to assist me in the execution of the plans."

"But it was *my* plan. *My* idea."

"Oh? And where is your proof? Do you have a copy of the report you gave me? No, I thought not. If you challenge me, I shall merely say I asked you to provide the documentary evidence to support my arguments." Sir Hereward walked to the door and opened it. "Now, if you have said your piece, you had best get back to the archives before your tardiness attracts attention. And besides, there are devilled kidneys for breakfast this morning and they will be growing cold. Good day to you, Spendlove."

Thus dismissed, Rudolph left the Towers and, with leaden feet, made his way to the Town Hall. His hopes, his dreams were in tatters. The honour of raising Little Piddling to new heights would not be his. He would not be lauded for his academic prowess. The townsfolk would not claim him for their saviour. Even if he told anyone of his efforts, they would think it vain boasting.

And Millicent would never think him other than a dull clerk. An office boy.

Somehow, Rudolph struggled through the rest of the day. When he emerged from his basement, everyone in the Town Hall was talking about Sir Hereward's great achievement. For once, Little Piddling commanded the front page with its announcement and had stolen the march on its larger neighbour. On his way home he called into the local stationer's to purchase more pen nibs to find Mr Ottery, the owner, who was already celebrating the extra business coming his way. Everyone would need more stationery, new invoices, business and calling cards, not to mention the guide books that would have to be reprinted. He would need to take on another apprentice to cope with the workload.

When Rupert arrived at Cosmo Terrace, Mrs Spendlove was entertaining Mrs Arbuttle, who had called to discuss the new developments and Rudolph was obliged to listen once again while Sir Hereward's praises were sung.

Excusing himself, Rudolph went for a walk. It was a fine summer's evening, but the promenade was not crowded, and he strode along, trying to clear his brain and his heart of its anguish. Everyone else appeared to be excited by the news of the change of name, yet his had been the work, the effort, the inspiration and he was not to receive any of the acclaim.

The beach huts were in sight and even at a distance, Rassendyll Lodge, at the very centre of the row, stood out like a sore thumb between the pastel hues of its neighbours. Rudolph strode on until he reached his mother's hut and, as he gazed up at the elaborate frontage, a change came over him. It might be brash, some might consider its excessive carving, its shutters and ornamented balustrade as vulgar, but it was certainly not *boring*.

He knew full well that his namesake was the noble English hero of Mr Hope's novels and any house Rassendyll might have owned would never have looked like this. The florid, overdecorated style of an Alpine chalet was more in keeping with the villain of the piece, and secretly Rudolph had always thought Rupert of Hentzau much more dashing than the hero.

Rudolph Rassendyll had been very noble, but where had it got him? Perhaps it was time for him to change his allegiance. In future he would not model himself on the noble, self-effacing hero. No, in future he would become more like Rupert.

He would have his revenge.

# Chapter Two

After a night's sleep, Rudolph was still determined to follow his plan to become more like the villain of Zenda, although he decided that changing his name to Rupert would not be feasible. For one thing, Mother would want to know why. However, he could change his appearance. He began to wax his moustache, encouraging the sides to grow while he stood before the mirror and practised twirling the ends between thumb and forefinger. His hair, formerly shorn neatly around the back, now grew longer and curled daringly over his collar. When he was not working, he left off his bowler hat in favour of a soft black trilby, which he considered gave him a rakish look. It was a good start, he thought. He felt more confident, somehow, and for the first time in weeks he walked with his shoulders back and an added spring in his step.

However, he was no nearer deciding how he was to punish Sir Hereward. Various plans came to him, only to be discarded. Revenge filled his thoughts. Even his Saturday morning bicycle rides passed in a blur. And when he accompanied his mother to church on Sunday, he quite forgot to speak to Mr and Mrs Simister or their daughter but spent the whole service with a crease in his brows, his thoughts very far from his surroundings.

Rudolph's behaviour piqued Millicent, who had grown accustomed to being the object of his attentions. When the service was over and her parents dawdled in the graveyard, exchanging pleasantries with their friends and neighbours, she hung back, waiting for Rudolph to emerge from the church. When he did so, she stood in his way, pretending not to notice him until he was almost upon her.

"Oh, Rudolph." She feigned a small start of surprise. "I did not see you there."

His distracted look was so far from the fawning adoration he usually bestowed upon her that she felt the first stirrings of alarm. She gave him her sunniest smile.

"I have not seen you all week, Rudolph. Have you been so very busy at the Town Hall?"

"What? Oh, yes, yes. Extremely busy. I have had a lot to think about."

His manner was offhand and she sought for something more to say.

"But you have still found time to ride out on your bicycle—I saw you setting off yesterday morning, you know."

"What? Oh well, yes." He waved a distracted hand. "One must keep up the exercise, you know."

"I think it looks very exciting, Rudolph. I should very much like to be able to ride."

For the first time, he showed a little interest. "You would? It's not that difficult, you know."

"Not for a clever man like you, perhaps," she told him, eyelashes fluttering.

"Oh, I don't know." He puffed out his chest, visibly pleased at her comment. He glanced past her. "Mother has turned for home with your parents. May I escort you back to Cosmo Terrace?"

She hesitated slightly for modesty's sake, then placed her fingers delicately on his proffered sleeve.

"My friend Lucinda Grayson has a bicycle, you know. She keeps it at Primly Court, Lady Bosomworth's residence."

Millicent added this last grandly, although she had been there but once, a few years earlier, when old Lady Bosomworth had been persuaded by the vicar to open her grounds for a garden party in aid of the Mothers' Union. It was there she had met Mrs Grayson. Although Lucinda was a widow and several years older than Millicent, their friendship had blossomed during one idyllic summer when Lady Bosomworth had owned a beach hut and they had enjoyed sea bathing together. But that was before Lucinda began her incessant travels, and since then they had kept in touch by correspondence.

Millicent sighed. It was inevitable, she supposed, that the great-niece of an intrepid explorer would want to have adventures of her own. Millicent wished with all her heart that she, too, might see something of the world but it seemed unlikely. Mama was desperate for her to settle down to a life of household duties and motherhood and Milly supposed she would have to do so, and soon, if she was not to become an old maid.

She continued, "Lucinda comes to the area so rarely now that she has offered to give the bicycle to me." Millicent peeped up at him. "If only I could ride, I am sure it would be extremely beneficial to my health."

She let the words hang and was gratified a few moments later when Rudolph responded.

"I could teach you to ride, Millicent."

She stopped and turned to look up at him, her hands clasped before her. "You could? Oh, that would be most kind of you, Rudolph. I will write a note to Lucinda immediately. I believe she is currently staying at Primly. If she is amenable, I could perhaps collect it from her."

Rudolph hesitated. For a moment he had been distracted from his plan to seek vengeance, but now it came back to him. What time had he for teaching young ladies to ride a bicycle? Any day now, inspiration might strike him and he must be ready to grasp the nettle and take his revenge upon Sir Hereward for his dastardly appropriation of all Rudolph's hard work.

However, since nothing had yet occurred to him, what harm could it do to spend a couple of evenings with Millicent Simister? He was sure Rupert of Hentzau would not turn his back on a pretty young lady. Teaching Milly to ride would be a pleasure. She would need a great deal of help at first, of course, and he might even be obliged to hold her while she found her balance.

That thought sent a tingle of anticipation running through him. He smiled.

"I should be delighted to teach you, Millicent. You let me know as soon as you have a bicycle, and we will begin our lessons."

A few days later, Rudolph was on his way home from a hard day at the archives when he saw a woman ahead of him disappearing into Jubilee Gardens. He recognised her as Mrs Lucinda Grayson and his fingers stole up to the spindly ends of his fledgling moustache. What was the beautiful widow doing, wandering alone in the gardens? Why, anything might happen to her. It was up to a gentleman to offer his escort.

Rudolph lengthened his stride and hurried after her into the deserted gardens. The sun had disappeared and the threat of an imminent rainstorm had persuaded nannies to take their young charges home, while those who worked for a living had not yet emerged for an evening stroll, having been obliged to go home and change first. Rudolph, however, even in his work suit, saw his duty clear. He continued to follow Mrs Grayson.

His quarry sat down on a bench and Rudolph slowed his pace, watching her. She dragged a handkerchief from her pocket and dabbed at her eyes. By Jove, she was weeping. A damsel in distress, and clearly in need of manly support. He walked up to her and cleared his throat to announce his presence.

"Mrs Grayson, may I be of any assistance to you?"

She started. "Oh! Do I know you, sir? Have we been introduced?"

Her cold tone would have unnerved the old Rudolph, but he was now more Rupert of Hentzau, and not a man to be intimated by a mere woman.

He smiled and tipped his hat. "Alas, I have not had that pleasure, but I saw you with Lady Bosomworth, when she visited the Town Hall. Rudolph Spendlove, at your service, ma'am." He schooled his features into what he hoped was an expression of sympathy. "I pray you will forgive the presumption, but seeing you are all alone, I could not pass without stopping to enquire if I could be of any help at all to you?"

She had wiped her cheeks and now regarded him with a little less hauteur.

"Oh, you live in Cosmo Terrace, do you not? Millicent has mentioned you in her letters. My carriage is to meet me in a quarter of an hour to convey me to Primly. I decided to stroll in the park while I wait."

Rudolph's chest swelled at the thought that Millicent should have mentioned him to her grand friend. He gestured to the bench and, when Mrs Grayson did not object, he sat down beside her.

"You look unhappy, ma'am, is there anything I can do?"

"No, no. I am merely a little sad at losing a very good friend." She touched her handkerchief to her eyes once more.

"Good heavens, you mean your friend is…has passed on?"

"No." She straightened and blinked, very hard. "He…he has gone away."

Ah. A man friend, thought Rudolph. The poor lady must surely be in need of consolation.

"Now, now, my dear, do not cry." He ventured to put his arm along the back of the bench so that it was almost around her shoulder. At the same time, he reached into his pocket for his own handkerchief. Thank heavens Mother always insisted he should have a clean one with him.

Amazed at his own temerity, he tilted Lucinda's flower-like countenance upwards and smiled at her. "You must not spoil your pretty cheeks with tears, my dear."

The lady recoiled immediately. "How dare you! Let me go this instant!"

Her indignation brought Rudolph to his senses. He jumped to his feet, his thin cheeks on fire with mortification.

"My dear Mrs Grayson, I humbly beg your pardon. Forgive me, I did not mean—"

"Did you not, indeed?" The lady was on her feet now, shaking out her skirts and glaring at him.

"No, no, I was merely— that is— Oh my lord, I had no intention of behaving in such an ungentlemanly way."

"Hah!" The lady gave a brittle little laugh. "In my experience you were behaving *just* like a gentleman! Rogues and scoundrels, all of you, and you care not a whit about how many hearts you may break. Good day to you, sir!"

With that she stormed off, leaving Rudolph red-faced and ashamed. Good heavens, what on earth had come over him? He was turning into more of a cad than even he had thought. He turned and slowly made his way back to Cosmo Terrace. It was becoming clear to him that it was one thing to admire the cunning and ruthlessness of Rupert of Hentzau, but it was quite another to emulate the man when it meant ignoring all the tenets that had been drummed into him since childhood.

He stopped as another horrid thought accosted him and his blood suddenly ran cold. What if Lucinda told Millicent of his attempted seduction? It was one thing not to be boring, quite another to be considered a Lothario. Alas, there was nothing he could do about that now. He walked the last few yards to his house with his shoulders slumped.

He had promised to give Millicent a bicycle-riding lesson once she was in possession of a machine and it was quite clear now that she had a bicycle, but would she advise him of the fact, as she had promised? He glanced at the Simisters' house as he turned onto the little path leading to his own front door. Well, if he did not hear from her, he would know the worst.

By Friday morning, Rudolph was quite prepared to believe that Lucinda had told Millicent of their encounter and that he had lost her forever. The day dragged. Even the discovery of a hitherto undocumented report on the failings of the 1899 sewage outfall pipe failed to rouse him from his lethargy and, when he saw Edward Simister waiting for him as he left the building that evening, he almost turned tail and scurried back inside. Too late. Mr Simister had seen him.

"Ah, Spendlove, there you are. I was waiting for you. Milly gave me a message for you, my boy."

"Sh-she did?" Rudolph braced himself for a tirade.

"Yes, she told me to ask if you were free this evening, at eight o'clock."

"Sh-she did?" he said again.

"Aye, she did. For a bicycle lesson. Only you are not to be wearing that scandalous racing suit of yours. Why, you might as well be naked, sir."

"No, no, of course not. I have a cycling suit. Knickerbockers and woollen hose, very respectable," Rudolph said, quick to reassure him. He added eagerly, "Not that I shall need to wear it whilst I am teaching Miss Simister how to ride. We could meet on Saturday morning, if that would suit better, sir."

"Millicent tells me you have your bicycle club meeting then and we would not wish to disrupt that. No, no, this evening will suit. Eight o'clock, Millicent said."

"Excellent, sir. Thank you."

"But only for an hour, mind you. I'll not have you keeping my girl out after dark."

"No, of course not, sir. I wouldn't dream of it." Rudolph knew that was not quite true. He dreamed quite often of strolling in the moonlight with Millicent. Even stealing a kiss...

"Well, Spendlove, are you free?"

"Y-yes, I can be."

"Splendid. Shall we walk home together?"

In silence Rudolph fell into step beside Edward Simister, feeling more than a little weak at the knees. It would appear that Lucinda Grayson had not told Millicent that he was a debauched rogue. Thinking back, she had told him he had behaved like all other gentlemen. And a beautiful woman such as Lucinda Grayson must know any number of gentlemen, so it must be true.

"Mighty good of you to give up your time for her, my boy," remarked Mr Simister. "Good little thing, Millicent, and if she wants a hobby, she could do worse than the bicycle. She has an excess of energy, you see. I was afraid for a while she might want to join these dashed females campaigning for votes for women." He was silent, shaking his head at the thought, then he turned to smile at Rudolph. "So, my boy, anything you can do to give her thoughts another turn would be very welcome."

Rudolph arrived at the Simisters' house on the dot of eight o'clock and by ten past the hour, he was pushing her bicycle towards Jubilee Gardens with Millicent walking beside him. She had been adamant that she did not wish to take her first lessons in view of her friends and family in Cosmo Terrace, so Rudolph had suggested the wide, flat paths around the gardens.

An hour later and Millicent was riding around the paths with Rudolph running alongside. True, she was a little wobbly and she needed Rudolph to steady her when she came to a stop, but she achieved a complete circuit of the gardens and Rudolph declared that the first lesson had been a success. He suggested they might meet the following Tuesday for another lesson and Millicent agreed with flattering eagerness.

"Would you like to ride somewhere different next time?" he asked her, as they walked back to Cosmo Terrace, wheeling the bicycle between them.

"Oh yes, if you think I might," she replied eagerly.

"Perhaps we could try the promenade." He added, when she hesitated, "It is usually pretty quiet at this time of an evening and there is plenty of space to avoid pedestrians."

"Then yes, if you think I will not be a danger to anyone." They had reached Millicent's gate and she stopped, a faint blush painting her cheeks. "I cannot thank you enough, Rudolph. I enjoyed that immensely."

"So, too, did I," He opened the gate for her and she wheeled the bicycle through. "Until next Tuesday, then."

"Until Tuesday," she called, adding with a little laugh, "if it doesn't rain."

With a cheery wave Rudolph made his way to his own front door. Rain? At that moment he thought this summer might be one of eternal sunshine.

The bicycle lessons fell into a twice-weekly routine and gave Rudolph some much needed relief from his fruitless attempts to devise some means of revenge upon Sir Hereward. Plans for the new town name were steaming ahead and at the Town Hall there was no escaping them. It seemed to Rudolph that everyone had a part to play, except himself, and that only rubbed salt into his still open wound.

By the end of June, Millicent was sufficiently practised for Rudolph to suggest that, since the racing club was having its summer break, they might take a Saturday morning ride onto the headland. The day dawned bright and sunny, and Millicent looked particularly fetching in her new cycling suit with its fitted jacket and knickerbockers. She wore a matching hat decorated with a blue ribbon, the ends fluttering like pennants as she rode along.

They saw no other cyclists on their route, and only a few walkers making the steep climb to the cliff top. When they reached Piddling Point, they stopped and walked to the cliff edge to take in the view. Below them, Piddling Bay basked in the sunshine.

Millicent took in a deep breath.

"Oh, Rudolph, isn't it wonderful up here? And look, you can see the beach huts." She laughed. "From here they look like a selection of my favourite fruit drops."

"Yes, very colourful." Rudolph could not help thinking that Rassendyll looked more like a treacle toffee in the middle of the row. "We should be getting back now. Come along, it will be easier going downhill."

"No, wait." Millicent touched his arm. "The lady over there. I think she is crying."

Rudolph glanced across at the woman. She was dressed in a black bombazine gown and bonnet and was standing near the cliff edge, looking out to sea. Unlike his mother's ethereal appearance, this widow presented a substantial figure and, although she was mopping her cheeks with a black-edged handkerchief, there was a determined look upon her strong features. He thought she looked to be the sort of matron who demanded young men move out of her way, or waved an umbrella angrily if they passed too close on their bicycle.

"Well, it is none of our business," he muttered. "We really should not intrude upon her private grief. Come along…"

"Oh, but we should at least ask if she needs help," replied the soft-hearted Millicent. "We cannot walk away and ignore her."

Before Rudolph had time to argue, she moved towards the woman.

"I do beg your pardon," she addressed the woman with kindly diffidence, "but I could not help noticing that you are distressed. Is there anything we can do?"

The matron finished wiping her eyes and turned to look at Millicent. It was a very considering look, and Rudolph kept his distance, feeling uncomfortable.

"That is very good of you," replied the widow, pushing her handkerchief back into her bag. "But there is nothing to be done, thank you."

That was good enough for Rudolph. He touched Millicent's arm and muttered that they should withdraw, but she ignored him and took a step closer to the woman.

"Oh, but it must be something to make you so unhappy," she said softly. "Sometimes it does one good to speak of it. In confidence, of course."

Rudolph braced himself for a rebuttal, ready to carry Millicent away, but the lady merely regarded Millicent for another long moment, then she sighed.

"It is my son," she said at last. "He died, four years ago."

"Oh, I am so very sorry." There was genuine sadness in Millicent's voice. "Was this a favourite spot of his?"

The woman shook her head. "No, but I come up here on the anniversary of his death to remember him. To see where he took his last swim. He loved the water, you see, and he became sick and died after swimming in the bay. He was only four and twenty."

"Oh, bad luck," murmured Rudolph, who was anxious now to set off on the return ride.

The old woman fixed him with a stare.

"Not bad luck at all, young man. It was due to poor sanitation. The outfall pipe for Little Piddling should extend beyond this headland, but it does not. It ends in line with Piddling Point and at certain times of the year, instead of being dispersed out into the sea, the effluent is washed back into the bay."

"But that is dreadful!" exclaimed Millicent. "The council should do something about it."

She looked to Rudolph, who spluttered, "I only work in the archives; I have no influence with the council at all."

"Perhaps Sir Hereward could help," Millicent suggested.

The widow gave a snort. "He could, but he won't, and the council are too frightened to go against him. Our Mayor will only support causes that reflect well upon him, such as this ludicrous idea of changing the town's name."

These disparaging remarks about what had, after all, been his idea, caused Rudolph to feel a certain amount of indignation, but it was somewhat diluted because he shared the woman's animosity towards Sir Hereward.

"I beg your pardon, I should not be taking your time with all this." The widow touched Millicent's arm and gave her a tiny smile. "But you are right, my dear, it has helped me to talk of it."

With that, the woman walked off.

"Oh, my goodness, what a tragedy." Millicent sighed as she accompanied Rudolph back to their bicycles. "I believe Mr Bretherson recently suggested they should make improvements to the sewage disposal system, but the council would not authorise further expenditure because Sir Hereward was so against it. Father came home and told Mama all about it and he almost *never* tells us anything about council business, which just shows how put out he was, doesn't it?"

Rudolph muttered sympathetic noises. The widow's complaint gave an added sense of justice to his own resentment against Sir Hereward, but, really, there was little he could do about it, except redouble his efforts to find a way to be revenged upon the Mayor.

The problem of revenge continued to haunt Rudolph. Every time he heard talk of the new town name—and it was mentioned a great deal in the Town Hall—he felt more aggrieved. How he longed for the days when one could challenge a fellow to a duel. Not that he had ever learned to fence, of course, and the idea of using a pistol was quite abhorrent, but he could not deny that defending one's honour with one's life had a very noble ring to it.

Two days after the outing to Piddling Point, Rudolph was returning a box of papers to the Archive when he saw Albert Kettlesing hurrying down the corridor. Albert worked in the mailroom at the Town Hall and generally had a cheery word for everyone, but today he was clearly agitated. However, when Rudolph paused to ask him what was the matter, Albert merely waved him aside.

"I cannot stop now, Mr Spendlove. I promised Mr Simister I would deliver these before the end of the day." He waved the letters in his hand and added importantly, "There's one for the sign-makers and one for Mr Lamb the stonemason."

Rudolph ground his teeth. There it was again, another twist of the knife. But it was not Albert's fault, after all, so he replied pleasantly. "Oh, well, there is plenty of time for that. It is not yet four o'clock."

"No, no, it is not getting them there," replied Albert, edging past him. "It is getting home afterwards. You see, I am taking Millicent Simister to the theatre tonight, to see *Floradora*, and I don't want to be late."

Rudolph blinked, his feeling of ill usage rising again. He had invited Millicent to go with him to see the musical comedy and she had refused. Rage boiled through him, heating his blood, filling his lungs with hot, angry breath, but it also scoured his brain of its fog and he saw with blinding clarity what he had to do. He caught Albert's arm.

"I can deliver them for you, if you like. That way you can get home in plenty of time to prepare for your evening out."

"Would you? That would be really kind of you, Mr Spendlove. Thank you."

Albert thrust the letters into his hand and went back to the postroom, whistling. Smiling, Rudolph watched him, then he continued on his way to the archives, his fingers twirling the ends of his moustache.

A period of unsettled weather prevented Rudolph and Millicent riding out together and it was almost two weeks before they met again, when they rode to the tea rooms in Much Piddling. This had been a daring suggestion of Rudolph's, but he was inordinately pleased when Millicent agreed to it. During the past weeks, his feelings had been swinging erratically between hope and despair. He was morbidly afraid Millicent might prefer Albert Kettlesing's company to his own, but surely, the fact that she had agreed to spend the whole of Saturday riding out with him was a cause for optimism?

Millicent certainly appeared to be in good spirits when they rode out from Cosmo Terrace, and by the time they were cycling along the lanes out of the town, Rudolph could stand the suspense no longer. He asked how she had enjoyed her visit to the theatre.

"Oh, you mean *Floradora*?" She glanced across at him, which made her wobble.

"Yes. Kettlesing told me he was taking you." He tried to keep the accusing tone from his voice but was not quite successful.

"I beg your pardon, Rudolph, but Albert invited me weeks ago. I should have told you that was the reason I could not go with you, but I thought you might be jealous."

"Me, jealous of Albert Kettlesing? Good heavens, no."

"Oh, I am glad about that," she declared, smiling with relief.

"And, did you enjoy *Floradora*?"

"Oh, yes," she replied sunnily. "As did Albert. He is such a comic and takes nothing seriously, does he?"

"No, he doesn't." Rudolph missed the doubtful note in her voice and his jealousy grew.

Kettlesing's endless joking was something Rudolph disliked intensely. It grated on his nerves and he thought it would serve the fellow right if he came to grief over it one day.

"It is less than a week now to the Little Piddling Festival," said Millicent, breaking into his reverie. "You will be there on the Friday, I suppose? Father says Sir Hereward has asked all the council to attend."

"What? Oh, the unveiling of the new town signs. Yes, yes of course."

"Mother has bought me a new dress to wear," Millicent went on. "Jonquil yellow. I only hope the sun shines and I do not have to cover it with a coat."

She chattered on and Rudolph responded suitably, but he was very glad when at last they reached Much Piddling and the busy streets gave them something else to think about. He treated Millicent to tea and cakes, and they cycled back in perfect harmony. It was only when Rudolph reached home that his sunny spirits dimmed slightly.

He wished he still felt as enthusiastic about his plan for revenge as he had a few weeks ago. As he went upstairs to change, he admitted to himself that he had been worrying about it almost since the day he delivered those letters for Kettlesing. When the truth came out, everyone would say that it was just the sort of thing Albert would do. They would be only too willing to believe it; and Rudolph was not sure if his conscience would allow him to let the fellow take the blame. Even if they were rivals for Miss Simister's affections.

Rudolph moved to the mirror and began to brush his hair. If he was to be completely honest, he was beginning to have doubts about the course of action upon which he had embarked. However, there was no way he could withdraw now without confessing the whole, which would not only cause him great personal humiliation, but it would almost certainly cost him his position as Town Archivist. Then what would Mother say?

*Forget your mother, what would Rupert of Hentzau say?*

The thought stopped Rudolph in his tracks and he stopped brushing. He snatched off his glasses and gazed, albeit somewhat myopically, at his reflection. With his dark hair swept back, and his waxed moustache now beginning to curl up very nicely at the ends, he looked very much like his vision of Rupert of Hentzau. He reminded himself that Rupert was the villain of *The Prisoner of Zenda. He* would not consult his mother about how to behave. A villain would also throw an innocent man to the dogs without compunction to achieve his ends.

Rudolph tried curling his lip and was quite pleased with the result. He replaced his glasses and went off to join his mother for dinner. No, he would have his revenge upon Sir Hereward and…and *to the devil* with the rest of them.

# Chapter Three

It was the first day of the Summer Festival. The day when, at noon, Sir Hereward would announce to the world that the town was no longer Little Piddling, but Little Piddling sur Mer. A week ago, the metal uprights for the signs had been erected on the roads leading into the town and the sign-makers had agreed they would not attach the new signs until twelve o'clock, by which time Sir Hereward expected the townspeople and invited dignitaries from neighbouring Much Piddling to be gathered outside Jubilee Gardens ready for the Great Unveiling. Even the monument, which had been carefully secured in place overnight, was shrouded in a thick linen sheet to prevent anyone enjoying its full glory before Sir Hereward had made his speech.

It was a beautiful July day and in Cosmo Terrace, Rudolph and his mother left their house just as the Simisters were setting off and together they made their way through Jubilee Gardens to witness the unveiling.

They spilled out of the gardens to find crowds already milling around the western end of the promenade, where a sparkling blue sea provided a stunning backdrop for the brass band that was playing jolly tunes, accompanied by the noisy gulls wheeling overhead.

Rudolph had spent hours before his mirror, perfecting his lip curl, ready to sneer at Sir Hereward's humiliation. Even the sight of Millicent in her yellow gown and chip straw hat could not quite overcome his excitement at what was to come.

A large area had been roped off, with red carpet placed before the monument for the Mayor and his invited guests, and space reserved behind it for members of the town council and their families, from where they would have an excellent view of the proceedings.

By eleven-thirty the promenade was filling up. Whole families were arriving, as much to listen to the band and take advantage of the summer sunshine as to witness the unveiling, Rudolph thought. Albert Kettlesing sauntered up, his hat pushed back at a jaunty angle. He waved at Millicent, who responded with a smile, and Rudolph felt the demon jealousy stabbing at his chest again. Once the town name was revealed, Sir Hereward would be looking for someone to blame. Then Kettlesing would find he did not have much to smile about.

The Mayoral party arrived, the gentlemen in their black frockcoats and toppers quite outshone by the ladies in their colourful dresses and large brimmed hats trimmed with lace and flowers. The Arbuttles arrived and Rudolph touched his hat to them while his mother made room beside her.

"Such a splendid day for it, Mrs Arbuttle," she declared, then dropped her voice a little. "I thought Sir Hereward might have invited you to join his party, you being such a good friend of Lady Wakeleigh."

A look of disapproval shadowed Mr Arbuttle's kindly face.

"We should have been," he said heavily. "Our names were on the original invitation list, but it was changed at the last minute."

His wife turned to Mrs Spendlove. "Dora Wakeleigh was most put out about it. She made a point of apologising to me, and told me herself that it was Sir Hereward who decided the matter. He is negotiating something with Mr Dumaine and wanted to keep him sweet."

"Is he really?" replied Mrs Spendlove, looking suitably outraged. "And Hermione Dumaine no better than she should be."

"Quite." Mrs Arbuttle took her husband's arm. "I wouldn't wish her anywhere near my Sydney."

Mrs Spendlove gave a very audible sniff. "She is a member of the Waifs and Orphans Relief Committee, too, but I have it on good authority that she has a closer connection to some of those waifs than she admits."

Mrs Arbuttle stifled a very unladylike giggle.

"Mother, really!" Rudolph protested, flushing.

Mrs Spendlove spread her hands. "I am only saying what I have heard, my dear. Why, you only have to look at her, flirting with Sir Hereward. And right in front of her husband, too. Look at them, it is outrageous."

Obediently, they all turned to look at the ripe brunette in the cherry-blossom pink coat. She was laughing up at Sir Hereward while behind her Lady Wakeleigh was struggling to make conversation with Mr Dumaine, who appeared quite bored by the whole proceedings.

"You are far better off here with us, Mrs Arbuttle," said Mrs Spendlove, patting her arm. "We shall be a very jolly party, and afterwards you must come back with us to Cosmo Terrace for tea."

Rudolph's attention wandered. He looked around to find that Mr and Mrs Simister had moved away, and he had only Millicent standing beside him.

"Lady Wakeleigh is to unveil the monument," he explained as they watched the Mayor organising his little party on the red carpet. His eye was caught by a mild commotion at the edge of the crowds. "And that is old Lady Bosomworth's carriage drawing up. I did not think to see her here today, not since the council changed its mind about a statue to her late husband."

"Lucinda told me she only agreed to come because she is convinced Sir Hereward will make a fool of himself," said Millicent.

"How right she is," thought Rudolph.

He had not imagined there would be such a large crowd but he was glad of it. The more people who witnessed the Mayor's very public humiliation the better.

Millicent broke into his thoughts with an exclamation.

"Sir Hereward is about to speak." She placed one dainty hand in its white net glove upon his arm. "Oh, isn't this exciting?"

"Yes, it is. And it is going to get a great deal more exciting yet."

Rudolph was very pleased with his drawl, very suitable for one who had masterminded the forthcoming debacle. He had wondered if he would actually be able to achieve a demonic laugh to fill the silence that was sure to follow the unveiling, but now, standing here with the beautiful Millicent on his arm and the sun shining down upon him, he thought he could achieve anything today.

Sir Hereward had moved to the small dais in front of the monument and was making his speech, thanking his honoured guests and describing in detail Little Piddling's maritime history. Rudolph had heard it all before—indeed had he not provided all the information?

As the Mayor droned on, Rudolph glanced down at Milly's hand, noting the small gap between the embroidered edge of her glove and her sleeve. Not now, perhaps (especially with Mother and Mrs Simister standing so close) but later, he would raise her hand and place a kiss upon the delicate skin of her inner wrist.

"And now, ladies and gentlemen, it is my pleasure—nay, my honour—to announce that henceforth, our magnificent town will be known as Little Piddling sur Mer!"

Even the Mayor's stentorian declaration was not enough to break into Rudolph's pleasant daydream. Millicent would blush adorably and raise her beautiful eyes to his face. Then she would say—

"Oh, Rudolph, look. The rope has snagged."

It was true. The cord had been designed so that a single tug would allow the sheet to fall gently into soft artistic folds at the base of the monument. However, when Lady Wakeleigh pulled at the tasselled end of the rope, nothing happened. Rudolph watched Sir Hereward stride forward and could almost hear him muttering, "Can you do *nothing* right?"

A quiet buzz of chatter could be heard as Mr Lamb and his assistant ran out of the crowd to help. They busied themselves with the rope, gave it a few tentative flicks, then nodded at the Mayor and retired again. Sir Hereward tried to make a joke of it, called everyone to order and invited his lady once more to unveil the monument.

This time Lady Wakeleigh's efforts were rewarded and as the cloth fluttered down, there were cheers and a smattering of applause from the crowds.

"And there we are, ladies and gentlemen!" the Mayor's voice boomed out as he turned towards the monument. "I have great pleasure in announcing that from today, visitors to our wonderful town will be greeted by this grand edifice. The inscription reads, *Welcome to Little Piddling sur...*"

His voice faded to silence. Even from a distance Rudolph could see the angry colour suffusing his cheeks. Those who were close enough to see the bold lettering on the monument began to mutter.

"Come on," shouted someone from the back of the crowd. "Finish your speech, why don't you?"

Sir Hereward himself had all the appearance of stone as he stared at the monument. Not so Mr Dumaine, who stepped up and read the inscription, his voice carrying with dreadful clarity over the crowd.

"Welcome to Little Piddling sur Mer*de!*"

And with that, he burst out laughing.

# Chapter Four

Rudolph did not know what he had expected to happen once the monument was unveiled, but for several moments, chaos reigned. A few people in the crowd began to laugh; those in the mayoral party looked dumbfounded. He stepped over the rope and moved a little closer in order to hear what was being said.

"I don't understand," cried Lady Wakeleigh, casting a bewildered look towards her husband. "Is this not what you ordered?"

Sir Hereward opened and closed his mouth in silence and looked as if he might be carried off by apoplexy at any moment.

"I sincerely hope not," said Mr Dumaine, between laughter and contempt. "*Merde* in French means—"

"Yes, yes, that is quite enough of that," snapped Sir Hereward, interrupting him. "Of course I did not order this."

"Oh yes, you did," said Mr Lamb, coming up. "That's exactly what it said on the order. I've got it here in me pocket, if you don't believe me."

"Poppycock! Where's Simister?" Sir Hereward spotted his quarry and beckoned imperiously. "Come here, man, and tell me, what is the meaning of this?"

"I-I really don't know how this could have happened, sir," stammered the hapless Clerk to the Council, who was as white as his shirt.

Mr Lamb drew a paper from his pocket and looked from it to the inscription.

"But what's wrong with it?" he demanded, scratching his head. "The lettering's right. Spaces are in the right place."

"It should read Mer, not Merde!" barked Sir Hereward. "It means Little Piddling on Sea, not Little Piddling on-on…"

"Sewage," put in Mr Dumaine helpfully.

Mr Lamb moved closer, eager to ensure that no blame for the error was foisted on him. Rudolph loitered and listened, twirling the ends of his moustache. The crowd was chattering now, the occasional shout of laughter ringing out whenever the translation from the French was explained to someone new, while Sir Hereward was growing ever more red in the face. It was all going very nicely. Very nicely indeed. He glanced across to where his mother was standing with Mrs Simister and Millicent. Soon he would be able to leave Sir Hereward to his chagrin and turn his attention to something far more pleasurable. Courting the lovely Millicent.

"Where's Kettlesing?" Mr Simister waved towards the crowd. "Albert, come here, if you please."

The post boy ran up and Sir Hereward pounced on him.

"So it's all your fault. *You* are the one who delivered the orders. I suppose you thought it was a fine trick to play, eh? Well, see if you think it's so fine to be out of work. You are dismissed, my boy. With immediate effect."

"What? But I—"

"Enough! I want none of your excuses."

It was then that the enormity of his plan hit home to Rudolph. In his dreams, the incorrect spelling of the town name should have led to much hilarity and ridicule for Sir Hereward, and perhaps a reprimand for Albert, but he had not considered that anyone would lose their post.

*What of it?*

The demon on his shoulder dismissed his scruples. Rudolph looked at Millicent, her hands pressed against her mouth and a look of horror on her face. He must escort her away, along with Mother and Mrs Simister. These ugly scenes should not be witnessed by gently-nurtured ladies.

Kettlesing was looking very shocked, and a little grey, too, as Sir Hereward continued to hurl insults at him. If Albert admitted that he had given the letters to Rudolph to deliver, he could always deny it. After all, he had been Town Archivist for the past ten years. Everyone would believe his word over that of a mere post boy.

*You have had your revenge. Take the ladies home and leave the fool to his fate.*

Rudolph twirled the ends of his moustache, for the first time in his life feeling very much like the character from a novel. He straightened his shoulders and stepped forward.

"Stop this!" His voice, usually a little thin, had found a hitherto unknown bass note and it boomed out, causing those gathered on the red carpet to freeze and fall silent. "It was not Kettlesing who scuppered your plans, Mr Mayor, it was I. I, Rudolph Rass— I mean Rudolph Spendlove."

He would normally have quailed to find so many eyes fixed upon him, but now he was fired up with energy and he gazed about him with haughty arrogance.

"I persuaded Albert to give me the letters and I made a few little alterations before I delivered them."

"Them?" Mr Simister stopped him. "Do you mean, the road signs, too?"

"Oh, yes," Rudolph declared grandly. "Everyone coming into the town will see them."

Sir Hereward gave an angry roar. "I see what this is, Spendlove. You think you deserved some recognition for looking up the town's history. You-you sabotaged my grand design out of spite!"

Rudolph was about to say that was it exactly, but at that moment he saw a black-clad figure in the crowd and recognised her as the widow he and Millicent had met at Piddling Point.

"I may have felt a little aggrieved that you stole my suggestion and passed off all my arguments as your own, but that is not it. No," he declared, warming to his theme. "I did this because this town *should* be called Little Piddling sur Merde." He raised his voice and addressed the crowd still gathered on the promenade. "The waters of our beloved bay have been allowed to become polluted, ladies and gentlemen. They are not safe for swimming."

"What nonsense!" blustered the Mayor. "Our waters are as clean as any on the south coast."

"Are they? The outflow pipe should continue some way past Piddling point, but in fact it stops short." Rupert swung round and pointed toward the council members gathered in the reserved area. "Ask them if it was not proposed that this should be rectified at the same time as the public conveniences were refurbished. And ask them who it was vetoed the proposal and declared it too costly."

"Aye, I remember," muttered Mr Arbuttle, nodding.

"Yes," Rudolph continued, encouraged. "Rather than spending good money on a costly monument to bolster your own self-aggrandisement, Mr Mayor, you should be encouraging the Council to improve the town's sewage system."

Rudolph drew in a deep breath, slightly shocked at his own eloquence. A murmur of agreement was rippling through the crowd and he saw that the widow was nodding her approval. He was trying to smile back at her when, with a bellow of pure rage, Sir Hereward flew at Rudolph and floored him with a hefty punch to the chin.

"No!"

Rudolph heard Millicent's shriek as he fell. Thankfully, he landed on the carpet rather than the hard ground but nevertheless, he was too shaken and dazed to do anything but lie still for a few moments. He groped for his glasses and, by the time he had retrieved them and breathed a sigh of relief that they were unscathed, Millicent was kneeling beside him, brandishing her rolled parasol at Sir Hereward like a sword.

"How dare you assault a poor innocent man, you-you bully!"

"Innocent!" Sir Hereward spluttered, incandescent with rage. "He has not only insulted me, he has cast a slight upon the whole town."

He took a step closer. Millicent screamed, and Mr Simister grabbed at Sir Hereward's arm to restrain him.

Lady Wakeleigh appeared. "Come away, dear, this is not good for your heart."

"Let go of me. It isn't my heart that's at risk here, it's my reputation."

Rudolph was climbing gingerly to his feet. He would have liked to say he could manage without Millicent's help but, in truth, her support was very necessary. Part of him—the old Rudolph—wanted to offer a grovelling apology, but that would undo everything he had achieved. He kept silent.

Mr Lamb and his assistant were already busy putting the cover back over the monument and the local constables were encouraging the crowds to disperse.

Rudolph stared at the Mayor, who was scowling direfully.

"You haven't heard the last of this, Spendlove. I'll see you are dismissed. I'll have you chased out of town—"

"Plenty of time for that later, Sir Hereward," muttered Mr Simister. "Best not to give the crowds anything else to gossip about just now."

The Mayor recollected himself and, after another baleful glance at Rudolph, he stormed off.

"Come along, Millicent, we must find your mother and take her home." Mr Simister turned to Rudolph. "And you had best do the same, my boy. Mrs Spendlove is looking rather shocked."

Rudolph's elation had quite evaporated by this time. He looked around for his mother. She was still in the reserved area, but whereas others were in little groups, talking animatedly, she was standing a little apart from everyone else and staring at him in horror. Millicent had left his side and gone over to take her father's proffered arm, so Rudolph made his way over to his mother.

"Oh, how shall I ever live this down?" she cried as he came up to her. "I have never been so humiliated in my life. How could you do such a thing, Rudolph? How could you do such a thing? How could you bring such shame upon our family?"

She continued in this vein as they made their way to Cosmo Terrace. Never had the walk taken so long. It seemed that everyone they knew was on the streets and they either cast sly glances in their direction or ignored them altogether.

By the time they reached their door, Mrs Spendlove was beginning to cry and Rudolph could take no more. He escorted his mother into the drawing room, called upon Elsie, her maid, to attend her, then made his excuses and left.

He had no idea where to go, all he knew was that he needed some time alone, to think. Exacting revenge was clearly far more complicated than he had first thought. His grand plan had upset everyone. Mother was distraught, Millicent wanted nothing more to do with him and his colleagues at the Town Hall would shun him in future. His ex-colleagues, that is, for there was no doubt that he would lose his position now. He was ruined.

Rudolph stopped. He might as well throw himself off Piddling Point. He turned and set off in the direction of the headland. He strode along, keeping his head down and ignoring everyone he passed. His route took him back to the promenade. The crowds had thinned now and the monument was once again under its shroud. It was very possible that workers had already been dispatched to remove the offending road signs, too. His gesture had been a feeble attempt at revenge. Sir Hereward would suffer a momentary upset and a small financial loss, but in a very short time he would bounce back. The other and unforeseen consequences of his actions were much more serious.

However, when he reached the end of the promenade and was about to strike out up the hill to the headland, his footsteps slowed. Was Ending it All the answer? Would that not make him a coward as well as a villain?

Instead of taking to the road up the hill, he struck out towards the beach huts.

Rudolph was sitting on the floor of Rassendyll Lodge, huddled into a corner, when he heard a soft knock at the door.

"Rudolph, are you in there? It is me, Millicent."

She need not have bothered to tell him; he would have recognised her soft mellifluous voice anywhere.

"Can I come in?" He did not reply, but she opened the door anyway. "Oh, I am so pleased to have found you. Everyone is very worried, you know."

"Are they?" he shrugged. "I cannot think of anyone who would care what happened to me."

"Now, there you are wrong," she told him, coming in and closing the door behind her. "Your mother is worried you have done something even more— that is—"

"Something even more foolish," he finished for her.

"Well, yes, that was what she said. But Father is worried, too. And Albert made a point of asking after you. He thinks you are quite a gentleman, to stand up for him like that."

"I could not let him take the blame."

"No." She sat down beside him. "I was very proud of you for owning up, Rudolph."

"Were you?"

"Yes. Many men would have allowed poor Albert to take the blame, and Father says he should have taken the letters himself because they were so important. Then none of this would have happened."

"But I *wanted* it to happen, Millicent. I wanted to humiliate Sir Hereward." His hands writhed together as he thought of it. "He came to me, you see, asking me to find something in Little Piddling's history to show that it was a very important place. And I did. I found all the information about its seagoing heritage, and the links with France. I even suggested changing the name. But he did not give me any credit at all. He made out that everything was his idea, his grand plan."

"It was very wrong of him."

"That's why I said I would deliver the orders. I retyped them, you see, and made sure any replies would come to me. That way I could stop anyone finding out about the change until it was too late."

To his surprise, Millicent giggled. "I thought changing *mer* to *merde* was very clever. It makes perfect sense, when you consider the sad story we heard from that poor widow at Piddling Point."

"But I didn't do it for her," he burst out. "Oh, I know I said the polluted water of the bay was the reason I did it, but it wasn't, Millicent. Those orders were sent off well before we met the woman on the cliff." He had gone this far, he must confess everything now. "I did it purely out of spite, to punish Sir Hereward. It was just that, when I saw the widow standing in the crowd, I thought it sounded far more noble to say I had done it for altruistic reasons rather than petty revenge."

"It may not have been your original reason, but everyone deserves to know the truth about the water, Rudolph, so what you did today was a very good thing."

"My mother does not think so," he said gloomily. "Nor does your father. And certainly not Sir Hereward. He knocked me down, remember. I am a failure."

"I am very proud of you for taking it on the chin," replied Millicent, no hint of laughter in her voice. She reached over and caught his restless hands, clasping them firmly in her own. "Perhaps your original motives were not quite what they should have been, but you gave a voice to the people, Rudolph."

Then, very daringly, she leaned over and kissed him on the mouth.

She drew away, blushing, and Rudolph stared at her.

"Good Lord. Are you...are you truly proud of me, Millicent?"

"Truly," she said, smiling at him.

For a moment his heart soared, then it plummeted again. He gave a groan and dropped his head in his hands.

"It makes no difference, I am ruined and by my actions I have hurt so many other people, too."

"Now that is where you are quite wrong," Millicent told him. "You see, after you took Mrs Spendlove away, Sir Hereward demanded that Father and the other councillors do something about the situation, and while they were all talking, Lucinda came over with a message from her great-aunt. She said Lady Bosomworth was willing to pay for replacing the monument with a statue of Sir Copson and, if the council agreed to it, she would also pick up the bill for having new and correct signs made for the roads into the town."

"I can see how that will save the council and Sir Hereward a vast deal of money, but the Mayor's reputation is in tatters, as I am sure he pointed out to everyone."

"That is where Father came into his own," she replied, smiling a little. "Father insisted you had a valid point about the outflow pipe and he persuaded Sir Hereward to change his mind about the proposals to upgrade the town's sewage system. Mr Flint says he still has the original plans he drew up with the engineers and he is willing to carry out the work for the same price."

"And the Mayor agreed to this?" Rudolph was incredulous.

Millicent's smile grew. "He did, once we…that is, once Father explained that the council would let it be known that he was the driving force behind the plan. Father is now drafting a report to the *Piddling Post* to say that no sooner had Sir Hereward grasped the nature of the problem—which, of course, he knew nothing of before today—he immediately set to work to rectify the situation."

"And your father thought of all this, on the spot?"

Millicent blushed. "Well, he might have had a little help, but he was very good at persuading all the councillors to back him up. So, you see, Rudolph, everything has worked out very well."

"Except that I am no longer the Town Archivist."

Millicent chuckled. "Father and I thought of that, too. The council have agreed to say that the incorrect name was a clerical error, and your outburst today will be put down to overwork. You will take a much-needed rest, but be retained on full pay."

Rudolph stared at her. "But how can that be? Sir Hereward will never allow it."

"Many of the crowd agree with you about the sanitation. Apparently, the protests have been growing for years and, once it was made clear to the Mayor that if you were dismissed from your post you would be seen as a martyr to the cause, and he would be the villain of the piece, he was all for your being allowed to keep your post."

"But this is marvellous!" cried Rudolph, jumping up. "But, if I cannot work, what am I to do? How long must I stay at home?"

"Oh, four months at least." Millicent stretched out her hand and he pulled her to her feet. "We must have time to let tempers cool."

"Four months. What on earth am I going to do with myself for four months?"

Millicent traced a pattern on the sandy floor with the tip of her parasol.

"I thought perhaps you might like to go abroad. Take a cycling holiday."

"Yes, by Jove, I suppose I might," said Rudolph, brightening.

"And..." she looked intently at her artistic creation "...I w-wondered if you might like a companion."

"I suppose that would be a good idea." He mulled over the idea for a few moments, then sighed and shook his head. "No, it won't do. All the cyclists I know have a job of work to do; they would never be able to take the time off."

"Not all of them are employed, Rudolph."

"Oh yes, they are. I— By Jove," he said again. "You d-don't mean *you* would consider coming with me?

"I would very much like to, if you think I wouldn't get in the way?"

"In the way? No indeed, I should very much like it, only, I thought you preferred Albert Kettlesing?"

"Albert? Oh no, he is a very sweet boy, of course, but far too frivolous. Too immature to be my sweetheart."

His face lit up. "Do you mean that? Oh Millicent, it would make me the happiest man in the world if—" He broke off as another objection occurred to him. "No, it won't do. Your mother and father would never allow you to come with me, unless..."

"Unless what, Rudolph?"

"Unless we were married."

"And we are not."

"No." He sighed, his shoulders drooping. "No way around that."

"You could try asking me, Rudolph."

He stared at her. "Do you mean, if I did ask you, you would say yes?"

"Yes, I do, you silly man. It would take at least four weeks to arrange everything for our trip, so there is time for the banns to be read and for our mothers to organise a wedding."

"But weddings take months to plan."

"Not necessarily." She clasped his hands. "Oh, what do you say, Rudolph, shall we do it? The bicycling trip can be our honeymoon."

Rudolph felt as if the world was tilting on its axis, but he also felt his battered spirits reviving more with every minute. He said cautiously, "Very well. If you are sure about all this."

"Surer than I have ever been about anything."

"Even though I have made such a mess of everything today?"

"You displayed great skill and cunning, Rudolph, and in the end you also showed that you are a very honourable gentleman because you would not allow another to take the blame." Millicent stepped closer and slipped her arms about his neck. "In fact, Rudolph Spendlove, I very much think you are my hero."

And with that, Rudolph relinquished all aspirations to be Rupert of Hentzau and gave himself up to the pleasure of kissing Millicent, his very own heroine.

# THE END

## *About Sarah Mallory*

Sarah Mallory is an award-winning author who has published more than 30 historical romances with Mills & Boon. She loves history, especially the Georgian and Regency periods, and when she is not writing, she spends her time exploring the remote Scottish Highlands where she has made her home.
Sarah also writes romantic historical adventures as Melinda Hammond.
You can learn more at www.sarahmallory.com and follow her @SarahMRomance. Sarah is also part of the Libertà hive: libertabooks.com/sarah

### *Want Sarah's latest book?*
You can get Sarah's latest book, and find earlier ones you may have missed, at author.to/SarahMallory
where you'll also be able to follow Sarah for her latest releases

# GOING HOME?
## *by Sophie Weston*

# Chapter One

Until the Visit, I was doing fairly well at Orwell College for Gifted Children. I was teaching chemistry at all levels. It was March 1973 and I'd been in post for seven months. I'd started extracurricular classes in astrophysics for half a dozen Sixth Formers. My Astronomy Club was so popular, I'd had to divide it into Juniors and Seniors, or nobody got enough time at the telescope. No takers yet for my classes in computer science. But Headmaster Abel said that would come in time.

"Your enthusiasm is too infectious, Selsis," he said kindly. "Lo, the unbelievers shall see the light." It was a private joke to make me feel better. And it did.

I watched *Star Trek* with the Orwell College addicts, staff and pupils alike, and managed not to correct the errors.

The food was strange but I'd got used to it, though alcohol was an issue. After an evening tasting Real Ale, hosted by the Headmaster, I said firmly that I was sticking to water. And I'd nearly mastered the knife and fork.

OK, Peter Abel wouldn't let me meet the parents yet. But that was partly because I was new and partly—well, parents were a new concept for me. There was always a risk that I'd say the wrong thing to them. Words, like the use of knife and fork, were still a work in progress for me. But I was getting there.

Or I thought I was. Until the Visit.

The first I heard of it was in the Staff Room. Everyone was in a fever of anxiety.

I couldn't understand. What scared them about a visit from a secretary in education? I knew the school secretary. Secretaries did top chaps' typing and organised meetings. They didn't have any power. I said so.

"You don't know Maggie," said the Art Master with feeling. "She's a control freak." He was a bit of a male chauvinist.

"A strong-minded woman," corrected the Head of Mathematics, who wasn't.

"You wait," said the Art Master. He was also a conspiracy theorist and brooded a lot.

Even Peter Abel was cautious. At least, he made sure the Art Master and the Senior Tutor in French—a Byronic character, still mourning the collapse of the French Revolution—were out of the way when she came. They went off with a school party to an exhibition of Impressionists that day. All day.

And he sent me out with a map and packed lunch to prepare a discovery walk for the Upper Fourth. So I knew he wanted me out of the way, too. And I would have been, only a landfall had blocked the bridle path and I nipped back for a different map. There were a good couple of hours before the terrifying secretary was due to arrive.

I was halfway across the kitchen yard, heading for the hills again, when a big limousine swept round the corner, swerved and jammed on its brakes.

Just in time, actually. I fell back against the wall, heart racing. I'd have a friction burn on my left hip, unless I was much mistaken. The car came to a halt just shy of the dustbins.

A man in a dark overcoat jumped out. He looked worried, poor chap.

I straightened and said soothingly, "I'm fine. Don't worry."

He looked blank. Clearly not worried about me, then.

Instead, he said, "Where are we?"

I was so startled, I reverted to default mode. "Earth."

Yes, I know it was a stupid thing to say. But it was the literal truth, from my perspective. And I hadn't prepared myself to encounter new people.

But he didn't complain that I was taking the piss, which he might well have done. Instead, he seemed panic-stricken and looked back at the car as if he expected it to burst into flames.

The driver put his head out of the window. "Can you help us, love? We've been going round in circles," he said nicely. "The Minister is looking for Orwell College."

Oh Heavens, I thought. And the dreaded secretary is due in an hour or so. Peter Abel will tear his hair out

So I was cautious. "Well, that's us. But everyone's in lessons now."

The first guy bridled and came round the car to put himself between me and the friendly chauffeur. "So which way to the main entrance?" he demanded.

I weighed up the situation. A surprise Minister from some unspecified religion! On about the worst day they could have chosen. Well, at least I could buy Peter Abel some time. The buildings were fairly complicated. I could send them round in a circle while I dashed inside and got Cook to alert the Headmaster's office.

So I did. Black overcoat got back in the front passenger seat and they drove off. Nobody said thank you.

As soon as they were out of sight, I pelted into the kitchen and scribbled a message on one of Cook's kitchen ordering pads. She sent the youngest and fittest of the kitchen staff galloping away with it.

I went back to the kitchen yard and set off for my nature-walk-plotting expedition again. I was quite proud of myself.

Only then the limousine nosed round the corner again. It didn't pin me to the wall this time. Instead it stopped in front of me, effectively cutting off my exit, like Smersh operatives out of a James Bond movie. And the back window rolled down.

A gloved hand beckoned. "Young woman, come here."

The chauffeur looked woodenly ahead of him, but the passenger beside him was clearly apprehensive. Neither of them said anything.

So I shrugged and went to talk to the window.

It was a woman. She seemed to have golden hair. Not like a princess, though. Maybe a queen, from her imperious manner. Not the British queen, I hoped. "I am here to see the school. Fetch the Headmaster." From her tone, she might as well have been saying, "Take me to your leader."

I was genuinely apologetic. It was really bad luck that she had chosen such a rotten day to descend on us.

"I'm afraid I don't know where he is. He's very busy today. But if you'd like to see something of the school, I could take you to the Art Studio while I track down his secretary. She'll know where he is. The children there are always so absorbed you wouldn't disturb them." And the Junior Art Master, *Goons* fan and demon bowler, could cope with just about anything, in my experience.

The magic word "secretary" must have swung it.

She debated for no more than a moment. "Very well. That is what we will do. It's always best to arrive unannounced. Godwin...?"

The man in the overcoat got out of the car at once and opened her door for her, like a footman out of a fairy tale. She got out. Regally.

I knew that Ministers often dressed in ordinary clothes when they weren't actually running religious ceremonies, but I boggled a bit at hers. She was wearing a fairly short navy blue skirt and jacket, with the most scrumptious silk blouse in a heavenly shade of violet, with a big floppy bow at the collar. Bishops, I remembered, wore purple. Was she a bishop, then? Yet that bow would have looked better on one of the Staff Room boxes of chocolates. She had no hat but her hair was set in sculpted waves like a warrior's helmet. Not a hair moved in the brisk March wind. A mitre? Was that what it was called?

It was too puzzling. I gave up.

"Would you come this way, Your Eminence?" Wasn't that what you called bishops? Or was that the Pope?

From the sharp look she gave me, I suspected I'd got it wrong.

Oh well, at least I'd shown respect. That had to count for something. Right?

I took them round the dustbins and in through the old Pantryman's Door.

"This is the oldest part of the building. Tudor we believe. We can take the back stairs. The Art Studio is on this side of the building."

Chatty and welcoming didn't come easily to me, but I did my best. I gave the Junior Art Master a good puff. At least, it was meant to be.

The Minister wasn't having any of it. "What do you mean, free expression? Education isn't about free expression. It's about training people to do something useful."

Here, at least, I was on solid ground. I had studied the education systems of several civilisations, after all. I said helpfully, "Only in very primitive societies. The real aim of education is to explore possibilities. To add 'why' and 'what if' to 'when, where and how', if you will."

She waved a hand, like a queen ending a debate. "Education is training."

But this was not a matter of debate, for me. This was my life's research. I couldn't let a fallacy like that go unchallenged. "Education is discovery," I corrected. Kindly, I hoped.

She swung round on me, her eyes snapping. I think she might have argued further, which could have been very useful to both of us, in my opinion. But her assistant had an explosive coughing fit just then and I had to divert to the upstairs pantry to find him a glass of water.

And the Junior Art Master came out of the Studio, stopped dead as if he'd been poleaxed and fled. I stared after him, astounded.

Then Peter Abel arrived, academic gown billowing behind him in his haste, as he rushed towards her, saying, "Secretary of State, you are very welcome."

And the whole ghastly business unravelled like a ball of wool tumbling down a mountainside. I had, in effect, kidnapped the honoured visitor, made her walk up two flights of rickety old stairs, laddering her stockings in the process and, above all, committed the cardinal sin of not recognising her.

According to Peter Abel, she was so shaken she behaved quite mildly for the rest of the visit. But she made it clear that I had to go. I was incorrigibly frivolous.

He put it more kindly than that. But he needn't have bothered. I'd overheard quite a lot of her remarks. Especially when the Junior Art Master gave me a plate of the ceremonial shortbread and a gentle push towards the honoured visitor, hissing, "Go and offer it to *Mrs Thatcher*."

I didn't. It seemed a waste.

She had a carrying voice. "Of course, she may be simple, poor thing. I understand that some geniuses often are. But is one happy to trust one's children to them?"

Subtext: give her the sack. Or I will close you down.

I don't think she actually said that. But it's certainly what the posse of governors heard. The new Chairman of the Board of Governors was an aspiring politician, according to the Staff Room. He heard it all right.

Peter Abel was gone within the week, by order of the Board.

I left the next day.

# Chapter Two

Oddly enough, it was Peter Abel who had told me what to do when I was thrown out. He'd been a bit drunk at the time, I suspect. And he'd been talking about himself and his beloved northern mountains. But I'd committed it to memory. Just as well, really.

So I packed a small knapsack, attached my state-of-the-art telescope to it, and got on a bus, any bus. And I kept getting off and joining the next bus until there were no more buses and nowhere else to go.

The buses got smaller and smaller and so did the towns. I ran out of road in a place called Little Piddling. At least that was what the sign at the side of the road said. *Welcome to Little Piddling.* It gleamed. It looked as if it got washed a lot.

The beach was beautiful, though.

It was one of those thunderous days when the sky seems like a low, dark roof with a hole in the top. Golden sunlight came streaming through and broke into about seven separate beams. Where they hit the sea, the water turned into a turbulence of diamonds. I knew I ought to imprint the image, for future reference if nothing else. At the Institute I could have done it in an instant. But my human eyes weren't good enough.

So I stopped trying.

That's what Peter Abel advised me to do when I walked into a wall of my own ignorance. "Stop trying so hard, Selsis. It's a waste of energy."

He was worrying a lot about conserving energy, by then. He was another Adaptive Life Form, like me, and he had a theory that the more we adapted, the more energy we used up that we couldn't replace. At the Institute we replenished it naturally, all the time.

Maybe he was afraid his energy was running out. I didn't know him very long. Just those last seven earth months before he, well, went home. Or not.

Home was not a concept either of us had encountered before Earth. Like parents, it presupposed too many new ideas. The Institute was—well, the nearest translation, I suppose, would be our "accustomed place". We worked there. We ate there. We slept there. But... well, Earth home was quite a bit more than that.

We both knew it. But I don't think Peter Abel understood it any more than I did, though he tried to get the Sixth Form to explain it a couple of times. Well, of course, what he did was to get the Sixth Form to *discuss* it in one of their philosophical debates. He didn't tell them they were teaching us.

Now I walked along the promenade looking out to sea and watching that cascade of particles falling and rebounding from the surface of the water. Instead of focusing and analysing and constructing a usable hypothesis, I just thought: maybe Peter was right. Maybe I've Adapted too much, too fast. Used too much life force energy.

If I'm already losing my powers, can I survive?

It felt oddly peaceful, like floating in a warm bath. I even closed my eyes and opened my palms to the sensation, rocking gently.

I'll say this for the human body, whatever I was losing in deductive and recording abilities, not to mention ability to take action, I was gaining in sensory awareness. They *feel* everything, these humans. Though mostly they seem not to know it.

I opened my eyes. There were steps off the promenade that took people over the sea wall and down onto the golden sand. I edged down them with care. Staring into those shimmering droplets had dazzled me. I didn't want to tumble. It would bring people running to help and Peter Abel had warned me that it was essential not to be noticed. I focused my energy and sent out a low-grade deflection signal. Partly to see whether I still could, if I'm honest.

*Nothing to see here. Just shifting shadows in the strange light.*

It seemed to work. There were probably a dozen people on the beach: a couple of runners; a group of women who had been for a swim, laughing; a man with binoculars staring out to sea; a woman with two feathery-tailed dogs. She looked in my direction once or twice. But I kept broadcasting *shadows, just shadows,* and she walked on, looking faintly puzzled.

The sun was glorious but it had no chance to warm the air. The wind took care of that. It kept whipping round me, making my all-weather jacket puff out and then cling like wet flannel. It felt as if it was trying to blow me back to where I'd come from.

But where was that? Orwell College? Just to think about it was like a physical injury, for some reason, a sore place under my breastbone. No wonder humans talked about breaking their hearts.

Or the Institute? To do that, I would have to walk into the sea and channel those sparkling particles. It would take most of my remaining energy. In practical terms, I knew I had enough for one shot. But if that failed—

It needed planning, taking stock of the position of the moon, prevailing winds, earth vibrations. It was not something to do on the spur of the moment.

And yet the wind, pushing me towards the sea.... Was that chance?

Or could it possibly be the Institute trying to restore communication?

Once I would have known, without having to think about it. Now I was floundering.

I stopped and half-turned so that the wind was behind me, the sea at my back.

The Institute had pushed me so hard to come to Earth. Had they really lost all interest? Or was this silence deliberate? Maybe they wanted to throw me back on my solo resources and force me to explore more than I'd bargained for.

I shook my head. It felt wrong. The Institute was what humans would call bureaucratic and controlling. But it was not usually devious. Never in my experience.

*What has happened? Why have they abandoned me?*

It burst out of me so ferociously that I stumbled and almost fell over. It was like a human cry of anguish, almost tangible. It appalled me. Before this body, I had never felt anything like it. It shook me.

And any telepath in broadcast range would be feeling pretty shaken, too. Humans didn't use mind-to-mind communication like we did, but they had a small number of natural telepaths. If there were one on the beach right now, that could present a problem.

I pulled myself together and revolved slowly, on the spot, looking for signs of distress among the now distant beach-walkers. Someone on their knees clutching their ears, maybe. Or one of the dogs, howling in pain.

But there was nothing. All was as it had been. As it should be.

It was a relief. I must have mistaken the force of my own feelings. Because I felt so much, I'd thought I was broadcasting. Yet another sign of how I was losing touch with who I really was.

Logic, I thought. Use logic. You haven't lost that.

I began to walk again. There were some brightly painted one-storey sheds to my left, with a sort of wooden way in front of them. They had shutters, as if there were windows behind them. They looked as if they had their eyes closed. Sleeping until summer, I thought, amused.

A gust of wind made me stagger and brought me out of my reverie. I looked around and saw that I was very close to the water. Either the tide was coming in or I had been walking towards it on an involuntary trajectory.

Chance again?

I suddenly had a nasty thought. Maybe the project was going so badly that the Institute had decided to discontinue it. With Peter Abel gone and me in no position to take over, maybe they had done so already. Both, of course, were my fault, one way and another.

Would they discontinue *me?*

Maybe there was no point in preparing careful calculations. Maybe I should just walk into the ocean and see what happened.

*Stop trying so hard, Selsis. Let what will be, be.*

Oh well, Peter Abel had ended in his mountains. The sea would do me fine.

I began to walk forward.

And a voice behind me said, "Are you all right?"

# Chapter Three

For a moment I thought it was a voice in my head.

But then I realised that it was real human man. Which meant it was much too late to try the *Nothing to see here. Just shifting shadows* trick. Mind suggestion only works when people aren't paying attention.

So I drew a deep, revivifying breath, squared my shoulders and turned round.

He was taller than me and very windblown. His hair must have been tied back, but now long fronds of it were blowing this way and that across his face, like seaweed over rock. All I could make out was a great beak of a nose and hard grey eyes. Not the sort of eyes that I—well, the human that it looked as if I was becoming, anyway—would have expected to ask someone whether they were all right. Especially not a stranger on a chilly beach just as it was coming on to rain.

"Can I help you?" I said, in the tone the School Secretary used to repel rampaging parents. It worked like a bucket of icy water emptied from a great height on their heads. Well, it usually did. When she did it, anyway.

I clearly didn't have her touch.

This man just looked impatient. "You called out."

"No, I didn't."

"I heard you. Right in my ear. It's still bloody echoing."

Ouch. "You're mistaken."

It started to rain in earnest. Maybe he'd run for shelter, I thought hopefully.

But he was one of the stubborn ones. "You said, 'Why have they abandoned me?' No, make that yelled. Nearly burst my eardrums. Real Maori warrior stuff."

Oh, shoot. The blasted man had to be a natural telepath. Just my luck to fall over one of the 0.0001 per cent of this world's population in Little Piddling on a wet Wednesday. I knew I was glaring at him. He glared back.

"My ears are still ringing," he said, as if explaining to a not very bright class of twelve-year-olds.

Not really helpful.

I swapped to Chairman of the Governors mode, bit of a bully, effortlessly superior. It was good, too. "How ridiculous."

It didn't have the effect I hoped for. He opened his mouth—to argue, I was almost certain—and then closed it again. Not intimidated, alas.

The wind dropped a bit then and he used both hands to push the hair away from his face. And I saw that what I had thought was a glare was more complicated than that. I might not understand humans very well, but I had been conscientiously recording my observations for a year now. This looked...personal.

How could that be? Did this man think he knew me?

I was floundering again. We habitually used mind communication in the Institute. But it had to be voluntary on both sides. We didn't read unexpressed thoughts. On Earth, where people lied most of the time, I'd learned to read faces a bit. But I was really only any good with people I knew. I didn't know him and I couldn't read him.

And then the ground under me gave one of those nasty little lurches that I never got used to and another thought skated into my mind in a whirl of cold panic. Did he think he knew me because we'd met somewhere and I'd forgotten him?

I knew I was losing familiar skills as I adapted to this life form. What if this new brain couldn't hold onto newly gained knowledge either?

My brain scanned this world's memories furiously. He wasn't the doctor with whom I'd made the first big mistake of the project. I'd never forget *his* face. But someone else? One of the island party, where I'd first floated up out of the water? I'd bonded with the girls, but there had been men there, too. Or one of the librarians who'd helped me in London? Or someone who'd given me directions at a station? Or...? Or...?

Or anyone.

For a moment, I couldn't think. Couldn't *move*. My thoughts were a total jumble.

Not so the interfering man's. He said, "Come away from the sea."

Now I was really lost. I gaped at him.

"Just three steps."

And he began to back away a little, holding my eyes. I'm not sure he wasn't patting his trousered thigh, the way the woman with the dog had done.

"What?"

"One step then. You can do that. One step towards me."

This sounded like total loopiness. I took refuge in gentle reason. "Why should I step towards you?"

He smiled. It was a surprisingly sweet smile. "Because if you don't, you'll get your feet wet. The tide's turning."

I looked down quickly. Feet. Oh yes. I'd forgotten feet. And he was right, the water was reaching for my boots, a little closer with each wave, then falling back in a spume of frustrated spittle. From that angle the sea didn't look magical at all. Just greedy.

"Not so nice," he said with a nod, as if he were agreeing with me.

Just for a moment I froze. Could he *hear* me?

In a way, it was not so surprising that he'd picked up my earlier howl into the ether. OK, the Institute had tuned me out, but I was still trying to re-open communication. And yes, sometimes it was involuntary, a sort of *Is anybody there? Talk to me.*

But overhearing a howl of anguish is a very different thing from eavesdropping on someone's private mind. The first is accidental. The second is deliberate spying.

I said, "I don't know you." And even a non-telepath would have got the message. Pure loathing.

Even so, it didn't deter him. He nodded pleasantly and went right ahead, as if we were in the middle of a cordial conversation.

"Anton. I teach at the crammers up the hill." He jerked his head at the landscape behind him. "Geography and music. I come to the beach most days. Pleased to meet you." And he put out his hand.

I wasn't pleased to meet him, not at all. But the body put out my hand in response, because this social thing of shaking hands seems to be hardwired. He seized it but he didn't shake it. Instead he started to pretty much haul me up the incline of the beach. I tried to dig my heels in to bring us to a halt, but the sand was too soft. I just ended up ploughing two great ruts in it.

From his point of view, it must have felt like dragging a huge rake up the beach. Or maybe landing an enormous fish.

"What do you think you're doing?" I yelled.

"Saving you from yourself. That sea is dangerous."

He was panting by the time he stopped on a sort of plateau of slightly paler sand. He hadn't got us even halfway up the beach, I saw. The slope up to the scrub and the rainbow huts looked steep. Much steeper than it had seemed coming down to the water's edge.

I had to tip my head back to see the road beyond. It seemed impossibly far away. And this end of the beach was deserted, I noted, assessing this new situation.

What's more, he hadn't let go of my hand. In fact, in that split second while I was taking my bearings, he'd grabbed my other wrist as well and pulled me closer, to face him. Not gently.

I thought: good gracious, he is going to hurt me. How extraordinary.

The body said: *run.*

So I did.

# Chapter Four

I don't quite know how I did it. Except that Adaptive Life Forms are known for adapting fast when there is a survival need. Of course, I had acquired data on the difficulties of moving in wet sand over the last few minutes. And, anyway, the sand was not so wet further up the beach. So the going was easier.

But even so, I didn't really expect to get away from my assailant. I had no plan of action. I just ran.

So, when I found I'd escaped, I didn't know what to do. What I wanted, desperately, viscerally, was a home to go to. Somewhere I would be welcomed. Somewhere safe.

That was unexpected. Actually, it was a nasty surprise. When I'd left the college, my only thought was to keep on travelling until I could work out the optimum departure point, date and hour to attempt a return to the Institute. I wasn't even thinking about a home.

But now I was.

Logically, I knew that I needed a place of safety to take stock. But I wanted more than that. I wanted comforting. I wanted a place I could curl up in and be warm and cosy; somewhere I could tell myself a story with a happy ending until I fell asleep, embraced by my dreams. I wanted a human *home*.

It had to be the effect of this planet and all its emotions. After the first shock, I recognised that.

Great! Just great!

But on that first burst of urgency, I'd reached the sheds with the pointed roofs and dived behind them. Now my chest was heaving and I felt as if I was going to throw up. You can't go into mourning for a home you've never had when you're trying not to vomit. Even this body had its priorities.

I don't know how long it took for the sick feeling to subside. When it did, I sat down rather suddenly, still expecting pursuit. But the man didn't appear. Eventually I got my courage together, crawled to the side of my chosen hut and peered cautiously round. There was no one on the beach.

Keeping low, I wriggled around the hut until I was in the shadowed gap between my hut and its neighbour. From this new position I could survey what looked like the whole beach, right back to the distant steps I had come down from the Promenade.

It was quite empty. Even the dogs had disappeared. There wasn't a living thing in sight except a couple of wheeling gulls against the gunmetal sky.

I couldn't believe it. I whipped round, in case the telepath had worked round behind me. But here the coast road had dwindled to not much more than a lane and it was deserted. So were the hills beyond.

It was raining quite hard by then.

Actually, that was probably the reason for the lack of people. I had already noticed that humans, at least the ones I knew, dived for cover at the first few drops of rain. But it was a new experience for me and I liked the stuff.

So, as soon as I saw I was alone, I stood up and waved my arms about. I may even have danced. I certainly turned my face to the sky and let the rain cascade over all its protuberances—eyebrows, cheekbones, nose, chin—in sybaritic excess. It was wonderfully reviving.

Pretty soon I was drenched. Rain was trickling down my neck. Fat raindrops clung to my eyelashes. They blurred the landscape into an Impressionist dreamscape. It was beautiful. For some reason, it made me feel like dancing some more.

I would have done, too. But then the sky went dark, thunder started and I realised how unpleasant wet clothes were.

My sheltering shed was shuttered and locked up tight. But the next one along was more tumbledown. The boards were rotting at the base and I could see where one of its doors was hanging slightly off true. Between brute force and a certain amount of applied geometry, I managed to pull the wood away from the hinge far enough to get my head and shoulders through at floor height. It was all I needed. I took off my backpack and wriggled through. The poor mistreated door fell back into place behind me.

I stood up and looked around.

It was magic.

I don't mean it was magic getting out of the storm, though that was welcome. I mean the place itself. I'd expected—oh, I don't know, maybe a store of tools, possibly fishing nets or even an old outboard motor, basically a glorified cupboard of hardly-ever-used things. But this was a little *house*.

I stood up and looked round, almost dazed with delight.

Yes, it was shabby and needed repair. But somebody had really loved it once. There were paintings on the wall, delicate watercolour studies of plants. Everything was small, perfectly fitted to its place. It was like a doll's house.

There was even a bookshelf, stuffed with books. They were mostly paperbacks and looked as if they had been read again and again. *Children of The New Forest, The Compleat Angler, Rogue Herries, The Lord of the Rings, Funeral in Berlin.* I saw that most of them were novels, a new concept to me. I wriggled with excitement. They would make a nice change from social research. I'd worked my way through six months' back copies of *Cosmopolitan* magazine on the journey and it had been hard work.

I retrieved my backpack and began to explore. At the back, which was darker, there was a cupboard with a scrubbed pine worktop and a plate rack above it. At the beach end, two folding chairs and a folding table stood propped against the wall. Against one wall there was a beautifully made chest. Someone had made a deep cushion to fit it exactly, with cushion arms and a cushion backrest, so that it was like a half-size couch. If you set up the folding table and set it in front of the couch, you could have four people eating a meal here.

Inside the chest there were blankets, and a patchwork quilt, all carefully folded in brown paper tied with string, and an embroidered tablecloth. They smelled of lavender.

Was there a cooking facility of some kind? I went back to the pine worktop, but no, nothing. That was when it occurred to me— where was the light coming from? I couldn't see any windows, not even above the doors.

I looked up. But there was a low ceiling above my head.

And then I realised—the ceiling only covered half the length of the shed. That was why the cupboard area was comparatively dark. I backed out from under it and saw the narrowest, steepest little built-in ladder that I could imagine. I ran up it. My head touched the ceiling before I got to the top step.

It was a wide balcony, constructed with the same loving carpentry as the chest below. It contained what I took to be a thin double mattress, encased in a sort of mackintosh envelope. So that explained the blankets.

There were four windows set into the gabled roof, two over the bed, and two over the dining area. You would have to crawl into bed from the foot and you wouldn't be able to sit up when you woke. And a night of passion, as recommended by *Cosmopolitan*, would probably mean that you risked falling six feet out of bed. But otherwise it was really cosy.

I turned round, leaned back against those doll's house stairs, and laughed until my stomach hurt.

Oh, it was magic all right.

Without even knowing that I was looking, I had found a home.

# Chapter Five

The thunderstorm was spectacular but soon moved on. As soon as it had gone, I went outside and scouted round. No one was about yet and all the other sheds were shuttered and locked.

Just beyond the last one, a wooden signpost pointed away from town. It said "Bridle Path". Underneath someone had chalked "NO motorbikes!!!" And underneath *that* was a weathered notice which flapped in the wind. It had taken a good deal of punishment from the weather and was mostly indecipherable. But by means of unfocusing my eyes, using my deep sight and applying all my remaining deductive powers, I managed to make out something useful. "For Beach Hut Rental enquire at Paper Shop."

Intriguing. It sounded just what I needed. If I could work out what a paper shop might look like.

I went back and stored my backpack out of sight, just in case someone noticed the damaged door and came investigating. Then I made my way up to the road and went back into Little Piddling.

I found the Paper Shop on a corner, one road back from the promenade. As I'd already suspected, it wasn't made of paper. It didn't even sell very much that was made from paper, though I tracked down a notebook of squared paper, which would be perfect for my lunar observations. But actually the shop sold *everything*. In fact, it was a dragon's hoard cave of new things, very few of which I recognised. But those I did—oh, they were exactly what I'd dreamed of when I first took this assignment.

Since my arrival, all my housekeeping needs had been provided for, at first by kind strangers who took care of me; then, after I joined the college, by my employer. Almost as soon as I got on my first bus, I realised that being on my own was presenting me with a whole new dimension of challenge. Now I saw that this Paper Shop was a place where I could buy all the things that I would need to feed, clothe and even keep myself warm in this strange hiatus of my expedition.

I was inspecting something which looked like a rock but felt like a vegetable when a voice behind me said, "Can I help you?"

I jumped. I mean I should have been aware of her before she spoke. Even humans could do that.

"Do you want that potato? Let me weigh it."

Potato! So that's what the thing was. It didn't look at all like the potatoes I had eaten at school. I put it back in its basket.

"Oh. No, thank you. I was just looking." A very useful phrase that Peter Abel had taught me. "I want to rent one of the beach huts. The notice said I should come here?"

"Yes, that's right." She came out from behind a tall stand holding bright plastic buckets and even brighter sombreros. She had long straight hair, greying at the temples, and steady eyes. She was wearing a shapeless robe in some very light, very pretty material that finished just above her shins. And wellington boots.

"Well, may I take the sky blue one? It's one in from the end of the row."

She bent her head, like a queen acknowledging a petition. "Forget me not."

For a moment I wondered wildly whether I needed a password to rent one of the things. "I'm sorry?"

"That beach hut is called Forget-me-not. Like the flower."

"Oh. How—er—charming." Another useful word. It covered everything from stupid-and-ugly-but-I-know-you-like-it to simply bonkers.

She produced a hard-covered notebook and began to leaf through it. As far as I could see, each beach hut had a page of its own, carefully ruled and divided into columns.

"Why that one?"

Um—because I broke in and fell in love with its patchwork quilt? Maybe not.

"It has a lovely vibe," I said, borrowing freely from our pupils' vocabulary. And waited for those eyes to bore into my guilty conscience.

But astonishingly, she smiled. "Yes, it does, doesn't it? Do you know the owners?"

I shook my head.

"They're lovely people." She sounded sad. I almost asked about them, but she had already removed a pen from behind her ear and said briskly, "How long do you want it? Just the day?"

"A month."

She looked up from the page, clearly confused. Maybe I hadn't been sufficiently precise?

"I mean a whole lunar month, starting today."

She put the book down. Not a good sign.

"Every day for a month? For how many people?"

"Just me."

"You're staying in Little Piddling for a month on your own?"

"Yes."

"Why?"

I didn't try to dress it up. "I'm studying the moon. I have to take regular observations every night throughout this whole moon cycle."

She believed me. She thought I was mad, but she believed me. "So you want the hut twenty-four hours a day for four weeks?"

"Yes."

"You do know there's no running water? No lavatory nearer than the public conveniences in the park? No heating?"

"That's what I assumed," I said carefully.

"One or two of the other huts have bottled gas and cooking facilities." She watched me, equally carefully.

But that patchwork quilt and the beautiful carpentry were both calling me. I shook my head. "Like I said, I love the vibe."

"Very well. I'll ask the owners. It's a much longer let than usual. They might want to use it themselves. Over Easter for instance. Oh, and can you provide references?"

My heart sank. But the new Headmaster had promised to give me a decent reference for any job I applied for. I could probably finesse that into supplying one for a beach-hut landlord. "Yes."

"OK. I'll ring them now and see what they say."

And she whisked out of sight. Somewhere behind the sombreros, a door closed with great firmness.

I continued to browse, collecting food that didn't need any additional preparation and three large bottles of water. I piled it all on the counter, to await her return. At least I had plenty of money, since my job at the school, I thought. It would be more than enough to pay for my rent and food for the next four weeks. And after that... Well, after that was unknown territory in so many ways. Money or lack of it was going to be a minor issue.

When she eventually emerged her face was completely blank.

"The owners have agreed to rent you the beach hut for the next four weeks."

The rent was to be paid weekly in advance, plus a deposit against breakages. The Paper Shop, in the person of the shopkeeper whose name was Judith Beaupère, would have the right to visit to ensure that I was the sole tenant. "That means no wild beach parties," she interpreted, without a glimmer of a smile.

Parties? Wild beach parties? *Me?* Oh, this independent living was so interesting.

I suppose I must have looked stunned.

She misinterpreted. "Little Piddling is a quiet place. We get families on the beach. Kids from the local schools, that sort of thing. If you want sex and drugs and rock and roll you'd be better off in Brighton." She sounded distinctly wistful, I thought.

I shook my head. "Not my scene," I said borrowing from a very cool sixth former from the Astronomy Club. Who had, indeed, introduced me to the whole concept of Cool.

She sighed. "Well, I suppose if moon watching is your thing..." And returned to the practicalities.

I paid her both for the beach hut and my shopping. She gave me a receipt and made me sign for the key. It was on a pretty blue ribbon instead of a keyring. She smiled as she passed it across.

"It's a dear little place. You're right. It has seen joy. I hope you'll be very happy there, Miss—er—Brown."

"Selsis, please."

"Selsis? That's unusual."

Ouch. Should have changed that.

"Family name," I said firmly.

"That's nice," she said, closing the book. "Well, you know where the beach hut is, so why don't you go along and make yourself comfortable? I can't leave the shop until closing time. But I'll be along later to see how you're settling in."

Ah. Better get on with repairing the damage I'd done getting in, then. Number one priority.

She gave me a string bag to carry my food purchases and I hurried away to find the necessary supplies.

Hurried? I damn nearly ran.

# Chapter Six

I thought I'd caught sight of a DIY suppliers down an alley on my way into town and so, indeed, it proved.

At Orwell College, I'd helped repair several small accidents engineered by enquiring minds. I loved it and the Art Master had been quite complimentary, too. He and the caretaker had taken me into the well-equipped school workshop as their very first pupil. Gifted children, apparently, didn't enjoy mending stuff. Adaptive Life Forms did.

So I knew a bit about basic carpentry. Actually, I was more comfortable in DIY places than I was buying food in a general store. I came clean with the two guys who ran it.

"I've done some damage to one of the beach huts and I need to repair it."

Cautious at first, the DIY guys soon came to the conclusion that I knew what I was talking about. By the time they found out that the first aid was for Forget-me-not, they were enthusiastic and helpful.

"Bert and Milly's place," said the older one. "If he'd been himself, Bert would have had it all shipshape and ready for the season by now." He shook his head. There was clearly some cause for sympathy there. Before I could ask, he added briskly, "But he doesn't lend his tools, you know."

"Of course not." I knew enough to be shocked at the idea.

They looked at each other and beamed.

"You could rent—" began the younger, whom I took to be the son.

"I was hoping you'd advise me on what I need and I could buy the tools to do the job."

But the older one dismissed such extravagance. "No need for that. Not on a little job like this. We can lend you everything you need. It won't take long. Bring the tools back tomorrow when you've finished."

His kindness silenced me. I felt tears backing up behind the body's eyes. Oh, these blasted humans, they cry so *easily*.

"Or I can pick them up," the younger one was saying casually. "And you'll want to match the paint. It was bluebell originally, but it's been up a while. Must have faded. What do you think, Dad?"

I blinked back the damn tears and made a private note that I was right about the family relationship. Maybe I was getting better at this human observation thing, after all. Even if I hadn't got control of the tear ducts yet.

The two of them put their heads together over several palette cards and came to the conclusion that the shade I wanted was Sea Whisper.

Very appropriate, I thought, and said so.

They put all my purchases into a box, with the borrowed tools, and the younger one offered to run me back to the beach huts if I was going back now. I decided that being a helpless female had some benefits I hadn't suspected, and thanked them with real gratitude.

It pays to be nice, Peter Abel always said. I would have liked to tell him he was right. Oh, I missed him.

So I got a lift home. And more.

Before he left, my driver, whose name was Colin, helped me wrench off the damaged wood, and replaced the distorted hinge with my new one. I thanked him and he went off whistling.

I pottered around my new domain, finding places for the food I'd bought and the few belongings I'd brought with me. I put my precious telescope in the chest and arranged the cushions on top again.

The rain had completely stopped by then. As I worked on the wood, measuring, preparing and marking it out, the grey roof of cloud disappeared. The sun came out and the sea sparkled in quite a different way.

It was hot work, especially when I had to rehang the door without Colin's help. I stripped off the last layer of my travel wear and was down to tee shirt, jeans and bare feet by the time I finished. The sand was positively warm under my toes. Good paint drying weather, then. Just as well, as I seemed to have signed up for putting on five coats of various sorts.

I took out my notebook and made a few basic entries. But Colin's dad had insisted that I apply the primer with even strokes, nice and slow. Nice and slow and hypnotic. I'd just about managed to put my brush into the jam jar (thank you, Colin) of turpentine and push it into the shade, before I opened my notebook. First it slipped, then it fell out of my hand as I slid down onto the sand. I didn't so much doze off as fall into a trance.

A trance with dreams.

I was in an art gallery. The Art Master was walking me round a group of Renaissance portraits, mostly of young men.

"Look at them," he said. "They're the cool kids of their time. Long hair, fancy jackets. Rock gods, every one."

Even in my not-quite-doze, I knew that I was tapping into recent memory; that it was not where I really was in time and space.

I was looking at one of the cool kids now. He was standing under a summer blue sky, with little puffs of white cloud. His red cap, almost like a fez, was crammed on top of waves of flowing auburn hair that touched his shoulders. The colours in it danced in the sunlight like spray above the sea. His eyes were brown? Green? The colour of a path through a wood where it gets lost under the trees, anyway. He was wearing a very smart jacket with a tight collar round his throat, and slashes of black and parchment and plum.

Something about the set of mouth and chin made me think he looked stubborn.

A great beak of a nose...

A great beak...

I jack-knifed out of my stupor.

It wasn't a dream. Well, he wasn't wearing plum velvet and a fez. But, apart from that, the Renaissance rock star was standing there in the flesh. Looking down at me. Flowing auburn waves and all.

Auburn? The last time I saw him his hair had been black straggly rat-tails. I remembered it clearly. Oh, I suppose that was the rain.

Anyway, there was no gainsaying that nose. Or those steady, unreadable eyes. I knew him. And, oh horrors, I was awake.

It was the telepath. He had found me.

# Chapter Seven

And then something really strange happened. I'd heard people talking about being in two minds. It always sounded like nonsense to me.

But now, suddenly, I understood. I was definitely in two minds. My immediate thought was: *danger, danger, danger!* But there was something else, too. It wasn't quite thought and it wasn't quite feeling. The best way I can describe it is a sort of dreamy what-the-hell curiosity.

I heard myself murmuring, "You're rather beautiful."

And he was. He certainly didn't look dangerous. Not with that long hair shimmering in the sun. Not to mention the sand on the bottom of his jeans. I knew they were sandy because, briefly shaking off the mesmeric fascination of his hair, I was staring straight at them.

"Hey, don't go back to sleep."

"Mmm?"

"Come on. Get up. It's going to rain any minute."

He was right. A great fat raindrop landed plop! on my bare arm, jumping me awake. I gave up and lurched into a sitting position, yawning.

"What do you want?" I rubbed my eyes, so I didn't have to look directly at him.

"And good afternoon to you, too." He sounded amused.

He held out his hand.

A second raindrop fell. Then, more. The sun darkened. His hair darkened with it. An unremarkable mid-brown. Ah, that was better.

I ignored his hand and tried to stand up. My left leg wobbled and I cried out in surprise. It really was just surprise. It didn't hurt.

But by then he had already caught me and was holding me up. Not at arm's length. And I had to look at him directly, after all. Right into his eyes, in fact.

Something changed. I'm not sure what. It was too quick for me to catch, though I knew it had happened. Maybe his pupils flared? Oh, I was slowing down so much in this body.

"Well, hello Selsis Brown," he said softly.

I couldn't look away.

No, he didn't look scary. And he wasn't trying to mindscan me either, as far as I could tell. Or was that me deceiving myself, because I couldn't cope if he was?

It was an effort, but I applied logic. Well, part of me did. The part I knew and was still comfortable with. He'd got my name from somewhere—the obvious source was me.

"How do you know my name?"

He withdrew a notebook from his armpit where he'd stuffed it when he caught me. *My* notebook, I now saw.

"Selsis Brown, Orwell College," he said.

I'd written my name inside the front cover, so it sort of made sense. But was that just a way of hiding that he'd peered into my mind?

Most natural telepaths are only in tune with people they are bonded with: a twin, someone they've survived death with, a profound love. A universal telepath, someone who could pick up a cry of anguish from a stranger, is rarer and more vulnerable. Even on a planet like this, where telepathy is rare and most people didn't believe in it anyway, a universal telepath would develop masking strategies out of sheer necessity.

All my own mind-communication was learned, the hard way. I had no natural telepathic abilities. But I'd worked with telepaths and I should be able to recognise the signs if this guy had been rummaging around in my mind. Or I would have done before this body. I slid a finger behind my ear and tapped. It was crude. But it ought to work.

Nothing. No echo.

Deliberately, I locked eyes with him. He didn't jump back, or flinch. His eyes remained steady. So he wasn't cloaking a probe.

Unless he had phenomenal control.

But could an Earth person have phenomenal control? Seriously? Without years of training and a Major Adept to mentor him?

AAAARGH.

He said, "Are you OK?"

"I don't know. My leg feels very odd." I tried to move it and my ankle went over, in a way that should have been painful and wasn't.

He looked down. "Pins and needles," he said. "The feeling's starting to come back. You'll just have to hang on to me for a moment."

He was right on both counts. The next minute or so was sort of alarming and sort of interesting at the same time. Not just because of the sensation in my leg. As soon as I could put weight on it, I limped—no, make that hobbled—back onto the boardwalk and into the beach hut.

He followed and stopped in the doorway. "OK, now? Are you sure?"

"Yes." But he was still searching my face for signs of…what? I swallowed and said the first thing that came into my head. "Who are you?"

How inane can you get? I mean he wasn't going to tell me he was the county druid with telepathic powers, was he?

"Name's Anton. We met earlier," he reminded me. I was almost certain he was trying not to laugh. "But for these purposes, I'm Next Door. I saw you flat out—" He gestured at the beach. "I thought you might have hurt yourself."

That puzzled me. "Why?"

He stopped being amused. "Well, you were trying to walk into the sea, earlier, weren't you? Fully clothed. I thought you might be—"

I bristled. "Off my head?"

"In some sort of trouble," he said soberly. He looked away.

"Oh."

His tone changed. "Anyway, I saw Judith at the Paper Shop and she asked me to keep a lookout for you. Forget-me-not hasn't been open since last summer. She was worried what you might find."

"Like what?"

He shrugged. "Mice? Squatters? Smuggled brandy? Your guess is as good as mine. Then, when I saw you on the ground, I didn't think. I just ran."

That embarrassed me. And *that*, in turn, made me realise that one part of me had already decided he wasn't telepathically spying on me. Because I wanted to believe it? *Damn.*

"I'm sorry?" He sounded startled.

So I must have said it out loud. Or…

Oh hell, it didn't matter whether I trusted him or not, did it? I didn't trust *me*.

I tried to say something sensible. "I spent three hours or so repairing the door. I just fell asleep. I'm fine."

He nodded, already turning away. "Great. Then I'll get out of your way."

"Um. Thank you." It wasn't what I wanted to say. I wanted him to *stay*. I don't know why. "Would you like a drink? I mean, I've got water. And water."

Anton stopped. Looked at the dark clouds and then his watch. "Or if you'd like something warm, we could go to the chippie?"

I had no idea what a chippie was, so this was a good opportunity to acquire new knowledge, equally useful for adding to the Institute's archives or assisting my survival on Earth, if that was my only option.

"I would like that. Thank you."

"Great. I'll lock up next door and we can go."

He pushed off. I tested the paint and wasn't convinced it was dry enough to shut the doors. So I tidied my tools away in a cupboard out of sight and propped both doors very slightly open. There were neat wooden doorstops for the purpose. Like everything else in Forget-me-not, they were beautifully made. And I loved them.

He came back, wearing a waterproof jacket. It was raining quite hard now. He stood on the boardwalk, looking in.

"Ready?"

I went to meet him, pulling on my own jacket. "Yes. As long as it's OK to leave the beach hut open?"

He turned to scan the beach. It was empty, even of dog walkers.

"It's fine. Nobody's going to come this far along the beach on a cold wet evening in the middle of the week. A warm weekend would be different."

I remembered Judith Beaupère's prohibition on wild beach parties and grinned.

He saw it. "What?"

I explained and he laughed. "She's a free spirit. She's been waiting for Flower Power to hit Little Piddling since 1968. Make that, looking forward to it."

I was pleased. "That's what I thought, too." At least I'd got *something* right.

He took me up the slope past the NO motorbikes!!! notice and turned left down the main street. Then almost at once, he turned into a small door bearing a handwritten notice: "Frying Tonight".

The chippie, I found, meant a narrow cave of a shop with a couple of tables in the window and a tall counter at the far end, with a trough of oil behind it. The air smelled...filling. I may have groaned.

He looked round and his eyes warmed with understanding.

78

"Hungry?"

I nodded.

"When did you last eat?"

I concentrated. I couldn't remember breakfast, though I had bought a coffee from a van outside the last bus garage. "Maybe yesterday evening."

"Right. You need to eat *now*. Can we have two cod and chips, please, Chandra?"

The young woman behind the counter smiled at him. "Not yet, you can't, Anton. The fryer isn't up to the right temperature yet. Come back in forty minutes."

I know I groaned that time.

Anton chuckled. "OK. We'll go to the pub and come back then. Bag us the table in the corner, will you?"

"Be glad to."

He led the way again. But the pub wasn't open yet, either. I could have wept. Now that I had remembered I needed food, I was starving.

Anton looked at his watch. "Ten minutes to opening time. Right, turbo tour of Little Piddling."

Our first stop was the pier. It was deserted. We ran along the wooden planks. They bounced and there were one or two gaps where I could see the water rocking below us. It was exciting, but I was glad of the lifebelts positioned at intervals along the railings. Anton ignored both sea and lifesaving notices.

"Please note the theatre. Bit down-at-heel but they do a great panto at Christmas," he said. "This way to the lifeboat." There was a shed at the end of the pier with Lifeboat Station painted in big letters on the door.

It had stopped raining but we'd had to dodge puddles. Now lights were coming on in the twilight. The little town was basically rundown and rather shabby but the lights made it magical. It was like one of the Art Master's Impressionist paintings, I thought, wincing.

"What's wrong?" asked Anton, looking down at me.

I tensed. If he wasn't a telepath, he was acute as hell.

"A sort of memory."

"One that makes you jump and wince? Doesn't sound like a good one."

"Neither good nor bad. Just...gone."

He muttered something about blue, remembered hills.

"I'm sorry?"

"Happy highways where I went and cannot come again."

"*Oh!*" Yes, that was it. That was *it*. My throat felt full and there was moisture on my face that had nothing to do with rain or even sea spray.

He put his arm round me and tugged me a bit closer. We stood looking back at the town, like two exiles saying goodbye to land.

He said abruptly, "I came here once when I was a kid. Exchange holiday. It's a good place."

Outside the pub there was a handwritten notice advertising craft beer. I patted it happily. "Ooo lovely."

He groaned. "For God's sake take care with Prime Piddle. It stinks." He opened the door for me. "How do you know about real ale, then?"

"Chap I worked for. Peter Abel."

"Abel? The genius kids man?"

I nodded. "Founder member of the Campaign for Real Ale, and very proud of it." I didn't tear up at the memory this time. It just made me feel warm.

Anton was right about the beer. It smelled like two-day-old rugby socks. The barman turned out to be kind Colin from the DIY shop who welcomed me cheerily.

As, back at the chippie, did Chandra and her quiet husband. They came and sat with us, in the frequent intervals between customers.

In fact, I had a really nice time. Anton was entertaining and had travelled widely. He made us laugh about his student travel in India and hippie days in San Francisco. Places, I suddenly realised, I would now never visit.

"Something wrong?" he said, seeing me droop.

There was no way to explain that would make sense to these kind people.

"Just tired."

"Let's get you home."

*Home.* It sounded lovely.

I stumbled a couple of times as we headed down the slope to the beach, and Anton took my hand. He also brought out a small torch and lit the footpath in front of us. It made me feel—well—odd.

At Forget-me-not I thanked him for the tour, the meal and his company. But he stopped me before I could close the doors on him.

"What?"

I wondered if he was expecting a good night kiss, which I had heard of but had no further information on. Or wild, exotic sex, given his San Francisco experience. Theoretically I knew more about that, though I couldn't see me flinging my underwear over the door handle, as I'd heard was *de rigueur*.

In the Institute, physical intimacy consisted of a rapid transfer of energy. It was practised with great secrecy and regarded with disdain by Management. And I didn't know anything about that, either.

In the dark, I couldn't see Anton's expression but I could hear from his voice that he was laughing. "No electricity. You'll fall off that sleeping platform if you don't have a light."

"Oh." On reflection, I saw he had a point. "I didn't think of that."

"I did." Not only laughing but smug. "The torch," he added with a bow worthy of a Cavalier, "is yours. Good night." And he pressed it into my hand and sauntered off under the stars.

I was very cold and nearly asleep on my feet but I stood in the doorway watching him out of sight. I had an uneasy feeling that Anton had read my goodbye anxieties very clearly. And that I had let him win a game I didn't know we were playing.

It was annoying.

I couldn't wait for our next match.

# Chapter Eight

It was very cold in Forget-me-not. It would be even colder outside with my telescope. I decided I couldn't face it. I would start my lunar observations tomorrow.

I kept all my clothes on, then grabbed all the blankets and the quilt out of the chest and wrapped myself in them like a mummy. By the time I'd done that, I couldn't face climbing the ladder to the sleeping platform, either. So I threw every single cushion I could find onto the floor, as far away from the draughty doors as I could get. They made a nest of sorts. It wasn't all that comfortable but I was beyond noticing. I collapsed into them and slept until morning.

Quite late morning, actually. When I woke, I was very stiff. And there was a great carpet of sunlight on the front half of the beach hut.

I untangled myself and faced the first day of my new, if temporary, life. And soon realised that there were practical matters to be sorted urgently. I couldn't march back to the Jubilee Gardens every morning to go to the loo and wash. They were spotlessly clean but they didn't even have a shower.

I was pondering solutions when I saw Chandra and her husband unloading their van outside the fish and chip shop. She waved. It gave me an idea. I crossed the road...

Twenty minutes later I had negotiated bathroom rental for the month, borrowed Chandra's transistor radio and bought a prawn salad, a coffee and a home-baked cinnamon roll for breakfast-well-lunch.

Not too bad, I thought, pleased with myself. Thrown back on my own resources, I hadn't lost all my problem-solving skills. Or maybe the people of Little Piddling were just kind to incompetent strangers. For, when I got back to Forget-Me-Not, there was a cardboard box on the boardwalk outside, with a note. It was from Judith.

*Sorry I missed you last night. Here are some things you might be able to use.*

It was heavy. I unlocked the doors and staggered inside with it. But even when I unpacked it, I didn't recognise much, except a small greaseproof packet of shortbread. For the first time, I remembered the Secretary without flinching. In fact, I laughed. Little Piddling was giving me Honoured Visitor treatment in spades.

I shook out last night's bedding and tidied my little home, leaving the doors wide open to the sea air, so I could apply the next coat of paint. By then the sun was directly overhead and it was really warm. So I copied former colleagues and took *Funeral in Berlin* with Chandra's prawn salad onto the beach and gave myself a proper lunch hour.

It astonished me that anyone could stop reading a novel and go back to work after only an hour. Or even two. I couldn't put it down.

I was still deep in double- and treble-crossings, when a voice above me said, "Good book?"

I looked up. The sun was already beginning to dip towards the horizon. For a moment it turned his remarkable hair to flame. And then I blinked and it was just hair again.

"What is it?" Anton said, looking behind him.

Ah. Very much not a telepath, then.

I pulled a frond of grass to keep my place in the book and closed it. "You startled me."

He squinted at the book cover. "Len Deighton? Good book?"

I considered. "It's terribly exciting. But I really hate the people."

He lowered himself down beside me. "Will you stick with it?"

I stared. "Of course. I *have* to know what happens. I've just always hated spies. Lying to everybody. Yuck!"

It was a sore point. That was how I ended up in Education and Research. I'd refused to train as a spy, which is what Adaptive Life Forms were originally bred for. The Institute had not been pleased. If they'd cut me loose now, that was probably why.

Anton stared. "Know a lot of spies, do you?"

I made a face. "How would one know?"

He hesitated, then said, "How indeed?"

I remembered Judith's box of mysteries and jumped up. "I'm glad you're here. I need help with something."

Anton came back to Forget-me-not and investigated obligingly. There seemed to be a lot of machinery.

He held one piece up. "That's a foot pump. Is there a Lilo or something?"

I didn't know what a Lilo was and said so.

I'm not sure he believed me. But he said, "An inflatable mattress for paddling out to sea, going too far and calling out the lifeboat." With some bitterness, I thought.

"Inflatable! Of *course*. There's a sort of rubber envelope on the sleeping platform. I suppose I have to blow it up." I looked at the machine doubtfully.

He ran up the ladder and investigated. "Yes, I can see the valve. Hand the thing up to me, will you?"

I did.

There was a certain amount of muttering and some experimental standing on chairs, then the table. But eventually he found the ideal configuration and Forget-me-not resonated to the sound of pumping. When he was satisfied, he tidied the pump away and said, "That's an awkward space. I'll finish what I've started. Where are the bed clothes?"

I indicated the blankets, still draped over chairs, cooking gently in the sun.

"Yes, but that can't be all. Isn't there a sleeping bag or something?"

Sure enough, they were in the chest, right at the bottom, a depth to which I had been too tired to plunge, or even notice, the night before. Sheets and pillow cases, and, oh joy, a couple of flattened pillows.

"Look," I said, emerging triumphant and just a bit dusty.

But he had found my telescope. I'd had to move it to get at the linen and I'd put it down beside the bookcase. It was still in its carrying case. Anton had opened it to inspect it.

"What on earth did Judith bring you this for?" he asked blankly.

"No, no, that's nothing to do with Judith. It's mine. A telescope. My hobby is astronomy." It was what I'd told the Orwell College governors at my interview. No one had ever queried it.

Nor did Anton, though he looked at me pretty narrowly, as he put it down on the table. With great care, I noticed. But he didn't say anything else, just gathered up the sheets and blankets and ran up the ladder with them.

I heard him whistling, as he thumped about. When he'd finished, he backed to the edge of the platform and swung round to sit on the top step. Then he slid down the ladder, arms and legs splayed, giving a great schoolboy hoot of glee and triumph.

It was infectious. I had to laugh in sympathy.

He stood up and dusted off his hands. "So let's see what else Milly's sent you, then." And started removing other stuff from the cardboard box.

"What? I thought Judith brought all these things?"

"Judith would just be playing postman. That pump for the airbed is pure Milly." He picked up the other bit of machinery. It had reminded me of an archaic chemistry lab, but he patted it as if it were a familiar pet. "Aha. Here's Bert's camping gas stove too. State of the art, that is."

"How does it work?"

"Propane gas. There'll be some somewhere."

"Gas?"

He was picking through the box but looked up and saw me frowning. He laughed softly. "Don't worry. It's basically lighter fuel. Bert won't admit it, but it's standard equipment these days. Boy scouts take them to camp, I'm told."

He might as well have been speaking a foreign language. I nodded.

"Now what's this?" He held up a small wooden box.

I took it from him. Like the blanket chest, it had been beautifully made. I turned it round, marvelling at the tongue-and-groove joints, the almost silky finish of the polished wood. It looked as if had been intended for a jewellery box. Opened, though, it proved to contain tea bags. When I looked more closely, I saw that there were four different types, tied together with different coloured ribbons. Each small parcel had a luggage label attached, with a handwritten inscription. The writing was copperplate, almost Victorian. The blue ribbon was English Breakfast.

"Look." I couldn't say anything else.

The woman who had sent me that home-baked shortbread had also gone to the trouble of sorting out my tea choices: Typhoo, Orange Pekoe and Nettle were also on offer. I felt as if my landlady had wrapped her patchwork quilt round me and given me a hug.

Anton was putting together the portable gas burner but he spared a glance at the contents of the box and smiled. "Milly takes her tea seriously."

I swallowed hard.

"There should be a kettle in one of the cupboards." He opened one and started to rummage. "Milly usually— Ah, here it is." He held up a shiny silver thing, with a stumpy spout. It had a sort of ski hat contrivance covering the end of the spout. "Kettle. It's a whistler. Scared the living daylights out of me the first time Milly brewed up for breakfast."

He located a bottle of mineral water and poured it into the kettle. Then he picked up the burner, a gas canister and the box of tea and headed outside.

I followed.

Anton was looking for something. "Ah," he said with satisfaction. "Here it is."

Beside Forget-me-not was a small brick-built shelter. I'd assumed it was for the storage of trash. But Anton was putting the burner on top of it, beaming.

"Perfect," he said. "Bert must have built it. See? It's level, out of the wind, just the right size. Now—" He checked to see I was watching. "We insert the canister like this. You don't have to force it. It just slides into position." He took it out again and handed the can to me. "Now you do it."

I did. I've always been a quick study.

"Oh, OK." Did he sound a bit deflated? "Now you turn the knob on the burner. And light your match. Like so."

There was a soft whoosh and the burner produced a steady circle of blue flame. Anton put the kettle on top of it. "Did Milly put in any biscuits, by any chance? I found the longlife milk."

"I'll look."

She had. Of course she had. After yesterday's shortbread, she'd followed up with chocolate chip cookies, possibly also homemade. They were wrapped in pretty blue and white napkins with pictures on them. Milly had sent me a whole packet of those, too. I took him the lot, napkins and all, along with a couple of mugs from the kettle cupboard.

He was wrong to tell me the kettle whistled. It screamed. Which was what it did the moment I turned the corner. I froze. Anton retrieved my burdens and began picking his way through Milly's loving selection of teas.

I knew my eyes were filling and there wasn't a damn thing I could do about it. Damn human bodies.

I tried. I really tried. I managed to say, "How very kind she is."

My throat hurt.

"You're kind, too. Why is everyone so kind to me? I—"

And that's when the body's leak turned into a torrent and I just gave up trying to control it.

# Chapter Nine

Anton was surprisingly competent in the matter of handkerchiefs and not trying to stop me weeping. Eventually I hiccupped and snortled my way into exhausted silence. Too exhausted even to feel ashamed of myself.

Some part of me was certainly appalled by this display of irrational emotion. Very uncool.

But I just couldn't seem to make it matter. So there I was, in two minds again. Twice in two days. Oh God, I was becoming so human.

"All done?" asked Anton.

I nodded.

He smiled. It was oddly companionable. "Good. That was my last handkerchief."

I looked down. I still had a damp and twisted rag clutched between my fingers. "Oh. Sorry."

He shrugged. "It's what they're for."

He pressed my forgotten mug of tea into my hands. I wrapped my hands round it, savouring the warmth. He made a great business of heating the screaming kettle again, making his own tea and then carefully turning off the burner. I looked away and shivered. The sun had disappeared behind clouds and a sharp breeze was whipping the sea into foam.

"You're cold. Take your tea inside. I'll pack up out here."

I nodded, grateful. Inside Forget-me-not, I tucked myself onto the chest in a nest of cushions and huddled the quilt round me. The tea was wonderful.

Anton raised his eyebrows when he came in. "Chilly?"

"Warming up." My voice was steady enough, now I was in my single mind again.

"There's a reason people don't use their beach huts in the winter," he agreed.

He closed the doors and bolted them. Then he looked round. "Milly's got a snake somewhere."

"Snake?"

"Draught excluder."

He rummaged in one of the cupboards and came back with a thick python-headed sausage, which he laid out with care along the bottom of the doors. Instantly, the place began to warm up. Maybe it was my imagination, of course. Or maybe it was because the python was scarlet and orange and Day-Glo pink.

I said so.

He chuckled. "Yup, next best thing to a log fire, old Selina Slithery." He patted the snake on the head and stood up.

"You must know her very well."

He looked startled. "*Selina?*"

"Milly."

"Oh. Well, yes. I suppose I do. Or she knows me."

He picked up his mug of tea and swirled it round and round for so long that I thought he'd forgotten me. He seemed a long way away. And not very happy about it.

But then he looked up and said abruptly, "You're in trouble, aren't you?"

It was so unexpected, I just gaped.

"I knew when I saw you psyching yourself up to walk into the sea."

My lips felt frozen. "*No!*"

He sounded half-angry, half-awkward. "I knew because I've been there. Actually, Milly was one of the people who sorted me out."

I shook my head. He'd thought I was trying to *drown* myself? "You're mistaken. I didn't..."

Dammit, where were the words when you wanted them? "I mean, it wasn't like that."

"Whatever. It's your own business. I don't need to know. But staying here—" He made a wide gesture. "No heating. No running water. That's desperation." The remarkable eyes bored into me. "Or are you going to tell me I'm wrong about that, too?"

It was a body blow. "No," I said, when I got my breath back. "No, I'll give you desperation."

We pretty much glared at each other. Then he gave a sort of explosive snort. "Well, thank God for that, at least." He put the mug down and looked at his watch. "I have to go. I'm supervising prep this evening. I'll see you tomorrow. Don't do anything crazy until we've talked. Right?"

He didn't wait for me to agree. He just unbolted the doors. I threw a cushion at him, Heaven knows why. It was too late anyway. Anton was long gone.

For the second night running, I couldn't face going outside to set up my telescope and look at the moon. I told myself it was because I was too cold. So instead I found the little torch I'd forgotten to give back to him and took *The Prisoner of Zenda* to bed.

# Chapter Ten

I had dreams full of glamorous swordsmen and woke as warm as toast. So warm, in fact, that I looked at my little travel alarm clock with loathing. The airbed was surprisingly comfortable. I *really* didn't want to get up.

But I did and pattered up to the chippie for my shower of the day. And, as it turned out, breakfast. Chandra was making samosas and her husband was out buying supplies, so she invited me into the kitchen for a coffee.

"I talk to myself when Ben's gone. I could really do with the company," she said, which made me laugh.

Coffee turned out to include delicious cinnamon buns, which were still warm, and a gossip about Little Piddling. Chandra, a city girl, loved it but she admitted that it was hard to make ends meet in what she called the off season. That's why they were only frying three nights until Easter, and she'd started to sell coffee and home-made buns to people coming in to work in the morning, as well as salads, sandwiches and soup from noon onwards.

"I'll remember that," I said. I hadn't taken to the camping gas burner, to be honest. I'd never encountered real flames until I came to Earth and they made me twitch. "In fact, could we change our deal to morning shower, coffee and a bun?"

She agreed and we were haggling in a friendly way over what I wanted to pay and the little she wanted to charge, when there was a *ping!* as someone opened the door to the shop.

"Customer. Stay and finish your coffee. Read the paper." She pushed it at me, as she grabbed a basket of cinnamon rolls and shot off. "I'll be back. The real breakfast rush doesn't start for another twenty minutes."

I poured myself another cup of coffee and settled back with the *Piddling Post*. It was an odd mixture of official stuff and local gossip. A half page had bios of People You Should Know: a pompous-looking town councillor called Dumaine; Brown Owl—which rather unnerved me until I realised that this was not a shape-shifter, but seemed to be a volunteer teacher of small girls in worryingly military uniform; and Anton, newest member of the lifeboat crew.

All three had answered emblematic questions. Anton, apparently, loved asparagus, hated exams, couldn't remember where he was born, coached pupils for university entrance and had been a Little Piddling resident for nearly five years.

Chandra dashed from shop to kitchen several times, but it was clear that the morning rush had started. I decided I was in her way—though she protested very kindly—and left.

I didn't go straight back to Forget-me-not. Instead I walked along the beach, thinking. Chandra was obviously having the time of her life, solving their off-season business problems by baking buns and serving coffee. How would I cope in her shoes? If the Institute wouldn't take me back, it might become a real issue.

No more putting it off. I had to start my moon observations tonight. No matter how cold it was. And try again to contact them.

I went into town and bought two of the warmest sweaters I could find. Also thick gloves, knitted socks and an ugly woollen hat which the assistant told me was a favourite with the lifeboat crew.

I wondered whether Anton wore one and rather hoped he did.

Back at my beach hut, I gave the doors another coat of paint. They gleamed beautifully in the sun but I could see that they would need another coat tomorrow.

Just after I finished, Judith came along the boardwalk. It was her lunchtime and she brought a large paper bag full of hamburgers, coffee and chocolate bars to share.

We sat inside, with the doors propped half-shut. Out of the wind, the temperature was very pleasant. I thanked her for everything she'd brought the day before.

She shared out the food between us. "Oh, that. All Milly's idea. Did you get the gas burner going?"

I explained.

"Anton helped?" She sounded disbelieving. "That's a first."

I was startled and a bit upset. Anton had talked as if she were a friend. "Don't you like him?"

She looked shocked. "Oh *no*. Anton's great. But he's kind of a loner, you know?"

"But surely, if he's on the lifeboat crew…"

"Yes, I saw that in the *Post*. Must be coming out of his shell." She inspected the burger bun thoughtfully. "Of course, I remember what he was like when he first came. Never spoke to anyone in town. Just wandered along the beach with those binoculars of his. To be honest, I thought he was a bit—well—strange."

I wondered what Judith would consider strange. Anton had struck me as interfering, bossy and just a bit scary. Only then he turned out to be surprisingly kind, as so many Earth people were.

"Seemed quite normal to me," I said.

But Judith was lost in memories. "Of course, he was a political refugee, poor chap."

"*Oh.*"

So Anton was an exile. Like me.

"Young, too. Still a student, he told me. Can't have been more than twenty-five. Milly said he was grieving for his home."

I shook my head. "He didn't tell me that." I didn't really say it to her. I was thinking.

But when I looked up, I saw she was back from the memory place, bright-eyed and alert. Our eyes met and she gave a little nod, as if I'd answered a question. Only then she started to talk about Milly and Bert and the beach huts and pretty soon she was looking at her watch saying she had to get back to open the shop.

She gathered up the remains of the picnic she'd brought, only leaving me with a bottle of something called cream soda. And she gave me an unexpected hug before she left.

"Good luck," she said.

# Chapter Eleven

After Judith left, I took stock of my situation. I had a month of research to do, to see whether I had any chance of returning to the Institute. And I'd already missed two nights.

Well, maybe I had genuinely been too tired on the day I arrived. But yesterday? That was what the Sixth Form would have called sheer funk. I could perfectly well have added more clothing against the cold and started my observations. Clearly, I was afraid of knowing the answer.

I took a firm line with myself. *No excuses tonight.*

I'd bought the right clothes to keep me warm. Now I needed to prepare this body for a night's wakefulness. I closed and bolted the doors and climbed that ladder to bed.

My last thought before I fell asleep was: *am I afraid that I can't get back? Or that I can?*

It was nearly dark when I took my telescope outside. I'd already realised that if I were to get a decent perspective on the sea, I needed a higher vantage point than Forget-me-not. So I followed an overgrown track up the slope towards the headland.

Fortunately I found a sort of ruined hut, pretty much overgrown. It looked as if no one had paid any attention to it for years, but it had two great benefits from my point of view: six feet of table-flat land in front of it, and brambles high enough to provide a serious windbreak. Perfect!

I set up the 'scope, checked the time, and made my first observation. The moon was maybe fifteen degrees above the horizon. No sparkling activity into the water at all. I made a note in my notebook and waited while the moon climbed another ten degrees.

It was a long, chilly night.

I went home around dawn and fell into bed, shivering. My last thought before sleep? *I must stop thinking of Forget-me-not as home.*

It was very cold when I finally woke. The only thing that got me out of bed was the prospect of the nice warm chippie for breakfast.

"Bad night?" asked Chandra's husband, passing me on his way out to the farmers' market.

"Cold," I said, clutching my jacket round me.

He grinned. "Tell Chandra. She'll know what to do."

I did. And he was right, she did.

"Hot water bottle," she said.

It was a sort of big rubber envelope. You filled it with not-quite-boiling water and put it into a cold bed at least an hour before you wanted to go to sleep. It warmed the sheets and, eventually, you.

I immediately went to Judith's shop and bought two.

"But what you really want is a stone pig," she told me. She disappeared into the back of the shop and returned with a thing that looked like the stone ginger-beer containers she had for sale. "You can put boiling water in these. Just don't put your bare feet on it afterwards. Wrap it in a sock or something. My advice is to keep one between the sheets all day, so that the bed never really gets cold."

I had to use the camping gas burner to heat the water. But needs must and it wasn't as difficult as I'd thought. Even so, I still disliked that real flame.

There were a lot of people on the beach—well, it was the weekend—but none of them was Anton. Several children and their parents came to my end of the beach, heading for rock pools. But most of the activity was at the other end: some swimming, a lot of games, one spectacular sandcastle and some truly brave consumption of ice cream. It made me smile. It looked like fun.

That afternoon I followed the hot-water bottle advice to the letter. It worked. And the next morning, after my night's moon watching, the bed was as warm and cosy as the basket of puppies I'd met in the caretaker's cottage.

At breakfast, Chandra said, "Anton came in for supper last night. Said he hadn't seen you."

I shuffled a bit. In the long cold intervals between taking readings, I'd been thinking a lot about Anton. Possibly too much.

I muttered, "Well, I've been busy."

Chandra nodded in silent sympathy. She gave me a box of cinnamon rolls to take away with me when I left.

It set the pattern for the next week. Anton and I never overlapped. From conversation in the chippie, I worked out that he had to be teaching all morning. By the time he normally came to the beach, I would be in bed. When I woke up to prepare my hot water bottles and a thermos flask of tea to take moon watching with me, he would be back in school to oversee the boys' prep and evening meal.

"It's a boarding school," explained Chandra with a shudder.

I nodded. So was Orwell College. I knew how the timetable worked. I couldn't see me and Anton meeting again, or not until I'd completed my observations, anyway. I regretted that. I was curious about him, after what Judith had said. But it was probably just as well.

Between triangulating moon, sea and sky, I made a series of calibrated attempts to contact the Institute. At first I was clumsy and forgetful. But to my surprise, my skills returned with use. A couple of times I thought there was a flicker of response from the Institute. But it always winked out before I could catch it. Still, as Peter Abel would have said, at least the boys were *trying*.

Although the real work was done at night, my days were pretty full as well. I listened to the radio a lot. I'd never had to clean house before or do my own laundry. Oh, the triumph of locating a launderette in a small back street of Little Piddling! The big machines had no terrors for me, of course. So I soon became the go-to adviser to a mixed group of bachelors and senior citizens. I began, dimly, to see the possibility of a useful career, if I decided to remain here.

In my spare waking hours, I read my way through Milly and Bert's bookshelf. Some were memoirs but most were novels. I *loved* them all.

It was like walking into multiple worlds, one after the other. Suddenly life was full of excitement. For those hours, I forgot the Institute and my future there as a returning failure. I even forgot about the cold, boring night ahead. For those hours, I *lived* those stories.

Eventually, I started to take a book with me when I went to the pub or the chippie for a hot meal before going out moon watching. I told myself that it kept difficult questions at bay. But really it was because I couldn't bear to stop reading.

In fact, the following Friday, Anton found me at a corner table in the pub, with a plate of *boeuf bourguignon* forgotten in front of me. I was far away in Middle Earth, absorbed in the clash of mutually suspicious life forms.

"Selsis?"

I surfaced slowly. "Mmm?"

He pulled up a chair and sat down opposite me. "How's life?"

I'd spent four straight hours trembling my way through *The Lord of the Rings*. "Wonderful," I said from the heart.

He looked amused. "No point in asking whether you missed me while I was gone, then."

I was confused. "Gone?"

"I had a conference in Oxford on Tuesday. Then I took the boys on a field trip. Only got back this afternoon."

"Oh," I said, enlightened. "Gone from Little Piddling. Um…welcome back?"

"Thank you." He sounded perfectly serious but I knew he was laughing inside. I just wasn't sure whether it was at me or at himself. "There's a spaghetti western on in Piddling Magna. Do you feel like it?"

I had absolutely no idea what a spaghetti western was. Or what he'd asked me to do with it. And I was too slow to hide it.

He laughed aloud at my blank expression. "I'll take that as a no. OK. What do you want to do tonight, then?"

That confused me even more. It sounded as if he expected us to spend the night—well, evening—together. As if we'd already agreed.

"I don't understand."

Anton sat back in his chair, still amused, but watchful, too. "I'm trying to ask you out, Selsis." He said it with just the right touch of rueful charm to disarm me.

But there was something a bit off about it. It was too calculated. Why should he want to disarm me?

"That's very kind of you," I said, because I'd read a lot of novels since the last time we met and I knew more about dating rituals now. I debated saying that I had to wash my hair, before remembering Forget-me-not's sad lack of the essential equipment. So I said, prosaically, "I'm afraid I have to work."

"What sort of work has to be done on a Friday night?" He sounded lazy, teasing even. But he wasn't either. He sat in front of me like an Inquisitor.

"Lunar observations."

He seemed sceptical.

I fell back on the Fourth Form's get-out-of-jail-free card. "I'm doing a project."

"Can I join?"

I was appalled. "*No.*" Then, remembering British manners, "Sorry, not mid-experiment."

He nodded slowly. "OK. I won't spoil your data set. What about tomorrow?"

I shook my head.

"Well, when are you free?"

He was serious! He really was asking me out. It flustered me. I stammered some rubbish about needing to stick to my schedule. Then pushed the book into my shoulder bag and gathered myself to leave.

Anton stood up. Oh, those British manners again. But then, for a moment, I thought he wasn't going to let me past.

That annoyed me. I raised an eyebrow.

He gave a little nod. Then stepped back. "OK. Not tonight. I'll see you around."

And I was out of the pub and heading for home and my telescope.

Phew.

# Chapter Twelve

I had the greatest difficulty in concentrating on the moon and the sea that night. I kept dropping things—the telescope cap, the notebook, my biro countless times. I nearly missed the four o'clock observation altogether and knocked the 'scope out of alignment, rushing to catch up. And all because I couldn't understand Anton.

What did he *want?* Was he suspicious of me, for some reason? I didn't see why he should be. I'd seen more of Judith, Chandra and Ben than I had of Anton, and they accepted me totally at face value.

I discarded the possibility that he might genuinely be attracted to me. Pretty much at once, to be honest. I'd read *Rogue Herries*, *Persuasion* and *I Capture the Castle* by then. So I knew about the conventions of human courtship. Though, based on the same evidence, my own reactions were distinctly suspect.

*Not going to think about that.*

Oddly, that was the first time since I'd arrived on Earth that the Institute communicated clearly. Or maybe I'd been trying too hard up until then. Anyway, it was deeply unrewarding, a bureaucratic classic in fact: Report in Full; we are Reviewing Options.

Gee, thanks, guys.

I was too stirred up and, frankly, too pissed off to get to sleep after that. I took my telescope home to Forget-me-not and dumped my stuff. Then I marched along the beach and off into the countryside to walk off my temper.

It didn't work.

Fortunately Ben and Chandra were both busy by the time I went for my shower-and-breakfast. I grabbed a bun and their biggest coffee to take home and set about cleaning the place. Ferociously.

Judith, who often wandered up around lunchtime, was much entertained. "Hormones," she said wisely. "Just don't kill anyone. There are tourists about."

I knew about hormones. I'd learned the hard way. When I arrived in the wrong place, I was taken in by a friendly bunch of girls, students on a Greek island holiday. So they were the life form I Adapted to. All my research told me that blood meant injury. I knew that. So when I began to bleed, I sought out a medical person.

"It happens," he said. "You are a woman."

That worried me. I'd already discovered that women were not respected. "Permanently?" I asked.

He was taken aback, but then he laughed as if I'd made one of their jokes.

So I learned about hormones in the field, as it were. Knowing why I was feeling like that didn't make me any more rational, though. I snapped Anton's head off when he turned up that afternoon. He'd even brought me a transistor radio of my own. It was a present.

I glowered. "Why?"

He gave me a bland smile and said, "Chandra would like her radio back sometime."

I couldn't argue with that. I gave him the borrowed radio and more or less drove him out of the beach hut at broom point.

He went, but he was laughing. I suspected Anton knew about hormones too. It made me want to throw things.

Anton turned up every day. He brought me books. I told him I would be reading *The Lord of the Rings* for the foreseeable future. He invited me to an evening of folk song at the Church Hall, a barbecue on the cliffs and another movie. I reminded him that I never went out in the evenings. *Never.* He came back with the offer of an Easter Sunday picnic at Milly and Bert's.

"No," I almost shouted.

"Well, it's not until the end of next week. You've got ten days to change your mind."

It wasn't just hormones that were driving my exasperation by then.

What's more, he was on the beach with his binoculars the whole damn time then. I fell over him morning, afternoon and evening. Maybe he was there at night, too, though of course I was busy then, so I didn't catch him.

On Thursday afternoon, he even walked in on me in floods of tears over *The Lord of the Rings*.

It was the last straw. "Are you spying on me?" I yelled, trying to blot my face unobtrusively.

He didn't even try to ignore my tearful state. "What's wrong, Selsis?" He hovered between the open doors, looking worried and awkward. He even sounded as if he cared.

I blew my nose hard. "Got to a sad bit." I stood up and closed the book firmly on the hobbit Meriadoc saying goodbye to the dead

Theoden. *As a father you were to me for a little while.* My eyes filled again. "Damn!"

I went towards Anton, certain that he would give way before me and back out onto the boardwalk. I think I wanted him out of my home, so I could howl in decent privacy. But he didn't move.

"Hey," he said, really gently. "Don't cry. It's only a book."

But it was a bit more than that. Meriadoc could have been me, bidding farewell to Peter Abel.

Anton lifted the book out of my hand and surveyed the cover. "Ah. Tolkien. Damnably good at grief, isn't he? Tolkien and the Dvorak Cello Concerto do it every time."

I couldn't speak.

He took my hand. It was a bit tentative. But I could feel the kindness.

"Come along. We'll walk down the beach and back again. Then you'll feel better. I'll buy you an ice cream, if you like."

He held onto my hand all the way along the sands to the Pier.

He bought each of us a big swirl of ice cream with a chocolate flake in it and made me sit on the sea wall to eat it.

Hoisting himself up beside me, he said, "You didn't tell me you were a giant killer."

"What?"

"I met one of your former colleagues at my course on Tuesday. He was telling me how you put the Minister for Education straight."

Ouch! "Secretary of State," I corrected, wincing.

"So it *was* you. I thought it had to be, since you'd mentioned Peter Abel."

My eyes filled. I stared resolutely at the sea. "I cost him his job."

"No, you didn't."

I was horribly tempted to push him off the wall. But at least it stopped the tears.

"You know nothing about it," I said, with dignity.

"I know that, whatever the Minister thinks, Peter Abel has taken a sabbatical. He'll be back."

I slewed round to stare at him. "What do you mean?"

He shrugged. "The Chairman of Governors is a politician. He says she won't be running Education for long. She's not interested and, anyway, she has her eye on higher things."

I remembered her dogmatic pronouncements. "She certainly isn't interested," I agreed.

"There you are, then. She moves up. Peter Abel quietly moves back. Meanwhile he's climbing the Munros. After which he's heading out east."

In my relief, words spilled out of me. "I thought he'd jumped. He was worried. He probably didn't have the energy—" I stopped dead, remembering too late that Anton was already suspicious of me.

But he wasn't looking suspicious. He was looking as if he'd found the answer to a puzzle. And deeply compassionate.

He said slowly, "That was why you were so distressed the first time I saw you, wasn't it? You thought Abel had thrown himself off a mountain."

"Sort of." I'd actually thought that he'd been ordered back to the Institute. I knew he would either break up in transit or, if he got back, break his heart, knowing he could never return to Earth. "He loved Orwell College. *Loves*. He loves that school."

Anton put his arm round me. "Well, you can stop worrying about him now."

I was saved from having to answer by the imminent collapse of my ice cream. I applied myself to salvage and the emotional moment passed.

Walking back, Anton said casually, "How did you get on with that spy book? Like the characters any better in the end? Or at least forgive them?"

"Yes and no."

"Why is that?" He sounded as if it mattered.

Anyway, I needed to explain to myself as much as to him. "I was educated with facts. I learned to experiment again and again until I knew the where, when, how of things. But nobody ever taught me to ask *why?*"

His eyes were very intent. "Not educated in this country, then."

I wasn't really listening. "The great thing about novels is they make you think *what if?* What if I could do this? What if I could feel that?"

"Your parents must have been very fierce."

*Define parents.*

That brought me back to reality with a bump.

I shut up like a clam. In the end, he gave up and walked back with me to Forget-me-not. I didn't ask him in.

Before he left, Anton said, "Are you star gazing again tonight?"

"Yes."

"Would you like company?" It sounded as if he expected a negative but was driven to ask anyway.

I shook my head, keeping my distance, expecting him to leave. But he didn't. "Selsis—"

"Yes?"

"I want to tell you something... Ought to..."

I blanked him. It was nothing to do with mind-communication. It was pure Staff Room.

"Oh, the hell with it," said Anton and stalked off back to college.

Well, that's what I assumed.

I should have known better. Look where my assumptions about the minister had got me.

Coming back from my night watch in the cold dawn, I heard steps behind me. I was too tired to run and, anyway, I should be able to broadcast a strong enough suggestion to deflect most would-be muggers and snoopers. So I sighed and turned to face my pursuer.

It was Anton.

He looked tired, too. I wondered how long he'd been following me.

He said, "I'm really sorry, Selsis."

A rather pretty pink blush was starting to infuse the sky behind him. I stared at it, trying to work out what to do, what to *say*.

In the end all I could think of was, "What are you talking about?"

"I've watched you all night. Yes, you look at the sky. Yes, you make notes. And then you scan the sea."

He stared at me as if I ought to be falling back in guilty surprise. I felt blank.

"So?"

"What are you looking for? A Russian sub?"

Was I hallucinating? Had I somehow fallen asleep and this was a rapid eye movement delusion?

"I know where you come from, you see. You're an enemy alien."

Alien! He *knew*. I went cold. And I was falling, falling, falling...

"And... That thing I was going to tell you? I'm a spy, too."

It was like a blow. My recoil was instant. I couldn't *think*.

After a moment, Anton said heavily, "The Prague Spring. I was born a Czech. In 1968 I was at Manchester University, post-doctoral studies in hardware address translation. If you went abroad to study, you reported to the Ministry. Even under Dubček. Until the Russians got rid of him."

In the grey dawn light, he looked haggard. *Grieving.* He half-turned away from me, looking at the brightening sky.

"The night after tanks rolled into Prague, I went to a concert. London. The Soviet State Symphony Orchestra." He nearly spat it out. "I wanted to kill them all. A Russian cellist was playing."

"*Oh.*" Suddenly I understood. "The Dvorak Cello Concerto."

He swallowed. "He cried. Rostropovich. He played it through to the end. And he cried. Afterwards, I— Well, that was my walk into the sea moment."

He turned back to me, remote, courteous. It was like a skull smiling. I shivered. The wind was very cold.

"They gave me political asylum. I changed my name," he said lightly, quite as if it didn't matter. "These days I'm attached to British counter-intelligence."

He looked at me steadily, waiting.

When I didn't—couldn't—say anything, he squared his shoulders. "So I'm afraid I'm going to have to turn you in."

# Chapter Thirteen

Of course, I didn't understand. Story of my life on Earth. Blasted *words*.

"Turn me into what?" It wasn't the most important thing, but it sounded worrying.

Anton gave a bark of laughter, more angry than amused. But he translated in a level voice. "Report your activities to my superiors. Take you in for questioning."

Even I could understand that.

"Oh."

I took a couple of steps back from him and nearly lost my footing on the rough path. I still had that sensation of falling, tumbling in free fall through the thinnest of air. I couldn't breathe.

In *Star Trek*, this would be where the Institute locked onto me and beamed me out of there. And I suddenly realised: *I really don't want that.*

Huh?

Anton had grabbed me when I stumbled. Now I looked at him properly, I could see that he was as shocked as I was. Yes, he was angry. But not, I thought, at me.

And that was when, rather late, my brain kicked in. I dissected what he'd said. It didn't make sense.

"You're going to report me as an enemy alien?"

He flinched. "Yes."

"But I'm not. I mean, I'm no enemy. I'll put my hands up to being an alien. But I'm here to *help*. Not to spy or do anything hostile."

Behind him the sun was rising in a surge of gold and cherry-blossom pink. It turned his hair to that fabulous Renaissance auburn again.

Suddenly the core of my body blazed into life. It was rather alarming, but it sharpened my wits.

Not before time.

"Look," I said. "Let's go back to Forget-me-not. We can heat some water on the burner and have coffee and talk about this."

He only agreed to come because he was so miserable. I knew that. But it was a start.

Sitting opposite him at the small table, I set out the full course of my career on Earth. Starting with arriving in the wrong place, because I thought I was aiming for somewhere called the Bibby Sea.

"What?"

I looked eloquently at his transistor radio.

Anton choked on his coffee. "You mean the BBC?" And he hooted when I recounted my exchange with the Greek island doctor. "And on top of all that, you patronised Margaret Thatcher!" And he was off again.

I could have smacked him. "I didn't patronise anyone. I told you. I'm here to *help*."

Anton sobered. I could see it was an effort.

"OK. You're very convincing so far. What was the game plan, then?"

"Earth, this world, is spending more and more of its resources on stuff that will destroy the planet. Weapons of mass destruction. Machinery that will bring about climate change. You can still change that. But it's getting a bit late. Basically, the Institute sent me here to encourage new young inventors."

Anton leaned back in his chair, eyes alert. "And why does your Institute care whether this planet blows itself up?"

"I don't think it does. They worry about repercussions. Especially intergalactic refugees. Beings with nothing to lose can be dangerous."

He stared at me for a long moment, not blinking. Then, finally, he nodded. "Makes sense." He thought about it. "Why you?"

"I'm a good researcher. Decent track record in teaching. And I've always been interested in Earth. Though I didn't know as much about it as I thought I did," I admitted ruefully.

His eyes lit with that lovely laughter. "So you said." But then he looked thoughtful.

"How are you going to do it?"

*Are*, I noticed. Not *were*. For some reason, my heart lifted another notch.

"Communication technology."

"Telephones?" Anton was frankly disbelieving.

"Telephones are in the mix, eventually. At the moment all the focus on Earth is on computer development. Particularly packet switching."

He jolted upright as if I'd zapped him with an electric current. "Explain!"

I remembered that he taught computer science. He would probably get it.

"Four years ago—29th October 1969, to be precise—two computers in California talked to each other. That could be the start of worldwide person-to-person communications. Or it could get lost in the US Department of Defense."

"Who told you that?"

"One of our researchers picked it up by chance in routine monitoring." No need to say it was me.

Anton wasn't deceived. "I thought you said you weren't a spy." He wasn't amused any more.

"I'm not. I only picked it up because, well—" I was faintly ashamed of this "—it made me laugh."

*"What?"*

"Well, everyone involved was so high tech. And the message was straight out of the seventeenth century." The King James Bible to be precise.

He stared at me, narrow-eyed.

"Lo," I said. "It's Tudorspeak, like 'behold'. Which is more or less what it means. It made me laugh and it gave me hope, at the same time. Like when the dove came back to Noah, after the flood. 'And, lo, in her mouth was an olive leaf.' As if chance had taken a hand and everything was going to turn out all right after all."

Anton said nothing.

"Of course, it was a mistake. The message was supposed to be LOGIN. Only it crashed after two letters." I laughed. I couldn't help it. I always did. "But that just made it better, somehow."

One look at his face made me realise I'd blown it. That incorrigible frivolity the bloody Minister had complained about. I wiped the smile off my face but it was probably too late. I waited nervously.

And the most terrible wailing started.

# Chapter Fourteen

Anton jumped to his feet. And staggered. "Damn. Got to go."

"Why? What's happening?"

For some reason—maybe it was his talk of Russian submarines—my first thought was *invasion!*

"Lifeboat launch. They'll be calling me at home. If I don't get there fast, they'll think I'm not available. Gotta run."

He was already out of the door before I'd stood up.

When I went outside, he was powering down the beach towards the pier. I followed, almost as fast. My brain ran an earworm at the same time: *too tired is dangerous, too tired is dangerous.* Not me, I realised. Anton.

Judith was already at the pier and other people were coming along all the time.

"Anton?" she said, as soon as she saw me.

I gestured to the figure disappearing into the boathouse at the end of the pier. "He shouldn't go out to sea. He's not slept."

She didn't laugh. She thrust a carrier bag at me.

"Sandwiches. Coffee. Take it down to them. Go."

I grabbed it and ran.

There were two men in the boathouse, apart from Anton. One was already geared up and on the telephone. Anton and the other guy were pulling on their gear, listening to the speakerphone. It sounded bad. A boat in difficulties. A man in the sea, injured.

Anton looked up and saw me. He looked like hell. There were dark shadows under his eyes and his cheekbones were like razors. Not surprising, really. He was running on two shots of instant coffee and pure adrenaline. He looked and sounded so calm. And it was all an act of pure will alone.

Why didn't his crew mates see the signs? Why was I the only one to notice?

And then it hit me. I could *hear* him, his exhaustion, his desperate self-monitoring.

*I, Selsis, the worst mind communicator in the Department, could hear Anton like any natural telepath.*

I sat down rather hard.

He had heard me, that first day on the beach. And he had heard true. Now I could hear him. Who did a telepath hear? Someone they had bonded with. A twin. A fellow survivor.

A lover.

Good gracious.

Two other crew members arrived, called greetings, got to work in a measured way that was much faster than it looked, cutting no corners. I realised I was still holding Judith's care package.

I went to Anton. "Judith said I was to give you this."

He took it, passed it to one of the others, who nodded and made a mark on the white board at the end of the hut.

Anton said, "Don't look so worried. We train for this."

I wanted to say: *Come back to me.*

I didn't. Instead, I said, "Did you tell them you've been up all night?" Oh God, I sounded such a scold.

His lips twitched. "Not really relevant."

I touched his face. It was cold.

And suddenly a thought occurred to me. Anton was running on empty. Maybe I could give him my energy. It would take the whole of my accumulated store. I could never go home to the Institute. But hell, what of it? The Institute wasn't my home. Earth had taught me the word and the feeling, too.

Only...I'd never done it before. And it was the ultimate intimacy. I went hot, then cold, then terrified.

It was worth a try.

Not looking at any of the rest of the crew, who should not have witnessed this, ever, I said, "Give me your hand."

Anton was zipping up his jacket with heartbreaking care. "What?"

I took his right hand and held it steady. I could see where the pulse throbbed in his wrist. I had no idea whether this would work. If it didn't, I'd look an idiot. If it did, I'd probably die of emotional exposure. Neither seemed to matter.

I gathered my energy into stillness. It was what I had done when I set out for Earth, before I dissolved into particles and launched out across space. This was not so different.

I put one finger on that pulse, found another behind his ear and stopped thinking.

The energy flash was instant. Anton's pupils flared. Suddenly he seemed to be standing straighter, more co-ordinated somehow. I felt his mind settle into orderliness. And something more. He hesitated, just a second, then joined the crew, jogging towards their craft.

I felt naked. But rather peaceful. I raised a hand, though I wasn't sure he saw it.

*Come back to me.*

And in my bones, my blood, my synapses, Anton replied.

*Count on it.*

I did. And so did he.

# THE END

# About Sophie Weston

Sophie Weston has written 50-ish romantic novels, published in 27 languages and more than 100 countries, as well as short stories and non-fiction. She lives in London and reads widely—as a result of which she occasionally whips fellow enthusiasts on a walk round Georgette Heyer's Regency Mayfair.
She can be found at libertabooks.com/sophie, where she blogs regularly; SophieWestonAuthor on Facebook; and @sophiewestonbks on Twitter

### *Want Sophie's latest book?*
You can get Sophie's latest book, and find earlier ones you may have missed, at author.to/SophieWeston
where you'll also be able to follow Sophie for her latest releases

# THE BODY AT SATIS HOUSE
## by Lesley Cookman

# Chapter One

"I don't actually believe in this place," grumbled Libby Sarjeant, as she struggled out of Fran's little Smart car.

She shook herself and stamped a bit to stretch her legs and settle her garments. Libby liked her clothes flowing and unstructured. But they had flowed a bit more than she bargained for in Fran's compact passenger seat. For the last few miles she'd been feeling like an Egyptian mummy.

"What do you mean?" Fran herself got out, much more elegantly. "It's there, look!" She pointed at the village sign.

Libby trampled across the unmown verge and held an overhanging branch clear of the waist-high sign. "Little Piddling sur Mer," she read out. "I mean—how ridiculous can you get?"

"And see what someone's added?" Fran approached the sign and peered at it.

"Oh!" Libby laughed. "Sur Merde! They've added a 'de'!"

"And someone else has painted it out. Or tried to."

"Serve them right," said Libby. "I bet it wasn't always 'sur Mer'. Pretentious buggers."

Fran sent her an amused look. "Someone's grumpy today."

Libby sighed. "I've been dragged away from home by someone who wants us to 'investigate' something and won't say what. Almost all of my friends and relations disapprove. And I've forgotten my laptop."

"Oh, stop moaning. I've got my phone if we need to look anything up," said Fran, responding to the only one of Libby's complaints she could dismiss. "We got here, didn't we?"

"Eventually," muttered Libby, who had her doubts about Fran's relations with her satnav. "Late."

"And it was a lovely drive," said Fran firmly. "Beautiful country and very little traffic."

Libby refused to be comforted. "Because we're at the end of the known world. How long is it since we've seen anyone?" She shivered. "And listen. There isn't a bird singing."

"It's the middle of the afternoon," said Fran practically. "The birds have all eaten themselves to a standstill and gone back to their nests to sleep it off."

"It's like the start of a horror movie."

"Nonsense." They'd both been professional actors but Fran, who was taller and had gone through a waiflike stage, had appeared in more than one horror movie and was inclined to laugh at the wrong moments. "You'll feel better when you've had a cup of tea." She strode back to the car. "Let's see if we can find this Satis House."

"Odd name—Satis House. I'm sure I've heard it before. Just can't think where." Libby climbed awkwardly back into the car.

Fran frowned and switched on the engine. "Yes, I thought that. I've been trying to remember ever since Cora got in touch." She glanced at the satnav screen. "Now, she said to keep straight on down this road without turning off. But it looks as if it goes into the sea."

"Horror movie," said Libby, pleased. "Told you."

Fran was unimpressed. "Keep your eyes out for a sign to Satis House. It could just be one of those homemade things, I suppose. I don't think there's a lot of money around."

Libby looked at her friend with affection. Fran had been her lodger for a while and they'd been friends ever since. "Is that why you said we'd come and help? Because they can't afford professionals?"

Fran shook her head. "No. Nothing like that. I can't really explain it…" She fell silent.

"Oh," said Libby, suddenly understanding. "One of your feelings."

Fran could be sensitive about her moments of intuition. But Libby had seen them in action and tended to trust them.

"Maybe a little," Fran admitted. "After all, I hadn't heard from Cora for years. The last thing we did together was a radio play back a while ago. I think she must just have picked up on the grapevine that you and I sort of looked into mysteries."

Libby peered out of the window in an effort to see what was on the other side of the high bank. There wasn't even a footpath leading off the road. No sign to Satis House or anything else.

"But we're not going to visit her?"

"I told you, she doesn't live here." Fran was testy. "You never listen."

Libby took a deep breath, opened her mouth and closed it again. "All right," she conceded. "But her *daughter* lives here. And Cora thinks she's in trouble."

"I'm not even sure about that. Cora just said Estella could do with help and would I—we—see what we could do."

It seemed a small enough request to get Fran to drop everything, bundle them both into the car and bring them all this way. Fran was definitely unsettled, Libby thought. It must be a really strong feeling. Oh well, she would tell more in her own good time. Probably.

"How old is she?"

Fran thought about it. "The daughter? Quite young, I think. Twentyish." Then added dryly, "Old enough for Cora to want her living somewhere else, out of the eye of the tabloids. Won't want people to start doing sums."

"But why does she have to live so far off the beaten track?"

"Oh, come on, Libby. We came cross-country. We haven't even seen the town yet."

"Just seems strange," muttered Libby. "It's not exactly a thriving holiday spot, is it? I'd never heard of Little Piddling until yesterday."

"It's a thriving holiday coast, though," said Fran. "Little Piddling is probably a sort of genteel offshoot. Full of retired colonels and City boys' grannies."

"Precisely. Not exactly exciting for your normal twenty-year-old."

But Fran was leaning forward, scanning the hedgerow on her side of the car, looking for a gateway.

Libby settled back in her seat. "Do you think this Satis House is some sort of country house hotel?"

"Could be, I suppose. I told you. I don't know anything more than Cora told me."

"Which is basically that her daughter was asked if she could identify a dead body and is freaking out?"

Libby scowled through the windscreen. Her children were made of sterner stuff. She couldn't see her metropolitan daughter Belinda calling in her mother's friends just because she might know a dead body.

"I think the police must be treating it as a suspicious death," Fran said slowly. "Cora said the daughter would explain everything when we met. Estella."

Libby suddenly sat bolt upright. "Estella! Of course. That's it!"

"Eh?" Fran shot a quick look at her friend.

"Estella—Miss Havisham's Estella!" shouted Libby.

"All right, all right! Who—oh!" Fran stood on the brake.

"Careful!" Libby lurched heavily against the seatbelt.

"Miss Havisham's house in *Great Expectations*—Satis House. Of *course*." Fran put the car back into gear and set off again. "Sorry."

The road levelled out and suddenly they were looking at the town. It wasn't large.

"Looks as if we've missed Satis House, then. What do we do now?"

"Cora said we could park on the promenade and call Estella to come and meet us there."

Libby sniffed. "Sounds as if she expected us to miss the turning."

Fran's phone began ringing. "Answer that for me, will you?"

Libby fumbled for a moment with the unfamiliar screen. "Hello? Fran Wolfe's phone."

"Oh! Hello—are you Libby?" a very young-sounding female voice answered.

"Yes." Libby raised her eyebrows at Fran, who took the opportunity offered by a Non-Residents' Parking sign to pull over and stop. She took the phone and put it on loudspeaker.

"Hello. Fran here."

"Oh, Fran. This is Estella. Are you in Little Piddling yet?"

"Yes. We seem to be at the top of the town. Where are you?"

"Stay where you are and I'll come and get you," said Estella. "Can you see anything like a road name?"

"No, but there's a strange pink house just ahead of us—"

"Oh, yes. I know where you are. Just stay there, then, and I'll come and find you."

"Why couldn't she just tell us where to go from here, if she knows where we are?" grumbled Libby. "Honestly, this gets sillier and sillier."

It was less than five minutes later when someone tapped on Fran's window. She was pretty, in a blonde washed-out way, a far cry from the glamorous photographs of Cora that Libby had looked up on the Internet.

"Hello," she said, when Fran opened the door. "I'm Estella Hope."

"Fran." Fran smiled and held out her hand. "Nice to meet you, Estella. This is Libby."

Libby grinned across at the newcomer. "Hi. Where do we go from here?"

"We turn off just down here." Estella looked doubtfully at the Smart car. "There's no back seat."

"Well, no. That's rather the point," said Fran. "Is that a problem?"

"I was going to get you to give me a lift," said Estella.

"You aren't very big," said Libby. "You could squash into the luggage space. Couldn't she, Fran?"

They both climbed out of the car and, with a good deal of pushing and shoving, managed to get Estella wedged uncomfortably in the back.

"Now," she said breathlessly. "Go down past the pink house, and turn left."

Fran did as she was told and stopped. "Are you sure this is actually a road?"

Winding away from the road they were on was what was little more than a track.

"Oh, yes. It's all right, and you won't meet anything coming up."

"Hmm," said Fran.

Libby lowered her window and salty air filled the car. She leaned out to see where the wheels were. There were deep ruts in places, but at least there was no mud that she could see.

"It looks dry enough," she told Fran.

The track led down, rather bumpily, towards the sea. The smell of ozone got stronger. They eventually met up with a much smaller cliff track.

"You can park just along here," said Estella. "See? There's a sort of lay-by."

Fran pulled in to the side of the path. "Are vehicles supposed to be here?" she asked. "It looks more like a pedestrian footpath."

"Well, that's what it is, mostly," said Estella, "but it provides access for emergency vehicles as well."

"Which is what we're not," said Libby, getting out of the car and preparing to extricate Estella.

"I'm not so sure about that," muttered Fran, who'd been casting worried glances at Estella in her rear mirror.

Libby helped the girl climb out.

"So where's Satis House?" asked Fran, when they were all standing on the path looking down at the beach.

"There."

"Oh."

Just below the level of the path stood a lone beach hut.

Libby stared. "So much for my vision of a country house hotel, possibly with spa," she said. "Why am I not surprised?"

But Fran was walking towards it. She turned and beckoned Libby to follow, grinning. "Look at that. This is not just any beach hut. This is a Tudor beach hut. It's got gables and everything."

Estella looked a bit guilty. "I'd better explain."

"I would," said Libby ominously.

"Come on, then, let's go inside."

Estella led the way down to the beach hut, and produced a complicated set of keys. "Attempted break-ins," she said excusingly, ushering them into a minimally-furnished interior.

"Sit down," she said, indicating two armchairs of antiquated appearance, while she perched on the Formica-covered table at the back.

"Welcome to Satis House. I'm afraid the name is my fault. We used to come here when I was a kid and I called it that. I was very proud of being named after the heroine of a novel, you see, and this was my special place."

Libby was speechless.

After a quick glance at her simmering friend, Fran said hastily, "So you really were named for the character in *Great Expectations*?"

Estella nodded.

"Odd choice," said Libby. She'd always thought Estella was rather a nasty piece of work. "A Dickens connection?"

Fran answered. "Cora was playing the character in a run of *Great Expectations* when she found out she was pregnant. That's right, isn't it?"

"Yes." Estella had clearly decided she had an ally in Fran and smiled at her. "I think she hoped it would inspire me to be a beautiful heartbreaker and save the family fortunes into the bargain. I'm afraid I've been a disappointment there," she added ruefully.

"Probably just as well not being a heartbreaker," said Libby bracingly. "Messy business, breaking hearts. Is it still your beach hut?"

"Yes. My grandmother left it to me when she died last year." She smiled reminiscently. "It had been in Dad's family since the war. He was long gone by then and my mother never much liked Little Piddling. So I got it in Granny Joan's will."

Fran looked round the bare little room. "But surely you aren't staying here?"

"Oh no. I'm up at Manor Farm. That's where Granny Joan and I lived."

"Where's that?"

Estella waved a hand towards the back wall of the hut. "A bit inland, near The Old Barge Inn."

"And is that where the—um—body was found?" asked Fran.

Estella shook her head. "No. No, that was here on the beach." She looked down at her hands and swung her feet. "It's just..." She stopped.

"What?" said Libby.

The girl shook her head. "I hate talking about it."

Libby could understand that, but it wouldn't help. And Fran was looking helpless.

Libby said gently, "Look, Estella. Your mother said she knew all about Fran and I helping out with the occasional police investigation. So she thought we might be able to give you a few hints on how the police do things. Help with your—how did she put it?—bit of trouble. Unless you tell us about it, we can't help, can we?"

Fran sent her a grateful look.

Estella nodded reluctantly.

Libby said no more.

Eventually Estella took a deep breath. "Last week a dog walker found a body. It—he—was lying right next to the hut. There was crime-scene tape and everything round it for a couple of days. The police made me go to the morgue and look at him to see if I knew him. But of course I didn't." She looked faintly sick. "The problem was that he had Satis House scribbled on a piece of paper in his pocket."

"And what else? ID? Credit cards?" asked Fran.

"Nothing. Just Satis House."

Libby and Fran looked at each other.

"What can *we* do about it?" asked Fran eventually.

"Mum said you can talk to people." There was the faint suggestion of a whine in Estella's voice.

Libby sighed. "We can talk to people on our own turf. We don't know anyone here. Or anything about the area."

"I'm honestly sorry," said Fran, trying to sound sympathetic, "but we aren't professional investigators."

"Even if there's anything to investigate," pointed out Libby. "I know it's odd that he had the name of your beach hut in his pocket. But it could have been a route reminder, like 'Turn left at Satis House'. Or someone could have told him to look out for its fine Tudor beams," she added, momentarily sidetracked. "Anyway, the police won't have dropped a recent investigation yet."

Estella shrugged. "Haven't seen them." She looked sulky.

Libby knew that look. Her son Adam had worn it when he swore it was someone else's fault that he hadn't done his homework. He had grown out of it, she reminded herself. So would Estella.

"Have you asked them?"

Estella shook her head.

"They'll be doing a lot of work behind the scenes, you know," she said kindly. "Just think of all those TV shows—you've seen how much the police do that isn't actually at the scene of the incident." Libby knew that this was slightly misleading, but it was true that there was a lot more done out of sight of the public—mostly boring.

"Why not call them if you're worried?" asked Fran reasonably. "I'm sure they gave you a business card with a number to get in touch with them."

Estella nodded but didn't otherwise answer.

Fran looked at her searchingly. "Are you *afraid* to call them, Estella? Why—?"

But the girl interrupted. She had lost all colour and her hands were trembling. "Because everyone's saying it's murder!"

# Chapter Two

"This begins to make sense at last," said Libby.

Fran said, "When you say *everyone*, who do you mean, Estella? Clearly not the police. So who's saying it? The paper boy? The village shop? Or have you had the local newspaper ring you up and ask for an interview?"

"No-o-o," Estella wailed. "They wouldn't do that, would they? They can't. I couldn't bear it." And she began to sob.

Fran got up and put her arms round the weeping girl.

Libby rummaged in her bag and handed over a helpful tissue. "Crumpled but clean," she said.

Estella took it and blew her nose gratefully. "I'm not really sure," she said at last. "It just seems to be on the grapevine."

"There you are, then. It's gossip. You'll only find out what's really going on from the police. Why don't you ring up whoever's name is on the card and ask? The body was found more or less on your property, so you've got a right." Libby also knew that this didn't necessarily carry much weight, but it was worth a try.

Estella sighed and slid off the table. "The card's back at home," she said. "Will you come with me? I've actually made up the beds in the annex for you, in case you want to stay." She looked at them both hopefully.

Fran looked at Libby. "Let's see what the police say and we can discuss it," she said. "Come on."

~~~~~

"This is more like it," murmured Libby as they pulled up outside a substantial stone house just outside Little Piddling itself.

"Welcome to Manor Farm," said Estella, after extricating herself from the back of the car.

"This is Manor Farm?" said Fran in surprise. "Where your grandmother lived?"

"Yes." Estella shrugged, turned and went up the shallow steps to the front door.

The hallway was wide, dark and slightly forbidding. Designed to impress, thought Libby, distinctly not.

"Definitely the house of a gentleman farmer," she said.

"You could say that." Estella didn't look at them.

123

Libby looked at Fran and raised her eyebrows. Fran shook her head.

"Come through to the annex." Estella smiled briefly over her shoulder, and led the way down an equally dark passage next to the staircase. At the end of this, a half-glazed door opened onto a glassed-in walkway that led in turn to another, small building.

"This is the annex," said Estella, opening the door straight into a pristine sitting room, complete with three-piece suite, stone-effect mock fireplace and large television.

"It's a mobile home," said Libby in surprise.

Estella coloured. "They're called residential park homes these days," she said.

"Why have you got one here?" asked Fran. "And attached to the house?"

Estella sighed. "Sit down," she said, waving at the sofa, while she subsided into an armchair. "I'd better tell you all about it."

For a moment she was quiet, staring at the carpet.

"I told you Granny Joan lived here. Well, she first came here during the war, as a land girl."

"It was still a working farm, then?" said Libby.

"Yes. She was very young." Estella stopped again. "It's a bit complicated, actually. My grandparents left together. They—um—weren't married. It caused a bit of a rumpus at the time."

"But then they came back?" said Fran, after another pause.

"Well..." Estella cleared her throat. "Grandpa Clive's mother sent for Granny Joan. When she heard about the baby, I think. And she needed help on the farm."

"Did your great-grandfather die?" suggested Libby helpfully.

"Yes," said Estella gratefully. "I don't think Grandpa Clive can have been around much, because his mother and Granny Joan always ran the farm together. There are photographs of them haymaking in the family album and there aren't any men around. Just my dad as a little boy."

"And your dad?" asked Fran.

"Oh, he died when I was very young. He was quite a lot older than Mum. She must have told you."

"Richard?" hazarded Fran.

Estella nodded. "Yes, that's right."

"I don't think we met. Cora didn't mention him when we spoke yesterday. And I haven't seen or heard much of her since we last worked together. So what happened then? Did you come back to live here after your dad died? I was under the impression that your mum didn't live here."

"No, she never has. As long as I can remember, the farm was going downhill and Granny Joan wasn't really coping, by the end. She left the estate to me when she died last year. My solicitor advised me to sell it, but I couldn't bear to."

"So what happened? The house looks very well maintained," said Libby.

"Well…" Estella took a deep breath. "The solicitor found me a white knight. That's what he called him. Arthur Strange. He owns The Old Barge pub. He had this idea of turning Manor Farm into a residential park homes village."

"Oh!" Libby sat back on the sofa. "Well, actually, on the face of it, that's quite a good idea. It would save the farm."

"It did." Estella looked a trifle defeated. "He bought all the homes and paid for the landscaping, and for all the services to be connected."

"And the licences? You have to have licences," said Fran.

"All of that." Estella nodded. "The solicitor deals with everything but—"

"Strange takes the lion's share of any profits?" said Fran shrewdly.

Estella nodded sadly. "I was in a panic. It seemed the only way out."

Libby was frowning. "Surely you don't think he had anything to do with this body?"

"I didn't. I just thought the body was some poor rambler who had lost his way and had a seizure or something. But if it's murder…" She looked scared again and said in a rush, "Well, I suppose it might be connected."

"Connected to what?"

Estella wriggled in her chair. "Well, then… Oh, I don't know. Mr Strange wanted to buy Satis House. He was really annoyed when he found it was mine, not part of the estate he'd leased. And then he started turning up here all the time. He'd never bothered much before. He does more at The Old Barge—acts as Mine Host, if you know what I mean."

"We do." Libby grinned at Fran. "We're seasoned pub goers. So this bloke started turning up here. What—and started poking his nose in?"

Now Estella was frowning. "A bit. Mostly just hanging around the office."

"Can't be bothered with the nitty-gritty, eh?" said Libby.

Estella sighed. "No. He doesn't even handle the sales. I do all that—I'm just the agent."

"Doesn't sound very fair." Libby scowled.

Estella looked uneasy. "His solicitor arranged a sort of agreement." She gave herself a little shake and sat up straight. "So do you think the—er—body could be anything to do with us at the residential homes park village?"

"Let's just ask the police what progress they've made first," said Fran. "Then we can see if there's anything we can do."

Estella left Fran and Libby in the mobile home, where they found double and twin bedrooms and two bathrooms.

"Quite swish, really," said Libby. "How about a cup of tea while we review the situation?"

"I'd like to get a look at the site first," said Fran. "Did Estella say we were near a river?"

"No!" said Libby in surprise. "Where did you get that from?"

"I don't know." Fran frowned. "Perhaps it was the name of the pub—The Old Barge, wasn't it?"

"Oh, yes. Probably," said Libby, eyeing Fran a little warily. She had that look she got when one of her hunches struck her. "Do you want to go and have a look?"

"Yes." Fran was decisive. "Did she say this Strange had chosen Manor Farm because it was near the pub?"

"No... But I suppose I took it that it was the main motivation. Estella didn't actually say, though, did she?"

"Let's go and look."

Fran led the way out through the French doors onto the veranda that ran along the side and front of the home.

The main "village" appeared to be on the other side of Estella's annex, but Fran led them over a piece of rough ground and up a slight bank.

"Well, I expect it *was* a river," said Libby, looking down on a nettle-filled ditch.

"And that would be The Old Barge," said Fran.

On the other side of the ditch stood a low, whitewashed building, looking like everybody's vision of the idyllic country pub. A few wooden tables were dotted outside. There was no sign of life.

"Hmm," said Fran. "Let's go and look at these—I don't know—bungalows? Units? What do we call them?"

"Park homes, I think, officially. They're quite well appointed, if ours is anything to go by."

"No room for book shelves," said Fran, dismissively.

"Well, no..." Libby began, as she slithered back down the bank in her friend's wake.

Fran led the way back to the annex and round the side, where they met a path leading to a cluster of more homes. Landscaped to within an inch of its life, the set-up struck Libby as too sterile for words, but she supposed it would suit those with an excessively tidy mind.

"No clues," she said. "Now can we review the situation?"

Fran sighed, nodded and went back into the annex.

"What do we know?" asked Libby, going to fill the kettle in the smart open-plan kitchen area.

"About Estella?" said Fran. "Well, it appears her Granny Joan lived at Manor Farm and left it to her. Satis House was left separately, so if the estate had to be sold or rented out, Satis House wouldn't go with it."

"And Joan had Estella's dad out of wedlock, although the family came round." Libby found a couple of mugs and teabags and stood looking at the mugs thoughtfully while the tea brewed. "Actually," she said finally, "I don't see what on earth it's got to do with this body. Or with this business bloke—what was his name?"

"Arthur Strange," supplied Fran. "No, neither do I. And I don't see how we're going to make sense of any of it, anyway."

"Or why," said Libby, adding milk to the mugs, "Estella is so bothered by it all."

"I suppose it's nastier having a murder victim found outside your beach hut than if the poor chap just had a seizure or something."

"Maybe. Perhaps he'd simply been told to meet someone outside Satis House. After all, it stands out, doesn't it? And it's isolated from the main town."

"True." Libby handed over a mug and sat down in one of the armchairs. "The police have probably found out more by now and just haven't bothered to tell Estella. Do you think she'll come back and tell us?"

"I expect so. Are we going to stay here?"

"Must we?" Libby sighed. "I can't see that it's going to make any difference."

"Mmm." Fran frowned, clearly still uneasy. "Let's wait and see what the police say."

A sharp rap on the French doors, and Estella came in, looking flustered.

"What's up?" asked Libby, sitting up straight in her chair.

"The police." Estella collapsed on to the sofa.

"What?" said Fran, when the girl fell silent. "You got through, then?"

"Eventually. The one who had given me their card wasn't there—or wasn't taking calls, at any rate—but they put me through to someone else in the end."

"And what did he say?" asked Libby.

"It was odd." Estella scowled down at her hands. "First of all he said the investigation was on-going, but there wasn't anything he could tell me at the moment."

"And then?" prompted Fran.

"Then he seemed to change his mind. He said he was going to ask his sergeant and he would call me back."

Libby raised her eyebrows. "Sounds to me as if he just wasn't sure if there was anything he was *allowed* to tell you."

Fran nodded agreement. She looked tense. Libby wasn't surprised. It had just got a lot more likely that the poor body really had been murdered. And Fran's bad feeling seemed to be getting worse.

"Does it?" Estella looked from one to the other. "But do you think that means there *is* something to tell?"

"Probably not much," said Libby, with a shrug.

"Tell me, Estella—" Fran leant forward, elbows on her knees "—why are you so concerned about this? And why do you think it has something to do with your grandmother?"

Both Estella and Libby sent her startled looks.

"I—er—I don't." Estella looked uncomfortable.

"But you told us all about your grandmother inheriting Manor Farm and Satis House."

"I-I was just explaining how it—um—had come to me."

"In case it had some bearing on the body and the reason he was where he was?"

Estella was silent for a long moment, staring beseechingly at Fran. "Yes," she said at last.

Fran sat back in her chair and nodded. "And why did you think that?"

"Oh, hell!" Estella burst out suddenly. "I didn't think this would be so difficult. I thought you could just come to Little Piddling and ask some questions. Mum said that's what you do."

"We've already explained," said Libby, with a sigh. "We don't know anybody round here, we know nothing about the town and we wouldn't have any idea of what questions to ask—or to who."

"We don't have the authority of the police, you know," said Fran, more gently. "Now just tell us why this is important."

"You think it was *murder*. Don't lie to me. I can see you do."

"Possibly. You'll know soon enough when the police call you back. But apart from having the name of your beach hut on him, why should the victim have anything to do with you?"

"I just said to Fran, perhaps it was just the venue for a meeting," put in Libby.

Fran said suddenly, "Does your Satis House have some special significance?"

"Er—" Estella now looked confused.

"If," said Libby, with sudden inspiration, "it was to do with something in Granny Joan's past, or even earlier, your body wouldn't have known the beach hut was called that, would he? You told us you named it when you were young."

"I called it that when I was little," said Estella. "I used to pretend..."

"And I don't see what it would have to do with a present-day crime," said Libby. "Too small and too inconvenient."

"I think," said Fran, standing up, "that we'll stay for a day or two."

Libby sighed inwardly. Well, she'd known Fran was going to stick with this to the end, hadn't she?

"We'll get our bags in, and then sort out where to have dinner," she said. "And you can tell us a bit more about your family history. There's more to it than you've told us so far, isn't there?"

"All right." Estella stood up reluctantly. "But I'll get your bags."

"No," said Libby. "We will. And then we'll make a reservation at The Old Barge for dinner. What do you think?"

"We might see Mr Strange..."

"Oh, that'll be fine," said Libby brightly. "I'd like to see him, anyway."

Bags brought in, Libby and Fran tossed for the double bedroom (Fran won) and Libby looked through the various brochures left for visitors about local amenities. The Old Barge was attractively portrayed and promised a quiet atmosphere among beautiful surroundings.

"Including a silted-up riverbed," said Libby, as she punched the number into her phone.

"Seven-thirty," she said, five minutes later. "I should have asked how we get across the ditch, shouldn't I? They surely don't expect us to climb across?"

"There's got to be some form of easy access," said Fran. "If Strange is promoting Manor Farm as a sort of adjunct to the pub. Estella will know."

Estella did know.

# Chapter Three

"He's built a sort of wooden bridge just a little way up from us," said Estella, leading them along the bank later that evening. "The road round Manor Farm leads directly up to it, this end." The park homes petered out after about fifty yards, and the tarmac led, sure enough, to a rustic-looking wooden walkway across the ditch.

"It's not too obviously modern," said Libby. "Does it fit with the rest of the town? We haven't seen any of it yet, remember."

"You can have a look round tomorrow," said Estella. "If you want to, that is. Not that there's much to see. Sir Hereward's sign at the end of the prom, the Jubilee Gardens and Sir Copson's statue. The pier, I suppose, although it's not like Brighton or Hastings."

"Who's Sir Hereward?" asked Libby. "And Sir Copson?"

"Oh, Sir Hereward's some councillor at the beginning of the last century, I think," said Estella, leading the way up to The Old Barge's heavy oak door. "And Sir Copson is famous for getting lost in India or Africa or somewhere at about the same time. I can't remember where."

"And neither of them mean anything to the modern generation," murmured Fran, as she and Libby followed their young guide inside.

The Old Barge was all small table lamps and carefully restored beams. A naval theme had been subtly introduced, but without going overboard. "Although it would have been more in keeping to have had some Canal Art," mused Libby.

"What's Canal Art?" asked Estella.

"Tell you when we've sat down," said Libby, as a little waitress in traditional black and white approached them. "Yes, hello. We have a booking. Sarjeant."

They were seated at a small table in a window overlooking what Libby still thought of as a ditch; the ubiquitous small table lamp stood right in the centre, on a pristine rose-pink tablecloth. They were presented with large mock-leather-covered menus and offered drinks.

"Bit pretentious," muttered Libby. "Think we'll try somewhere else tomorrow."

Estella grinned. "It is, isn't it? Dumaine's is a lot better."

"What's Dumaine's?" asked Fran.

"Wine bar in the town. On the corner of Brewery Square. That's an old family, too. So come on, what's Canal Art?"

Libby explained about the beautiful hand painting with which the canal dwellers decorated their boats and tinware.

"Oh—I've seen that. Like the fairground rides?"

"Same background." Libby sighed. "As an Old Barge Inn, that would have been more appropriate."

"He's not looking for appropriate," said Fran. "He's aiming for gastro-pub status, possibly with a Michelin star."

"He's not going to get it with this menu," said Libby, scanning the careful calligraphy inside the faux-leather cover. "I wonder just how local 'Locally-sourced charcuterie' really is."

"Wild boar salami," murmured Fran. "Or possibly a nice farm-bred Large White."

The waitress arrived with their drinks and asked if they were ready to order.

"What would you recommend?" asked Libby.

The waitress looked confused.

"What's the special?" asked Fran.

The waitress's face cleared. "Oh, the sea bream."

They all chose the sea bream.

"We're probably being very unkind," said Libby. "I've no doubt this place—and Mr Strange—are well intentioned. So come on, Estella. Spill the beans."

"First of all," said Fran, "did the police call back?"

"No. Do you think they will?"

"I expect so." Fran nodded slowly. "Carry on, then."

"Well." The girl sat back in her chair and twirled her wineglass between her fingers. "This was really mum's idea."

"What—the whole thing?" Fran was startled.

"She wasn't close to Granny Joan, you see. She was dad's mum, but mum was often away working, so I used to come here."

"So you should know a lot of the people here, after all?" said Fran.

"Some, but Granny—well, she kept herself to herself."

"You said they weren't married, Granny Joan and Grandpa Clive?" said Libby. "So they got together when she was a land girl and Clive was—what? The son of the house?" Libby nodded to herself. "Not unusual. Exactly the same as my own mother-in-law. So they ran away together?"

Estella heaved a sigh. "I suppose so. She never talked about it much. I don't think they were very happy." She took a large gulp of wine. "Eventually Granny Joan came back with my dad in tow. Grandpa Clive's mother wanted to keep the farm in the family, despite the fact that Dad was an illegitimate son." She sighed. "Doesn't that sound ridiculous today? Half the children in Britain would be 'illegitimate' if we still believed that."

"So was everybody pleased about that?" asked Fran.

Estella made a face. "What do you think? Half the town wanted to—oh, I don't know—"

"Run her out of town?" suggested Libby. "I bet. And in a backwater like this, it would be even worse than in a big city."

"Anyway, that's the background," said Estella.

"But why do you think all this has something to do with the murder?" asked Fran. "Is there a connection with Satis House?"

Estella looked uncomfortable. "Granny Joan once said it was good that I'd taken to the beach hut, because it needed exorcising. I thought it might have been where she and Grandpa Clive used to meet."

"That's not a reason to suspect murder." Libby frowned at the younger girl. "There's something else that you're not telling us."

The sea bream arrived and discussion was postponed while it was sampled and pronounced satisfactory. Then Fran spoke.

"You said Joan was young. She must have been very young; practically a child."

Estella looked up sharply. "Yes, she was young, but she was independent. Granny Joan volunteered as soon as there was a call for the Land Army. She always said she wanted to do her bit. They grew up quickly in those days."

"They did." Libby smiled kindly. "Don't worry—we aren't criticising. So how did they actually meet, Joan and the son of the house? She wouldn't have been living in the house, would she?"

Estella shook her head. "The Land Army girls lived in a sort of dormitory in one of the barns. My great-grandmother had it demolished later. And I don't know how Granny Joan and my grandfather actually got together in the first place." She frowned. "Granny Joan was a bit mysterious about it. I always assumed they used to meet at the beach hut, because of what she said. But she let me play down there whenever I wanted to."

Libby was frowning too. "When she met Grandpa Clive, the beach would have been protected, wouldn't it?"

"Protected?"

"Oh, yes." Fran nodded. "Barbed wire, possibly even tank traps."

"So how did she get down there in the first place?" said Libby.

By now Estella was looking thoroughly bewildered. "Barbed...?"

"Oh, you must know," said Libby. "You can't live here and not know."

"During the war years, the beaches all round Britain were protected in case of German invasion," Fran explained. "Big coils of barbed wire, and dragon's teeth tank traps, as well as the straightforward stone bollards."

Estella brightened. "Oh, of course. Barbed wire and stuff. I remember now. And I know there was some kind of lookout hut at the top of the point..."

"Where's that?" asked Libby.

"The headland at the end of the bay. Piddling Point. It's all boarded up now. But I didn't know about the beach."

"Did you really not know?" asked Libby, marvelling. Local history was life-blood to her. "People weren't allowed to go on to the beaches, either, which is why I wonder how Granny Joan got down to the beach hut."

Estella pushed her plate away. "Oh, I wish she was still here and I could ask her. Perhaps that was why she was a bit mysterious about it?"

"Could be," said Libby. "Do you know much about Grandpa Clive? What he did in the war, for instance?"

"I don't know." Estella frowned again. "I thought he would have been called up or something. Wouldn't he?"

"Conscripted," said Fran. "Yes, unless he was in a protected occupation."

"Farming," said Libby suddenly. "That was a protected occupation. I wonder why he didn't marry her?"

Estella looked surprised. "She never said. I suppose I assumed it was the old class thing."

"But his mother actually asked Joan back after Clive's father died," Libby pointed out.

"Yes." Estella's frown deepened. "That *is* odd, isn't it?"

"You said she needed help on the farm," Fran reminded her. "And she got her grandson, too. I wonder what her husband died of?"

"I don't know," said Estella. She hit the table with a fist. "This is so frustrating!"

"It would be on the death certificate," said Libby. "You could get a copy."

Estella looked rather daunted.

"And it gets us no nearer the body," said Fran.

Libby sent her a sidelong look. "Oh, I don't know..."

"Ladies!" A hearty voice spoke behind Libby's back and made them all jump. "Estella, my dear. Friends of yours? Won't you introduce me?"

"Mr Strange." Estella smiled rather unwillingly. "Mrs Sarjeant and Mrs Wolfe. Libby, Fran, this is Mr Strange, who owns Manor Farm. And this place, of course."

The man standing behind them inclined his head with a smile. "My dear Estella, you own Manor Farm—I merely lease the land for my park homes." He turned to Libby and Fran. "Have you seen them?"

"Yes, we're staying in one," said Libby.

Arthur Strange's eyes widened and he opened his mouth, but before he could say anything, Estella said hurriedly, "In the annex. They're my guests. Friends of my mother."

"Ah." Arthur Strange's florid face lost its watchful look. "And what do you think? Quite luxurious, aren't they?"

Libby opened her mouth, but Fran forestalled her. "Indeed. Who do you find buys them? Mainly retired people?"

"We've limited the site to the over-55s," said Strange, taking the unoccupied chair uninvited. "We sometimes have difficulty with the holiday rentals, but..."

"Most people get round it by bringing the grandparents along if they want to bring children," said Estella with a grin. "The children love it here, and of course we aren't far from the beach."

"No," said Strange, not looking thrilled. "So what brings you to our part of the world, then?"

Estella looked outraged at this question, but Libby got in first. "Oh, so you're a native, are you? Little Piddling born and bred?"

Strange gave her a curious look. "Not quite. I only lived here as a child. Very interesting area."

"Yes. Quite a lot of wartime activity round here, wasn't there?" said Libby innocently.

He looked at her sharply. "Oh—n-not that much," he said, standing up clumsily. "Well, I shall leave you to enjoy your—er—"

he looked down at their almost empty plates "—er—yes. Good evening, ladies."

He turned and made his way between tables to the back of the room.

"Well," said Estella. "What was that all about? What did you do to him, Libby?"

Libby grinned. "Shot in the dark. If he's here for some other reason than business, it might just date back to the war years. Looks as though that might be the right guess, doesn't it?"

Fran sighed. "You love stirring, Mrs S, don't you? You might be wrong."

"From that reaction? Well, even if it isn't the war, I struck a chord, didn't I?"

Estella shook her head.

"Don't try and understand," said Fran. "Now does anyone want any dessert? Coffee?"

They saw no more of Arthur Strange until they left, when Fran noticed him watching them from a small sitting room on the left of the main door.

"Much as I hate to admit it," she said, "you were right, Lib. He's down here for a reason other than business."

"And I think it's to do with Manor Farm and the war," said Libby. "Bet you."

"Honestly, I don't see how...?" Estella gazed at them in bewilderment.

"Can we go and have a look around the beach hut tomorrow?" said Libby.

"Yes, of course, but there's nothing to see there. Do you want me to come with you?"

"No, you're all right," said Libby. "We'll go and have a rootle, then we'll wander up to the town and have lunch at that wine bar... What was it called?"

"Dumaine's. OK, if you're sure." Estella was reluctant. "Do you think you're going to be able to help at all?"

"No idea," said Fran cheerfully. "But we'll do our best. I doubt very much if we'll find out anything about our victim, to be honest. Though it will be really interesting to know whether the police have identified him yet."

# Chapter Four

Estella disappeared down the glassed-in tunnel to the main house and Libby went to dig out the half-bottle of whisky she had packed with her luggage.

"What's she scared of?" she said, waving it at Fran, who shook her head. "Why ask us to ferret things out and then act scared that we might actually find something?"

"I think it's simply what she said earlier," said Fran, going to fill the kettle. "She didn't realise it would be so difficult, remember? She thought we would just come and ask questions. *She* wants to know, but she doesn't want the rest of the world to know."

"Really? She's that naive?" Libby topped up her whisky with water and collapsed into an armchair.

"She's never been involved with anything like this before. Most people haven't," said Fran. "Why are we going to look around the beach hut?"

"Oh, just an odd idea I had." Libby stared into space. "Where was it we heard about the Special Duties groups?"

"Oh, those secret cells during the war... Was it something to do with tunnels?"

"Maybe. Anyway, a lot of the people in them were farmers, weren't they? People in protected occupations."

"And especially near the south and south-east coasts," murmured Fran. "Do you think there's a secret tunnel from the beach hut?"

"Maybe not that, but perhaps a secret wireless station. Lots of the women manned those."

Fran looked at her friend wide-eyed. "Good heavens, Lib. And you think Grandma Joan could be a secret operator and Grandpa Clive a member of the unit?"

"They were usually kept secret from one another, weren't they? But one or the other, perhaps."

They were quiet for a moment, Fran sipping tea and Libby sipping whisky.

"Have you called Guy?" Libby asked.

"No need. He texted me. He knew that I would stay, even though I didn't," Fran said ruefully. "Husbands."

Libby laughed. "Ben said he'd put money on it, too," she said affectionately. "He won't be surprised when I call him and ask him to go round and feed Sidney tomorrow."

Estella had thoughtfully left bread and eggs as well as milk, coffee and teabags in the kitchen, so in the morning, after boiled eggs, toast and tea, they set off to find their hostess, who was discovered sitting mournfully at her own kitchen table, being stared at by a large, fluffy tortoiseshell cat.

"Who's this?" said Libby, making a beeline for the cat, who flicked a haughty tail and disappeared.

"That was Queenie," said Estella, pulling herself together. "Coffee?"

"Just had tea, thank you," said Fran. "Any word from the police?"

Estella shook her head. "Do you still want the key?"

"Key? Oh—to Satis House. Yes, please." Libby sat down at the large pine table and gave it a friendly pat. "We've got one of these at the Manor."

Estella looked startled. Fran laughed.

"Libby's mother-in-law lives at the Manor in Steeple Martin. That's a farm, too, more or less. Libby's partner runs it."

"When he can spare the time," sighed Libby.

"Er—oh," said Estella.

"He's very busy with his brewery and hop garden, as well as his new Brewery Tap," explained Libby. And feeding my cat, she thought, warmed.

"Oh! We've got one of those, too," said Estella, brightening up. "On Brewery Square, where Dumaine's is."

"So you've got a brewery, too?"

"Yes, Bascombe's. I don't know much about beer," said Estella apologetically.

"Don't worry about it." Fran smiled. "We'll just take the key and leave you to get on."

"Keys," said Estella, taking a set off a board on the wall. "You have to use both at the same time and turn them in opposite directions. You can walk, by the way. Just follow the path along the old river bed. It branches to the left to get to the hut."

"Thanks," said Libby. "We'll see you later."

The morning was what people called fresh—not exactly hot, but not cold, and enlivened by a salt-laden breeze. The built-up bank that ran beside the river bed flattened out the nearer they got to the coast until, by the time they reached the path down to Satis House, it wasn't there at all.

"Must have flooded badly down here," said Fran. "Perhaps that's why Satis House is on stilts."

"Not very tall stilts," said Libby. "You can only just get underneath it. Which is why I don't think there's a tunnel here."

They climbed down to the level of the beach hut.

"It's quite lonely, isn't it?" said Libby, looking round at the deserted beach.

"I guess this path turns into the promenade further down," said Fran, turning round to get a better view. "More beach huts down there."

"We'll go and have a look after we've had a look in here," said Libby, fishing out the keys Estella had given them and inserting them into the complicated locks. The door creaked open and she stepped inside.

"Smells musty," said Fran, wrinkling her nose. "I didn't notice that yesterday."

The walls were clad halfway up with tongue-and-groove panelling, although it looked to Libby's eyes rather the worse for wear. "Looks as if it was thrown up later than the hut," she muttered.

"Probably to help insulate, or protect from damp," suggested Fran, prising one plank a little way away from the wall. "Look, it's on thick battens. Quite a space between the panel and the outer wall. It's a bit of a fortress for a beach hut."

"Don't do that!" said Libby. "You'll have the whole lot off."

"No—look." Fran sounded excited. She turned to Libby. "I think you were right."

"Right? About what?"

Fran pointed. "Wiring."

Sure enough, tucked down behind the panelling was some old, fabric-covered electric wiring.

The two women looked at one another.

"What do we do now?" asked Fran.

"See how far it goes," said Libby.

Very carefully, they pulled more of the panelling away, until they had traced the wiring all the way round one wall to where it had been roughly cut, or torn off.

"Wireless station," said Libby.

"Do you think we could find out?" Fran sat back on her heels.

Libby used one of the armchairs to help haul herself to her feet. "There's a website. I'm sure we looked it up when we were over on the Isle of Wight. Don't you remember? They might be able to help. A lot of stuff is no longer secret now it's over 70 years—or 75—or whatever it is."

"What's it called?" Fran pulled out her smartphone.

Libby looked at it dubiously. "I can't find things out on that thing."

Fran grinned. "I can. What's the website called?"

"Special Duties Branch, as far as I can remember."

They sat in the two armchairs, Fran scrolling away on her screen and Libby staring through the open door to the sea throwing itself at the pebble and sand beach.

"Here we are. You were right." Fran scrolled up a bit further. "There were actual branches—civilian observers and secret wireless networks."

"And you should be able to look it up on a map," said Libby. "I think they were called Out Stations."

"It's just a list," said Fran, peering at the screen. "You can't always get the right place. They aren't all live links. There's one that says Beach Lane Out Station in the right area. Do you think that could be it?"

"Might be. Wouldn't hurt to poke around a bit more." Libby looked round the bare walls of the hut. "Up there, see? Looks as though something like an electricity meter's been pulled off the wall. And there's what looks like an old Bakelite switch."

"And that's unusual, isn't it? Most beach huts haven't got mains electricity. And there's no sign of a generator." Fran put her phone back in her pocket and stood up. "I don't think there's going to be anything more to find here, though. It's been cleaned out—at the end of the war, I would guess."

"Oh, I wish there was someone still alive we could talk to," said Libby with a sigh.

"I doubt if anyone would tell us anything," said Fran. "There was something on that website that said civilian operators and observers never spoke to each other, even up to when they died."

Outside, Libby turned and looked up towards Piddling Point. They could see little but a shape and a tangle of vegetation. "That's where Estella said the lookout post was. Isn't it a bit odd to have a lookout post *and* an Out Station so close to each other?"

"Perhaps they simply felt they couldn't have a secret wireless station in the lookout post," said Fran. "Although they would have to have had wireless, too, wouldn't they?"

"And we still don't know what this place had to do with our murder victim," mused Libby, as they turned away from Satis House to walk towards the town.

They followed a boardwalk where the coastal scrub met the sand and finally came to the row of beach huts.

"Very individual," said Fran. "All got names."

"Forget-Me-Not," said Libby. "And Rosa's Retreat."

Further along, "And look! Rassendyll. So Satis House isn't that unusual."

"There are some newer ones, though. They haven't got names." Fran turned and looked seawards. "I like the look of the pier. Do you suppose that's a theatre at the end?"

"Looks like it," said Libby. "Nice little place, isn't it?"

"It is. I wish we had a pier in Nethergate."

"You've got the jetty. No room for anything else. Look—that probably leads to the square." Libby pointed to a side road between the shops that lined the promenade.

They made their way past the huts, across the promenade and past the fish and chip shop on the corner, and finally came to the square.

"Is this it?" said Libby, stopping by the building on the corner.

"Dumaine's, yes." Fran peered through the doorway. "Is it open?"

"Yes, ducks," said a voice behind them. "Bit early, though."

They turned to see an elderly woman who looked as though she had stepped fully formed out of a 1940s photograph, crossover pinny and all.

"Too early for lunch?" asked Libby.

"Yeah. Better off down there." The woman jerked a thumb over her shoulder in the direction of the fish and chip shop. "They'll give you a drink, though."

"Were you just going in?" asked Fran. "Will you have a drink with us?"

Libby raised her eyebrows but said nothing.

The woman stuffed her hands into the pockets of her pinny and shrugged. "Don't mind if I do."

Libby pushed open the door and held it for Fran and their new friend to go inside. Fran winked as she passed.

Settled at a table where they could look out over the square, Libby went to the bar to order drinks.

"That'll be a stout for Lil, then," said the barman with a smile.

"Will it?" Libby looked over at the table where Fran was speaking animatedly. "OK. And a white wine, please, and a half of lager."

"Bascombe's lager?"

"Do you recommend it?" asked Libby dubiously.

"I prefer this one," whispered the barman, tapping a pump. "Don't tell anyone."

"Ah." Libby nodded wisely. "OK, half of that one, then."

She looked over at the table. "Stout all right, Lil?" she called, and received a nod and a grin in reply.

"Do you come here often?" she asked as she set the drinks on the table.

"Yeah." Lil picked up her glass and raised it in Libby's direction. "They know me."

"Lived here a long time?" asked Fran.

Lil smiled knowingly and took a healthy swig of stout.

"You know everyone, then?" said Libby.

"Know who you are."

Libby and Fran looked at each other in surprise.

"But we only arrived yesterday," said Fran.

"Met that Estella. Gone up that Manor place."

This time, Libby's mouth dropped open and Fran drew in a sharp breath.

Lil grinned smugly down into her stout.

Libby was first to recover. "Do you mean Manor Farm?"

"Used to be."

"But it still is," said Fran.

"Not a farm, is it?"

"Well, no..." Libby conceded.

"Caravan park."

"Why do you say that?" asked Fran.

"You know. That's what they are, ain't they?" Lil sat back in her chair and cocked her head on one side.

"They're a bit more than that," said Libby.

Lil snorted.

"You can live in them," put in Fran.

"Nasty piece of work." Lil gazed out of the window.

"Who?"

"Him at the pub."

"Oh, Arthur Strange," said Libby.

Fran was frowning. "Who is he, Lil?"

"Bad lot."

"I'm going to have to look him up," said Fran. She turned to Lil. "And how do you know so much about it?"

Lil shrugged. "Know why you're here."

Libby bit down on increasing frustration. "That doesn't answer the question."

Lil stood up. "You come down to help Estella. That's good. Stop 'em ganging up on her." She pushed in her chair and went to the door.

"Who's ganging up?" Libby got to her feet.

"Ought to know." And Lil was gone.

# Chapter Five

Libby sank down again. "Well! What on earth was that all about?"

Fran was gazing into space. "I think we've been taken for a ride," she said slowly.

"What do you mean?" said Libby indignantly.

Fran was quiet for a moment.

"Do you remember what you said when we first arrived?"

"No." Libby scowled at her glass.

"You said, 'I don't believe in this place.' Why did you say that?"

"Well... The stupid name for a start."

"That's real enough," said Fran. "Unlikely, but real. And what did you say then?"

"Er..." Libby cast around in her memory. "Something about how we'd been hauled down here?"

"Exactly. Cora asked us down here to help her daughter and, if necessary, investigate something. Only we weren't told what."

"So what are you saying? Your mate Cora is doing a number on us both?"

Fran leant forward, elbows on the table. "Not just us. Frankly, I don't think Estella ever wanted us here."

Libby frowned. "She's a bit shifty about answering our questions, I agree. But then she seemed really anxious we should stay. Told us she'd made up rooms for us and everything. I had the feeling she was scared."

"Ye-es," allowed Fran. "Me too. She certainly didn't want us to go home last night. Actually, I've had this very bad feeling right from the start that Estella really needs us. But she doesn't seem to think so."

Libby thought about that. "She does seem to blow hot and cold," she agreed. "Do you think maybe what she really wanted was her own mother?"

"You mean get Gorgeous Cora to come and hold her hand while she talks to the police?" Fran hooted. "Not a chance. It could well get into the media."

"So? There's no such thing as bad publicity, remember."

"Huh. Professionally, Cora's been clinging on to her early thirties for the last fifteen years. She can't afford to break out a grown-up daughter now."

"Ah," said Libby, understanding. "I see. Of course. So if I'm right, Estella asked Cora to come. Only Cora chickened out and sent us instead. Poor Estella."

Fran nodded. "And told Estella we were expert investigators. Which has made her jumpy as a cat."

"Yes, it has, hasn't it?" Libby pondered. "Do you think that she's lied to us? At times she seemed downright shifty, now I come to think about it."

Fran looked unhappy. "And what did Lil mean, about people ganging up on Estella? Who? Why?"

Libby peered out of the window of the wine bar at the empty square. There was no sign of Lil. "Lil was a bit unbelievable herself, if you ask me."

"Putting on an act." Fran nodded.

"And dressed for it."

They sat in silence for a few moments gazing out at the square. On the opposite side from the wine bar was The Brewery Tap, a little more down-at-heel than Dumaine's.

Then Libby sighed. "Shall we see if they've started serving lunches yet?"

"I'm not really hungry yet," said Fran. "It's not that long since breakfast."

"I just thought," said Libby, turning an innocent face towards her friend, "we ought to ask the barman about Lil. After all, he seemed to know her..."

Fran grinned. "Do we want to burst her bubble this soon? Let me talk to Cora first."

"Shall we explore a bit more of the town, then? What did Estella say...? Jubilee Gardens?"

"Come on then." Fran stood up. "Let's go and be tourists."

They emerged into the square and made their way back to the promenade.

"The beach huts have stopped," said Libby. "I suppose we go along the other way."

The Prom was lined with small shops and a couple more food outlets, while between them were the entrances to what were obviously flats up above. A reasonably-sized car park was situated next to where the main road led away towards the town.

"And these are the Jubilee Gardens," said Fran, coming to a halt before a riot of municipal planting, "and Sir Copson's statue."

"And that's Councillor Whats'isname's stone." Libby wandered over to look at it. She stared at the uninspiring stone erection for a moment, then swung round.

"The war," she said. "What could we find out online?"

Fran stopped admiring the planting and joined her. "The war here, you mean?"

"Of course. Or is there a museum, do you think?"

"I'll have a look." Fran moved over to a bench and took out her phone.

Libby fidgeted.

"Not much," said Fran after a moment. "It doesn't say anything about the Auxiliary Units or beach defences."

"I haven't noticed any tank traps or pill boxes round here," said Libby, going to peer over Fran's shoulder.

"Not the easiest place for tanks to land," said Fran.

"Good place for secret landings or launchings, though." Libby perched next to Fran and looked out thoughtfully over the sea. "Is that why Satis House was set up as an Out Station, do you think?"

"Possibly." Fran put her phone away. "But whether it was or not, that doesn't explain why someone was murdered, or why Arthur Strange is sniffing around."

"To be fair," said Libby, who often wasn't, "we've only got our own suspicions about Strange, haven't we? He could just be a crafty businessman, with an eye to the main chance. There was Manor Farm, run down and idle, the land going to waste. All he did was come along and turn a profit from it."

"Hmm." Fran stared at the Councillor's stone. Then she turned to look at Libby. "Did Estella go on her own to look at the body? Do you remember?"

Libby shook her head. "She didn't say. But it obviously upset her."

"Yes," said Fran slowly. "I think she went on her own."

"So?"

Fran leaned forward eagerly. "Well, think about it. If you had to go and identify a body, would you go on your own? No, you wouldn't. You'd phone a friend. Ben or me or…loads of people."

"Who was Estella going to phone? Arthur Strange?"

"Exactly." Fran was triumphant. "She hasn't mentioned a single friend. Except for the police, nobody's called her while we've been here. I'm starting to wonder if Estella's got any friends."

"Someone told her the gossip about it being a murder investigation," Libby pointed out.

"Do you think that was a *friend?*"

Libby remembered the girl's panic. "No. No I suppose not."

"Well, then. I think we need to make Estella tell us exactly what is going on." Fran jumped up.

Libby followed, more slowly. "That includes Arthur Strange. I don't like the sound of that mysterious arrangement she has with him."

"You're right." Fran snapped her fingers. "With all the work Estella is putting into that caravan park, she ought to be a partner, or at least earning a salary."

"And it was another one of the things she didn't want to talk about," concluded Libby, pleased. "I got distracted last time. This time I'm jolly well going to ask her."

They started to walk back the way they had come. It was a gorgeous day, with a fine crop of daisies in the meadow.

"You know I still have that feeling that this all dates back to the war," said Fran, as they crossed over an old-fashioned stile on the last leg of the path towards the Manor.

Libby sighed. She knew there was no point in asking why.

Anyway, Fran was pursuing her own thoughts. "It seems to start with Estella's Granny Joan who came here as a land girl."

"But," said Libby, "the family connection starts farther back. When Joan arrived, the Hope family already lived at Manor Farm. Gentlemen farmers. Remember that gloomy old Victorian hall?"

"Quite grand, though," said Fran absently. "And the 'gentleman farmer' thought Land Girl Joan wasn't good enough for his precious son. So he ran Joan off and Grandpa Clive went with her. Pair of illicit lovers, shacking up somewhere…"

"London probably," said Libby, caught up in the drama of it. "Of course, they'd need to have had their ration books. But you can always hide in a big city like London if you want to."

"Maybe they didn't have to. No sign that his old man wanted Grandpa Clive back," said Fran crisply. "The mother didn't invite them home until the old man died." She stopped dead.

"What?" asked Libby, stopping so abruptly she narrowly avoided a cowpat.

"Gentleman farmer. Fairly grand house. Clive's mother wants an heir..."

"Yes?"

"So what happened to the money?" demanded Fran. "You don't care about an heir if the farm is bankrupt and the house is falling down. Something happened. I want to know what. And the first thing I want to know is when Old Man Hope died."

They turned to start walking back to Manor Farm and Libby stopped.

"Look," she said. "Up there—is that Arthur Strange?"

Outlined on the skyline stood a lone figure.

"Is he watching us?" said Fran.

"Certainly facing this way." As they watched, the figure turned and disappeared from view. "Well, it needn't be suspicious, I suppose."

They walked back along the dry riverbed in silence. When they arrived at the annex, Libby went to put on the kettle while Fran pulled out her phone and settled down to search for death certificates.

# Chapter Six

Knowing that Fran was deeply absorbed, Libby made tea for both of them and put Fran's mug within recovery distance. From time to time Fran made little "Aha" noises, which sounded promising. Eventually she sat back and stretched.

"Success?" asked Libby.

"I've found Estella's Dad and Grandpa Clive. I can't find a marriage certificate. But Clive is down as the father and Granny Joan is named as 'Joan Mary Hope' on Richard's birth certificate."

"Is that legal, using the name if she wasn't married to him?" said Libby, surprised.

Fran shrugged. "Who knows?" She thought a bit. "Wonder if Clive knew she put him down as the father? I suppose Joan could have changed her name by deed poll. For the moment, I'm assuming it doesn't matter." She looked hopeful. "Any more tea before I start looking for Old Man Hope?"

Libby retreated to the kettle and returned with two mugs. She put them on the coffee table and sat down on one of the sofas.

Fran looked up from her notes. "Oh, lovely. And tonight, we can walk down and have fish and chips, if you don't mind having fish two nights running."

"Great. I'll be ready for it. It looks as if you've found a lot," said Libby.

"Fairly easy, so far," murmured Fran. "There were rather a lot of Richard Hopes, but finding Clive was a piece of cake. And Old Man Hope was Frederick Ethelred. I bet there aren't a lot of them about." And she started tapping her phone again.

"Blimey. Wonder where that came from," said Libby.

But Fran was getting used to the website now and her fingers fairly flew. "Here he is. Frederick Ethelred. Birth certificate: born 28th June 1880. Gosh. His father is down as Land Agent of Primly Court. Definitely a Gentleman Farmer."

"I think I saw a signpost to that on the road in," said Libby.

But Fran wasn't listening. "Ah, here we are. Died 10th September 1941." She looked up. "So Joan and Clive were gone by then. I think that may be important."

"Another feeling?"

"The same one really," said Fran ruefully. She sipped her tea. "You know—I think I'll phone Cora. She'll want to know that Estella is OK. Or she's going to, anyway," she added with a grin. She picked up her phone and scrolled to find the number, pressed the link and gave Libby a decisive nod while she listened.

"Hello? Cora? Yes, hi—it's me, Fran... Well, we're here in Little Piddling, but we don't know what's going on... No, Estella doesn't seem to know, either. I think you gave her rather a false impression... No, she's not telling us much. Did you know Joan well? No? So you can't tell us anything about the family? Oh—" her eyes widened as she looked across at Libby "—*did* he? Really? Well! Yes, I'll certainly ask her. Well, thanks, Cora. Yes, I'll keep in touch." She ended the call. "That was interesting."

"What?" Libby was on tenterhooks.

"Richard hardly ever talked about Grandpa Clive. Made it sound as if he was a real bad boy. Cora said Richard was oversensitive about being illegitimate. She thought it was funny."

"I wonder if Estella does," said Libby. "She was here a lot as a kid, wasn't she? I think we ought to ask her. Time she started talking."

Fran regarded her friend with a frown. "You're right. I'll ring her now."

Libby stood up and wandered round the sitting room.

Fran said into her phone, "Estella? Oh, hi—are you busy? We were just wondering if you could spare a moment to talk to us about Joan...? No, we just thought, if we are to go on looking into this whole business, we ought to get a feeling for the Hope family. Perhaps we could come up to the house...? Yes, fine, we'll be there in five minutes." She put down the phone. "She was a bit reluctant—"

"Surprise, surprise."

"—but she said yes. Finished your tea?"

Ten minutes later, Fran and Libby were sitting at Estella's kitchen table facing a very uncomfortable-looking Estella.

"We have rather a lot of questions," said Libby.

"And we'd like to start with Grandpa Clive," said Fran. "What happened to him after the war?"

Estella looked blank. "I don't know."

"Did Granny Joan leave any papers behind? Anything that might tell you?"

"Well..." said Estella after a pause.

"Come on, Estella," said Libby robustly. "We said we'll help and we will. But we can just as easily give up now and go home."

There was another silence.

"I notice," said Fran, slowly, "that you haven't asked us what your family history has got to do with this murder. So you think there's a connection, too, don't you? What is it you're not telling us, Estella?"

"Oh, God." Estella had gone perfectly white. She looked terrified.

Fran and Libby exchanged a startled glance.

"Have you told the police?" Estella whispered.

Fran put an arm round the shaking girl. "Of course not. But you'd better get it off your chest."

"Yes," said Libby, who was beginning to suspect that she knew what Estella's secret was. "It's eating you up. I can see it." She fished in her bag to hold another paper tissue in readiness.

The story was very simple and rather sad. Estella *had* known the murder victim, after all.

"I knew it," muttered Libby.

Fran frowned. Estella didn't seem to hear. She took the proffered tissue but instead of mopping her eyes, she twisted and twisted it, staring down as if it mesmerized her.

She'd first met him the Monday before his body was found. She always banked any cash and cheques on Mondays and she bumped into him outside the bank. He asked her for directions and, when she showed him the way to the cliff path on the map, he wanted to buy her a coffee to say thank you.

Fran and Libby looked at each other. It was clear that this was a novel situation for Estella.

"I didn't really *know* him," said Estella. "He said to call him Dave. He was nice enough. But pushy—you know?"

"We know," said Libby kindly.

"I just didn't quite trust him. He asked me to meet him later, for a drink in the pub. I couldn't think of an excuse and—well—he made me feel silly. So I agreed."

Fran was worried. "And did you meet him?"

Estella shook her head violently. "No. Oh, I was going to. Just to say that I had to work that evening and couldn't stay. But when I set off—"

"Yes?" they both said, impatient.

"Well, I was down in the dried-up river bed. It's quite overgrown in places. I suppose I was hidden. I saw Dave on the skyline and I thought, oh dear, and was going to hide. Only then I saw Arthur Strange. They'd obviously arranged to meet. They didn't look like friends, though. Arthur just gave him an envelope. And then they laughed."

"And you thought they were laughing about you," said Libby, in quick sympathy.

Estella nodded. "I waited until they'd gone and then I went back home. I locked the door," she added.

"Very sensible," said Fran.

Estella looked at her gratefully. "And then the next day the police came and said a body had been found beside Satis House. And would I come and see if I could identify it. And it was him." She looked sick. "I probably should have said that I'd met him. But I was scared. And I didn't know who he was, did I? So that's what I said."

Libby and Fran looked at each other. Both knew that Estella was going to have to tell the police that she'd met Dave and seen Strange talking to him. But she wasn't ready to hear that yet.

Libby said, "What about the paper in his pocket with Satis House written on it? You didn't give it to him?"

Estella looked appalled. "No. I can't understand that at all. When he asked me about the cliff path, he didn't even know where Piddling Point was. I was supposed to meet him in the pub."

Libby looked at Fran. "Maybe Arthur Strange gave it to him."

"It's a possibility," said Fran cautiously.

"I didn't like him," said Estella suddenly. "Dave, I mean. I know I'm shy—I was always the girl nobody picked for their team—but he sort of took me over as if I was *nothing*."

Libby looked at her with sudden approval. This shrewdness was unexpected. "Is it possible that he was lying in wait for you when you came out of the bank?" she asked.

"Why...? You think he deliberately set out to pick me up?" Estella sat up straighter. "Yes, it's definitely possible. Lots of people in Little Piddling could have told him my routine." She looked a lot happier suddenly. "So I wasn't just being paranoid?"

"Probably not," said Libby.

"My mother says I'm paranoid."

"It sounds to me as if you have damn good instincts," said Fran, keeping her feelings about Cora's maternal advice to herself.

Estella almost beamed. Instead she said, "But you wanted to ask me about family history. I don't know much. Though I do know that Little Piddling didn't approve of Granny Joan having a baby out of wedlock."

Libby nodded. "Did she tell you?"

"She didn't have to. I spent a lot of my childhood here, remember. She was a sort of pariah. And so was I."

Fran clicked her tongue sympathetically.

Estella took a deep breath. "The town didn't like it much when she came back here. Or when she inherited, either. There was some massive row after the war. Local rumour says that Grandpa Clive stamped out and Old Mrs Hope changed her will the next day. So Granny Joan got the lot."

"So..." said Fran slowly, "you think the murder has something to do with you? Because you've now inherited?"

"But I don't see why!" Estella sounded almost defiant. "The farm was so run down when Joan died that it was losing money. That's why I thought I was so lucky when Arthur Strange made me the offer. At least, I did at the time."

Libby heaved a sigh.

"Estella—" Fran stood up "—are you afraid that something about Joan will come out if the investigation into the murder goes on? Something disreputable?"

Estella stared at Fran. She was a rabbit-in-the-headlights again. She didn't say anything.

Fran went on, but gently, "Some old scandal that you thought you'd put behind you?"

"Look," said Libby with patience, "you didn't trust that Dave. You thought he had an ulterior motive. I'd say you were on to something. So what if this is all rooted in the past, like Fran thinks? What if someone else comes here on the same errand as Dave?"

Estella recoiled. "*No!*" she shouted.

And she jumped up and shot out of the room.

# Chapter Seven

"Oh dear," said Libby guiltily. "That didn't come off, did it? Not quite the reaction I expected."

Fran was looking thoughtful. "I think you may have spelled out exactly what Estella is frightened of."

"Ouch. Poor girl."

Fran was philosophical. "Better out than in. She was going to have to face it at some point."

"But what do we do now? Come on Fran, time for one of your 'moments'." Libby leant forward across the table.

Fran smiled. But they both knew that she couldn't call up one of her intermittent flashes of psychic intuition to order. "I think she'll get over it. Hope so, anyway."

"So we just sit and twiddle our thumbs until she comes back?" said Libby, dissatisfied.

Fran grinned. "Yes. Or until the chippie opens. Whichever comes first." And she started to tap away at her phone again.

Libby prowled round Estella's kitchen, opening cupboards. Queenie the cat ate the same food as Sidney and looked as if she had a Dreamies habit. There were a lot of postcards propped up on the mantel over the old kitchen range. Whatever the residents might be like, lots of visitors wrote friendly thank-you notes to Estella, it seemed.

"Oh," said Fran suddenly.

Libby put a postcard of Windsor Castle back. "What?"

"I've found Primly Court. It looks as if it's owned by some City Chap now. But the local history society has a fair bit on its website." Fran was clicking through web pages. "It was a school in the 70s. And— No, hang on. It was requisitioned by the Army in 1941. Looks as if it was pretty much wrecked by them."

Libby went and peered over Fran's shoulder at sepia-tinted pictures of devastation. "Ouch. I read a book about that. Everyone dreaded having their stately homes requisitioned. The Army were the worst of the lot. Used Van Dycks as a dart board and drank the cellar dry, apparently."

Fran had pulled out her notes. "1941... 1941... Yes, here it is. September. Frederick Ethelred dies. Hmm."

But the kitchen door opened and they both looked up. Estella was back. She was carrying an old biscuit tin.

"Here," Estella said, seating herself at the table. "This is Granny Joan's box." She looked up. "She gave me this just before she died."

"When was that?" asked Libby gently.

"Last year. She—um—she was tired. Well, she was well over 90 and she had pneumonia. She kept falling asleep. But she was making sense. She said—" Estella swallowed, then went on bravely, "She said not to look in here until I was ready." She pushed the box across the table.

Fran opened it. Estella sat back, clearly not wanting to look.

"Photographs?" asked Libby, who'd seen biscuit tins like that before.

Fran investigated the contents with care. "And papers. And press cuttings. And… Is that a bunch of heather?"

The photographs were all small, dog-eared, black-and-white and of what appeared to be family groups.

"Who are they?" asked Fran, showing one to Estella. She pointed to a girl in a summer dress and sandals, standing next to a grumpy-looking younger boy beside a farm gate.

Estella didn't touch it but looked at the photograph cautiously. "That must be Amy."

"Amy?" repeated Fran and Libby together.

"Amy Hope," said Estella. "Grandpa Clive's sister."

"So that's Clive?" asked Libby after a pause.

Estella nodded.

"What happened to them?" asked Fran. "Did they die?"

Estella looked evasive. "Why do you say that?"

"Well, we haven't heard of Amy before. And I can't find a death certificate for Clive."

"Is it important?" Estella kept her eyes down.

Libby rolled her eyes. But Fran said kindly, "It may be."

"I don't know what happened to Amy. I think she went into the Wrens. She'd gone before Granny Joan got here."

"And Grandpa Clive? Come on, full story," said Libby.

"Granny Joan said his mother spoilt him," said Estella unexpectedly. "Every time he got into trouble, she made excuses. Said he'd got into bad company."

"Bit of a wide boy, was he?" Libby guessed.

Estella looked bewildered. "Granny Joan told me that when his father threw Clive out, she went with him because she wanted to get back to London. He left her almost at once. Then she found she was pregnant. After the baby was born, she sent Clive a letter telling him he had a son and she was going to call him Richard."

"Where did she send the letter?" asked Libby.

Estella nodded, as if she made a good point. "To Manor Farm. She assumed Clive would slink home when he ran out of money."

"He sounds charming," said Fran.

"Only old Mrs Hope opened the letter. She came up to London. Found Granny Joan and begged her to bring the baby home to the farm." Estella was lost in memories for a moment. "Granny never said so, but she must have been desperate, because she said yes."

"Understandable," said Fran.

"I suppose so." Estella came back to the present. "You know the rest. Old Mrs Hope took Joan in on condition my dad was brought up as a Hope."

"Interesting," said Fran. "Joan had already registered Richard as Hope, with Clive named as his father. I can show you the certificate online."

Estella surprised them by beaming. "Oh, that is so like my Granny Joan. She was very straight. 'Tell the truth and shame the devil,' she used to say." Her eyes filled suddenly. "I miss her."

Fran patted her shoulder.

"So what happened to Grandpa Clive? Did he die in the bombing?" asked Libby.

Estella looked surprised. "Oh no. He used to come back to Manor Farm from time to time. My dad met him a couple of times, as a boy. Then there was a massive row and he was never seen again."

Fran and Libby looked at each other.

"I think you may find what happened to Grandpa Clive in Granny Joan's box, Estella," Fran said. "Would you like us to go through it with you?"

There was a silence.

Then Estella was suddenly decisive. "Yes. Yes, I would. I've been a wimp. Granny Joan would be ashamed of me. Let's look now."

They spread the contents out across the table. There were about two dozen photographs, some yellowing press cuttings, two long narrow envelopes and a hard-backed notebook, with a red cloth spine.

"Very 1940s," said Libby, whose grandmother had been a hoarder.

Estella opened it. There were pages of closely written prose. "*Oh*. It's Granny Joan's writing. I didn't know she'd written a book."

But it was more than a book, as it turned out. It was a diary.

More than that. It was evidence.

# Chapter Eight

They extended the kitchen table to fit it all in.

"We need a timeline," said Libby, moving round the table like a 1940s Air Force plotter. "Where do we start? Granny Joan's diary?"

"Might as well," said Fran. "Estella?"

Estella was in charge of the notebook. She skipped back to the beginning. "She says she got to Manor Farm in October 1939. She was sixteen but she lied about her age. Nobody cared."

Estella had brought in some blank record cards from the Manor Farm office. Fran wrote the details down on one and put it at the far end of the table.

"Then what?"

Estella was speed-reading. "She stays for Christmas, because she hasn't any family. Clive goes off to London and there's a huge row when he gets back. His dad says he's been gambling and threatens to throw him out." She looked up. "It sounds as if the row frightened her. She says, 'I told the Land Army woman I wouldn't stay if the men were too free with their fists. And I won't.'"

"Sounds heartfelt," said Fran, writing it down and giving the card to Libby.

Libby put the card at the end of the table. "Maybe Clive didn't have a fling with Joan at all. Maybe his father threw him out for some other reason."

"You could be right," said Fran, much struck. "Maybe they got together later. What next?"

Estella thumbed her way through farming activities. "Ah. Primly Court has been requisitioned. The family only has 48 hours to clear out. The Women's Institute rally round to help and Mrs Hope organizes a roster." Estella looked up. "There should be a list somewhere of what went where and how it got there."

Fran hunted round.

"One of the long envelopes?" suggested Libby.

She was right. There were five foolscap sheets of accounting paper, covered in meticulous spidery writing.

"Joan helps ring round to find petrol. Only gets a bit. So they pack up anything small enough into parcels and people on bikes take it to where it's got to go."

"I'm beginning to see the light," said Libby. "Clive was one of the cyclist couriers, right?"

Estella turned pages fast. "Doesn't say. Oh, hang on. There's a note here in pencil. Yes, I think you must be right, Libby."

Fran flourished one of the press cuttings. "Here we are. 'Thieves at Large. Mr Clive Hope of Manor Farm was riding his bicycle on the Piddling Magna Road on Thursday evening, when he was set upon by two thugs and his bicycle was stolen. Mr Hope was found unconscious and is now recovering at home.'"

"Ho yus?" said Libby. She had taken against Clive in a big way. "What date is that?"

Fran peered at the very top of the cutting. "1940, 25th August, I think." She picked up another card and scribbled it down.

"Two thugs, my eye," said Libby trenchantly. "What if shifty Clive made off with the small valuables and threw his bike in the hedge? *That* could be why his dad kicked him out the following month."

"Possible," said Fran, giving the card to Plotter Libby to place on their timeline column. "What's next, Estella?"

The girl was looking stunned. "Oh. Um. An Inspector comes. Farmer Hope complains that he keeps having to fill in forms. He and Clive argue. Joan asks to go to the pictures. Mrs Hope agrees, but Farmer Hope says they have to keep working while it's light. He's in a bad temper all the time." She turned the page. "Oh. *Oh no.*" She snapped the notebook shut and almost threw it at Libby. "You read it. I can't. I just can't."

Fran put her arm round Estella.

"He *hit* her, Fran." The girl was shaking.

Libby said, "Why don't you make her some tea? I'll have a quick read of this."

It wasn't quick, but eventually Estella had calmed down, Fran had gone through the loose papers in the box and Libby had enough markers in the notebook to make sense of events.

"Farmer Hope said Joan was a lazy baggage. And he hit her."

Estella gulped.

Fran patted her absently but said, "He must have been at the end of his tether. When, Libby?"

"Fifth of September. Joan left the next day, telling Mrs Hope why. Clive went with her. She was grateful but surprised. No, definitely not lovers—at that stage, anyway."

Fran scribbled and added the card to the timeline.

With Libby reading out diary highlights, they pieced the story together.

When they got to London, Clive and Joan shared digs in London for a few weeks. Then he went off, saying he had to see a friend. Joan got a job, the bombing was bad and Joan didn't realize she was pregnant until very late. Afterwards, she wrote to Clive, care of the farm, to tell him he had a son. Mrs Hope came to London, told Joan that Farmer Hope had died and persuaded her to come back, with the baby.

Neither of them knew where Clive was. Mrs Hope thought he'd joined up. Joan didn't.

Clive didn't figure much in the diaries. He didn't deny that he was baby Richard's father, but didn't seem very interested in him. In 1947, he came to Manor Farm for Christmas, had a fight with his mother and left. Mrs Hope told Joan she was cutting him out of her will and saw her solicitor on Monday 30th December.

Five years later, Clive arrived uninvited, this time with a friend. He claimed they were spending their summer holiday on a walking tour and he'd dropped in to meet his son. Joan was suspicious. But Clive and his friend walked on the beach with Richard and offered to help the eleven-year-old restore the derelict beach hut for him and his mates. But after a couple of days, young Richard said he didn't want to go to the beach with them any more. Joan told them to go and they went.

The last time was the nastiest. After Mrs Hope died, Clive tried to contest the will. Fran found a collection of legal letters about it, along with a doctor's letter confirming that Mrs Hope was of sound mind when she died. After that, Clive came to Manor Farm, but Joan had gone away for a rest and Richard, now nearly thirty, was running it until she got back. Joan's diary recorded that Richard found Clive in the house, stealing the keys to the beach hut. Richard took back the keys and threw Clive out.

All three of them looked at the timeline, set out in cards along the kitchen table.

"Poor Granny Joan," Estella said softly. "Poor love. She never told me."

"The beach hut," murmured Fran.

"Wish we could find out what small valuables he pinched," said Libby, not attending.

"It's there," said Fran. She waved at the long thin envelope at the far end of the table. "Full list of three loads, transported by bike.

Clive was carrying the smallest. Jewellery, mostly diamonds, two enamel boxes, a jewelled fan—" she paused dramatically "—and a Fabergé egg."

"Blimey," said Libby. "They're all one-offs, aren't they? Must be priceless."

Estella's eyes were as big as saucers. "Wow," she said. "Just—wow."

"Assume Clive stole it," said Fran. "Then hid it in the beach hut for safe keeping. And that last time, Richard caught him at the farm before he could retrieve it…"

Libby digested this. "You mean that's what Dave, or whatever his name was, came here to look for? The proceeds of an 80-year-old theft?"

Somewhere outside there was an almighty crash. Fran jumped and Libby rushed to the window.

Estella, clearly no longer frightened of anything, waved a nonchalant hand. "That'll be Queenie. She's learned how to pull the dustbins over to get at fish bones."

Sure enough, a series of thumps and tinklings followed the crash.

"I can't see a cat," said Libby. "But to be fair, I can't see anyone else either." She came back to the table, a touch reluctantly.

"Clive came back three times. Maybe he was selling it off, a piece at a time. How would we find out if any of the stolen things have surfaced?" asked Estella.

She's starting to think like us now, thought Libby approvingly. From Fran's suppressed grin, so did she.

"Ask the police," said Fran reasonably. "You need to tell them that you'd encountered Dave, anyway. Show them the box as well and tell them what you suspect."

Estella looked from one to the other. "What if they don't believe me? I sort of didn't tell them everything, after all."

"So you're putting that right now," said Libby. "Just tell them."

"Do it now," said Fran. "Libby and I will come with you to the police station and wait outside, if you like."

"No need," said Estella. She swallowed but picked up her mobile from the large dresser.

When she ended the call she looked thoughtful.

"Well? What did they say?" asked Libby.

"Someone would come along to take my statement, possibly this evening, but more probably tomorrow morning."

"We were going to go out for fish and chips this evening," said Libby. "Should we stay here instead?"

"One of us can go and collect them," said Fran. "For all three of us. If Estella wants to eat with us?"

Estella's eyes were shining. She looked like a different girl. "Oh, yes, please." She picked up the book. "And now I'm going to be brave and read this properly."

# Chapter Nine

Libby and Fran left her to it. They went back to the annex and Fran tried to get a signal to call her husband, while Libby set off with her basket down the path to the town.

It was still light, and very quiet. When Libby reached Satis House and set off along the walkway towards the prom, there wasn't a soul about. She shivered and quickened her steps.

None of the beach huts appeared to be occupied, although there were lights on in the building at the end of the pier. When she reached the lane leading to Brewery Square, with the fish and chip shop on the corner, she saw that here, at least, there were signs of life. Not many signs of life, but some. Libby went into the chip shop, and to her surprise, found Lil sitting at a table.

"Hello," she said. "You treating yourself to fish and chips, too?"

Lil shrugged and picked up a large mug of tea. Libby surveyed her for a moment, then turned to the counter to place her order.

"Where is everybody?" Libby asked the man brightly.

"Low season," he said, portioning chips expertly. "And our girl's on *Search for a Star*. Semi-final night. Everyone's at the screen on the pier or home watching on TV."

"Interesting." Libby turned to include Lil in the conversation. But Lil had gone, as swiftly and quietly as she had earlier from Dumaine's.

It was appreciably darker when Libby finally left.

"You watch yourself walking back up that Manor," came a voice from the darkness. Libby whirled round, and there was Lil, sitting on the wall.

"Why? Is it dangerous?"

"Could be." Libby saw the outline that was Lil give another shrug.

"I'll keep my eyes open," said Libby, after waiting for further words of wisdom. None were forthcoming, so she turned back towards Satis House and the river path. When she looked back over her shoulder, Lil had gone.

By the time Libby reached the Tudor beach hut, she was definitely spooked. She turned up the path along the dry riverbank, looking all round her and imagining all sorts of strange figures on the skyline. She fairly ran the last hundred yards to Manor Farm.

Fran was outside, frowning at her phone. She looked up, eyebrows raised in surprise. "Hello? What's up?"

"Nothing," panted Libby. "It's dark."

"Well, let's go and put the fish and chips in the Aga to keep warm. Estella's got an Inspector Danby with her."

"Oh!" It was Libby's turn to be surprised. "Somehow I didn't expect anyone to turn up tonight."

"No, neither did I." Fran opened the door into the warm kitchen. "So what were you so nervous about out there?"

Libby started to unpack the fish and chips and handed the packet to Fran, who was opening drawers and cupboards. "I saw Lil."

"Oh?"

"And she warned me to be careful coming back up here. She didn't say why."

"Perhaps she was just concerned about you being out after dark on a lonely path."

"Hardly," said Libby, propping herself against the dresser. "I don't think she's the motherly type." She banked the problem for later. "Is Estella OK on her own with this inspector? What's he like?"

"He's a she," said Fran, extracting a roasting tin from the back of a cupboard. "Only met her in passing while I was wandering round the garden, stalking a signal. Seems OK. I think reading Joan's diary has put heart into Estella. She went off with the inspector and her sergeant quite happily."

Fran put the food in the warming oven. Libby went back to the annex and fetched the bottle of wine they had brought with them.

"Getting dark now," she said, switching on the overhead light and twisting the cap off the bottle. "Where are the glasses?"

Fran had already found them. Glasses of wine poured, they sank gratefully onto a couple of kitchen chairs and contemplated.

"I wonder what happened to Clive's sister, Amy," mused Fran.

Libby looked round at the kitchen table. It still had the extension out but the top was completely bare. "Never mind that. What's happened to our lovely timeline display? Did Estella tidy it away?"

Fran followed her eyes. There was a pause. "I'm sure she must have," said Fran in a voice that said she wasn't sure at all.

Their eyes met.

"That crash!" they said in unison.

They both fled outside to the bin store. The outside light came on. And, sure enough, one of the bins had toppled over and spilled its contents across the yard. There were horrid red marks across the cobbles, where someone in trainers had run towards the footpath.

Fran grabbed Libby's arm. "Is that blood? Did they hurt the cat?"

But Queenie was sitting on the wall, watching them disdainfully, as Libby pointed out, consolingly.

Fran breathed again. "Baked beans or sauce," she decided, from long experience.

Libby looked at the position of the bin, measuring angles with her eye. "If he was standing on it and leaning to the right he, or she, could just about have seen in the window."

"And heard what we were saying?"

"Maybe."

"And then, when we all left, he nipped in and stole Granny Joan's papers," said Fran in a hollow voice.

Libby straightened her spine. "We're going to have to go and tell that inspector. *Now.*"

In the just-this-side-of-shabby sitting room, Estella seemed to be holding her own. When they entered, a small, slim woman with dark hair stood up, a friendly smile on her face. At her side, a large gloomy presence loomed.

"Your support group, I see, Ms Hope. Detective Inspector Danby," said the woman, holding out a hand. "And this is DS Brooks."

"Fran Wolfe," said Fran, offering a cool smile of her own.

"Libby Sarjeant with a J," said Libby, with a grin. "But I'm afraid we might have bad news." She turned to their hostess. "Estella, did you put away all the papers we left on the kitchen table?"

Estella sat bolt upright. "The timeline? No, of course not. I was going to show Inspector Danby what you—we—had worked out, once I'd finished explaining Granny Joan's notebook." And she patted the book on her knees.

"Oh, thank goodness you've still got that," exclaimed Fran. "Everything else has gone. We think someone must have been standing on a bin in the farmyard, listening to us."

Estella led the pack, grabbing a torch from the dresser on the way. The detectives were a very respectable second and third.

"We've left the fish and chips in the Aga," said Libby, turning a woebegone face to Fran as they sped through the kitchen.

"They'll be fine. That's what warming ovens are for," puffed Fran.

"They won't be the same, though," Libby mourned.

Outside, the other three were staring blankly at the overturned bin and the red-stained cobbles.

"It's OK," said Estella, mistaking Libby's mournful expression. "I'd thrown away a ketchup bottle that had silted up. Whoever he was, he must have jumped on it and shifted the blockage." She was very pale. "The keys to Satis House have gone, too."

"Told you," murmured Fran.

DS Brooks looked at the intermittent prints with a frown. "Took a risk, didn't he? Ran away when he fell off the bin. Then came back, by the looks of it."

Inspector Danby nodded. "May have had Manor Farm under surveillance, waiting for his moment."

"Listening to us piecing the timeline together. He would have heard us say that Clive must have hidden the loot in Satis House."

Inspector Danby exchanged looks with Sergeant Brooks. "Have you seen anyone else hanging about? Apart from Dave, of course," she asked Estella.

Getting that white, pinched look again, Estella shook her head.

"We-ell..." said Fran.

"Oh, great Heavens," said Libby, remembering.

Fran looked at her in surprise. "When we came back from Little Piddling, we saw someone on the skyline. He was watching us. I thought he looked like Arthur Strange. Didn't you, Libby?"

Libby moaned.

"What is it?" demanded Fran, half-irritated, half-concerned. "You were the first to catch sight of him, after all."

"It isn't that," said Libby, feeling dreadful. "I didn't say. I mean I meant to, but then we got talking about whether any of the stolen stuff had been recovered, and I forgot. I *forgot*," she almost wailed.

"Forgot what?" Fran almost shouted.

"The name of the friend who came with Clive Hope when they started to restore the beach hut for Richard."

Estella and the detectives looked blank.

But Fran said, "Oh yes. The walking tour companion. What about him?"

"His name," said Libby in a hollow voice, "was L'Estrange."

# Chapter Ten

Inspector Danby was impressive. "In that case," she said coolly, "we'd better get up to that beach hut right now. Come on, Brooks."

And the next moment, the police car roared off into the darkness.

"Oh," said Estella.

"Don't be disappointed," said Fran. "The police like to do things their own way. And they couldn't have taken all three of us, anyway. Only one car."

"But it's *my* bloody beach hut," said Estella, a martial light in her eye.

Libby blinked. Was painfully-polite Estella Hope *swearing*?

"Yes, but it's empty," said Fran soothingly. "Even if Arthur Strange is actually up there, the police won't find anything incriminating. It was too long ago. Everything from those days has gone."

"Not everything," said Libby. "There's all that panelling that you started to pull off the wall. There could be something behind that."

"So there could." Fran looked brighter. "We'll have a look tomorrow."

"We'll have a look now," said Estella, bristling. "We'll get there quicker than that damn car will. Come on." And she shot off along the old riverbed path, lighting the way with her torch.

Fran and Libby stared at each other, in the yard's motion-triggered spotlight.

"We look like zombies," said Libby, her lips twitching.

"What happened?" said Fran, bewildered. "One minute she's a rabbit who can't say boo to a goose."

Libby choked.

"Well, you know what I mean," said Fran crossly. "The next minute she's Wonder Woman."

Libby patted her friend consolingly. "I think Granny Joan's book put some gumption into her. Now, if we're going up that damn cliff in the dark, I want the torch I saw in my bedside drawer."

Estella was nearly at Satis House by the time they caught up with her.

"For once in my life, I'm going to confront that snake, Arthur Strange," said Estella with determination. "You know, now I've got used to this, it's quite exciting, isn't it?"

There were no lights up ahead. The police had certainly not arrived yet. Except...

"Is that a firefly or something?" muttered Fran.

"It's a pencil torch," whispered Estella absently.

She was very focused, thought Libby, a bit alarmed.

Suddenly Estella surged forward. Fran took off after her up the rutted path.

"Bloody hell," panted Libby, following suit. "I'm not built for this any more."

The door of the Tudor beach hut was wide open. Inside there were people, but they were difficult to see because of the two tracking beams that seemed to be duelling in the darkness.

"I'm armed. Put your hands up," yelled Estella.

And astonishingly, both—for there were only two—combatants did.

"Hell's teeth," muttered Libby, leaning against the side of Satis House, with a hand to her side. She had a horrible stitch and she was quite sure someone was going to get hurt. Make that, even more hurt. That stitch was a bastard.

But Estella was quite fearless. She turned her torch onto its widest beam and played it across the far end of the hut. In the spotlight, Arthur Strange blinked, dazzled.

"I can explain..." he began.

"Crook!" yelled his adversary.

Suddenly, there were police sirens. Strange's face turned into a mask of panic.

"There's nowhere to go," said Fran calmly, from somewhere in Estella's shadow.

But Strange bared his teeth, like a cornered wolf. "You ridiculous old woman," he said to Lil. And hit her, a real punch under her ribs, with the full force of his body behind it, as he tried to barrel past her.

Estella gave a scream of fury, jumped in front of him and hit his neck with her torch. She used a sharp chopping backhand that was clearly powerful. It sent him staggering back. He swayed for a moment and then fell forward until his forehead rested against the wall. He was clearly more than half-dazed.

A large chunk of panelling fell off the wall and hit him again, across the shoulders this time. Lumps of plaster thumped onto the floor around him.

Strange groaned. He shook his head and slid to the floor.

From the floor, Lil croaked, "Great shot, Batwoman."

And the police arrived.

Inspector Danby summed up the situation in one look and told Sergeant Brooks to call for backup. She helped Lil up and eased her into a chair.

"What happened?" asked the inspector.

Estella, Fran and Libby all began.

The inspector held up a hand. "One at a time."

Lil beat the others to the draw. "He killed that young man," she said, still breathing hard. "They were both... looking... for the stash... from the big house... started fighting." She broke off, coughing painfully.

Inspector Danby was sceptical. "And how do you know this?"

"Saw them," said Lil and leaned back and closed her eyes.

Estella said excitedly, "I *told* you I'd seen Dave talking to Arthur Strange. I bet they were working together."

"Until they fell out," mused the Inspector. She went across to Strange.

He opened one eye and groaned theatrically, nursing his jaw. "Estella Hope attacked me!"

"He hit Lil," said Estella indignantly. "And he was getting away."

"Citizen's arrest?" suggested DS Brooks, looking at his superior.

"Possibly," said Inspector Danby.

She made a gesture and DS Brooks helped Strange to his feet. The man gave an odd shuffle and DS Brooks looked down.

"Hello, what's this?"

Arthur Strange opened his mouth, looked round and shut it again.

DS Brooks picked a squashy envelope-sized object off the floor. It was grey with age. He turned it over and coughed as dust flew everywhere.

"Looks like a jewellery roll," said Libby, craning forward.

DS Brooks started to unwind it. Once inside the dusty outer layer, it turned into a faded plum-coloured velvet grid. DS Brooks plunged a finger into one of the hand-sewn pockets and brought out a dangly earring, with a blue stone suspended from twisty grey metal.

Inspector Danby drew in a long breath. "That looks like platinum. We need to bag it."

"Better have a good look," said Fran practically. "There should be a Fabergé egg and other stuff somewhere here, as well. Unless Clive Hope already sold it, of course."

Arthur Strange winced.

As soon as the backup arrived, Inspector Danby cautioned Arthur Strange and sent him back to the station with an escort, while other officers took photographs and carefully removed the panelling, searching for more stolen items.

Fran, Libby and Estella fell over themselves to explain what had happened. But then Lil struggled up in the old chair.

"I followed Arthur Strange here, Friday before last," she said slowly. "The young man was already here. Strange was furious. They fought."

"His neck was broken," said DS Brooks, before Inspector Danby could shush him.

Lil said, "Pure bad luck. Must have hit his head when he went down."

Inspector Danby frowned.

"The L'Estrange family built this hut originally, during the war," Lil went on. "Perfect place to hide the Primly Court haul."

"Primly Court haul?" Inspector Danby repeated, bewildered.

Libby said, "Wartime theft. Eighty years ago. We've pieced it together. We can show you."

Inspector Danby looked at her watch. "I need to get back to the station. DS Brooks, would you take Mrs Lil to A&E and…"

But Lil refused to go to hospital. "It's just bruises," she said.

"Look," said Fran, "it's dark and cold and Lil needs a cup of tea. Why don't you take us back to Manor Farm? We can look after her there. And you can take statements in comfort."

Lil graciously indicated that she would go to Manor Farm. The inspector agreed impatiently and hurried away. So DS Brooks transported all four women in a slightly crowded squad car, leaving the crime-scene team to finish their work.

Back at the Manor, DS Brooks stuck to Lil like glue.

Libby followed Estella into the kitchen when she went to make hot drinks. "Can I help? Congratulations on the Wonder Woman act, by the way."

"Batwoman," said Estella with a faint smile.

"What? Oh, yes, that's what Lil called you, wasn't it? Do you know her then?"

Estella shook her head. "No. But when Arthur Strange hit her, it was somehow as if he was hitting Granny Joan. It made me so *mad*. I'd let him walk all over me, but he wasn't going to get away with hurting someone like that. So I just launched myself at him." She was shamefaced. "Sounds crazy, doesn't it?"

"Perfectly reasonable," said Libby, meaning it. "Let's take in the tea and see how she's doing."

Fran had found Granny Joan's notebook, still with Libby's markers in it, and was explaining it to Lil and DS Brooks, who had his phone out, photographing pages.

Lil looked round when Estella eased through the door, carrying an old-fashioned tray with a massive brown teapot on it, as well as mugs, milk and sugar.

"I need to explain," said Lil, not taking her eyes off Estella.

DS Brooks said firmly, "And I need to take notes."

Lil shrugged.

It was as if she had stopped playing a part, Libby thought.

"Whatever. I'm sorry, Estella. I should have talked to you before." Lil's voice suddenly sounded different—more educated, somehow. "That's what your grandmother would have wanted."

Estella said, "What's Granny Joan got to do with it?"

Lil looked sad. "She left my mother some money. She wanted to be fair. And that's what put Arthur Strange onto my mother's trail."

Estella seemed puzzled. "What?"

Lil was clearly marshalling her thoughts. "My grandmother was Clive's older sister, Amy."

"*Oh*. So we're some sort of cousins." Estella positively glowed. "How lovely."

Lil looked surprised, then shyly pleased. But she said, "You'd better hear me out before you say that. The thing is—my mother's in her seventies now and ill. But in her day she was a real wild child. And she got mixed up with the L'Estrange family through glamorous Uncle Clive."

Fran said, "Oh dear."

"Quite. Joan's solicitor put a notice on one of those Trace Your Family websites and bloody Arthur Strange picked it up and found her. Started blackmailing her about her past. She was—is— terrified." Lil smiled. It wasn't a nice smile. "Well, IT is my game. I tracked him down."

DS Brooks said, "And followed him here?"

"Yes. Disguised myself as an eccentric fan of the 1940s and started surveillance on him. It worked, too. Strange always looked right through me," she said with satisfaction. "I followed him to Satis House several times. I thought he was probably looking for a drugs stash. I was going to photograph him and take the evidence to the police. The fight made me think twice, at least for a bit."

"There could be a charge of failure to report a crime," mused DS Brooks.

Lil was unimpressed. "I wasn't going to report him for something that would only get him a small fine." She looked a bit shamefaced. "I didn't realise it was that lad who'd died until today. The paper said it was the body of a walker."

Estella said in a small voice, "Did you know that Clive was responsible for a big theft and had hidden the stuff in my— in the beach hut?"

Lil said, "My grandmother always said he got pushed into it by the L'Estrange clan. She said that Clive was just a stupid gambler with a big education and no conscience."

Estella closed her eyes and let out a long sigh.

DS Brooks patted her kindly on the shoulder. "It was a long time ago. I reckon we've got all we need. Don't need to listen to your family history as well. Someone will type up your story, madam, and I'd be grateful if you'd come into the station tomorrow to check it for accuracy and sign it."

He left.

Estella said slowly, "Lots of people round here blamed Granny Joan for Clive staying away." She swallowed. "When I was at school, no one from my class would ever come to Manor Farm."

Fran's eyes met Libby's. "Ganging up?"

Libby nodded.

Estella seemed not to notice. "And Clive told the whole town that Richard was illegitimate because he'd refused to marry Granny Joan."

Libby stared open-mouthed. "*Told—?*"

Fran said, "Oh, of *course*."

Estella came out of her memory trance. "Why 'of course'?"

Fran spread her hands. "It's obvious. Joan was already calling herself Hope. Clive's mother accepted her. Why would anyone question it? But you said all the locals knew that they weren't married, Estella. *Someone* must have spilled the beans."

"Your Granny Joan sounds like a good egg," said Lil gruffly. "She deserved better than that shit Clive."

Estella sat up. "Do *you* know what happened to him?"

Lil nodded. "My mother said he died in Macau. Probably still gambling."

It didn't seem to upset Estella, however. She and Lil were soon deep in reminiscences of Estella's grandmother. Clearly, in Lil, Estella had found family and friend in one.

Libby touched Fran on the arm. "Are your feelings OK now? Can we go home tomorrow?"

Fran laughed affectionately. "Dear Libby. You're a stalwart friend. We can go home tonight, if you want to."

"What? And miss fish and chips?" said Libby with mock horror. "Very warm, rather old, fish. And *chips*. And home tomorrow. Bliss!"

# THE END

## *About Lesley Cookman*

Lesley Cookman wrote the bestselling Libby Sarjeant Mystery series, and the Alexandrians, an Edwardian mystery series. A former editor, air stewardess and nightclub disc jockey, she lived on the Kent coast with two cats and occasional returning offspring. Very sadly, Lesley died on 29th June, 2025.

### *Want Lesley's books?*
You can get Lesley's last book, and find earlier ones you may have missed, at author.to/LesleyCookman

# PAST ECHOES
## *by Liz Fielding*

## DEDICATION

To a group of friends with whom I've shared writing days, party nights and soul-nourishing shepherd's pie and who never fail to keep my eyes on the deadline.

# Chapter One

Rose slowed as she saw a road sign that read, "Welcome to Little Piddling sur Mer."

Despite the postcard and the website, she had still half-believed that it was a comic opera fantasy, but she'd already driven through the narrow streets of Piddling Magna. It was real enough.

She pulled into a lay-by and climbed out of her van to take in the sea stretching out until it became one with the horizon. Below her, the town was tucked into the lee of the hill that stretched out to a headland.

The town was huddled around a sandy beach, empty this early and—though it had not been evident on the website—there was a small island half-a-mile or so offshore that was topped with a picturesque ruin.

She had never, to her knowledge, been here before; like "Adlestrop" she would surely have remembered the name and yet that island chimed in her memory.

Maybe it had been used as a setting for an episode in one of those not-so-cosy crime series. The kind where the body count reaches massacre proportions before the detective finally has a lightbulb moment.

With its narrow streets, it had the old-fashioned charm to have been used in an outing for Poirot or Marple.

Or maybe it was simpler than that. The view from here was very like the retro cover of one of her grandmother's childhood books that Rose had devoured as a child.

She'd found it when she'd been clearing the bookshelves in her father's house and, unlike the rest, which had gone to a charity shop, she'd put it in her keeper box.

The one thing she could be sure of was that it hadn't been on the postcard.

She'd been running a vacuum cleaner around the bedrooms, clearing away the last of the dust that had settled behind heavy old furniture that hadn't been moved in years, when she'd spotted it stuck in the skirting board.

She'd plucked it out and wiped off the dust to reveal a row of brightly-painted beach huts.

It was just an old holiday postcard but, as she'd looked at it, her heart had begun to beat a little faster and she'd had one of those goose-walked-over-your-grave moments.

Less to do with the postcard than the fact that it was the last time she'd ever be in her childhood home with all its memories, good and bad, she knew, but she'd turned the card over to see who it was from.

*"Weather great. Katy can't wait for her birthday. Jules."*

There was a single cross that looked like an afterthought.

Katy?

Her name was Katherine Rosalind Redmayne, but she had always been called Rose. Rose Red when she was little. Cute when she was at primary school. No fun at all when the mean girls at High School had found out.

The card was addressed to her father but not at this house, which meant that it had been sent before she was born. But the postmark was smeared, the date undecipherable.

It must have fallen out of one of the boxes of photograph albums, cards, school reports, stored on top of the heavy walnut wardrobe that had been a fixture of her parents' room for as long as she could remember.

She'd go through them in the dump-save-or-pass-on to her brother and sister triage when she had more time.

Matt and Lisa had, of course, been "much too busy" to stay and give her a hand once they'd been through the house to grab what they wanted in the way of furniture, pictures or anything else of value.

Too busy to help with the funeral arrangements or any of the endless details that had followed their father's death.

All they were interested in was their share of the house sale, accompanied by grumbles about how much she intended to rip them off for her expenses as executor. She'd been too weary to fight with them, would have let it go. Their father's solicitor, realising how it was, had been firm on the subject at the will-reading, but a difficult time had been made a lot worse by their whingeing.

Heaven help her if she threw away some cherished piece of their history.

They wouldn't want this old postcard, though, and she slipped it in the back pocket of her jeans, intending to drop it in the rubbish on her way out.

She found it there when, hours later, she stripped off her dusty clothes before sinking into a hot bath.

The Beach Huts, Little Piddling sur Mer.

The name was ridiculous, but it made her smile, which after the last grim months was worth a great deal. Her father was famously allergic to the sea but it must have meant something to him and, instead of tossing it into the wastepaper basket, she put it on her bedside table.

Later, limbs weary but her mind churning with the emotional fallout of the day, she picked it up and, seeking a distraction, tapped Little Piddling sur Mer into her tablet's browser.

She half-expected a "not found" response—a place with a name like that belonged in a comic opera—but the town was real enough and a list of links immediately popped up.

There were the usual cricket, bowls, rugby clubs, a couple of pubs and restaurants with websites, a brewery, an arts festival, a group called The Piddling Players...

She clicked on the town's official link and there it was on the header, the kind of seaside town that you saw in art deco posters. The golden era when families took the train to the seaside for two weeks' holiday in the summer.

The photograph, taken from the sea, showed a curve of sand, and a tastefully preserved promenade that gave the impression of municipal gardens and afternoon tea, rather than amusement arcades and hot dog stalls.

There was a pier, too, with a little theatre, and a slipway for a lifeboat station.

The town, intentionally or not, appeared to be aimed firmly at the nostalgia market and the row of colourful beach huts was very much part of that image.

She clicked on the link and, in a close-up photograph, she could see that some of them, the older ones, she thought, had been individually decorated and given names.

One, called Rassendyll Lodge, had been trimmed to give it the look of a Bohemian hunting lodge. There was a Blenheim, an Arundel, a Chatsworth, but in amongst the stately homes there were huts with candy stripes and some named after flowers. A pale blue Forget-Me-Not, and a Marguerite that had been painted yellow and decorated with large white Mary Quant daisies. Very nineteen-sixties.

But it was the pink hut that caught and held her attention. Not just because the roof ridge had been adorned with an exquisitely-carved wooden garland of roses, but because it was called Rosa's Retreat. And at that moment, a retreat with her name on it sounded very appealing.

She was aware that there was a big demand for beach huts with some, in the most desirable places, fetching ridiculous sums.

A few of these were available to rent by the day, the week, the season. Some, including Rosa's Retreat, were for sale and, without the stately-home pretentions of its neighbours, at what seemed to be a very reasonable price.

There was a button to click for more details that seemed to pulse, inviting her touch.

You've had a rotten year, it seemed to be saying.

Your fitness fanatic dad dropped dead while out running and you had to deal with the coroner, arrange his funeral, sort out probate and sell the house without any help from your shit of a partner.

On the contrary, while you were dealing with grief, overwhelmed with paperwork and working all hours in an effort to keep your clients happy, he was consoling himself for your lack of attention with extras from a woman at the gym.

You've got money coming from the house sale and there's nothing to keep you in Maybridge. Your clients are all over the country, you can work from anywhere, so come and sit here, breathe in the sea air, dip your toes in the sea, have an ice cream from the little kiosk on the front.

It would be a fresh start.

A beach hut is an investment...

"Nice try, Rosa, but why would I buy a beach hut in a town I've never heard of?"

Rolling her eyes, she shut down temptation. Talking out loud to a beach hut was a sure sign that she really did need a break.

Somewhere warm, she thought. On one of the Greek islands, maybe, with a what-happens-in-Santorini-stays-in-Santorini holiday fling.

Two days later, searching for a sock, she found the postcard under the bed.

Rosa's Retreat seemed closer this time, a little brighter than the others; and when she ran a thumb over it, she could almost feel the texture of the carved roses.

She blinked and it was just a faded old postcard, but hadn't there been a gull on the roof? She shook her head.

It had been in the picture on the website, she told herself, propping the card against the lamp on her bedside table, hoping for sleep.

She hadn't taken on new commissions whilst she was dealing with the aftermath of her father's death, but there had been unmovable deadlines, contractors and suppliers to be chased. She'd spent hours travelling between sites to sort out problems, hours online, sourcing the perfect fabric, light fitting, antique rolltop bath. Time spent calming a client who, when she saw the colour she'd chosen on the wall, had burst into tears.

Rose had finally signed off on the last outstanding job, but the stress had taken a toll.

The cheating ex was history, but Rose missed the warm comfort of someone beside her in the dark and she wasn't sleeping. When she did manage to nod off for a few minutes, her mind had not shut down but had been chasing down corridors, searching for something. Trying to call out to someone who was always just out of sight, who couldn't hear her, because the sound was on mute.

She'd been avoiding the emotional minefield of the boxes that had been cluttering up the hall since she'd cleared her father's house and one night, afraid of slipping back into the dream, she got up, went downstairs and dragged them into the centre of the room.

It took a while. She was continually ambushed by memories. Her mother's last birthday before the cancer took her. Pictures of graduations, holidays, birthdays going back through the years. A photograph of the twins making their promise when they'd joined the Cubs brought her to a halt.

Why hadn't she been a Cub? Or a Brownie? She searched her memory but there was nothing there, and now there was no one to ask.

She was torn between a smile and tears when she found the photograph of a birthday cake her mother had made. She'd picked out Rose's name in little red roses and there was a single candle in the shape of an eight.

And that was it for her.

Every step of Lisa and Matt's lives had been recorded from the first moment of birth. There were photographs of her playing with them in the garden, on holiday, older, but there were none of her before they arrived. None of her as an infant in her mother's arms, a toddler. There was no first-day-at-school picture.

It was as if her life had started on her eighth birthday.

Had she missed an album somewhere? Thrown it out in a box of rubbish?

She swallowed down a lump in her throat and, as she climbed back into bed, something made her reach for the beach hut postcard, a distant connection with her father, and tuck it under her pillow.

It didn't stop the dreams. If anything they became more intense until, weeks later, in a moment of terror, she woke herself up, screaming.

She reached for the comfort of the postcard, clutching it against her chest until her heart stopped hammering.

She had to get away from everything that had been happening and, as the first streak of dawn lit the horizon, she was in the fast lane, on her way to Little Piddling sur Mer.

# Chapter Two

Rose arrived as Little Piddling was lifting its shutters for the day. She parked her van in the pay-and-display, found a café on the front. She hadn't been eating much, wasn't hungry, but she sat outside with a restorative coffee and forced herself to eat a croissant warm from the oven, while she checked out accommodation.

Her dash to the coast had been a crazy impulse. She had no idea if she was fleeing the last few dreadful months or racing towards something waiting for her in this town with a ridiculous name.

Right at that moment, it didn't seem to matter.

She booked into a B&B in the Regency terrace overlooking the bay, but the room wouldn't be available until two o'clock. It didn't matter.

After days of rain, the seafront and beach were sparkling in the sunlight and she couldn't wait to take a look at the beach hut.

Arthur Kettlesing, a partner in Kettlesing & Flint, the agency handling the sale, leapt to find her the details.

"Has there been much interest?" she asked. "I would have thought most beach huts would have been snapped up by Easter."

"It's still early. There's always demand at the beginning of July, when the school holidays begin but, once the weather picks up, people aren't looking for a fixer-upper. They want something they can use straight away."

Fixer-uppers were right up her street, but she wasn't about to tell him that. Instead she pulled a face.

"A fixer-upper? How bad is it?"

"It needs painting inside and out, but the condition is reflected in the price." When she didn't reply, he added, "I'm sure the owner would be open to a reasonable offer."

"Can I see it now?"

"I can't leave the office right now," he said, with obvious regret. "My partner is conducting a country house auction and he'll be away all day, but I'm sure I can trust you with the key. If I can just take some details?"

She handed him her card.

"Rosalind Redmayne Designs?"

"Yes. I'm staying at Queen Charlotte House on the promenade."

"Good choice. Flo will make you very comfortable." He handed her a keyring with the agency tag attached. "No need to rush back with it, Miss Redmayne. It's a lovely day. Take your time, try it out. If we're closed when you're done, I'll be at Dumaine's Wine Bar this evening. We could seal the deal over a glass of something."

His optimism warranted a smile, but no guarantees. "I'll see you later, Mr Kettlesing."

"Arthur..."

He waited for her to reciprocate, but Rose preferred not to mix business with pleasure. "I'll see you later, Arthur."

Rose could have walked along the promenade, but she took the steps down onto the beach which, apart from a couple of mothers with pre-school children, was deserted.

Further along, a group of older children in bright red school sweatshirts were poking about in tidal pools under the supervision of a couple of adults and, in the distance, where the beach gave way to shingle, a man was throwing sticks for a large black dog to retrieve.

This was all very new. Rose's parents had been deaf to the children's pleas to join their classmates on the annual summer exodus south to the beaches of Spain and Portugal.

They had favoured rugged camping and pony-trekking holidays in the Highlands and in the mountains of mid-Wales. Beautiful, but about as far from the coast as it was possible to get.

Older, Rose had been more attracted to cities—Rome, Paris, New York—and the ex was a winter sports fan.

Slipping off her shoes, Rose caught her breath as the cold water rippled over her feet. Offshore, a sailing dinghy was tacking in the wind and in the distance, blurred by the haze, was the outline of a container ship making its way west.

The tide had turned, leaving behind smooth wet sand and, as she walked along the water's edge towards the beach huts, she picked up small shells and stones, worn smooth as they'd tumbled in the sand.

Completely absorbed by the faint trace of an ammonite in the surface of one, she didn't notice the little boy clutching the blow-up alligator twice his size until, unable to stop his mad rush for the water, he blundered into her.

Rose caught him before he fell, steadied him. Checked that he was OK.

"Gator!" he cried. "My gator!"

She looked around and saw that his toy had bounced into the water and was in danger of being swept out into the bay.

The boy began to wail loudly and, dropping everything, she splashed into the sea to rescue it. It skimmed over the water at surprising speed and, already up to her knees, she missed it a couple of times as it was jerked out of reach.

In the distance someone shouted for her to leave it, but she called back, "It's OK, I've got it." And, at the third lunge, she grabbed it by the tail.

She hauled it in, waded back to the beach and handed it over to the boy's mother, who sighed and said, "This thing has been nothing but trouble since his dad bought it."

Rose, whose crops were now soaked to well above the knees, the edge of her shirt dripping from that last lunge, was only half-joking when she said, "Maybe you should stick a pin in it."

The woman gave her an odd look before bustling the boy away.

"Just trying to be helpful..." Rose muttered, shaking her head at the woman's lack of manners and sense-of-humour vacuum. Then, when she bent to retrieve her bag and sandals, something half-buried in the sand caught the sunlight as the wavelets retreated.

A piece of blue-green sea glass...

She dug it out with her fingers, swilled away the sand, smiling at this little treasure, but when she stood up, the man who been throwing sticks for his dog was looming over her.

"Didn't you hear me?" he demanded.

The sun was at his back, his face in shadow, a close-cropped beard adding to the illusion of darkness. The only light came from eyes, the same blue-green as the sea, and they were blazing with anger.

Startled, she dropped the glass and took a step back, before gathering herself.

"Was that you shouting at me?" she asked. "It was OK, I'd got it." For all the thanks she'd got.

"More's the pity. Never," he said, forcefully, "ever go into the sea after a blow-up toy."

"And leave it for some poor creature to choke on? There's too much plastic in the sea already," she replied, seriously irritated now. What was his problem?

"Too much plastic and too many bodies of people who think the ocean is just a big paddling pool," he retaliated.

Bodies?

Rose looked out across the bay, remembering how quickly the toy had been sucked away, tugged out of reach. How easily she'd been drawn in, up to her thighs before she knew it.

How much further would she have gone?

Maybe he had a point. Clearing her throat, planning to tell him that she'd told the mother to stick a pin in the wretched thing, that his message had been received and understood, she was confronted by his retreating back.

"Terrific," she said. "Piddling Sur Mannerless..."

His huge, bear-like dog, who'd been sitting quietly during this exchange, gave her a sympathetic look.

"Nigel!"

Nice dog. The verdict was still out on his man. Undoubtedly, he meant well but, like the child's mother, his social skills could do with a little work.

Her crops were soaked up to her thighs and she needed to change, but she'd have to pass the beach huts to get back onto the prom, so she decided to take a quick look at Rosa's Retreat on the way.

She didn't need to get up close to see that the agent hadn't been kidding about the condition. Familiar with estate-agent speak, she understood that it was shorthand for anything from in-desperate-need-of-renovation to falling-down.

Rosa wasn't falling down but, walking slowly around it, she could see that the paint, so bright in the postcard, had faded and was peeling off in strips where it faced the sea. The door was hanging a little out of true, one of the windowpanes was cracked and a chunk of the wood carving was missing from the roof ridge.

Nothing that she wasn't able to fix and, close up, it excited her to see that the garland had once been painted.

Most of the colour had been scoured by wind-blown sand and salt water, but there were still traces of it in the deeper crevices of the petals—rich pinks, greens and the sun gleamed on a touch of gold.

It didn't take much of a leap to imagine what it must have looked like when new. It was what she did. She'd tackled anything from a simple cupboard to an entire house, bringing the dilapidated back to beauty, upcycling the past-it.

All her instincts were telling her that this would be a great holiday project. A lot more productive than lying on a Greek beach. A lot less trouble than a mindless flirtation.

"Can I help you?"

She'd been so absorbed in her thoughts that she hadn't heard anyone approach and jumped nearly out of her skin, grabbing for the safety rail as she stumbled.

The door to the dark green beach hut next to Rosa's was open and one look confirmed her worst fears.

Usually she'd have given someone with a very nice dog the benefit of the doubt, but she'd been awake since before dawn, driven more than a hundred miles with a satnav that seemed to doubt the existence of Little Piddling sur Mer and it was about par for the day that Mr Grumpy, whose "Can I help you?" had been more along the lines of "What the hell do you think you're doing?", was going to be her next-door neighbour.

"Are you determined to give me a heart attack?" she demanded.

"What? No... I'm sorry, I didn't mean to startle you."

"And yet it's getting to be a habit," she snapped, and immediately regretted it.

He was clearly taken aback by her reaction and maybe she had been a bit quick to judge, based on their earlier encounter.

She turned to apologise, but the words died on her lips when she saw the way he was staring at her.

"Katy?" he said, uncertainly.

Her heart missed a beat at the name.

"It *is* you! I'm so sorry, I didn't recognise you back there but... It's so good to see you."

She just stood there, at a loss, not knowing what to say.

"It's Daniel," he said, grinning now as he rubbed his chin. "I've grown a beard since you were last here."

"No!" She said it sharply enough to stop him in his tracks as he stepped towards her, arms outstretched, as if to wrap her in a bear hug. "No," she repeated, but her legs were shaking a little as she took a step back. "You've mistaken me for someone else. I've never been here before. My name is Rosalind," she added, a little desperately.

"Rosalind?"

"Yes!" She only used her full name for business, but it was more emphatically not Katy than plain Rose.

"But I could have sworn..."

His grin faded as he dragged his fingers through the unruly mop of dark hair. "I'm sorry, it's just that the way you turned your head... For a moment I was sure you were someone I knew a long time ago." He shook his head, as if to clear the illusion. "We were just kids," he said. "She used to come to the beach in the summer with her mother and she did that thing with her chin."

"What thing?" she asked, before she could stop herself.

"That thing you just did." He lifted his chin up in a little sideways movement to demonstrate. "When she was annoyed. I was a vile ten-year-old and I used to tease her."

"I'm sure she loved it." Still would... "But you haven't teased me," she said, making a conscious effort to keep her chin from doing anything.

"Not teased," he admitted, "but I was a bit abrupt back there on the beach."

"A bit? You yelled at me and then stomped off before I could tell you that I understood."

"People don't realise how easy it is to get into trouble. In the sea," he added, to be clear. "Shall we start again?" He offered his hand and, with the sun on his face, his sea-glass eyes softened by a welcoming smile, he looked not so much threatening as dangerously attractive. "I'm Daniel Black." There was a slight lift on his name, as if he thought it might prompt her to remember him.

"The sea is something of an unknown quantity, Daniel," she said, taking his hand. "You were right. I hadn't realised how far out I'd gone." His hand was big, square and calloused and the word *safe* popped into her mind as she took it. "I'm Rosalind Redmayne. Most people call me Rose."

"Redmayne?" he repeated, as if still not totally convinced and expecting something else.

"No relation to the actor." She shook her head, shivered a little. It was still early and in the shelter of the hill the sun wasn't making much impression on her damp crops. "Ignore me, I didn't get much sleep last night and I'm not making a lot of sense today."

# Chapter Three

"Would coffee help?" Daniel asked. "I'm about to make some."

"Thanks," she said. "It would be very welcome."

With the formalities out of the way, Daniel disappeared into his beach hut, but his dog stayed to keep her company and gave a little grunt of pleasure when, having offered him her hand to sniff, she scratched him behind the ear.

"He's a Newfoundland, isn't he?" she said, when Daniel emerged with a couple of chairs.

"More or less. His original owners underestimated how big he'd get and I took him in when they panicked. What brings you to Little Piddling, Rose?"

"Is it that obvious that I'm a visitor?"

"You said you hadn't been here before," he reminded her, "but you don't have the trappings of the average holidaymaker."

"No blow-up alligators here," she assured him.

"That one belongs to a local who should know better," he said. "I will have words when I see his father."

"Are you a policeman?" she asked.

"No, much worse. I'm on the crew of the lifeboat."

"Oh." If he was one of the volunteers who put their lives on the line when people got into trouble, his attitude to safety was understandable.

"So?" he prompted. "You don't have small people clinging to your legs and the arts festival isn't until July. Unless you're scoping us out in advance for television coverage?"

"Nothing that exciting. Would you believe me if I said I had been lured here by an old postcard?"

"Which one?" he asked. "We should use it on the town website."

"It was a picture of these beach huts and this one had my name on it. When I discovered that it was for sale, it seemed like fate."

"You're thinking of buying it?"

A moment ago he had been on the verge of flirting with her, but now he was frowning and she sensed a sudden reserve in his manner.

Immediately back on the defensive, she said, "Do you have a problem with outsiders buying property here?"

"Not all the beach hut owners are locals. Some just come for a few weeks in the summer and let them out for the rest of time," he said, "but that one..."

"What about it?"

"Every year, at the beginning of the season, someone comes along full of plans to give it a make-over, but by the end of the summer it's back on the market in a worse state than before. The last people arrived full of enthusiasm, but they said it had an odd atmosphere. Almost as if it didn't want them there."

"That's ridiculous," she said. But was it any more ridiculous than her own feeling that it had been calling her? Her mad dash down the motorway... "It has to be an excuse for realising that they didn't want to waste their precious holiday wielding a paintbrush."

"Possibly. Why don't you take a look while the kettle boils and see how it feels about you?"

"Don't you mean how I feel about it?"

"I'll have that cup of coffee waiting for you when you're done," he said. "I'll even open a packet of biscuits by way of apology for yelling at a visitor."

"That has to be against the by-laws," she said, in an effort to get back to the flirting.

"If it gets out," he assured her, "I'll be drummed off the town council."

He smiled so that she would know he was joking. It was the kind of smile that, if you were short of sleep, emotionally vulnerable and not entirely sure what you were doing, could seriously disrupt the steady 58 beats a minute that, according to her Fitbit, was her normal.

If he put up for election in her ward, she'd vote for him. And if she was in trouble at sea, that smile...

There was a glimmer of something, a tug of recognition, and she visibly shivered.

"Rose?"

"Make that two biscuits," she said. "Anything but bourbons, and I promise not to tell."

"You still hate them?"

For a moment everything seemed to stand still, until the silence was broken by the thump of a seagull landing on the roof.

"I think it must have heard you mention biscuits," she said, then, when he didn't respond, "I'll—um—just go and take a quick look inside the hut."

Unsure what had just happened, Rose tried the key in the lock, conscious that Daniel was watching her.

"The door's dropped," she said, taking the handle and lifting it so that the lock lined up. This time the key moved but met resistance. "And it's not locked."

"Maybe someone else viewed it and left in such a hurry that they didn't stop to lock up."

She gave him a sideways look. "Are you trying to put me off?"

"No..." There was the sound of a kettle whistling. "I'd better get that."

She waited until he'd disappeared, then pushed at the door. It had swollen a little and it needed a firm shove, but having pushed the door all the way open, she hesitated, half-expecting to be repelled by some malignant force.

Instead she was enveloped in the scent of dry seaweed, sun-baked wood, the lingering mustiness of a damp towel that had been left behind at the end of the summer.

It was the first-day-of-the-holidays smell, full of anticipation and sunshine and, as she stepped inside, the compact interior seemed to open up in welcome, almost as if it had been waiting for her.

She reached out, put her hand flat against the wall. The wood was cool and dry and she felt the tension seep from her shoulders.

"Yes..." The word escaped on a breath. "Yes," she repeated, although what she was agreeing to, she couldn't have said.

There was a child's bathing suit lying in a crumpled heap, on the floor. She stooped to pick it up, expecting it to be stiff and dry, but it was quite wet, as if some little girl had just run in from the beach, peeled it off and left it there.

She looked up at the roof, wondering if there was a leak, but there were no water stains, only a swathe of cobwebs hanging in a gauzy curtain in front of a sleeping loft.

Evidently someone was taking advantage of the unlocked door which, considering how quick Daniel had been to challenge her, suggested that they had to be pretty light on their toes.

Her first job would be to change the lock, she thought, as she reached behind her and hung the swimsuit on one of the useful hooks near the door. Then frowned as she looked back. How had she known they were there?

Good design. It was where she would have put them and, with her designer's hat on, she set about thoroughly examining the interior.

The structure appeared sound enough, but like the exterior, it had been neglected. The cupboards were solid but hard used and one of the hinges had given way so that the door was hanging open to reveal an assortment of mugs. A tall narrow cupboard contained a broom, a dustpan and a cricket bat. No ball.

Across the rear, there was a long storage bench. The cushion had been covered in a heavyweight retro chintz—roses, fuchsias and leaves on a dark blue background. It had faded and begun to rot where it had worn thin.

With luck—and perseverance—she might be able to trace some of the same fabric to replace it. Old curtains for sale on eBay were a good source.

Inside the seat, there would be a pink beach umbrella, a blow-up bed with a foot pump, a striped blanket and last year's rubber flip-flops...

The image had been so vivid that it was a shock when she lifted the lid and saw an umbrella, its frame rusty, the cloth disintegrating. The flip-flops were there and the foot pump, but no blow-up bed and no blanket.

Sand crunched beneath her feet as she dropped the lid, took a step back, grabbing for the nearest thing to steady her as she stumbled over something that had gone over with a clatter.

The final screws on the cupboard door gave up their precarious hold and it came away in her hand. It was heavy and it slipped from her fingers, narrowly missing her foot.

She muttered an expletive, took a moment to catch her breath, then spotted the cause of her stumble.

It was a small plastic bucket for making sandcastles, but it had been filled with shells, smooth pebbles and sea glass, collected by some young beachcomber and now scattered across the floor.

She had no sense that she was being rejected by the hut, despite the bucket and the door, and knelt to gather up the treasures, still damp from the sea. But that moment, before she opened the storage seat when, in her head, she'd *seen* what was stored inside, was just a little bit weird.

It would have been weirder still if the contents had matched the vision, but it had just been her imagination working overtime.

Since she was down on her hands and knees, she took the opportunity to check the floor for any sign of damage or rot.

It was obvious that the surface had been scoured by years of sandy feet. It would need sanding and sealing, but it appeared to be sound.

She had just reached to push the door closed so that she could see behind it, when she spotted a bare foot, the nails painted with badly chipped red polish.

She froze, for a moment horribly afraid that she'd stumbled across a body, but then the foot began to inch back behind the door.

Whoever was hiding there was very much alive, and Rose let out a huff of relief as she realised that it had to be the child who'd discarded the bathing suit.

Trapped by the unexpected arrival, she must have dived into the only hiding place available and, over the initial shock, Rose peeped around the door, her lips formed to say "boo".

The sound stuck in her throat.

It wasn't a child curled up behind the door. Looking back at her was a young woman, wearing a pretty blue polka-dot sundress.

Her dark hair was curled damply about her face and her mascara had run, but she had that fine bone structure that would still look good when she was eighty.

There was something oddly familiar about her, a bit like spotting someone in the street that you couldn't quite place until, hours later, you realised that she was the dentist's receptionist. But Rose hadn't met anyone in Little Piddling apart from Daniel and Arthur Kettlesing; and the woman who'd served her with a croissant had short blonde hair.

Before Rose could ask who she was and what she was doing there—the damp hair, the child's wet bathing suit made that fairly obvious—the woman said, "There you are, Katy. What's taken you so long?"

Katy...?

Rose, whose heart was getting more of a workout than was entirely welcome in one morning, replied sharply, "I'm not..." Damn it, it was no business of this woman who she was. "Look, the hut was left unlocked and you took advantage, but you have to leave now."

"That is no way to talk to your mother."

*What?*

"No... That's enough." Rose had sat for long hours holding her mother's hand while she lay dying of the cruel cancer that had taken her from them. She stood up. "You have to leave. Now."

"I can't do that, Katy. Peter asked me to wait for you..."

"Peter...?" Rose repeated, confused. "Look, my name is Rose and my father died three months ago." And then, because there could be no other explanation, "Are you Jules?"

"Mama to you, young lady. And why are you calling yourself Rose?"

"It's my name."

The woman shook her head, sighed. "I called you Katy after a book I loved, but your Nanna Rose will love that you're using her name. Have you been to see her, yet?"

"No, no, no!"

Pauline, her father's mother, had died in a plane crash with the rest of his family when he was at university, but her maternal grandmother, Margaret, was very much alive and running a complex of gîtes in the Dordogne with her second husband.

"You know this was Nanna Rose's beach hut, Katy. She gave it to me for my twenty-first birthday and it should have come to you."

Daniel tapped at the door. "Coffee's ready," he said, pulling a face as he looked up at the ceiling. "This is a mess."

He couldn't see Jules where she was sitting behind the door, shaking her head vigorously.

Jules didn't want him to know she was there and, for some reason that she couldn't explain, Rose stepped back out into the sunlight.

"I'll leave the door open to let in the fresh air." Allow her unexpected tenant to escape.

"What do you think?" he asked, looking up at the roof.

"It needs cleaning up and painting inside and out, but it's basically sound."

"Well, that's a start. Did someone stop to see what was going on?"

"No..."

"Oh. I thought I heard you talking to someone."

"Did you?" She managed a shrug. "I was probably thinking out loud. I do it all the time when I'm weighing things up. Trying to come to a decision."

"And have you? Made a decision?"

# Chapter Four

A few minutes ago, Rose had been happily planning the restoration in her head. She knew the exact shade of pink she'd use on the exterior. How she'd restore the cupboards to retain the retro look. The bunting she'd make to hang along the sleeping loft. How she'd fix solar-powered fairy lights and restore the carving along the roof ridge...

Realising that Daniel was waiting, she said, "I should probably sleep on it."

"You're not going to do that," Jules muttered. "It's been here all this time, waiting for you. I understand why your father wanted rid of it, but it wasn't his to sell. At least he kept the money for you."

*Money?*

Her father had given her some money when she'd left art college to help her start her own business. Money that had been their little secret...

"You were always his little princess..."

Rose looked at Daniel, but he didn't seem to have heard. She rubbed her hands over her arms, suddenly cold.

"Are you OK, Rose?"

She shook her head. "My dad died recently and I haven't been sleeping very well." She shrugged. "Not much at all, if I'm honest."

"I'm sorry."

"Thanks. It was such a shock. He had a heart attack when he was out running." The coroner's officer had assured her that it had been a massive event and he would have been dead before he hit the floor, but she hadn't been able to get the image of him lying on the cold ground out of her mind.

"The coffee will help," Daniel said, walking back to his own hut.

"He's right. Bring me a cup, there's a good girl," Jules called. "And a couple of biscuits. A woman could starve..."

Resisting the temptation to stick her fingers in her ears, Rose shut the door with a bang, desperate to block her out.

With a steaming mug of coffee in her hand, Rose began to relax. "The plan was to take a break in the Greek islands," she said. "I'm not sure how I ended up here."

Daniel laughed. "That must have been some postcard. Who was it from?" he asked, casually.

She glanced at the pink hut with its peeling paintwork and rose garland. Looked away.

"It was old," she said. "Rosa's must have been freshly painted when it was taken."

"I remember Katy's grandmother repainting the garland," he said. "I must have been six or seven. Katy was just a toddler, but she wouldn't rest until she was given a piece of wood to paint so that she could be an artist like her Nanna Rose."

*She was an artist?*

"Your family have had this hut for a long time?" Rose said, telling herself that she didn't want to hear about Katy or her Nanna Rose.

"Since it was new. The oldest ones were converted from bathing huts that were pulled out into the sea by horses so that gentlemen could go nude bathing."

She laughed. "That's quite an image. I hadn't realised they were that old. It's no wonder the atmosphere in Rosa's Retreat is so layered with memory."

"Is it?"

"There was definitely something." She looked across at the faded pink hut. "I can't wait to bring it back to life." Once her squatter had realised the game was up and moved on.

"What happened to sleeping on it?"

"That was the plan," she said, but outside in the sun, sipping warm coffee in good company, she had no doubts. "But I've learned over the years that when something calls you so strongly, there's no point in fighting it."

"And Rosa is calling you?"

"Something is. Finding that postcard was not just chance."

"No..."

She turned to look at him. "You believe me? You don't think I'm crazy?"

"You believe it," he said, not quite meeting her gaze. "That's all that matters, but you're right to get an estimate of how much it's going to cost to repaint the exterior before you make an offer. Unless you have someone to help you?"

The question hung there for a moment and there was no mistaking his meaning. He was asking if she had a partner and a pulse of heat swept through her body as trillions of cells quivered in response.

"I have a very good idea how much a contractor would charge," she said, once she'd remembered to breathe, "but I'll be doing the work myself."

"How good are you with a paintbrush?"

There was nothing like a condescending man to provide a lust-quelling bucket of cold water.

"Men seem to manage," she said, glancing over the rim of the mug she was holding. "How hard can it be?"

He opened his mouth as if to tell her, but something in her expression must have warned him that it wouldn't be smart.

"I'm sorry, Rose. I didn't intend that to sound quite so patronising."

"I'm equally sorry to tell you that you failed." She reached into her bag and handed him her card.

"Rosalind Redmayne Interiors." He glanced up. "You're a decorator?"

"These days I mostly work on the designs and employ other people to do the serious physical labour, but I'm no stranger to sandpaper."

Her business was Internet based. She could work anywhere and, with her father gone, Matt and Lisa busy with their own lives, there was nothing to keep her in Maybridge.

She could let her cottage, rent somewhere in Little Piddling for the summer and bring the hut back to life in between design contracts. It would give her the break she needed, and a project that she could sell on for a profit when it was done. Or maybe she would keep it and rent it out.

And while she was at it, she could find out more about the hut and its past owners. Look for the connection between Jules and her father. Maybe let Daniel help her rub down the exterior of her hut. Rub down her own exterior...

"Rose?"

She blinked. "Sorry, did you say something?"

"I said we're going to be neighbours."

He made that sound so intimate. Aware that her cheeks had become a little warm, she said, "I'm afraid it will be a bit noisy for a while. Are there likely to be objections from the other hut dwellers?"

"Everyone will be glad to see Rosa looking tidy and if you promise to throw a really good party when you're done, we all might just pitch in and help."

"I'll bear that in mind. And next time the coffee is on me."

"You're going?" he asked when she put down the mug and stood up.

"I have a beach hut to buy, but first I need to get out of these damp clothes. I'm hoping the B&B will take pity on me and let me into my room early."

"Where are you staying?"

"Just across the road at Queen Charlotte House."

"Of course."

"There's no *of course* about it," she snapped. "It popped up in my search, the reviews were good, it's just across the road from the beach huts and there's parking, all of which make it ideal."

"Which is why it's the obvious choice," he said.

"Oh. I thought you were... It's just that..."

"It's OK," he said. "It's very popular with beach-hutters for all those reasons. You'll be very comfortable there—" A pager at his waist began to buzz and he was on his feet even before he'd glanced at it. "Tell Flo that you're a friend of mine and she'll sort you out," he said, backing away. "I'll pick you up at eight and take you to the Wine Bar for supper. Stay Nigel!"

He didn't wait for an answer but was running, the boardwalk bouncing under the pounding of his feet as he headed for the pier.

She looked at the bear-like dog who'd leapt up at the sound of the pager, but was now standing like a statue as he watched Daniel weave between the promenade strollers.

"Don't worry, sweetie," she said. "He'll be back soon."

His tail twitched as he looked back at her, then flopped down, his huge head between his paws.

A few minutes later, an inflatable inshore lifeboat was speeding across the bay. It was too far away to see who was at the helm, but from the stance, the angle of the head, she knew it was Daniel. And she knew, in her bones, that someone was going to be very happy to see him heading in their direction.

Rose took the biscuit tin and cups inside and rinsed them in the hot water left in the kettle, trying very hard to resist being a nosy neighbour, but with everything almost touching-close, it was impossible.

Dan's Den, clean, neat, freshly painted, couldn't have been more different to the interior of Rosa. There was a lot of plain dark blue fabric, including a roomy hammock slung beneath the sleeping loft, which appeared to be used for storage. There wasn't a lot of headspace up there and Daniel would undoubtedly have knocked himself out if he'd sat up too quickly.

There was a small desk with a stool tucked underneath and, above it, a corkboard thickly pinned with photographs.

She leaned closer to take a better look. There were photographs of lifeboat crews, parties on the beach with friends and family. In quite a few he was with a pretty girl. Laughing, serious, distracted... In one it was a redhead, another had a sleek dark bob, and there was one with an enviable waterfall of silky blonde hair.

It seemed that her neighbour with the pulse-raising smile was a bit of a player. She would have to watch herself.

About to turn away, she spotted a small photograph, curled at the edges, a little cracked, almost hidden. It was a snapshot of a boy, about ten years old and unmistakably Daniel. He was grinning at a little girl who had to be two or three years younger and who was gazing up at him with total adoration.

Was this Katy?

Her hair was an explosion of fair curls and Rose could see why Daniel might have thought she might be this little girl.

Her own hair had darkened as she got older, but the curls had tormented her throughout her teens. She'd been so desperate for sleek straight hair like her little sister that, once, she'd cut it all off as close to the roots as she could, hoping that it would grow back like Lisa's. Her mother had hugged her, understanding what had driven her to such a desperate act, but her father had turned away, unable to look at her.

At uni, she'd had it straightened, but no amount of conditioner could ever achieve the desired result and since then she'd left it to do its own thing.

She took the photograph out into the sun for a better look, but it was too faded for her to tell if the likeness was more than the hair.

Rose replaced it, taking care to leave it exactly where she had found it. She hesitated about leaving the hut open, but decided that, placid as he was, Nigel was sufficient deterrent to anyone hellbent on mischief and, having topped up his water bowl, she left him in charge.

Ten minutes later, having collected her van from the car park, she was at Queen Charlotte House.

"Are you Flo? I know I'm too early for my room," she apologised, "but I had a close encounter with the sea and was hoping there might be somewhere I could change. Daniel Black said to tell you that I'm a friend," she added, hopefully.

"Did he?" The tall elegant woman who'd responded to the reception bell gave her a professional smile. "I'm Florence Black, Miss Redmayne. Daniel is my son."

"Oh." She flushed with embarrassment. "His pager went off and he didn't have time to explain."

His mother sighed and looked out of the window at the bay, lost for a moment.

"It's really calm," Rose said. "I'm sure he'll be OK."

"I know, but you can't help worrying. People do such stupid things." She shook her head, dismissing the thought and said, "Redmayne? I don't know the name but you seem very familiar. Have you stayed here before?"

Rose swallowed. "This is my first visit to the town, Mrs Black. Maybe you've visited Maybridge?" she suggested. "Or bought something I've upcycled? My business is on Facebook and Instagram."

"Is that how you met Daniel?" she asked. "On the Internet?"

Rose relaxed. This wasn't going to be another "Katy" moment. Florence Black was just a mother making sure her boy wasn't getting into bad company on a dating app.

"Actually we met this morning when he yelled at me for chasing after a toy that had blown into the water. It's how I got wet."

"Then we must certainly do something about that." Her face softened into the smile that her son had inherited. "Your room is ready. Just sign the book and leave a note of your car registration number, then you can go up." That done, she swiped Rose's credit card and then handed over her key. "It's number two, on the first floor. Breakfast is from seven until nine-thirty. If you need it earlier, just let someone know and we can organise it."

"Thank you. I've only booked for tonight—I wasn't sure about my plans. Would it be possible to extend that, until I find somewhere to rent locally?"

"You're going to stay in Little Piddling?"

"Just for the summer. I'm buying one of the beach huts," she explained. "It needs some work."

Mrs Black frowned. "The pink one next to Daniel's?"

"Yes."

"It's in a bit of a state."

"I know, but it has my name on it," Rose said. "It would be rude not to."

Mrs Black looked as if she was about say something, but instead glanced at her computer screen. "I can let you have the room until the end of the week, Miss Redmayne, but after that I'm fully booked."

"It's Rose," she said, "and I'm sure that will do it. Thank you, Mrs Black."

"Call me Flo. Everyone does. Including, apparently, my son."

# Chapter Five

Rose shook out her damp crops and top and hung them over the towel rail to dry. Then, having showered off a surprising amount of sand, she slipped into a dress and returned to Kettlesing and Flint.

"Miss Redmayne." Arthur Kettlesing greeted her with enthusiasm. "How did you find the beach hut?"

"I walked across the beach, Arthur, and there it was, tucked between Forget-Me-Not and Dan's Den."

He grinned. "That's a relief. I was afraid it might have blown away in last week's storms."

"But not bothered enough to go and check? It's sound enough, but you might be less relieved to hear that it was not locked. I found a damp bathing suit inside, which suggests that someone has been using it. Maybe someone else to whom you loaned the key?"

He frowned, shook his head. "There hasn't been anyone else."

"Maybe Mr Flint?"

"James would have mentioned it."

She shrugged. "Then it's a mystery, but perhaps it would be advisable to get the lock changed?"

"I'll see to it. I'm sorry it wasn't suitable."

Rose sat down. "I didn't say that. Do you have the historic paperwork on the hut? A list of previous owners?" she asked.

"I imagine it'll be in the file."

He fetched it, watching with a thoughtful frown as she went through it, making a note of names and addresses.

The only possible Rosa had to be Rosalind Jarvis who had bought the hut in 1946, just after the war. Rose Mary Graham (nee Jarvis) had taken possession in 1961—not a sale but a transfer of ownership from mother to daughter. Was she Nanna Rose?

And then her heart began to pound as she saw the next transfer was to Juliet Rosemary Graham in 1988.

Was this the Jules who'd written the postcard to her father? Katy's mother. The dates were right, but the Jules in the hut was a lot nearer Rose's own age. Possibly younger.

"As you can see, Miss Redmayne, everything is quite in order."

"There's nothing wrong with the paperwork," she agreed. "How long have your family lived here, Arthur?"

"In Little Piddling? Forever," he replied, with every evidence of satisfaction.

"So maybe you know the Graham family who bought the hut just after the war? Or Jarvis?"

He shook his head. "I don't recall anyone at school with either of those names. I could ask my mother, or you might find something in the *Piddling Post* archives. It's just a free news-sheet these days, mostly adverts, but it used to report on anything that happened here. You'll find the office tucked away in the maze of little streets behind Brewery Square."

"Thanks. I'll check it out."

"So, the beach hut?" he prompted. "Are you thinking of making an offer?"

"It is going to need a thorough cleaning and then repainting, inside and out," she said. "The floor requires sanding and resealing and the cupboards are in a shocking state. One of the doors fell off in my hand," she added. "It narrowly missed my foot."

"I did mention that the condition was reflected in the price," he reminded her, refusing to be suckered by a near miss.

"Even so, I think your owner is being a touch optimistic." She offered a rough estimate of the costs involved in putting the hut into a usable condition.

"Is this for a client, Miss Redmayne?" he asked. "I checked out your website. It's very impressive."

She smiled. "Thank you, Arthur. Why don't you call me Rose?" She preferred to keep business contacts on a more formal footing, but an estate agent was a good contact, and Arthur Kettlesing wasn't quite as soft as he would have her believe. "This isn't a commission for a client," she said. "It's for me."

"Oh, well... I'm sure the present owners would be open to a reasonable offer."

She made one, he winced convincingly and then made a counter-offer. Rose split the difference and he shrugged. "It's worth a try."

He made the call and, twenty minutes later, the legal work was under way.

"May I keep the key?" she asked. "I'd like to make a start on cleaning it up."

"No problem. It's been a pleasure doing business with you, Rose. Is there anything else I can help you with?"

"Actually, yes. Since I'll be staying in Little Piddling, I'm going to need somewhere to live. And space that I can use as a workshop.

A lock-up garage would do. Do you have anything suitable on your books?"

He looked doubtful. "It's all short-term holiday lets from Easter onwards, but I'll check around and see what I can find. In the meantime, I'll get that lock changed for you."

"I'll see to it. Is there a DIY shop in town?"

"There's Jackson's. It's not one of those big out-of-town places," he warned, "but the service is personal, and they'll get you anything you need within 24 hours. It's on the other side of Brewery Square. Turn left..." He pulled a face. "As I said, it's a bit of a maze, but anyone will direct you."

"Is it next to an old-fashioned sweet shop?" she asked. "The kind that still sells sweets out of a jar?"

"Well, yes," he said, beaming. "Well done on finding your way around so quickly."

Except that she hadn't "found her way around". She hadn't been anywhere but the car park or the prom. She must have seen it on the town website...

"Did I mention that I'd checked out your website?" Arthur said as he walked her to the door.

"What? Oh, yes, you did."

"I'm not sure if you'll be taking on commissions while you're working on the beach hut, but I do know someone who could use your expertise. Would it be in order to mention your name?"

"Yes. Thank you, Arthur."

Jackson's had a narrow frontage, but it stretched a long way back and stocked pretty much anything she might need.

Rose chose a lock and some cleaning materials and, having introduced herself to the manager, she produced her VAT number and opened a trader's account.

That done, and for no reason that made sense, she went into the sweetshop and bought 100 grams of ginger liquorice. Feeling oddly unsettled by the experience, she found a very modern mini-supermarket and bought a six-pack of bottled water before collecting her overalls and toolbox from her van.

Nigel was no longer taking up most of the space in front of Daniel's hut and the door was shut.

She quelled the little jag of disappointment.

And anxiety.

She'd left Rosa's hut unlocked, giving her intruder the chance to leave. Common sense suggested that Rose should have told Arthur what she'd seen and insisted he deal with it before she went ahead with the purchase. Unfortunately, nothing that had happened since she found the postcard had made common or any other kind of sense.

How had she known where to find Jackson's? Why had she bought sweets that she didn't like? And why, as she walked through the town, had she known what would be around the corner? Whose name would be on the statue on the prom?

And then there was the B&B.

She'd told Daniel that she'd checked it out, chosen it for its closeness to the beach huts, the car park. But that wasn't true. She'd clicked "book" the moment the name popped up as if she knew...

The weirdness was piling up, which was why she would have welcomed Daniel's reassuring presence in the hut next door. Someone who would come running if she screamed...

She gave herself a mental backbone-stiffening, don't-be-silly pep talk. She had never screamed in her life. Apart from the scream that had woken her from a nightmare and brought her racing down here.

She took a deep breath and pushed the door, but the only thing to greet her was a swirl of dust and the faintest stirring of cobwebs where she'd disturbed the air.

The hut was empty.

The breath escaped a little shakily, but relief was touched with dissatisfaction.

There were so many unanswered questions rattling around in her head. Jules had known so much about the people who had owned the hut. Knew her father...

Except that couldn't be right.

She was far too young to have sent that postcard. To be Katy's mother. But there had been a child who'd collected shells and worn that swimsuit. Where was she?

Telling herself to forget it, just be grateful that Jules had taken the opportunity to make herself scarce, Rose closed the door.

In the dim light from a skylight above the sleeping loft, she slipped off her dress, climbed into her overalls and wrapped one of the muslin cloths she kept in her toolbox around her hair, tying it in a little knot at the front, like a nineteen-forties housewife.

That done, she tackled the door first. She used the handle of a hammer to prop up the dropped end, then tightened the screws in the hinges. Once it was hanging properly, she oiled them and then replaced the lock.

Satisfied that it would now be secure against anyone but a squatter armed with a crowbar, she put her bag and toolbox in the broom cupboard and moved what little furniture there was outside.

With the floor clear, she pulled on her Marigolds and set to work with the long-handled broom, sweeping down the cobwebs so that she could get to the sleeping loft without being enveloped in soft stickiness. She'd need the stepladder to reach into the corners and do a thorough job, but it was clean enough and she brushed the floor clear of sand and dead flies.

The air was full of dust and she stood outside, slaking her thirst while it cleared, conscious of curious glances from other hut dwellers. There were a couple of nods, but no rush to welcome her to their midst. Maybe they were waiting to see whether she'd stick, or disappear after a month or two, like the previous owners.

She smiled back, then returned to the job, clutching a dustpan and brush as she climbed the stepladder.

Jules, sitting on a mattress that was covered with an old striped blanket, was painting her toenails. "You've been a long time," she said. "Have you been to see Nanna Rose?"

"What? No! Why are you still here, Jules?"

"You need to go and see her. And when you come back, you can bring me an ice cream from the kiosk on the corner." She looked up. "The espresso coffee flavour. In a cone, not a tub."

"I'm not going anywhere," Rose said. "You have to leave. Now."

"I can't do that."

"Why? Are you homeless?" Jules didn't look as if she slept on the streets. Was she hiding from someone? "Do you need a shelter?" Rose asked. She could probably find a number online. Or Flo might be able to help...

Jules frowned, apparently struggling with the question. "A shelter?"

"Come on, Jules. You're obviously in trouble and I'll help if I can. Where do you live?"

She concentrated on getting the nail polish smooth before she said, "I live here."

"No..." Rose took a breath. "You can't live in a beach hut. It's not allowed."

Jules rolled her eyes, returned to the business of painting her toenails. "I don't see why not? It's warm and dry."

"There's no running water or electricity," Rose said, a little desperately. "And the nearest loo is on the promenade."

"The convenient conveniences."

"Oh, for heaven's sake. If you don't leave right now, I'm going to have to call someone."

"Call Nanna Rose. She is so lonely."

Rose sighed and was halfway down the ladder when a thought struck her. She went back up a step. "How did you get up here without disturbing the cobwebs?"

Jules, who'd started on a second coat, didn't look up. "Don't forget the ice cream. You'll find some money in my purse."

Rose sighed. The last thing she wanted to do was call social services, but the woman was clearly in need of help.

Maybe, if she bought her an ice cream, Jules would open up, say what she was really doing here.

Rose opened up a couple of wooden fold-up chairs that she'd moved outside and wiped off the dust. Then she stripped off her rubber gloves and tugged off the muslin hair net.

"OK. I'm going for the ice cream now," she called up. "Is there anything else you want?"

*Some proper food might be a good idea.*

There was no answer, which was new. Rose shrugged, took her bag from the broom cupboard and went back to the mini-supermarket for a sandwich and fruit, then headed for the ice cream kiosk.

It wasn't your usual mass-produced stuff. The ice cream was artisan produce from a local dairy and the flavours were luscious. She bought the espresso flavour for Jules and chose salted caramel for herself.

"I've got your ice cream, Jules," she called up. "You're going to have to come down if you want it."

There was no reply, but there was no way Rose was taking it up to her. The whole point was to entice her down and out into the sun.

She licked her own ice, which was already beginning to melt and then, after a minute or two called, "Jules!"

"I'm tired."

"Nobody is ever too tired for ice cream. Come on, it's melting."

She finished her own ice and licked her fingers where the other had begun to trickle over them, practically swooning at the dark, coffee taste that stirred something on the edge of her memory...

"Jules?"

This time there was no answer and with a sigh, Rose climbed up. "If you don't hurry up, I'll eat it."

"You always wanted mine," Jules said, stretching out on the mattress and pulling the blanket around her. "You can bring me an almond croissant from Queenies in the morning."

"Jules..." And this time, when she didn't answer, Rose whispered, "Mama... I've brought you some food. A sandwich, fruit."

"I'm tired. I'm going to sleep now, Katy. Don't disturb me, there's a good girl."

Rose finished the espresso ice, puzzled, concerned and full of sympathy for this woman who seemed to be suffering from some kind of mental breakdown. Unsure how to help.

If Jules was still in residence tomorrow, Rose would ask Daniel for help, but for now, Jules appeared to feel safe in the hut.

Before Rose left, she took up a bottle of water, the sandwich and fruit and she put the sweets she'd bought close to Jules' hand.

Then she took in the stray bits of furniture, the broken cupboard door. And in case Jules wanted to leave, or slip out to use the convenient conveniences, she left a key on the worksurface.

# Chapter Six

"What would you like to drink, Rose?"

"I can recommend something cool and refreshing from my cellars," said another voice.

Rose looked up at the man standing beside her.

"Henry Dumaine, Miss Redmayne."

"Ignore him," Daniel said. "If you drink his wine, he doubles his profit. Next thing we know, he'll be buying the brewery."

Rose smiled. "Another time, Henry. It's been a long and eventful day and I haven't eaten more than a couple of ice creams since breakfast. If I drink anything even remotely alcoholic, I'm likely to fall asleep with my face in my food, so I'll stick to a pineapple juice topped up with fizzy water."

"On the house," Henry said to the young woman who was hovering to take their order. "And a pint of best bitter for our gallant coxswain," he added, taking a chair from an adjacent table and sitting down.

"Thanks for the drinks, Henry. But you don't have to stay and watch us drink them."

"Arthur called me this afternoon, Rose," he said, ignoring the encouragement to leave. "I can call you Rose?"

She conceded the familiarity with a nod.

"I've been thinking about some radical alterations to the wine bar and he suggested I talk to you."

"That's very sweet of him, but how did you know I'm Rose Redmayne?"

"Arthur told me that you were staying at Flo's and, when I called and asked for you, Flo told me that you were here with Daniel."

"The joys of small-town living—"

"—are overrated," Daniel said.

Rose handed Henry her card. "Why don't you give me a call tomorrow and we can fix a time to talk through some ideas?"

"I'll do that," he said, getting up. "And, by the way, the baked crab is superb."

"I'll settle for that," she told the waitress.

"Your usual steak, Daniel?"

"Thanks, Lucy."

When she'd gone, Daniel shook his head. "How long have you been in town, Rose?"

"A little over twelve hours and already I have a potential client."

"Oh, I think Henry has his sights set a little higher than that."

"Then I'm afraid he's going to be disappointed. I never mix business with pleasure."

"That's a sound rule, especially around Henry," he said.

"What about Arthur?"

"Arthur, too?"

"I'd speculate that there's a shortage of eligible women in town, but the photographs in your beach hut would suggest otherwise."

"You made yourself at home when you were washing the dishes?"

"They were hard to miss in such a small space."

"Janine is my cousin and Molly is a member of the lifeboat crew, as is her husband. I'm sure he was in the background of that photograph."

"And the third?"

"You counted?" He shrugged. "Sarah was offered a job in Hong Kong. She wanted me to go with her, but I couldn't leave Little Piddling."

"And she couldn't stay?"

"It was a once-in-a-lifetime opportunity."

"I'm sorry."

"There comes a time in all relationships when you have to make the big decision. It was the right one for us. What about you?"

"The big decision?" She pulled a face. "Does putting his stuff into black plastic bags, leaving them outside and changing the locks count?"

"He cheated on you?"

"Thanks for sounding so surprised. To be honest," she said, "the fact that he wouldn't take time off to come with me to Dad's funeral hurt more, which tells you everything you need to know." She shrugged. "I should have ended it sooner, but when you're busy, it's easier to stay in a relationship that has gone past its sell-by date than face the upheaval. He did me a favour."

"If that's even part of the reason you're here, he did us all a favour."

"I'm glad you think so. What do you do, Daniel? Apart from volunteer for the lifeboat and do good work on the town council."

"I work with my dad. He has a boatyard on the far side of the bay. I design the boats and we have a team of craftsmen to build them."

"Is there much demand for custom-built boats?" she asked.

"There's always a demand for quality," he said. "People don't pay you to paint their houses in magnolia."

She laughed. "That's true."

"Have you sewn up the beach hut deal, yet?" he asked.

"Your mother didn't tell you?"

"I haven't seen her today. I have my own place, just around the corner."

"That's convenient."

"Yes."

As they looked at each other across the table, there was a mute acknowledgement of the possibilities that was broken only by the arrival of Lucy with their drinks and cutlery.

"Thank you, Lucy," Rose said, just a little breathless. Then, when she'd gone, "I made an offer on the beach hut and it was accepted. I've even made a start on cleaning it up. How did your day go?"

"Better than average. I met a lovely young woman and was getting to know her, but then my pager went off and I had to dash off."

Not before he'd made a date. Daniel Black was fast in every sense of the word.

"I wasn't sure what to do when you left. I didn't want to shut Nigel out of your hut in case he needed the shade. I hoped he was big enough to make anyone think twice."

"You did absolutely the right thing."

"Can I ask what happened? Why you were called out?"

"A local man out sailing with his wife had a heart attack. Fortunately, she was able to perform CPR until we arrived with a defibrillator. He's going to make it, but it was a close call."

"That's a good day in anyone's books. How long have you been a member of the lifeboat crew? Henry called you the coxswain. Isn't that like the captain?"

He nodded. "My dad was the cox until his leg was crushed during a rescue. I joined the crew as soon as I was old enough."

"Is he OK? Your dad?"

"They managed to save the leg, but he frets when a call goes out. It was his life."

"But hard on your mother. She must have worried about him every time he went out." She took a sip of her drink. "I know for a fact that she worries about you."

"Oh? Did she say something?"

"It was more in the look she gave me. She seemed to think that I was some Internet hussy with wicked designs on her boy."

"Oh, please, let that be true."

Oh, lord...

Rose took a long, cooling swig of her drink and said, "Arthur was happy to let me make a start on cleaning the hut."

"He didn't volunteer to help?"

"His partner was at a country-house sale so he couldn't leave the office," she said. "I spent the afternoon straightening the door, changing the lock and removing my bodyweight in cobwebs. I'll start stripping out the cupboards tomorrow..." She was talking too much and was relieved to see their food arrive. "Oh, that looks so good."

Lucy made sure they had everything they needed, then left them to it and, for the first time in weeks, Rose ate with enjoyment.

"Wow," she said, sitting back a little while later. "I haven't eaten that much in weeks."

"It's the sea air."

"Actually, I think it was the ice cream."

He thought about it for a moment, then said, "No. You're going to have to explain that."

"I would if I could, but actually I don't understand it myself." She didn't understand a lot of things that had happened recently.

Apart from some seriously wicked ideas about what she might do with Daniel Black. They were very clear indeed.

"Shall I bring the dessert menu?" Lucy asked, as she cleared the table.

Rose was giving it serious thought when Arthur saw her and made a beeline for their table.

"Flo told me you were here, Rose." He nodded at Daniel. "Good job today, cox."

"Arthur..." Daniel's acknowledgement had the barest touch of warning.

"I won't stay," he promised. "I've just got a couple of things to tell Rose."

Daniel raised a hand in surrender, but said, "Next time we're going out of town."

*Next time?*

Rose struggled to contain the smile threatening to break out all over her face and said, "I'm about to decide on dessert, Arthur, so can you make it quick?"

"Of course. First, I may have found somewhere that has everything you want and a bit more."

"How much more?" Daniel asked, irritably.

"It's attached to a shop," Arthur continued, ignoring him, "but the owner is having cash flow problems so he might be prepared to do a deal on a short let. The only problem is that it's in Piddling Magna."

"Why is that a problem?" Rose asked. "It looked a perfectly nice little town when I drove through. And it's—what?—five minutes in a car?" She glanced at Daniel for confirmation and he nodded.

"Oh, it's nothing," Arthur said, reassuringly. "Just a bit of local rivalry. It started when smuggling was the lifeblood of the town back in the eighteenth century. The Little Piddlers charged a toll for those upstream to access the Piddle. There were incidents."

"The Piddle?" Rose asked.

"The River Piddle. It's silted up now."

"And there were ruffled feathers," Daniel continued, "when Little Piddling decided to give itself a style upgrade and add *sur Mer* to its name—"

Rose snorted.

"It was not a laughing matter. Arthur's great-great-grandfather very nearly lost his job when someone changed all the new town signs to Little Piddling sur Merde."

"Merde? But that's...!" She shook her head. "Gilbert and Sullivan would have had a field day, but what has this to do with Piddling Magna?"

"It used to be called Much Piddling—"

"No. Stop. No more." She held up both her hands. "There's only so much piddle one can take. Tell me about the property, Arthur."

"It's detached. There's a big flat, a workshop and parking."

"Is it the old forge?" Daniel asked.

"Well, yes..."

"We'll pick up the key in the morning and take a look."

"Oh, but..." Daniel raised an eyebrow and whatever Arthur was going to say, he thought better of it. "Right. Tomorrow."

"Arthur," Rose called as he backed away. "What was the other thing?"

"Other thing?"

"You said there were a couple of things? Is there a problem with the hut?"

"What? Oh, no. Sorry... You were enquiring about the Graham family. I asked mother if she knew the name and she said there was a girl called Juliet Graham a couple of years below her at school. Her family had a beach hut."

"Does she still live in Little Piddling?" Rose asked.

"I'm afraid not. A little girl was swept out into the bay on a sunbed and Juliet was drowned trying to rescue her."

Rose felt the colour drain from her face. Katy... "What happened to the little girl?"

"I don't know. Sorry."

"How to kill an evening, Arthur," Daniel said, grimly.

Utterly confused by their reaction, Arthur said, "Yes. Sorry... I'll, um..."

"Just bugger off!"

"But there was something else—"

"Now!"

Daniel reached for her hand. "Rose? Are you OK?"

"Yes... No..." Confronted by something she had, on some subconscious level, already known, she was still struggling with the reality. "Do you believe in ghosts, Daniel?"

# Chapter Seven

"Let's get out of here." Daniel signalled to Henry that he was leaving and, having helped Rose to her feet, he headed for the door.

"D-Daniel! We can't just walk out. We haven't paid the bill."

He stopped, but only to take off his jacket and put it around her shoulders. Until she was surrounded by his warmth, she hadn't realised that she was shivering.

"Henry knows I'm not going anywhere."

"Of course not. You already said that you can't leave Little Piddling, but I want to pay my share," she said, concentrating on something tangible, something that she could understand.

"You can pay for lunch tomorrow after we've checked out the Old Forge," he said, his arm around her as he guided her into the street. "Right now, we could both do with some air."

"Where are we going?" she asked, as they crossed the square and turned the corner, but not in the direction of her B&B.

"Nowhere," he said, punching in numbers on a keypad beside the front door of a four-storey town house. "We're here."

Rose expected to find herself in the entrance of a flat conversion, but there were a couple of jackets and a dog lead on a stand in the entrance hall, boots and running shoes where they'd been kicked off. There was nothing to suggest communal living and she was just taking in the fact that Daniel's "place around the corner" was a rather fine house, when Nigel padded in from the rear.

Daniel opened the door to a large living room and bent to light a gas fire. "I'm going to make tea and then you can tell me about your ghost. Take care of her, Nigel."

Nigel wagged his tail as she slipped off Daniel's jacket and hung it beside the others, followed Rose to the sofa and then, once she was safely enveloped in soft leather, settled down over her feet like a warm comfort blanket.

The sun had set and the light had nearly gone when Daniel returned with a couple of mugs. "Hot sweet tea for you," he said, handing one to her. "Good for shock."

She tipped towards him as he sat beside her, and he put his arm around her and it felt like the most natural thing in the world. As if she'd known him all her life.

She sipped the tea but it was the warmth of his body, the steadiness of his breathing, his patience, waiting until she was ready to talk, that calmed her until the shivering subsided.

"This morning..." Had it only been this morning? She felt as if she'd been in Little Piddling forever. "When you thought you heard me talking to someone, you were right."

"I didn't see anyone."

"She was behind the hut door."

"She?"

"Jules. Katy's mother."

Daniel drew her closer as her voice snagged on the word. "Jules?"

"I didn't notice her at first. She was sitting behind the door and all I could see was a foot. I thought for a moment that she was a body, but when I moved the door she was just sitting there."

"When did you realise that she was a ghost?"

"I didn't. Not until Arthur... She was quite irritable. Asked me what had taken me so long. She called me 'Katy', too."

"What did she look like?"

"She was about my age, maybe a bit younger. She had dark curly hair. It was damp, as if she'd been in the sea and her mascara was running, but she had..."

"Had what?"

Rose swallowed. "I thought she looked familiar," she said, "and now I know why. It's because she looks like me."

"You always looked like her, Rose."

"Did I?" Just because it was all beginning to make some kind of crazy sense didn't make it any easier to believe. To accept. "There was a child's wet bathing costume..." And in that moment, the reality hit her. If Jules was her mother, the bathing costume, the bucket of shells, belonged to Katy.

To her.

"You knew!" She turned in his arm so that she could see his face. "You were just pretending to believe me when I said I was Rose."

"I could see that you believed you were Rose," he said, "but yes, I had no doubt that you were Katy."

"Jules wrote a postcard to my father." She pulled free and fished it out of her bag to show him.

He looked at the picture then turned it over and read the message.

"I don't know that address," Rose said. "I didn't understand why Dad would have kept it and I meant to throw it away, but it kept turning up."

"I imagine that he always meant to tell you the truth."

"When? I'm twenty-nine, for heaven's sake. And what is the truth? Jules told me that she was my mother but she's younger than me."

"She was twenty-six when she drowned, Rose."

A lump formed in her throat. "And Katy. How old was she? How old was I?"

"Nearly eight. You were excited because you were going to get a new bike for your birthday."

"I did," she said. "It was red, but I don't remember being here. I don't remember anything." She took a breath. "When I cleared my father's house there was a ton of stuff for the twins. Baby shoes, congratulations cards, baby handprints. It was as if every day of their lives had been filled with memories. But there was nothing of mine earlier than a photograph of me with the cake Mum had made for my eighth birthday."

"Twins?"

"Matt and Lisa. They're nearly six years younger than me but I don't remember Mum being pregnant, or her bringing them home. I only remember them as toddlers."

"Didn't you ever ask?"

"Dad told me that I'd had an accident, banged my head, but that isn't true, is it? Do you know what happened to me, Daniel?"

"Only what I was told afterwards. I'd joined the Sea Scouts that year and I was at a sailing camp on Brownsea Island. My dad was in bits about it when I came back, wouldn't talk about it, but Mum knew I wouldn't give up asking where you'd gone."

"I lived here?"

"Yes. You and your mother lived with your Nanna Rose—"

"In a pink house?"

"You remember it?"

"No... Yes... There's something..." A big pink house and a garden that looked out over the bay. "I had a swing," she said, "and if I sat on it, I could see the island."

"I think your Mum and Dad met when he was working down here in the summer vac from uni."

"And she had a baby? Where was he?"

"They obviously kept in touch."

"By postcard?" she demanded, then muttered an expletive as she realised its relevance. "The beach hut... That's where it happened. That's why he kept it."

"It looks like it. Maybe she was the one who didn't want their relationship to be permanent, Rose. Or maybe she just didn't want to leave Little Piddling."

"I was wrong about Gilbert and Sullivan," she said. "This place is more like Brigadoon. I'll bet if anyone born here ever leaves, it will disappear."

"You left," he reminded her. "Mum told me that your Nanna broke down when she was told what had happened and you were barely conscious when you were picked up. Someone must have called your dad, because he collected you from the hospital and took you home with him."

"To his wife and babies? She accepted me so completely, Daniel."

"If Jules was sending postcards to your father, his wife must have known about you."

"I suppose, but why can't I remember?"

"The memory is a tricky thing. It can blank out trauma."

"Permanently?"

"With nothing to remind you, no one to tell you..."

"And they didn't. Was that why they moved house?" Rose swallowed. "To somewhere no one would know, or would ask me who I was and where I'd come from? New neighbourhood, new school..."

"Or maybe with an extra child, they needed a bigger place," he suggested. "Were you happy with them?"

"Yes..." The woman Rose had always known as her mother had been handed her husband's love child out of the blue and given her the same love that she'd given her own children. "Mum..." Her throat tightened as she thought of the lovely woman who'd accepted her as her own. "I would never have guessed in a million years that I wasn't her own daughter. And Dad... Did you ever meet him? Did he come here?"

"Not often. He came on your seventh birthday and Jules threw a party in the beach hut. He called you his little princess."

"That's what Jules said."

"Do you remember anything else? Apart from the pink house and the swing?"

She leaned against him. "Not remember, but walking around town today... When Arthur told me about a hardware shop, I knew where it was. And I remembered that there was a sweet shop next door."

"Sweet Dickens. Your mum used to give us both money for sweets, but you always had to buy her something weird—"

"Ginger liquorice. I don't like it, but I bought some today. I left it for Jules."

"Do ghosts eat sweets?"

"Probably not. She asked for ice cream today but she didn't eat that."

"What flavour?"

"Espresso. She loved it and I used to beg her for a taste..." She grabbed his arm. "Ohmigod Daniel, that was a memory! Not just a feeling. I can remember the shock of it. The bitterness and then the sweetness. I couldn't decide if I liked it or not..." She swallowed. "That's why she asked for it. She wanted me to taste it so that I'd remember." She looked up at him. "Will you tell me what happened, Daniel?"

"Are you sure you want to know? If it jolts your memory it could be painful..."

"That's why the postcard brought me here," she said. "So that I could find out the truth. That's why Jules is here. She said Peter asked her to wait for me."

"OK..." He took a moment, then said, "Your mother was a bit of a sun-worshipper and she bought a blow-up sunbed so that she could lie out on the sand in comfort. One day, while she was in the hut, it seems that you took it into your head to take it down to the water."

"I drifted out?" Rose swallowed. "It was my fault?"

"No, Rose, you were a child."

But as it came rushing back at her, swamping her, stealing her breath, just as it had that day, she knew exactly who was to blame.

"You'd gone off on an adventure and I wanted one, too," she said. "I'd looked at the island for so long and I thought, if I went there, I could tell you about it."

"No—"

She put a hand on his arm. She had to get this out.

"Mama was busy painting her toenails so I sneaked off with the sunbed. It looked a bit like a raft and I thought I could paddle out there. At first it was OK, but then it started to get rough, tossing me about." She could feel it now, the sick fear... "The sea began to swamp the bed and I couldn't hang on..."

"Don't, Rose. Don't think about it," Daniel said, wrapping his arms around her as if he could keep the memory back, but there was nothing that could do that.

"The water kept coming over my head and I wanted my mother, but the water was coming over my head and I couldn't open my mouth to scream. I've been having nightmares about not being able to scream..." It was waking up screaming that had brought her racing to Little Piddling. "I couldn't scream but she came anyway. I saw her blue dress as she pushed through the people standing on the beach and ran into the water. Someone tried to stop her, but she shook them off and dived in and I knew it was going to be all right. She was going to save me..."

She was sobbing now, clinging to Daniel as he held her, rocking her as he whispered soothing words. Telling her over and over that it wasn't her fault until, finally, she managed to get a grip, calm down enough to draw back.

"Someone had called out the lifeboat as soon as they noticed how far out you were. By the time the radio message got to them to look for your mother, it was too late."

"Your dad's face is the last thing I remember," Rose said. "You look so much like him."

"He'll be very happy to see you."

"Will he? He won't shout at me?"

"He never shouted at anyone in his life. I don't normally, but this morning..." It was his turn to swallow. "This morning felt different."

She sniffed, wiped her palms across wet cheeks, then searched in her bag for a tissue to blow her nose. "I must look a sight. I bet you wish you'd left me with Henry or Arthur now."

He took her hands, held them in his. "Katherine Rosalind Redmayne, this would be a very good moment to tell me if you'd rather I'd left you with Henry or Arthur."

The warmth that trickled through her veins had nothing to do with the fire, or with Nigel lying on her feet.

"Why?" she asked. "What will you do if I tell you that I'm glad that you didn't?"

"I'd tell you that there was a reason I couldn't leave this town with its ridiculous name," he said. "I had no idea what it was, until I saw you standing in front of your beach hut with your curls and your chin and I knew then that I'd been waiting for you." He kissed each of her hands then cradled her face in his palms. "And once I'd said that, I'd kiss you."

"I'd like that."

"Would you?"

He was searching her face, wanting more and she said, "Henry and Arthur are both sweet men, Daniel, but we were soulmates. I'm sorry that I forgot you for such a long time," she said, "but I'm home now and I won't be leaving, so yes, I'd really, really like you to kiss me. Now, please."

# Chapter Eight

Daniel's lips descended with what felt like agonising slowness but it was worth the wait.

The first touch sent a whisper through her body. He took his time getting to know what pleased her, to respond to her sighs, her moans, his touches becoming more intimate.

At some point they rolled onto the sheepskin rug sending Nigel running for his basket. Everything stopped then and looking up at her, he said, "Bed..."

"Are you OK, Rose?" he asked, much later, when they'd regained their breath.

"I think I might need some more hot sweet tea."

He laughed, kissed her. "I can't believe that just happened."

"Me neither. Maybe we should do it again to be sure." Somewhere in town a clock struck eleven. "But not now. If I'm not tucked up in my own bed by midnight," she said, "your mother's worst fears will be realised."

"I'll call her and tell her you're staying here."

"And confirm them? She recognised me today. She had no idea who I was, but she knew she'd seen me before."

"Then I'll put her out of her misery. Seriously, Rose, a lot of memories have been stirred up and you were already having nightmares. I don't think you should be on your own." He leaned across, kissed away any possibility of argument, then peeled himself off the bed.

"Hey!"

"Stay right there. I have to take Nigel for walk around the block, but I won't be long."

"No, wait," she said, scrambling up after him. "I'll come with you. I want to see Jules."

"Won't it keep until the morning?"

"I want her to know that I've remembered."

"I'll get a torch."

It took her a moment to locate her clothes. Her bag had fallen over, spilling her purse and phone and when she picked it up she said, "Arthur has sent a text."

"An apology, I hope."

"No. His mother told him that Nanna Rose is still living in the pink house. That's what he wanted to tell me. She's a bit of recluse but she's alive, Daniel."

"I didn't know." He gestured at the painting over the fireplace. "That's one of your Nanna's. It belonged to my dad, but he knew how much I loved it and he gave it to me when I bought this house..."

Rose touched it. "It's beautiful."

"Come on," he said, offering her one of his jackets so that she wouldn't get cold. "You can tell Jules that you're going to see Nanna Rose tomorrow."

They walked arm in arm across the beach, Nigel bounding ahead of them, the stars dimmed by a full moon.

At the hut, Daniel said, "Do you want me to come in with you?"

"Yes, please."

She gave him the key, he unlocked the door and they stepped inside.

"Jules?" she called. There was no reply. Daniel handed her the torch and she climbed up to the sleeping loft.

Jules was curled up under the blanket.

"Mama...?" she said, uncertain whether she should touch her, but then letting her fingers whisper over her mother's cheeks.

"Katy..."

"Yes, Mama."

"Thank you for the sweets."

"I remembered."

"I told your dad that it would be better if you didn't, but he said it was time..."

"I'm so sorry, Mama."

"It wasn't your fault. I should have been taking better care of you. I relied on Daniel but I'd forgotten that he was away."

"He's here now and he's going to take me to see Nanna Rose tomorrow. Do you want me to tell her anything?"

"Tell her to start painting again."

"I will. Is there anything I can do for you? "

"No. I'm just going to stay here for a little while longer, thinking about Peter. We had such lovely times, but Nanna needed me and Peter had commitments..." She sat up. "Daniel?"

He stood on the ladder so that she could see him. "Hello, Jules."

"Will you take care of Katy for me?"

"Always."

Jules reached out a hand and touched his cheek. "Such a good boy."

"I'm going to stay with her, Daniel," Rose said.

"Do you want me to stay with you?"

She shook her head and he learned forward to kiss her. "I'll be next door if you need me."

He left her the torch, but she turned it off and lay in the dark beside her mother. They talked, laughed, remembered and cried a little until Jules' voice grew too faint to hear. And, when the scent of coffee tempted her from sleep, Rose was alone.

Matt walked Rose down the aisle to Daniel, with Lisa, thrilled to be her bridesmaid, following them. They had been stunned by her story and were just a little bewitched by Little Piddling.

Nanna Rose had repainted the rose garland and it glowed with pinks and greens and gold in the setting sun when, after their vows were made, Rose and Daniel threw the biggest beach party that Little Piddling had ever seen.

Rosa's Retreat and Dan's Den had been linked with more roses and fairy lights than anyone could count. There was fabulous food and lashings of champagne laid out in what had to be the smallest wedding reception venue ever, and they all danced barefoot in the sand as the sunset faded into twilight.

Later, they sat around a bonfire, eating hotdogs and watching fireworks—the silent ones that didn't frighten the animals—light up the bay.

And in the shadows, where only Daniel and Rose could see her, Jules looked up from painting her toenails and smiled.

# THE END

## *About Liz Fielding*

Bestselling author Liz Fielding writes contemporary romance and
has sold more than 15 million books. Recently she has turned to
crime and has published three murder mysteries. When not writing,
she is busy in her garden, fighting the flab in the local pool, or
doing stuff with a crochet hook or knitting needles. You can see the
results on Facebook/lizfieldingauthor or Instagram/liz.fielding, and
check out her blog at lizfieldingblog.com
Liz is also part of the Libertà hive: libertabooks.com/liz


### *Want Liz's latest book?*
You can get Liz's latest book, and find earlier ones you may
have missed, at author.to/LizFielding
where you'll also be able to follow Liz for her latest releases

# I, VAMPIRE
## Romance with Bite
### by *Joanna Maitland*

## DEDICATION

To the two people who inspired me to write a vampire:
the late Sir Terry Pratchett and David,
both of whom made me laugh.
And to my fellow authors in this anthology.
It's been a huge pleasure (and an honour) to work with you.

# Chapter One

"I, vampire. You, human. We have a relationship, you know?"

The boy nodded. He didn't look worried.

I was going to have to be more precise. It was time this little urchin showed some proper respect to a vampire. Fear, even.

"Vampires drink blood. Human blood. You are human. Worried now?"

He shook his head. "Nope. I know all about vampires. I've read Terry Pratchett."

"Terry who?"

"Pratchett. Don't you read in your vampire world? Oh, I suppose you're a bit short of light in your coffin."

"*I Don't Live In A Coffin.* I live in a—" Oh. Um. I glanced over my shoulder at beach hut Number 23a.

"Anyway, you don't have to drink human blood to survive. You can reform."

"I can *what*?"

"You can reform. Like Angel in Buffy."

"What the h—? Um." He was a child. No swearing. "*Who* is Buffy when he's at home? And where does the angel come in?"

"Buffy," he responded smugly, "is a *she*. She's a Slayer. Of vampires."

"Eh?"

"And Angel is a vampire."

"So she slays him?"

"Nnnooope. She falls in love with him."

My head was beginning to hurt. "So the Slayer doesn't slay the vampire? Does the vampire drink her blood?"

"Nope."

"So how does he survive?"

"It's complicated. You need to watch the box set."

The only boxes I knew were coffins – which don't come in sets. Besides, I'd given up on coffins in favour of beach hut Number 23a.

I'd picked my hut for its simplicity. Some of the others – like Rassendyll Lodge further along – were ornate beyond belief and stuffed to the gills with human junk. Barely room to stand, far less lie down and sleep during the daylight hours. But Number 23a was as spare as its name and suited me admirably. It had a long bench down each side, a low cupboard at the back, and a couple of deckchairs, neatly stowed.

"Look," I said, "I am a vampire. And I do need a regular resupply. Right now, you look plump and pink in a way that's very enticing."

He sighed. "I don't believe you. If you were a proper bloodsucking vampire, you would have done the fang bit long before now. Proper vampires don't get into discussions about Terry Pratchett."

That was a low blow. I tried to regain a little dignity. "Bloodsucking vampires can be extremely polite and logical, you know. Charming conversationalists, even. When they are *not* out for blood. But just at the moment—" I narrowed my eyes at him, trying to look threatening. He didn't flinch. "Just at the moment, I'm beginning to feel the odd pang."

This time, he didn't sigh; he laughed.

Being laughed at by a little boy of about seven is pretty insulting when you're several hundred years old and have, basically, seen it all. Correction, not *absolutely* all. Clearly I'd missed out on Terry Pratchett and the blasted vampire slayer but I'd catch up, eventually. What mattered now was that this mouthy little human was beginning to annoy me.

I let him see my fangs.

He had the sense to recoil a couple of steps. But he hadn't allowed for the uneven sand on the beach. He lost his balance and fell in a heap.

My turn to laugh.

"It's not polite to laugh at others' misfortunes." That came out instantly, like something he'd learned at his mother's knee and was repeating by rote. But he managed to scramble back onto his feet and stood facing me like a boxer, fists raised.

"If you're so well up on vampires, you'll know that we have enormous physical strength. Hmm?" I waited.

In the end, he let his fists drop.

"Better. And while we're on the issue of politeness, might I mention that boys of your age should have a little more respect for their elders?"

Something in my tone must have reassured him, because the tension left his shoulders and he grinned at me. "Boys of my age are a bit small to make a decent meal for you, aren't we? And how old are you, anyway?"

I ignored that. Though he was right on the size issue. I'd called him "plump and pink" but actually he was small and skinny and freckled. Barely a snack, really. And I was intrigued by his ability to resist the abject terror that most victims show when they see my fangs. "How old are you, boy? And do you have a name?" I rapped out, trying to regain the initiative. He was too cocky by half.

"William."

"William what?"

"Just William," he said with a smirk.

That certainly fitted. The freckles, plus a snub nose and too-innocent blue eyes. I hadn't read his blessed Pratchett person, but I *had* read Richmal Crompton. Even when I use a coffin, I don't spend all the sunlit hours sleeping, you know. After a century or so, meditation can get boring. So sometimes I read – I used candlelight at first, but nowadays I have an electric torch. And I'm thinking of getting one of those backlit tablet things – to save having to keep putting the torch down to turn the pages. Over the decades, I've read everything from kiddy picture books to Plato. Pratchett had now gone on to my To Be Read list.

"Just William," I repeated, returning the smirk. "As you wish. And your age, Just William?"

"Nine."

I raised a single eyebrow at him. I've perfected that over the years. It unsettles people, almost as much as the fangs.

Just William was unsettled enough to redden a little. "Well, nearly nine," he admitted. "More than eight and a half, anyway. Nearly eight and three-quarters."

I thought it didn't seem fair to quibble.

And then I realised what I was thinking. Since when did I, vampire, act fairly towards humans? Weren't humans simply fodder? Looking down at this small, skinny, *insolent* example of the species, I found that I'd lost my appetite. I wasn't interested in his warm, red, gloopy stuff. I was more interested in how his mind worked.

That was a first. For more than a century.

And his mind worked pretty well, it seemed. He got over the minor embarrassment of lying about his age and went back on the attack. "Do you have a name, Mr Vampire?"

That was certainly a first. *MISTER Vampire?* I choked down a laugh. I'm not *Mr* anything, of course. Over the centuries, one, er, acquires stuff. Money, land, mansions. That sort of thing. And titles. I have lots of those, bestowed by different royal houses, some quite willingly. My titles are mostly German-sounding. Many of them include *von* or *zu*; some of them even include *von und zu* as a job lot. *Theobald Victor Heinrich, Graf von und zu Oberuntermittelbergthal* has quite a ring to it, don't you think? And that's only the start of them.

"Mr Vampire? You *do* have a name, don't you?"

The little squirt was back in impertinent mode.

I resisted the urge to squash him. "Theo," I said.

"Theo what?"

Oh, William would take the gold medal in the cheek Olympics.

"If I told you, Just William, you'd be bored stiff and nodding off before I got to the end of the list. It goes on for hours. So let's stick to just Theo, shall we?"

He nodded.

"And while we're at it, what are you doing on the beach at this time of night? Aren't little boys supposed—?" No, not tactful. "Aren't young gentlemen of nearly nine supposed to be in bed when it's dark?"

"Oh, I did that hours ago. Bedtime story, goodnight kiss, the whole nine yards."

I gave him the eyebrow again. "Nine yards?"

"Sorry, Mr Theo. Naval slang. My father was in the Navy, you see. It means the whole kit and caboodle."

"Kit and caboodle. Uh. Right. I'm sure it does." I allowed myself a sigh. "And less of the *Mr Theo*, if you please. Let's do a deal, shall we? I'll call you William and you call me Theo. Just Theo."

He stuck out a hand. "Fair enough. Just Theo." He grinned. We shook.

"So, William, if you did the whole kit and caboodle in your bedroom, what are you doing here on the beach, making idle conversation with a passing vampire, may I enquire?"

"Ah." He frowned, as if considering something momentous. "If I tell you, you have to promise to keep it a secret. OK, Just Theo?"

"If you call me 'Just Theo' one more time," I said through gritted fangs, "I will change my mind about the succulence of nearly nine-year-old boys. Got it?"

"Hm. OK. Got it. And do you promise to keep my secret, Theo?"

What could be such a big deal for a child of his age? "I promise."

"Cross your heart and hope to die?" That seemed to come out automatically.

I drew in a long noisy breath through pursed lips. Theatrical, I know, but sometimes one does have to belabour the point. "Vampires can do many things, young man, but dying isn't one of them."

"Oh. Um. Yes."

"Not even to keep a promise to you. I've pledged you my word. And the word of a vampire is worth something. So now...give. What are you doing here? And how did you, er, escape?"

"It's no biggie, but you mustn't let on to the grown-ups. I wait till Mum and Dad are sitting in front of the telly with a bottle of wine and I climb down the tree outside my bedroom window. Dad's a bit deaf – didn't always wear his ear defenders when he was in the Navy, Mum says – so he has the sound turned up loud. They wouldn't hear me if I was a herd of elephants."

I resisted the urge to point out that elephants don't generally climb down trees. Instead, I asked very politely, "Don't they ever check up on you when you're supposed to be asleep?"

"Come on, Theo. Didn't you ever heap up the bedclothes so it looked like you were still in there, fast asleep?"

It was a very long time since I'd been William's age so I couldn't remember much. One thing I was sure of. As a child, I'd never, ever had a bedroom to myself. "When I was a lad, William, I was working so hard all day that I was asleep the instant I hit the mattress. So I had no energy left for silly pranks like yours."

"It's not a silly prank," he protested. "I come down here at night because there's things to see. Weird things happen around this beach hut. I even saw a vampire, once." He was looking very knowing, all of a sudden.

I'd had about enough by that stage. "If you keep on making clever-clever comments like that," I snapped, "this vampire may be the last thing you ever see." I flashed the fangs again, but this time he didn't show any fear at all. He just shook his head at me.

"Oh, I didn't mean you, Theo. I meant the other one."

# Chapter Two

William couldn't tell me much about the other vampire. It didn't sound like anyone I knew. In fact, it didn't sound like a vampire at all.

"What did you actually *see*, William?"

"He was wearing one of those huge black swirly cloaks. Like yours. But he had a big hat, too, so I couldn't see his face."

"Huh. No face, no fangs, no vampire, I'd say. You saw someone in a cloak and you assumed he was a vampire. You've got too many fantasy stories tumbling around in that head of yours, young man."

"No, I haven't. I *know* he was a vampire. Like I knew *you* were a vampire. I did, didn't I? Straight off."

He had me there. I changed the subject. "Where did you see him? *When* did you see him? More than once?"

"Only the once," he admitted sadly.

"So what made you decide he was a vampire? Rather than – oh, I don't know – a ghost, or something?"

"Because ghosts don't turn into bats and fly away."

Ah. "He, um, did the bat bit, did he?"

William nodded. "Just the one bat, mind." He sounded disappointed.

"Did you expect more than one?" Honestly, I was mystified by the way this lad's mind worked. Sometimes, he seemed far too clever for eight. Sometimes, like now, he was just plain daft. "One vampire, one bat. Tends to be the way things pan out."

"Not necessarily," William said very seriously. "Well, I read a theory that a full-sized vampire body needs to convert into the same mass of bats. Which would be quite a lot of bats, I suppose."

"Where on earth did you get that nonsense from?"

"Um. I think...I think it was Terry Pratchett. It might have been a joke, though." He sniffed.

"The joke would be on the vampire. How on earth would one vampire brain run a whole swarm of bats? I'm beginning to think your man Pratchett isn't worth adding to my To Be Read pile after all."

"Oh, he is. Honestly. And he's funny, too."

I drew myself up to my full height. "I don't approve of making jokes at the expense of respectable vampires, William."

My dignity act didn't seem to work. "Respectable, *bloodsucking* vampires, you mean, Theo?"

"Cheeky little toad," I said. "Yes, I suppose I do. But you should be aware, in case you meet this other vampire again, that our kind can be a little, um, thin-skinned when it comes to people who take the p—" I stopped in mid-word, reminding myself yet again that he was only a child.

"Take the piss, Theo?"

"That's not the sort of expression that a lad of your age should know."

"Oh, I know much worse than that. I know—"

"*That will do*, William. If we are to be friends, as you might say, I will promise not to fang you, but you will need to remember your manners."

"Must I? Oh. All right then."

"And it's really very late now. Tomorrow's Monday. I presume you have to go to school? So don't you think you should be climbing back up your tree?"

"I s'pose so. Can I have a look at your coffin first, though? Where do you keep it? In our beach hut?"

*His* beach hut? That was a complication I hadn't bargained on. "I told you, ages ago, I don't sleep in a coffin. Not here, anyway. I sleep in this excellent beach hut. Number 23a. There's a *Welcome* sign on the door inviting people in, so I took your family at their word. Kind of you all to ask me to stay. And it's very well sealed. It's even got wooden shutters on the windows. No sunlight problem during the day."

William considered. "Yes, I can see why you like it. But what will you do when my family want to use the hut? My sister Sylvie likes to come down in the Spring, as soon as there's a sunny day. So does my Mum. If Mum finds you…"

"If she finds me, I'll deal with her."

William grabbed my arm. "Don't kill my Mum, Theo. Please don't."

That's the problem with being fair to humans. You decide to be fair – kind, maybe? – to one of them, and they tie you up in knots. I shook off his hand. "I won't hurt your mother, boy." He didn't know as much about vampires as he thought. Like most vampires, I don't make a habit of killing humans. And I never turn them into vampires, either. I might indulge in a little gentle blood-sucking, but it never does them any real harm. No different from donating blood to a blood bank, really. "If she starts to open up the beach hut, I'll transform into a bat and hide in the roof. With luck, she'll get such a fright, she'll run away and I'll be left in peace."

"But wouldn't the sunlight get to you, even in the roof?"

"Nope. Or not enough to do me any real harm. I'm not daft. I did a decent recce on this hut before I moved in." I shouldn't have told him that. Because then I got...

"Why did you come here anyway? It's not exactly... I mean, you said you've got all these titles, and money, and stuff. Haven't you got a Dracula's Castle in Transylvania or somewhere to hang out in?"

I laughed. "Several, actually. But they keep being invaded by tourists. And it's impossible to get a wink of sleep."

"But you could turn into a bat, couldn't you?"

I sighed. "That can be a problem, these days. Either the sight of my leathery wings sends the poor dears screaming for the hills – which makes the chaps running the tour companies very stroppy and difficult to manage. Or they start cooing over me and wanting to conserve me because I'm an endangered species."

"Oh. Like great crested newts, you mean?"

Definitely too clever by half. Especially for eight.

"You, young man, are a precocious and annoying brat. And it's time you were back in bed." I pointed imperiously in the direction of the town where I assumed his home was.

He didn't move a step. "Can I come and see you again, Theo? I'd really like to—"

"Only if you go back to bed now." I was still pointing.

William finally took the hint. "OK. I'll go home now."

Result! "*And* back to bed," I added sternly. I knew about logic-twisting little boys. I'd tried to be one, once.

"OK. Back to bed," he agreed. "But I'll be back as soon as I can. You *will* still be here, won't you, Theo?"

I nodded. "For a while, anyway. Now, get lost, boy, before I change my mind."

He grinned and ran up the beach towards the road.

It was well after midnight. Not safe for little boys to be out on their own. Especially if there were unknown and unpredictable vampires about. So I translated into a bat – just the one, I would stress – and followed him. I wanted to make sure he got home safely.

Yes, OK. I also wanted to find out where the owners of my temporary residence were to be found.

He didn't run all the way home. After a while, he simply strolled along, whistling to himself. I overtook him easily as he got to his tree, outside Number 23, Gaol Street. Which explained the beach hut. Clever, but not pretentious.

By the time he started to climb, I was neatly suspended from one of the highest branches, doing a passable impression of a shrivelled leaf.

He was a good climber, I'll give him that. Up that tree in a trice and hardly a sound while he did it. The branch nearest to his window didn't look strong enough to bear even his slight weight but he crawled along it without hesitating. Until he got to his window and had one leg over the sill. Then he turned round, grinned up at the top of the tree, and whispered, "Night, Theo."

Any sharper and he'd cut himself. But he'd won that round.

I shrugged.

Well, no. Actually, I tried to shrug. But bats can't.

So I flew back to William's beach hut where I could shrug to my heart's content.

# Chapter Three

Sylvie ran across to the beach hut. She was late. She'd told Karl ten o'clock and it was long past that. Would he be waiting, tapping his foot and frowning?

He wasn't there at all.

Relief flooded her. Then annoyance. Then uncertainty. Maybe he'd stood her up?

She'd give him ten minutes, tops.

She opened the beach hut door so she could wait out of the wind. Her eye was caught by something on the floor, shiny in the light from outside. Sylvie looked closer. It was a piece of bright gold embroidery thread. But no one in her family did embroidery, so how had it got there?

Footsteps sounded on the duckboards outside. She turned instantly. And was bowled over by what she saw. "Wow!" Her breath came out long and slow, full of amazement. Talk about fit!

Karl doffed his gleaming top hat and bowed low, in a very old-world way. He'd told her he was an actor. From London. She hadn't known whether to believe him then, but she did now. He had the moves. And the glamour.

"I take it you approve?" He waited for her smile of agreement. "So may I come in?"

"Course." She stood aside and then closed the door behind him. She wanted to have him all to herself. And she would. The beach hut was a much cooler place to meet him than last night's noisy wine bar.

At first, she simply gazed wide-eyed at the apparition filling Number 23a. "Wow," she said again. "Just wow. Where did you get all that fabulous gear?"

He said nothing but he spun round slowly so that his long black cape billowed into sensuous folds. They seemed to absorb the light. And the upright collar cast a shadow on his face and neck. The effect was overpowering. And a tiny bit sinister.

"You like?"

She reached out to stroke a hand down the fabric. It felt silky smooth. And almost alive. "What's it made of? And what's it for?"

"Whitby."

Sylvie was stumped. "Whitby? What's Whitby?"

"Don't you know?" He shook his head at her. "Your education, sweetie, is sadly lacking."

He was being patronising. Again. OK, he was a fair bit older than she was – and a lot more sophisticated – but that didn't give him the right to treat her like a child. And there was nothing wrong with her education. In fact, it was probably better than his. She'd won a scholarship to the best school in the county *and* she had an offer from Oxford. Had he done anything like that? She wasn't sure he'd even been to drama school. She narrowed her eyes at him. Would he get the message?

He didn't. He droned on, like the worst of her teachers. "Whitby is famous. It's where Dracula landed in England. The vampire, you know? You *have* heard of Dracula, haven't you?"

"Course I have. But I haven't actually read the book. Horror's not my thing."

"You should. It's good. There've been some fantastic plays, too."

She ignored that. "And Whitby? What's Whitby got to do with your flashy new threads?"

"I'll be wearing this at Whitby. At the next Goth weekend. Whitby does them twice a year, April and October. Loads of people go. And it matters – a lot – what you wear. Like to come with me?" He raised one eyebrow at her. But before she had a chance to get a word out, he went on, "You'd need to have the right gear, of course. Lots of black lace and stiff petticoats. High-heeled boots. Black make-up. Probably a corset. With your black hair, you're a natural to be a Goth."

Her pulse had begun to race. They'd only known each other a week, and he was inviting her to take a trip with him. Whitby's Goth weekend sounded exciting and very grown-up. Miles away from boring old Piddling, too. But April was bang in the middle of final revisions for her A-levels.

"Um. The timing's not great. I've got exams to think about. If I don't get the right grades, I won't—" She stopped, remembering she hadn't told him about Oxford. He'd probably be patronising about that, too. "Anyway, I've never really fancied being a Goth," she finished. "All that posturing and play-acting." She hoped it came out as a challenge.

He ignored it. "No big deal. I'll take someone else if you want to wimp out."

She gave him her best death stare. "I don't give in to threats. Not from anyone."

He shrugged. "Whitby'll be a blast. Stupid to miss it."

"I'll think about it. But no promises, Karl. OK?"

He gave her a half-smile. In the dim light, his black hair gleamed like satin. She found herself wondering idly what kind of gel he'd used to get that 40s-film-star look. And then wondering why she was being so logical. Why wasn't she grabbing him and kissing that gorgeous mouth? After all, she'd spent most of the night dreaming about him. And most of the day anticipating the moment when they'd be together again.

Dracula. That was it. The thought of Dracula – and fangs – was a real turnoff. Especially when the man on offer looked too much like one of the undead himself.

And then she remembered what she'd been intending to ask him, before. "Why didn't you answer my text last night?" She'd sent him directions to the beach hut almost as soon as she got home. They'd been apart for less than half an hour by then. Had he ignored her because she sounded too needy?

"I was busy."

"At one in the morning?"

"I'd gone for a walk. And there was no signal. By the time I got back, it was too late." He smiled down at her. "Didn't want to spoil your beauty sleep, Sylve."

"Yeah, right. And don't call me 'Sylve'. You know I hate it."

"Why? It's no worse that 'Sylvia'."

"I hate my name. Especially 'Sylve'. It's old-fashioned and everyone laughs at it. When was the last time you met anyone called 'Sylvia'?"

He chortled. "What *were* your parents thinking about?"

Sylvie groaned and shook her head. "My mother. My culture-mad mother. I think she was going through her Schubert phase when she had me. Used to go around the house, Dad says, singing 'Who is Sylvia?' She has a really good voice, too. Had lessons and everything."

"Um. '*Who is Sylvia?*' Doesn't ring a bell."

"If that was a joke, it was rubbish." Sylvie grinned up at him. "Shakespeare. You must know it. You're an actor. It's a song in one of his plays. And Schubert set it to music. Schubert, the composer? He has to be at least as famous as your precious Dracula." Still grinning, she reached up and patted him gently on the cheek.

He didn't react. For a moment, he was like a marble statue shrouded in black silk. Then the statue spoke. "Don't you have a middle name you could use instead?"

"Yes. And no."

"Oh?"

"Perdita."

"Ugh. More Shakespeare?"

She nodded miserably.

"Well, Sylvia Perdita, you could refuse to answer to 'Sylvia'. Choose your own name. Why not something normal like 'Anne' or 'Mary' or 'Liz'?"

Sylvie made a face. "If I'm honest," she admitted slowly, "I'd like to be – don't you dare laugh, Karl – I'd like to be a 'Kylie'."

He was definitely pressing his lips hard together.

She punched him lightly on the arm. "I told you not to laugh, you beast."

He ignored that. "I don't think 'Kylie' is you at all. You deserve something with more, um, more *atmosphere* to it. Especially if you're coming to Whitby."

"I said I'll think about it. I'm still thinking. Don't push your luck."

He ignored that, as well. He stroked his forehead with two long white fingers. "Something with a bit of history to it. Medieval, maybe? Yup! Got it! Your mother picked the wrong composer." He smiled at her in a way that made her go all warm and treacly inside. "Wagner is your answer, sweetheart. History and myth coming out of his ears. Change your name to 'Isolde'."

Something gave a tiny squeak. Sylvie jumped. "Oh, God. Are there mice here somewhere?" She shivered. "I hate mice. They give me the heebie-jeebies."

"You're imagining it," he said reassuringly, without even glancing round to check. "It was probably my boot squeaking on the floorboards. Fancy patent jobs—" he lifted one foot to show off his shiny black boots "—and leather soles do squeak. I'll try not to do it again. Promise." He opened his arms to her and, without a moment's hesitation, she walked into his embrace. She let herself be enveloped in the silky black folds so that he could kiss his newly christened Isolde into forgetfulness.

# Chapter Four

After a whole day of reading Pratchett, I'd been enjoying a bit of low-key hunting well away from the beach. Nothing to panic the locals, of course. Taking a little blood from a sleeping victim does no long-term harm and most of them don't even notice the puncture marks when they wake up.

But then I'd had second thoughts. What if William turned up again tonight, looking for me? So I came back early, just in time to see my visitors going into the beach hut. Not good. What if William opened the door and saw? I knew he was pretty clued-up for eight, but did he know what really went on between a man and a woman when it came to hand-to-hand combat?

I didn't want to be responsible for educating him if he didn't already know about the way the (human) world went round.

So I hung around – not as a bat all the time, in case you're wondering – on the off chance that the boy would turn up. I had a feeling he would.

And he did. At ten minutes to midnight.

He was at the door before I realised. He even had his hand on the knob.

"William," I hissed, not wanting my voice to carry into the hut, "I'm over here."

He swung round and grinned. He looked delighted to see me, which was a bit of a turn-up. Humans aren't normally delighted to see vampires, even humans who know they're not potential prey. Was I really going to have an eight-year-old human for a *friend*? It was going to take me a while to get used to that. Weird, or what?

"Theo." Being so young, he had a high-pitched voice and he wasn't trying to keep the decibels down either.

"Shhh!" I put my finger to my lips and beckoned him over.

He trotted obediently across the sand. "What's going on, Theo?" William was clearly a born conspirator. He'd dropped his voice to a whisper. His eyes were eager.

"Your beach hut's, um, occupied. There's a couple of people in there."

"How did they get in? Did you leave the door unlocked?"

For once, I was totally innocent. I'd never used a key. A bat can wriggle through the tiniest of cracks. But William's question made me realise I'd overlooked something vital. How had they got inside? There was no sign of forced entry.

I decided to be a little economical with the truth. At least until I knew more about what was going on. "They were inside the beach hut when I got back." That was true enough. I'd heard their voices. And I'd caught a glimpse of the girl as she closed the door. "A man and a girl. I think—"

"Ah," said my friend in a voice that sounded much too worldly-wise for eight, "I see. You didn't want me to open the door in case I caught them *in flagrante*."

For a moment, I couldn't say a word. It wasn't only his precocious knowledge of sex that got to me; it was the casual use of Latin. I began to wonder how many books this minuscule brainbox might have read. And which library he'd got them from.

He talked on to fill the silence. "What are they like? Young? Old? Is she pretty?"

"Aren't you a bit young to be interested in girls, William?" I was trying to delay the moment when he would start adding two and two.

"Academic interest only, Theo. Puberty's still a few years off for me. Especially as I'm small."

His lending library clearly included medical books as well as Pratchett. So I decided to stick to facts and see what conclusions my budding Sherlock might come to.

"She's very pretty. Black curly hair and a beautiful peaches and cream complexion. Blue eyes. Long legs in tight jeans."

"But that sounds like—" He screwed up his eyes at me. "Does she have a name, Theo?" He sounded mistrustful. And also a bit annoyed.

"I heard him call her 'Sylve', I think." Well, it was the truth. And he *had* asked.

He plumped down on the sand and dug his fingers into it, drawing vague patterns. After a while, he said sadly, not looking up at me, "Sylvie. I told you, she's my sister. She's using the beach hut because she's got a spare key."

I'd suspected as much. And now, to be brutally honest, I hadn't a clue what to do. Why was he upset that his big sister was, er, cavorting with her boyfriend? William had seemed so grown-up before. Now, not so much. Playing for time, I suggested we both go for a walk along the beach. I was hoping, I admit, that the couple would have left by the time we got back. I didn't want William's sister to have an encounter with a vampire. It might get messy.

And a bit too shrill for comfort.

We'd gone a good two hundred yards before William said anything at all. "What's Sylvie's boyfriend like?"

"Sorry, William. Can't help you there. I didn't see him. Only her." Strictly speaking, that was true, though I knew a lot from what I'd overheard while I was clinging to the roof outside. William was already pretty down. I didn't want to push him any lower.

"But you heard his voice?"

"Yes. But you can't tell much from voices. Except that he's a grown-up. He sounds older. And quite educated."

"That figures. Sylvie's really clever, you see. She gets bored with people who can't keep up with her. She's going to Oxford in the autumn." He sounded very proud of her. Was he worried that a boyfriend might spike her plans? If so, he was even shrewder than I'd thought.

"Oxford, eh? She must be very bright." I didn't tell him that she might be going to Whitby first. I'd overheard her muttering about preparing for exams so it seemed she knew the risks, too. More than one young lass had got carried away by the joys of the full Goth experience, especially in the company of a persuasive lover. Would Sylvie throw away her future for a fantasy in black make-up?

William would want me to stop her, if he knew what she was planning.

Should I tell him?

No point. She hadn't made up her mind yet. Besides, she might get bored with lover-boy long before the Goth weekend. If she had any sense, she'd dump him. He was a complete pillock. Patronising *and* pretentious. *Isolde?* Honestly, I ask you!

I admit I had an ulterior motive. If the lovebirds planned on being in the beach hut every night, it would limit my nocturnal options more than somewhat. Vampires do need privacy, you know, and I'd planned on the beach hut providing mine when I wasn't out hunting. It would do nothing for my image if anyone found out that I do needlepoint when I'm at a loose end.

Change of plan?

Nah, not if I could help it. Perhaps I could nudge Sylvie towards ditching lover-boy? If I needed a partner in crime, I was pretty sure William would be up for it.

He broke into my mental planning with a new suggestion. "You should meet Sylvie, Theo. You'd like her."

I shook my head. "Don't think that's a good idea, William. Females don't react too well to vampires. Lots of screaming, usually. Tends to rouse the neighbourhood."

"But—"

"No. I like being in Little Piddling. It's peaceful here on the beach. And I want it to stay that way."

Even by moonlight, I could see that William wasn't convinced. More trouble. What had I let myself in for when I befriended a human? I should have remembered how badly it had turned out the first time.

"You wouldn't…you wouldn't *fang* Sylvie, would you, Theo?"

First his mother, now his sister. Great. For an eight-year-old, he was pretty demanding. But I didn't have a choice, did I? "No. I promise your sister is safe with me."

"Oh, good. Well, in that case, I'll tell her all about you. And you can meet her some other night. When she's not with…*him*." He glanced back towards the beach hut. And there was real, focused venom in that look.

"That's all very well, but will she believe you? Grown-ups tend to think that vampires aren't real, you know. If I have to show her my fangs to, er, get the point across, she'll probably faint on the spot."

"Your puns are rubbish, Theo. Didn't anyone ever tell you that?"

"Thank you," I said politely.

"You're welcome." He grinned up at me like the evil little demon he so clearly was. "Anyway, Sylvie's not a wimp. She wouldn't faint. I don't think she'd scream, either. She'd probably try to slug you. She does kick-boxing, you know."

That was certainly different. "Does she now? I'll bear that in mind." His sister was becoming more intriguing by the minute. "How old is she, by the way?"

"Nearly nineteen."

That was a big age gap. "Are there any more of you at home? Besides Sylvie, I mean?"

"No. Sylvie was an only for a long time. And I was an accident." He was very matter-of-fact about a failing of birth control.

That was when I made my mind up. If anyone could convince Sylvie that Theo the vampire was real but – crucially – no threat to her, William was the one to do it. I took a long, slow breath. "I'll meet her—"

"That's great—"

"—but there are conditions. Your beach hut door stays open. She has to feel she can run away. You'll have to bring her at night, too, well after midnight. We don't want there to be anyone else around."

William nodded wisely. He didn't seem to have noticed the problem.

"Won't that betray your great secret? You know – the tree?"

William chuckled and shook his head. "Sylvie used to do it herself when she was my age. Who do you think taught me? Sylvie would never tell on me."

Oh. Not so grown-up after all, if she did nothing to stop a little boy going off on his own in the middle of the night and tangling with all sorts of undesirables.

Like vampires.

But I'd been well and truly suckered in. "And you have to do your very best to convince her that I really am a vampire. *Before* she comes. Think you can do that?"

He didn't hesitate at all. "Oh yes."

"Cocky little blighter, aren't you?"

He beamed. "Yup. That's just what Dad says. But if you think I'm bad, wait till you've met my sister."

Sometimes, even centuries of experience aren't enough to prepare you for dealing with humans.

# Chapter Five

Sylvie turned up the following night, with William in tow, at about quarter to one. She was wearing a long skirt instead of jeans. Disappointing. It meant I couldn't admire her stunning legs.

Does that surprise you? I may be a vampire but I can still admire a good-looking woman, you know. We vampires are famous for our love of beauty, in all its forms. And Sylvie certainly qualified.

She looked me up and down assessingly. I couldn't see any signs of fear, or even caution. Perhaps that was to be expected. William had warned me that she was like him, only worse. And she was a kick-boxer, too.

"Nice gear, Mr, er, Theo." She waved a hand at my cape. "You getting set up for Whitby, too?"

I had to laugh. "No. Whitby's for people who like play-acting. I imagine William has told you? I'm not putting on an act. I'm the real deal."

She smiled indulgently in the direction of her little brother. "Yes, he did try very hard to convince me that his friend Theo was a real vampire but – you know what? – he didn't *quite* manage it."

"No? How come?"

"Because if you were a real vampire, William here would be a bloodless corpse on the sand by now. And he's not, is he?"

"That's because Theo promised not to fang me," William protested before I could get a word in.

"Oh. Oh, right." She was trying not to laugh at him.

"And he promised not to fang you, either, Sylvie. I wouldn't have brought you here if he hadn't."

"Good of you, Mr Theo."

"I prefer Theo," I replied politely. "Just Theo." I could see where this was going. So I needed to keep things calm and restrained. Until they weren't.

"And you should call her 'Sylvie', Theo."

"No, he shouldn't. My name is 'Isolde'. I'm not going to answer to Sylvie any more. I've always hated it. So I'm changing my name."

William grinned wickedly as he considered that. "Have you told Dad?" He chortled. "No, you can't have. We'd have heard the explosion from here."

Sylvie had reddened a fraction. "I'll tell Dad when I'm good and ready. And don't you dare say anything in the meantime, you little monster."

William drew himself up. He was still more than a foot shorter than she was. "The only monster in this beach hut," he said, with emphasis, "is Theo." He turned to me. "You're going to have to give her the fang bit, Theo, or she'll never believe in you."

I didn't move a muscle.

He tugged at her arm. "But whatever you do, Sylvie – Isolde – please don't scream. Promise you won't?"

Sylvie shook him off with the sort of look that only much older sisters can give to little boys.

William ignored that and turned expectantly to me.

Well, what choice did I have? To borrow William's picturesque naval slang, I gave her the full nine yards.

Her eyes widened so much there was almost no blue to be seen. She made a noise that was a cross between a strangled gulp and a groan but, thankfully, nowhere near a scream. She recoiled a few steps, too, and grabbed for the wall. On the whole, she reacted as staunchly as William had predicted. No screams, no fainting. No attempt to slug me, either, which was just as well, since I'd rashly promised she'd be safe with me. I was beginning to regret that. What's the point of having superhuman strength if you can't fight back when someone punches you?

William had clearly decided he now needed to take charge of the proceedings. "Told you so. Maybe next time you'll believe me?"

Pompous little toad. I thought for a moment that she was going to thump him rather than me. He would have deserved it, too.

Instead, she took a deep breath and straightened. She still had one hand on the wall for support, though. "I...I think I owe you both an apology," she managed, with commendable dignity. "I didn't believe vampires existed. Now I...I think I do."

Remarkable. And not at all what I'd expected.

I bowed to her. I knew it was the only thing to do. "In my very long life, Isolde, I have met only one adult human – another lady, as it happens – with as much courage as you have. I salute you."

She coloured again, more than before. "I, er— Um." She swallowed hard. "Thank you, Theo." Like her brother, she had obviously been brought up to be polite.

I smiled at her. No fangs. Definitely no fangs. "Please don't be afraid, Isolde. I promised your brother you'd be safe with me." I frowned down at William. "I promised he would be, too, though there are times when I rather wish I hadn't."

"That's one of his jokes, Sylvie," William said quickly. "Sorry – Isolde."

"No, you'd better stick to 'Sylvie'. Until I've told Dad." The corner of her mouth quirked into a rueful smile.

William had said she was clever. But she was practical, too. In my experience, the two don't always go together. But Sylvie/Isolde was both, and easy on the eye as well. I wondered idly how Oxford would cope with this phenomenon.

She looked me up and down. She'd recovered a lot of poise very quickly. "I take it," she said, musingly, "that I'm not supposed to let on that there's a vampire squatting in our beach hut?"

"Of course not." William sounded outraged. "You—"

"Keep it down, William. I'm sure your sister wouldn't betray your trust. Or mine." I was trying to sound confident but, if William hadn't had the nous to extract a promise of secrecy from her in advance, we could both be in deep trouble. Had he?

Sylvie smiled.

I knew then that William had failed me. I didn't trust that smile one inch. It was a conspirator's smile.

"Well, I *could* keep your secret, Theo. But there are conditions."

No surprise there. "Let's have them," I said.

"First, you have to agree to vacating the beach hut on the evenings when I might want to use it."

"Every evening, Isolde?" I didn't ask what she wanted the beach hut for – I thought I already knew that – and I didn't mention lover-boy, either.

"No. Every other night should do, I think. I've already got plans to be here later, so you can start the day after. OK?" When I nodded, she went on, "And secondly, you have to tell me all about the other female with courage."

"What? No. No way. It's none of your business."

She crossed her arms and stared me out. "That's the deal. You tell me, or I start to scream the place down. On the count of three. One…"

I couldn't shut her up without using force. What choice did I have?

On the count of two, I gave in.

Then I struggled for a bit to get my thoughts in order. Vampires don't have bosom buddies to confide in, you understand, so I'd never done this before. The truth was I really, really didn't want to go there. But the memories and feelings came flooding back anyway. They hurt. Like the devil.

In the end, I couldn't shut out the pain, but I certainly wasn't going to tell Sylvie about it. Especially not with William latching on to every word. Sylvie could have the bare bones of my time with Lucinda. And why we parted, more or less.

Less, if I could get away with it.

"You want to know about another female with courage like yours? Well, OK, Isolde, you win. I'll tell you her story, warts and all. It doesn't matter any more, in any case, since everyone involved is safely dead. It was a long time ago, you see. In the Belle Époque before the First World War.

"We met in Paris. And the lady's name was Lucinda..."

# Chapter Six

*Theo's story*

Theo heard about Lucinda long before he met her. She was the toast of Paris. She wasn't conventionally pretty. Some women admitted, grudgingly, that she was handsome. One sour-voiced lady, talking about Lucinda Grayson and men, was heard to refer disparagingly to "bees" and "honey-pots".

But Theo knew the only cliché that fitted a woman like Lucinda was "moths to a flame". Men didn't stop to think of words to describe her. They simply flocked round her, eager for a look, a word, a smile. And any man who came too near was likely to get burned. Even a vampire.

The first time Theo saw her was at the Paris Opéra. He had been living in Paris since 1906 and he'd taken a box at the Opéra every year. He told people it was because he enjoyed the performances. But, like so many vampires, Theo was handsome enough to draw the eye. And vain enough to enjoy being seen and admired.

Lucinda seemed to be alone in her own box. But he could see that gentlemen were parading in and out all the time, bowing and kissing her hand. Not just in the intervals, either. It was a fascinating procession. Theo couldn't stop staring.

His companion, Comte Edmond d'Evreuil, commented on Theo's odd behaviour. "Ah, you have spied the Lovely Lucinda. Madame Grayson, I should say."

"Madame? She is married?"

Edmond smiled knowingly. "Widowed. And very rich. She has, I would guess, no intention of entering into the married state again. She enjoys her freedom too much."

"What does she do with this freedom, Edmond? Take lovers, perhaps?" Theo glanced back at the lady's box. A uniformed officer was bowing to her at that very moment. "It would seem that she has plenty of choice if she wishes to, er, experiment a little."

"More than that, Theo. When she is not here in Paris, she is an intrepid traveller. Her model, I gather, is her countrywoman, Isabella Bird. Travelling the world is easier now than it was in Miss Bird's day, but it's still a challenge for a woman alone. I believe

Madame Grayson's most recent destination was Japan. And China before that. I doubt she is daunted by much."

"You know her?"

"We have been introduced. I would not say that I *know* her."

"But you could introduce me to her?"

Edmond smiled, pityingly. After a pause, he said, "It will do you no good, you know, Theo. Lots of men have fallen at her feet over the years. And been discarded. Or stepped on. You, of all men, would not want that."

Theo brushed the warning aside. "Will you introduce me, Edmond? Soon?"

Edmond tried to dissuade him, but Theo was adamant. And eager. Eventually, Edmond shrugged and gave in. He agreed to introduce Theo to the bewitching Lucinda the very next afternoon.

In an artist's studio.

In Montmartre.

Theo did not ask whether she would be modelling in the nude. But he did wonder. The lady seemed capable of anything.

It was well into autumn by then and Paris was blanketed by a heavy mist that obscured the sunlight. The locals were surprised that it lasted all day. But the locals didn't understand the powers a vampire could wield. Especially when he was determined to risk going outside during the hours of daylight.

The building Edmond sought was a little way down the hill from the Sacré Coeur. The street door was not locked. Edmond went in without ceremony and led the way through a maze of dark and dirty corridors to the studio. He threw open the door without bothering to knock. "No point," he explained. "When Modigliani's painting, he ignores everything else."

And there she was. Sitting for a young artist Theo didn't recognise – Modigliani.

Lucinda was not modelling naked. She was fully dressed. She hadn't even taken off her hat.

"Sit over there and keep quiet," Modigliani ordered, waving a brush towards a rickety sofa with a grubby, paint-spattered rug on it. Theo reckoned it was the cleanest thing in the place. "I must get on while the light lasts."

So Modigliani was obsessive about the quality of the light. Theo wasn't surprised. He'd known many artists and they were all the same. On that day, though, because of the persistent fog, there was very little light at all and it was fading rapidly. It clearly annoyed

Modigliani, but he refused to stop painting. And there was something manic about the way he kept working, which struck Theo as unnatural in one so young. He was to learn, decades later, that Modigliani was already suffering from the TB that would kill him and hiding his infectious state behind a flagrant addiction to alcohol and drugs. But that afternoon, in Modigliani's decrepit studio, Theo saw only the drink and the demonic glint in the painter's eye. The man wouldn't stop even to entertain two wealthy gentlemen who might be prepared to buy some of his work.

Theo took one look at the way the man was painting Lucinda – with a nightmarishly elongated face and neck that somehow nullified every facet of her striking beauty – and decided on the spot that Modigliani's paintings were not for him.

Theo and Edmond waited nearly half an hour. From their vantage point, it wasn't possible to see what Modigliani was doing to his portrait. There was a lot of huffing and puffing, and regular swigs of spirits in between brush strokes. Lucinda, though, was patience itself. She didn't move, she didn't speak, she didn't complain. She sat. And sat. Until Modigliani told her he had finished with her for the day and she should leave.

And that was it. He didn't thank her or say goodbye. He didn't arrange a time for a future sitting. He was paying all his attention to his canvas and completely ignoring his stunning model. Theo thought the man must be possessed. He had to be that – or mad – to be ignoring Lucinda Grayson.

Modigliani ignored his visitors, too. Theo concluded he'd forgotten them completely.

Edmond and Theo rose when Lucinda did. Edmond bowed politely. "Madame Grayson, we are delighted to find you here. Might we escort you home perhaps? Or offer you dinner?"

Oh. Problems. The undead do not eat. Theo knew that he would have to make his excuses – an unbreakable appointment elsewhere – and take his leave before the first course was laid out on the table. But he would remain in her company until the last possible moment.

Lucinda bowed her head a fraction in acknowledgement of Edmond's polite greeting. "Monsieur le comte. How delightful to see you again. Will you not introduce your friend?"

"Graf Theo Heinrich," Edmond said, waving Theo forward to bow over her hand.

When Theo raised his head again, she said, smiling, "A German title, monsieur?"

"No, madame, my title was bestowed by the Austrian Emperor, as King of Hungary." That was not the whole truth but Theo was not using all his titles in Paris.

"Graf Theo." She seemed to savour the words. "Would you prefer it if we conversed in German, perhaps?"

They'd been talking in French, which she spoke beautifully, with almost no accent. Now it appeared that she spoke German as well. Clearly a woman of many talents. A very unusual Englishwoman.

"It is not necessary, madame, unless it is what *you* would prefer. Or we could speak English instead?"

Her grey eyes flashed. "Touché, Herr Graf. Thank you, but no. I prefer to speak the language of the country where I reside. In France, I speak French."

Theo couldn't resist the temptation to tease. "And in Japan…?"

She gave him a searing look. Then she breathed deeply and allowed herself to smile. "In Japan, Graf Theo, I speak Japanese to the best of my ability. Which is to say, not very well at all." She glanced across at Modigliani who was paying absolutely no attention to any of them. So she settled her jaunty little hat more securely on her fair hair and tucked her hand through Edmond's arm. "Well, gentlemen, you offered me dinner? Shall we go?"

They strolled up the hill to one of the restaurants in the Place du Tertre, chatting amiably. On the threshold, Lucinda paused to stare in fascination at the day's uncanny view of the Sacré Coeur. Its great dome seemed to be floating above the blanket of mist, unsupported, indistinct and ghastly white.

Theo was not admiring the view of the basilica. He was admiring the view of Lucinda. He was beginning to realise he'd never seen a woman so alive. And that he wanted her. But he was one of the undead. His kind should not care about any living human being, except as a potential source of sustenance.

Lucinda truly was full of life. She revelled in it, in every tiny scrap of it, from the fallen leaves crunching beneath her boots to the sparrows dodging round the table legs in search of crumbs. She was mesmerising. Edmond seemed to be at least halfway smitten, as well.

By the time the trio took their seats inside, Theo knew he had every intention of keeping this extraordinary woman in his life.

Whatever it took.

Theo knew how dangerous Lucinda was, but it didn't stop him. There was something about her willowy figure, her long-legged mannish stride and her penetrating grey eyes that drew him in. He tried to unravel his reactions to her, but he failed, totally. And for some unfathomable reason, he never for a moment considered making her one of his victims, even while she slept. She was unique. The life-force in her had to be sacrosanct. He accepted it as fact; but he didn't understand it at all.

Theo and Lucinda met many times after that first encounter, but never again in the daytime. If Lucinda noticed, she never mentioned it.

Theo had been surprised to discover that she lived in a large apartment near the Moulin Rouge. Even in those pre-tourist days, the Boulevard de Clichy was always busy and very noisy. When he asked her about it, she dismissed his concerns. She liked the bustle, she told him, and loved the vibrant life that surrounded her, to be seen and heard and *felt* through her very pores.

The apartment itself was an oasis of calm elegance. Lucinda didn't indulge in the fashion for covering every available inch of surface with knick-knacks and curiosities. There were a few beautiful pieces of furniture, including a lacquered chest that she must have imported from Asia, and a Chinese screen, cunningly painted with lapis blue birds on a golden ground. Every piece was a work of art; and placed so as to be appreciated on its own merits. There were paintings on the walls, mostly modern, including a Renoir and two Picassos. Nothing by Modigliani, Theo noted. The paintings should have clashed with the older-style furniture but, somehow, it all looked right. As did the starkly simple Japanese flower arrangement that always decorated the table. For Theo, Lucinda's apartment was unique and special. As she was.

His visits tended to follow a pattern. They would start by exchanging Paris gossip and chatting about her travels. Both of them enjoyed that. Over the weeks, they had become increasingly intimate. She'd even confided, once, that she had an aristocratic great-aunt whom she visited every other year at Primly Court in England. Theo was intrigued. It sounded like a very grand country house. But Lucinda merely joked that Primly's nearest town had an even more absurd name – Little Piddling.

On their last day, there was no chat and no jokes. Lucinda's little French maid came in to offer him refreshments. Theo declined; as he always did. And Lucinda did not betray, by even the quirk of an eyebrow, how strange it was for a regular visitor to refuse the hospitality of her house. But nonetheless, she was nervous. She lit a Gitane with shaky fingers and drew the smoke deep into her lungs. The mellow scent of the tobacco quickly filled the room.

As soon as the maid left them, Lucinda stubbed out her cigarette. She went to Theo, put her arms round him and pulled him close.

That was unexpected.

This meeting was different. Theo recognised it. With a sense of foreboding.

She took his hand and led him across to the satin-covered chaise longue. She sat down unusually close to him, so close that he could feel the length of her strong leg muscles against his thigh, in spite of her petticoats. Then she dropped her head onto his shoulder for a moment.

One of her fair curls tickled his cheek. He gulped audibly and began to reach for her. But she pulled back and turned to face him.

"Theo, I have something to tell you. I have been putting it off, I must admit."

He raised an eyebrow but said nothing. He simply studied her face.

"I should have told you before. I am going off on my travels again. Soon."

He dropped his gaze and studied his fingernails for several seconds. "How soon?"

"Tomorrow."

"But you can't—" He stopped in mid-sentence. "May I ask where?" he managed at last.

"Canada. And America. I plan to explore the Rockies. I have read so much about them over the years. And now is the time."

"In winter?"

She shrugged. "I am not afraid of a little snow, Theo."

He laughed but there was no joy in it. "In Canada, I dare say you will meet more than a little of it. Several feet, I should have thought."

She shrugged again. "I can cope. But you, Theo?"

He wasn't sure what she meant. Was she hinting that he should accompany her? Or wondering how he would cope without her? The truth was that he knew he'd be lost. But going with her was equally impossible. No vampire could travel across the snowy, sunlit wastes of North America. Not without a willing accomplice. And Lucinda could never be that.

"I will miss you," he said. The words sounded utterly lame and inadequate in his own ears.

He sensed that she was too shrewd to ask him outright to go with her – or too proud to risk a refusal. "I am sorry, Theo," she said finally. "But this trip has been arranged for months – since before I met you, in fact – and I cannot change it now."

"I would not ask you to," he replied immediately, though it was a lie.

Perhaps he should confess to her, tell her what he was? He had a sudden, entrancing vision of the two of them together, sharing a future, as lovers, and as friends. For him, it would mean peace and an end to his solitary existence. The weeks with Lucinda had shown him that loving companionship might not be impossible, even for a vampire, and that his life did not have to be ruled by loneliness. For her, might it not mean the same? He had sensed from the start that she, too, was lonely, in spite of the social whirl that surrounded her.

His vision lasted for all of about three seconds. Lucinda was human. And mortal. She needed love – of course she did – but, for a human woman, real love could come only from another of her own kind, a lover to give her children and to cherish her as they grew old together. Lucinda deserved nothing less, but a vampire could provide neither of those things. And if she knew for certain he was a vampire, a monster, she was bound to recoil from him. With fear and even hate in her heart. Better for them to part altogether than to risk such an ugly end to their affair.

He rose to take his leave, with as much good grace as he could muster. He kissed her formally on both cheeks. He wished her the best of travels. And he strode to the door.

"Theo—" She followed him and seized his hand before he could wrench the door open. "Theo, do not leave me like this."

"I must."

Her eyes were full. A single tear began to slide down her cheek. He wiped it away with infinite gentleness. Then he raised her right hand to his lips and kissed it. "*Adieu*, Lucinda."

He never saw or heard from her again.

He told himself it had been the right thing to do. There couldn't be a relationship between a human and a vampire. Not even where there was love. Because a human would age and die, while a vampire remained the same.

Lucinda was in the prime of life, the toast of Belle Époque Paris, but she couldn't stay that way. Eventually, she would age. One day, she would die and the vibrant essence Theo had loved and treasured would be gone from his world.

It took him a long time to understand all that. Tormented, and miserable, he swore never to return to Paris. He resolved never to have feelings for another human being. And he kept those vows for more than a hundred years.

Until the day he gave in to his curiosity about Lucinda's Little Piddling.

And met Just William.

# Chapter Seven

Sylvie walked home very slowly, thinking about everything she'd heard.

William, trailing along at her side, was obviously doing the same. "I don't get it. Why didn't Theo just turn her into a vampire? Then they could've—"

"He told you why," Sylvie snapped. "More or less. At least, it was there if you read between the lines. But I suppose you're too young to understand."

"No, I'm not. I—"

"Quiet! I need to think." Sylvie did need some breathing space. Besides, she wasn't going to admit to her geeky little brother that she had no idea how to turn a human into a vampire.

"But—"

"*Zip it*, William. Or Dad might find out about you and your tree." She wouldn't really shop her brother but, as a threat, it seemed to do the trick.

He clamped his lips together, looking mulish. And he finally stopped talking.

Sylvie let out a long breath and tried to sort her thoughts. Theo was a vampire. Definitely a vampire. Those fangs hadn't come from a joke shop. They were the real deal – he'd said it himself. Vampires really did exist.

So Sylvie needed to get genned up on them. And on how they could be created. She would start by reading *Dracula*. She'd probably be able to download it to her phone. Not till the morning, though, since horror stories gave her bad dreams. Right now, she didn't want anything to remind her of the sight of those fangs.

She shivered.

She tried to concentrate on Theo's friendlier side instead. And how hot he looked – right up there with Chris Hemsworth and Robert Pattinson. Perhaps all vampires were drop-dead gorgeous? Theo had charm, too, oozing out of every pore. Well, he would, wouldn't he? What could be better for getting close to his victims? Close enough to do what vampires do.

Reading between the lines of his story, she was pretty sure Theo and Lucinda had been lovers. He'd let slip the word "affair". With luck, William hadn't twigged exactly what that meant, though her brother didn't usually miss much.

Theo had resisted his normal vampirish urges with Lucinda. No bloodsucking at all. How had he managed to do that? *Why* had he done that?

Had vampire Theo really fallen in love with a human female? Because of her courage? The whole thing sounded very strange. But then, Theo was strange. Uncanny, even. It sort of went with the territory.

Sylvie still couldn't get her head round the fact that she'd just spent an hour or so with a real live vampire.

Actually, no – with a real *undead* vampire.

She swallowed a nervous laugh. What was happening to her?

She looked down at William, trotting along beside her. And silent. Her brother was real. He was part of all this. So Theo must be real, too.

Poor Theo. He certainly still loved Lucinda, even though she must have been dead for at least fifty years by now. How sad was that? Crazy, too. But then, how could Sylvie tell what was crazy in a vampire's world? Vampires lived for ever, didn't they, unless someone put a stake through their heart? Maybe time was different if you knew you were never going to die.

Little Piddling had to be Theo's very last link to Lucinda. Was that why he'd decided to come here? To be close to the woman he'd loved and lost? It seemed the only possible explanation. But Sylvie knew that was not something that Theo would discuss with her. Or anyone, probably.

She parked that thought. She had a more urgent problem – her meeting with Karl, earlier. She still had to decide what to do about him. She'd been mega impressed by his vampire act, with the cool gear and the film-star looks and the smooth manners. His kissing wasn't an act, though. It was the real deal. It turned her knees to water.

None of her other boyfriends had kissed like Karl, but they'd all been much the same age as Sylvie. Whereas Karl was old enough to have been around. He knew all the famous actors in London. He even told stories about some of them. And he'd turned heads as soon as he appeared in Little Piddling. All Sylvie's friends fancied him rotten, but she'd been the one to pull him. He'd said she was the only girl in the place worth looking at.

She sighed again. It was all so difficult and she couldn't quite make up her mind about going to Whitby. She was very tempted. And she did like the kissing. But when he did his know-all, patronising bit, it made her want to kick him where it hurt. Next time, she might do it. It would serve him right.

She could see that one day she would have to dump him. And she would. Eventually.

Once she'd had a lot more of the kissing.

# Chapter Eight

Thursday night was my turn for the beach hut, so I wasn't expecting visitors. But then I saw that William was back again, racing across the sand to Number 23a. I was going to have to discourage him from doing his midnight stunt quite so regularly. A boy of his age needed his sleep. Without it, he might get ill and I didn't want to be responsible for that. Perhaps I could get Sylvie to have a word in his ear?

"Theo. Theo! I've seen the other vampire again." William was panting so much he could hardly get his words out.

"Doing his bat thing again, was he?" I said calmly, leaning nonchalantly against the beach hut. I wasn't about to go haring off after a fellow vampire who might not even exist. Besides, William needed time to catch his breath.

"No. No bats this time. But it *was* him."

"Are you sure?"

"Come on, Theo. It *must* have been the one I saw before. Can't be *three* vampires in piddling Little Piddling."

He did logic pretty well, for eight.

"Hmm. I suppose... Anyway, did you see his face this time?"

"Nope. Same problem. Big swirly cloak. Hat. Didn't want to get too close."

"Very sensible." If he *had* sighted another vampire, he needed to be careful. He'd made a friend of one, but two would be pushing his luck. "What was your other vampire doing, this time?"

"He was with a woman."

"Was he, now?" Was it significant that he'd said "woman" and not "girl"? Possibly. "And what were they doing, the vampire and this woman?"

"Um." William reddened a bit. "All that lovey-dovey stuff. You know?"

"I, er, I know." I paused. Discussing sex with a child can be difficult. "Are you sure it was only the lovey-dovey stuff? He wasn't taking a little blood on the side?"

"Oh. Um. I'm not sure. I suppose he *could* have been. He was, um, all over her."

I laughed. "We vampires don't generally do 'all over', William. We're rather partial to necks. Easiest access, you know?" He'd gone a tiny bit green, suddenly, but I didn't comment on that. "Any idea who the woman was?"

"Never seen her before. I think you'd have said she was quite a looker. Tall, thin – well, no, actually she was sort of rounded in places." He made a crude cupping gesture with both hands, something he'd probably copied from much older boys.

I let that pass. He was already embarrassed enough. "Colouring?"

"Light brown hair. Or maybe fair. Couldn't see very well 'cos the light was bad. Quite a lot of hair, anyway."

"Eyes?"

"Wasn't close enough to see."

"Did they just stand there, doing their lovey-dovey bit?"

"No, actually. After a while she took his hand and led him off."

"Any idea where to?"

"Dunno. Didn't dare to follow. They'd have seen me. To her place, maybe? Or his? He'll have a coffin about somewhere, won't he?"

"Possibly. But if she was doing the leading, they wouldn't be going there, I'd have thought."

He nodded.

As I said, he was good on logic, my young friend William.

"So what are we going to do now? Shouldn't we go out and hunt for them?" William was breathing normally now and very much up for the chase. Of course, he hadn't a clue what chasing a vampire might entail. Nor how dangerous it would be for a vulnerable human like him.

"You don't know where they went, William, so we'd have very little to go on." He looked so disappointed that, against my better judgement, I gave in and said, "But why don't you show me where you saw them? Maybe we might find some clues about who he is. Or even who his woman is."

"Oh, yes. I've got my torch so we can scour the ground for evidence." He took hold of my arm and tugged. "Come on. This way. Before the trail goes cold."

There wouldn't be a trail. I was absolutely sure of that. But I went anyway.

"I'm intrigued, William," I said as we walked briskly along the beach. "How do you recognise your vampires? I mean, you got it bang on with me, but what about the other one?"

"Well, the swirly cloak helps." He reached out and lifted one of the folds of mine before letting it drop again.

He seemed to be assuming that vampires always wore the classic gear. But we don't. Some vampires never wear it at all; and most of us like to ring the changes. In Paris, for example, I'd worn the same clothes as everyone else, so as not to stand out. William should have realised that but, for once, he didn't seem to have put two and two together.

It occurred to me then that there was at least one male wearing a long black cloak who was *not* a vampire. At least, I didn't think he was. To be honest, it had never occurred to me to check. But surely no bona fide vampire would be as much of a pillock as Sylvie's Karl?

On second thoughts, I'd known some vampires who were not all that bright. And if they were relatively new arrivals among the undead, they did sometimes take a while to learn the ropes.

I decided it wasn't the moment to put William right about what vampires wore. Instead, I said, "So anyone wearing a long swirly cloak is bound to be a vampire?"

William shook his head fiercely. "Course not. I'm not daft, Theo. You can hire gear like yours in the fancy-dress shop. They do lots of it at Halloween, you know."

"Fine. But you didn't answer my original question. How do you recognise a vampire, William?"

He hesitated. "Well, to be honest, I just do. A feeling, you know? Then I watch to see if I'm right. He did his bat thing, the first time, so it was a no-brainer."

His feeling, however it worked, had been spot on with me, too. He'd easily recognised me as a vampire. And I hadn't done the "bat thing" while he was around. Not at first, anyway. Just William definitely had hidden depths.

But something didn't smell quite right about this other so-called vampire, in spite of the "bat thing".

"OK, you were right the first time. The bat thing proves that. But this time? You saw a man in a swirly cloak. You assumed he was your other vampire. But was he? Couldn't he have been just a man in a swirly cloak? Dressing up?"

I expected an immediate denial. But William wasn't your average eight year-old. He thought about it for a good minute or so while we plodded along the road from the beach. "I'm pretty sure it was the same one. It was the hat, you see."

"What kind of hat was it? You never actually told me."

"A top hat. I've seen them on TV. Mum likes Fred and Ginger films, you see. *Top Hat*'s her favourite."

"Can't you hire top hats from your fancy-dress shop, too?"

"Well, yes. But it's how this guy wears it. Always at a cocky angle. And no matter what he does, the hat doesn't seem to fall off."

I didn't think that was a slam-dunk. If a top hat fitted well enough, it would always stay on. Mine does.

On the other hand, what chance is there that a top hat hired from a fancy-dress shop would actually fit well? William might be right after all.

Then again, William's other vampire sounded a lot like Sylvie's prat. In a hat.

Prat in a hat? That gave me an idea.

"You don't like Sylvie's boyfriend much, do you, William?"

He coloured a bit. "Don't know him. Sylvie hasn't let any of us near him."

"But you still don't like him?"

"Talking about him makes Sylvie go all gooey. It's gross." William made a disgusted face – pulled down lower lip, protruding bottom teeth, screwed-up cheeks and eyes. The whole nine yards, to coin a phrase.

I got the message. And I reckoned William was my man. "You'd like it if she dumped him, wouldn't you?"

He nodded. Then he went very quiet. Waiting. And looking expectantly at me.

I didn't ask him to explain why he was so anti – I wasn't sure he really knew, anyway – and I didn't want anything to put the kibosh on my plan. Like William, I was sure Sylvie would be much better off without lover-boy, but I also knew that she had to decide that for herself. She wouldn't take advice from anyone, not even a well-intentioned vampire. At the moment, she was all gooey about the pillock. So, what would make her ungooey?

I was pretty sure I knew. Well, it was obvious, wasn't it?

"William," I said slowly, "I've got an idea how to get Sylvie to dump the boyfriend. But I'd need you to tell Sylvie a story that isn't…um…exactly true. Not total lies, but not the whole truth either. Does she usually twig when you tell her porkies?"

"Depends."

"Well, if you did it right, you wouldn't have to tell her any actual lies. You'd have to tell the story a bit hesitantly, leaving gaps, letting her fill in the missing bits. If she jumped to the wrong conclusions, that wouldn't be your fault, would it? It might involve a bit of play-acting, though. Think you could do that?"

"Oh, I can do that." He smiled a conspirator's smile. I realised that he and Sylvie were even more alike than I'd thought. "I can be very convincing when I need to, you know. I worked it all out, years ago. You gaze up at them, open your eyes very wide—" he did exactly that, turning himself into an innocent and vulnerable little boy in the process "—and they melt. Believe every word you say, too."

That shook me up a bit. "Have you heard of a guy called Machiavelli, William?"

"Oh, yes. Haven't read him yet, though. He's a bit difficult for me." The innocent look had vanished in a split second.

I think I may have gasped.

William didn't pay any attention. He went on, blithely, "My technique works a treat. But I can't use it too often, of course. Mum might twig. And Sylvie certainly would."

"Oh. OK. Right." I tried to get my brain back in gear. It took a moment. "This is what I think you should tell Sylvie," I began. Then, looking down into his conspirator's eyes, I rejigged what I'd been going to say. "Nothing's set in stone, of course. If you've got a better idea, we can go with that. Feel free to suggest changes."

William nodded and smiled. Then he got impatient. "Come on, Theo. Give. What *is* this great plan of yours?"

# Chapter Nine

Sylvie had heard enough. She put her hands on her hips and scowled down at her little brother. "So what did she look like, this woman Karl was all over?" she demanded.

William swallowed and looked away. Sylvie almost felt sorry for him. He was embarrassed, talking about grown-up stuff like sex. But she needed to know what Karl was up to. And William was the only person who could tell her.

"Tall? Short? Fat? Thin?" she snapped. "You must know what you saw, William."

"Um, tall. Not fat. Blonde hair. Didn't see what colour her eyes were."

Sylvie swore. Then wished she hadn't. Not in front of William. But, honestly…! "A blonde, eh? Well, she'll make a fantastic Goth, won't she?"

Oops! She shouldn't have said that. But at least she hadn't mentioned Whitby. William would certainly have picked up on that.

William might not have noticed her slip. He was sidling towards the bedroom door.

"And don't you think of nipping down your tree to see Theo tonight, either," Sylvie said sharply, before he could creep out. "He'll be long gone. It's my night for the beach hut. I'm meeting Karl. And he'd better have a really good explanation." She ground her teeth. "Or else!"

When the door closed behind William, Sylvie slumped down on to her bed. If William's story was true – and why wouldn't it be? – Karl was cheating on Sylvie, taking her for an idiot. She wasn't having that. And she certainly wasn't going to be taken for a ride by a two-timing two-bit actor dressed up in fancy Goth gear.

She'd make him admit the truth.

And then she'd kick him. Hard.

When Karl arrived at Number 23a, he wasn't wearing his vampire kit. He was wearing tight jeans and a red T-shirt that clung enough to show off his biceps and his abs. He certainly kept himself in shape, but budding actors probably had no choice, she decided sourly.

She didn't think the sexy look was only for her. Probably any passing female would do. Especially if she was blonde.

"Nice abs, but aren't you cold in just that T-shirt?" He frowned at her. Good. She'd intended to get under his skin. "You'd be warmer in your black vampire gear. Like last night, hmm?"

"What d'you mean? I didn't see you last night."

"No, but William saw *you*. You were all over a blonde last night, he said. I can well believe it. It's what you do. You were all over me the other night, too."

He backed off a step and shook his head. "Not me, sweetie. Not with a blonde. Not my type." He shook his head again. Then he took a strand of her black hair between finger and thumb, stroking it lovingly. "I prefer brunettes. None of your bottle-blondes for me. Your little brother was seeing things."

"There's nothing wrong with his eyesight," Sylvie snapped. "He recognised you."

"Did he? Well, that's clever of him, because I was busy last night." He smiled down into Sylvie's eyes. "What made him think it was me?"

"He described you. The vampire kit. The top hat. The cocky angle you wear it at."

He chuckled. "Somebody else, darlin'. Maybe even a real vampire? You never know."

Sylvie swallowed. Could it have been Theo with the blonde? No. William would have recognised Theo. It must have been Karl.

"You weren't with me," she insisted. "So what were you so busy at? Hmm?" His story better be good.

"I was rehearsing."

"Ho, yus?"

"What do you think I'm doing here, in this piddling little hole? I'm an actor, remember?"

"So you say. But you never told me about any plays you'd been in, or films, or anything. Why should I believe you? Besides, Little Piddling doesn't have a theatre. The one on the pier won't be open until the tourist season."

"Huh. Don't know much about your own town, do you? Haven't you heard of Primly Court?"

"That's not in Little Piddling. It's miles away." It was a minor stately home, out in the country. Sylvie had never been there.

"Well, the City type who bought it fancies himself an actor. He's rebuilt its private theatre – no expense spared, but then he's stinking rich. He wants to put on plays, for a very select audience. And guess who's to be the star?"

Sylvie's eyebrows shot up. "You?"

"No chance. Himself, of course – Jacob Pringle-Coot."

She tried not to laugh. How could anyone have a name like Jacob Pringle-Coot? It was even worse than Sylvia.

"Anyway," Karl went on, "my job is to teach him to act. Or at least enough so he won't make a complete fool of himself when he puts his play on."

"What play?"

"I'll give you one guess. Long black cloak, top hat, fangs?"

"*Dracula*?" Sylvie gasped.

"Got it in one, sweetie. Where else did you think I'd got the gear from? Anyway, last night, I was giving acting lessons to my host, Jacob Pringle-Coot. So I couldn't have been shagging some passing blonde in the street in Little Piddling, could I?"

"Host? Are you staying there, at Primly Court?"

"Yup. Bed and board. Goes with the acting lessons. *Paid* acting lessons."

"And I suppose there aren't any slinky blondes lurking around?"

"Well, his wife is blonde. But she's nothing to look at. She's got a younger sister, though, who's tried it on a couple of times. But I've told you, blondes aren't my thing. I much prefer long-legged brunettes. Especially ones who kiss as well as you do."

He smiled a long, slow smile. Then he reached out and ran one finger along Sylvie's bottom lip, a caress so gentle she could barely feel it. It shivered all the way down to her toes. "You have the sexiest mouth, Isolde. And sometimes you don't use it half as well as you should." He pulled her into his arms. "Shall I show you what it's really for?"

Sylvie was having second thoughts even before she reached her front door. Karl had the gift of the gab. No doubt about it. And when he was kissing her, she couldn't think straight. He'd pretty much convinced her, back there in the beach hut.

But now she was on her own, she could see the flaws in his story. She hadn't mentioned that William had seen the couple in the street. But Karl had said "a blonde in the street". Coincidence? What's more, Karl had actually admitted there was a blonde at Primly who'd been trying to get off with him. Maybe she was the one he'd been with? As for the acting lessons, how would Sylvie ever know whether that was true or not? She couldn't very well present herself at the gates of Primly Court and demand answers from Jacob Pringle-Coot.

She was going to find out, though. If Karl was cheating on her, he was for the chop. The more she thought about it, the more doubts she had.

She locked the front door and climbed the stairs slowly, chewing at her bottom lip while she worked out a plan. By the time she was ready for bed, she had it sewn up.

She would text Karl to meet her at the beach tomorrow night. Really late, so he couldn't use rehearsals as an excuse. And surely he didn't give acting lessons on Saturdays anyway? She'd ask him to wear his vampire gear. She'd even tell him that it turned her on. That should do the trick! Flatter his outsize ego.

She chuckled. She was sure William wouldn't take much persuading to come down to the beach with her. Especially if she told him he was to be the key witness for an identity parade. He'd like that. Cops and robbers stuff. He could hide behind the beach hut until Karl arrived in his vampire gear. And then William would be able to say for sure whether it was Karl he had seen in the street with the obliging blonde.

Provided Karl bothered to turn up.

He might not. He didn't like it when he wasn't in control. If he thought his two-timing was going to be found out, he'd probably wimp out. He'd called her "a wimp" over Whitby, but she'd show him – she was nothing of the sort, even if he was. She'd tell him to his face he was dumped.

And then she'd kick him in the balls.

# Chapter Ten

I spent most of the next two days in the darkened beach hut, reading by torchlight. Pratchett again, as it happens. I was still trying to catch up on Just William.

The Discworld concept was interesting, though I recognised the myth about a turtle and elephants. Being the sharp little tyke he was, William probably knew where Pratchett had got the idea from. But if he didn't, I was going to have fun enlightening him about his hero's borrowings.

Pratchett's stuff about vampires was original, though. And about werewolves. I've known some werewolves in my time, but none of them was quite as sexy as Angua. Pratchett seemed to have decided that all the potential destroyers of humans should have their instincts damped down. Angua included. She had settled for chickens, it seemed. Well, that wasn't the way the universe worked, in my experience, but it obviously worked for Pratchett readers.

There might be something in the idea of black-ribboner vampires, I had to admit.

Vampires need blood. But it doesn't absolutely *have* to be fresh, or even human. Then again, getting it from a blood bank wouldn't be the same at all. That's what William suggested I do, when he sidled into the beach hut, not long after the sun went down.

I shook my head vehemently. "I may have sworn off you, William, but there's a limit to what a self-respecting vampire can tolerate. And blood banks is it!" He didn't seem impressed, so I tried to explain. "Think of it like being a coffee lover," I began.

He started to protest that he didn't like coffee – well, boys of his age don't, normally – but I was getting into my stride on this, so I kept on talking. "You want your coffee fresh and hot, with a zinging aroma that makes your taste buds stand on end, jostling to be first to savour the Arabica hit. You wouldn't want your favourite drink defrosted, after months in the freezer, would you? No aroma there. No real punch. A bland, unnatural beverage that could be anything. Certainly not the real deal." I put my book down and began to pace.

"The same is true for us vampires. We want it fresh. From humans. And alive. We want it so that our taste buds lap it up – fresh, and warm, and luscious." I gestured at the Pratchett book. It had the female werewolf on the front cover. "And I don't think a quick suck through a mouthful of chicken feathers would be in the same class, either. Not for a vampire. Not even for a werewolf."

William didn't say anything. He was staring at me. Not scared exactly, but certainly a bit more wary than before.

"Look, William." I crouched down so that I wouldn't be towering over him any more. I didn't want him frightened. "However good your precious Pratchett's jokes – and I'll admit I did chuckle at some of them – he clearly didn't know any vampires very well, or he'd have come up with a different solution to his fang dilemma."

"What solution?" William asked quietly.

Trust clever-clogs to put his finger on my weak spot.

"Um. I'll need to get back to you on that."

He relaxed then. "You know what, Theo? You may be a real vampire, but you're a right old softie underneath."

Now that's not the sort of description to endear a small boy to a vampire. I bared my fangs at him.

But I'd promised. And the little blighter knew I wouldn't break my word. He winked at me and made for the door. "I came to tell you that our plan's working, at last. Sylvie didn't dump the prat last night – he must have talked her round – but she's having second thoughts now. She's told him to meet her here again tonight, wearing his vampire kit."

I was tempted to remind William that tonight was my turn for the beach hut, but I didn't. If Sylvie was so fired up about Karl that she'd forgotten our agreement, I wasn't going to interfere.

"She wants me here, too," William went on, "watching from behind the beach hut. So I can identify him. If I say it was lover-boy I saw with the blonde – and I will – she's going to dump him on the spot." He grinned wickedly. "And I really, really hope she kicks him where it hurts."

He opened the door a crack and slid out. "See ya later, chicken-hater."

I threw the book at him. It bounced uselessly off the closing door.

It was after half-past midnight when Sylvie arrived at Number 23a. William was already there. He and I had been talking over our plan for more than an hour. This had to be the night when the prat in the hat got the boot.

Literally, we both hoped.

"Oh, hi, Theo." Sylvie gave me a half-smile. She looked a bit anxious suddenly. "What are you doing here? William's the only witness I need."

I managed not to smile, though I couldn't resist the chance to tease her. "Actually, tonight's my turn for the beach hut, Isolde. You had it last night, remember?"

The moonlight was pretty dim but I could see that she was now blushing slightly.

"Don't worry," I said quickly. "I do understand. I'll keep well out of the way." I was a bit sorry for her. She was young and vulnerable and hypersensitive. And she'd been humiliated by a smooth-talking rat. It was probably bad enough that her clever little brother knew she'd been taken for a ride. Of course she didn't want to broadcast it to anyone else.

William and I went round the side of the beach hut, with William in front so he could peek round the corner as soon as the prat started along the beach. Sylvie stood on the duckboards, waiting. She tried leaning nonchalantly against the door, but it didn't last long. She was too tense. She kept going to the other side of the hut, looking up towards the road in case he came that way.

"He's coming," she whispered after about five minutes. "Along the beach."

William leaned forward and peered round the corner. "Yes. That's him," he hissed instantly. "That's the guy I saw with the blonde."

I thought he'd overdone it there. He hadn't taken enough time to look. No one could identify a man that quickly, at that distance, especially when the light was so bad. Would Sylvie work out that William was lying to her?

She didn't. The sound she made in her throat – a bit like a dog's growl – proved that she'd abandoned thinking altogether. She was reacting on pure instinct. And fury was driving her.

She ran along the beach to confront him.

We couldn't resist. We came out to watch.

Even from a distance, we heard what she called him. None of it fit for William's ears. "And you're dumped!" she finished triumphantly.

"Yes!" That was William, of course. He was bouncing up and down, eager to see what his sister would do next. She was so wound up that anything might happen.

Karl had stopped dead. If he said anything, we were too far away to hear.

And then Sylvie attacked him.

"Get him, Sylvie!"

William yelled it. I thought it.

She landed a couple of good kicks. Karl didn't seem to flinch. It was as if he were made of solid granite. Oh-oh. That wasn't how our plan was supposed to pan out. Was Karl a fighter, too?

At my side, William gasped. "Theo, that's not Karl. That's the other vampire."

Seeing a human trying to fight off a vampire was a revelation to me. Sylvie was really good. She was trying all her kick-boxing moves and she was even managing to land a few blows. But the vampire was toying with her. He was definitely pulling his punches. I wondered how long it would be before he got bored and starting punching in earnest.

Sylvie wouldn't have a chance, of course. Not against vampire strength.

That was a pity. But there was nothing I could do. It's not done for vampires to fight each other. I had to stand and watch. Or leave.

I hadn't allowed for William. He grabbed my arm and pulled hard. "Do something, Theo! He's going to kill Sylvie. Stop him!"

"Can't interfere, William. Not allowed. Sorry."

"Yes, you can. You have to. You promised she'd be safe. You promised! You can't break your word."

The little tyke was right. And I was screwed. Vampire law forbids killing fellow vampires. But it's big on honour, too. A vampire's word, once given, must be kept. I sighed. I was in trouble, whichever way I jumped.

With William nagging and pulling on my arm, the scales were being tipped in Sylvie's favour. I would have to weigh in. To fight.

Not to kill. Killing was forbidden.

I'd got almost within striking distance when Sylvie aimed a flying kick at the vampire's head. It connected. And the vampire's top hat flew off. A mane of fair hair tumbled out.

The vampire – a female, clearly – gave a shout of outrage. She didn't stop to push the hair back from her face. She simply felled Sylvie with a single blow.

Sylvie slumped in a heap at my feet. Was I too late to save her?

Before I could move, William dashed forward and flung himself over his sister's body. So now I had him to protect, as well. Great.

I rounded on the vampire. I was angry now, too. "Back off," I yelled. "She's under my protection." I bent to check on Sylvie.

"Is she, indeed?" said a voice from under all that hair. It sounded familiar. I must have met this vampire before.

"Yes. I gave my word she'd be safe. You know as well as I do how much that counts."

She didn't speak. She didn't move, either.

Sylvie groaned. She was starting to come round. So it hadn't been a death-blow after all. She would recover. "William, get your sister out of here. This *lady* and I have things to discuss. Vampire things. In private."

For once, he didn't argue. He pulled his sister to her feet and half-dragged, half-carried her back towards the beach hut. It looked weird, since he was so much smaller than she was, but he managed her weight incredibly well. There were clearly more muscles in that skinny body than I had suspected. Or maybe adrenaline was working miracles on them.

I turned back to my opponent. "Do I know you?" I asked. If we were going to fight a duel, we had to do the honours first. Vampire etiquette is strict.

"Oh yes, I think so." She pushed aside her mane of hair and turned so that I could see her face. And she smiled. "You are looking as handsome as ever, Theo."

*Lucinda?*

# Chapter Eleven

I don't remember exactly what happened on the beach after that. I probably stood stock still for ages. I know that I couldn't stop staring at Lucinda. A result of the shock? Possibly. Even vampire strength has trouble dealing with something that momentous.

I had rediscovered the lover I'd been mourning for over a century.

Lucinda was patient, and kind, though she did insist on going back to the beach hut, to avoid prying eyes. But she'd forgotten about William and Sylvie. We found them huddled in the far corner, gaping at us as if we'd grown horns.

By then, my body was working fine, but my brain still seemed to be stuck in neutral. Everything was really hazy. And questions were crowding in on me.

Eventually, I began to think straight again. There was only one question that mattered, I realised. How had Lucinda come to be in Little Piddling?

The answer was obvious enough, though it took me a while to get my head round it, partly because I didn't want to admit the truth to myself. Lucinda had become a vampire – somehow – and was now part of the assembly of the undead. As I was.

But when? And how? I had been so determined that I would *not* turn her from the light and the vibrancy of life, even though it meant I'd been condemned to lose her.

Someone else – one of my kind – must have had fewer scruples.

"Lucinda. I don't believe this. Is it you?" I probably still looked as shocked as I felt.

"*You're* Lucinda?" Sylvie pushed herself up and stomped across to us. She'd clearly recovered quickly. No surprise there. Sylvie was tough. "*You're* Theo's Lucinda?"

"Yes," Lucinda said simply. "And, in case you have any remaining doubts, I am a vampire, too."

Sylvie shook her head. She wasn't cowed any more. She was seething. "I don't understand what's going on. William said he'd seen Karl on Thursday night – in his vampire gear, with a blonde. Did William get it wrong? Were you the vampire he saw?"

"In a way. I did have an encounter with your young man, Sylvie."

"He's *not* my young man."

"Really? Very well. If you say so." Lucinda shrugged. "It is of no moment. Whatever he may be to you, he was easy prey for me. Very easy, in fact."

Sylvie snorted. "So if that was *you*, in the cloak and hat, where was Karl? And who was the blonde?"

Lucinda chuckled. "You do not understand much about vampires, do you, my dear? *I* was the blonde. I was dressed in ordinary clothes. It was your Karl who was wearing the cloak and hat. He probably thinks a Dracula costume makes him irresistible to females. And perhaps it does?" She raised an eyebrow at Sylvie.

Sylvie swallowed and looked away. There was a slight reddening on her neck.

"We will not pursue that," Lucinda went on, more gently. "Let us simply say that I took him to a place of seclusion. He *imagines* we had sex there. His fantasy, of course. I took what I wanted from him and he remembers none of it. Human males like Karl go along for the ride so easily, I find. And then they forget where it has taken them."

Sylvie squared her shoulders again. "He told me he was at Primly Court on Thursday night, giving acting lessons to the owner," she protested.

"Oh, he was. Earlier on."

"How do you know?" Sylvie demanded suspiciously.

"Did Theo ever mention bats at all, Sylvie?"

"Ugh. Gross."

"To you, perhaps, but useful to me. Primly Court has been my daytime roost for weeks. My great-aunt promised I would always be welcome there, you see. So I have had plenty of opportunities to watch Karl at his play-acting, though he has never noticed me. One tiny bat is not at all conspicuous." Her mouth quirked into a knowing smile. "I had only visited Little Piddling once so far this year – no need when there are lots of humans around Primly Court – but I was curious about Karl and his nocturnal wanderings. So I followed him down here on Thursday. He was clearly in search of new female company. I suspect he was even prepared to pay, but in the end there was no need. He had a late-night encounter with an obliging blonde. Me. I assume he lied to you about that, when he met you last night?"

Sylvie swore.

From his corner, William chuckled wickedly. "And he didn't even have the guts to turn up tonight and face you," he said. "Wasn't he supposed to be here? Wearing his fancy vampire gear?"

From Sylvie's expression, she didn't want to be reminded of any of that. "I was going to tell him to his face what I thought of him. And that he was dumped."

In fact, she had done so. To the wrong vampire.

"Very commendable," Lucinda murmured. "No more than he deserves, perhaps?"

"Too right. And he *is* going to get dumped. Now." She pulled out her phone and started stabbing at the screen.

I slumped down on the bench and laughed. Oh, yes. Dumped by text message. I really, really liked that.

"That girl. That human girl. Sylvie. You said she was under your protection. What does she mean to you, Theo?"

There had been a hint of friction between Lucinda and Sylvie earlier. And now that Sylvie was fully recovered and both she and William had gone home, Lucinda was going to insist on hearing the truth. Was she jealous, perhaps? I hoped so.

I told her everything that had happened. It was mostly about William. And about how he'd conned me into protecting the rest of his family. Lucinda asked a couple of questions, but in the end she nodded, satisfied. Why would she not be? She knew what she and I had meant to each other. And she'd seen me with Sylvie. No comparison at all.

Sitting on the bench beside me, she stroked my face and smiled into my eyes. "We have found each other again, Theo. And we have all the time in the world now."

"But—"

"Shhh. You have told me about your human friends. So it is my turn. And I can see that I have a lot of explaining to do. I could do it now, if you want?" When I nodded, she touched her lips to my cheek.

I sighed and closed my eyes. This was happiness as I had never experienced it before.

She began softly. "I came back to Paris, after Canada, to look for you. I was going to confess that I suspected what you were. To be honest, I had guessed almost from the first. I visited Transylvania early on in my travels, you see, and so I understood a little about vampires. It could not stop me loving you, though I only discovered how much once I was high in the Rockies and alone again. By the time I got back to Paris, no one knew where you were."

She sighed. "I spent a small fortune on enquiry agents but it was a total waste of effort. You had disappeared completely. I suspect that was what you intended?"

I nodded again. I couldn't speak. And I didn't want to open my eyes.

"I was in despair at having lost you, Theo. And very, very lonely. Because of that – it is no excuse, I admit – I did something unforgivable." She dropped her voice almost to a whisper. "I am ashamed to tell you that I began to model for a man called Jean-Claude Gratton. He fancied himself a great painter, but I soon realised he had very little talent. Once I began, I could not abandon him, though. Not when he saw me as his muse." She stopped and swallowed hard.

"Since I am trying to be honest with you, Theo, I should confess that modelling for him also helped to fill the void in my life. And I liked him, though I could never love him. Later, I learned that he was dying of heart disease. I pitied him then – he was so desperate to keep on painting and he could not bear the thought that he would never finish all the great works that he knew were in him. Ha! 'Great works', indeed!

"Someone must have told him about Transylvania. I have no idea who. *I* certainly did not tell him anything. He immediately rushed off east in search of the solution to his problem. And he came back a vampire, of course."

I straightened and opened my eyes.

I needed to be able to read her face when she talked about Jean-Claude, the vampire.

"He was exultant," Lucinda said. "He would live – and paint – for ever." Her shoulders slumped and she shook her head sadly. "Poor Jean-Claude. He had failed to grasp that he would have to give up the light."

"So this Jean-Claude made you as you are? You wanted it, too?"

"No. Not without you, Theo. Jean-Claude did it without my consent, to keep me exactly as I was. He insisted on painting me over and over again. He was obsessed with creating the one great portrait."

"Did he?"

"No. And in the end, being a painter, he could not exist without the light. He kept venturing outside to look, to see the world, in spite of the burning pain it caused him. One day – one bright, fierce, sunny day, in the first year of the Great War – he went outside again, glorying in the light and the colour and the pain. I heard him in the garden – he was singing – but when the sound stopped, he failed to come back inside. He had turned to mist. And the harsh sun melted him to nothing."

All vampires know what sunlight will do to them. Jean-Claude could not have been ignorant of the risks he was running. He must have willed his own end.

"Can you forgive me for betraying you, Theo?"

"Can you forgive me for abandoning you, Lucinda?" I replied without even pausing to draw breath.

We were silent for several minutes after that.

I think we both knew we were equally guilty. Recriminations would achieve nothing, for either of us.

"What happened to your portraits?" My jealousy had melted away, but I was curious to judge the man's talent for myself.

"I burned them. They were not great art. Barely even mediocre, if I am honest. Besides, I wanted nothing to remind me of Jean-Claude. I knew what a mistake I had made there." She paused. "I try to forget him, but I am reminded of him every day because of what he made me. Could *you* not have done it for me, Theo? We could have been together for all these years." There was grief and longing in her voice.

I responded with the whole truth. From my heart. "No. No, I couldn't. Because for me you *were* the light, the sunshine, the colour – the whole human world. I couldn't take that away from you. I knew you needed love in the light. The kind of love that could only come from a living, human man." I shook my head sadly. I had been so very sure. Back then. Had I been wrong? "I thought that, if I left you, you would find that love. And happiness. And children. That you and your lover would grow old together."

Lucinda laughed softly. "How much you thought you knew me, Theo, and how little you did. It was you that I loved. And love still, even a century on. I was no artist. The light was not vital to me. I have had decades to discover that."

Oh. More than a century wasted. I'd been such a fool. And Lucinda had suffered so much, because of my arrogant belief that I

282

knew best. "Where have you been all this time, love? I never heard Lucinda Grayson mentioned by others of our kind."

She was relaxing now. She even smiled. "In Paris, to begin with. I could not be as I was before, of course, enjoying Paris society from dawn till dusk. And a vampire, lurking in the gloom, is no real artist's muse, either. I kept myself hidden. When the war ended, I started travelling again. Carefully. To be honest, I was looking for you, Theo, though I never once admitted it, even to myself. England – here – was my only remaining link to human life, so I continued to visit fairly often. I still came, even after my great-aunt died. Dear Little Piddling. The name always amused me. And even more, once they added *sur Merde*." She gave a peal of silvery laughter. "So very appropriate, do you not agree, my love?"

I had recovered now. I pulled her into my arms and began to kiss her, exploring her luscious mouth. She responded eagerly. We took a very long time over it, delighting in being together at last. Well, why not? We had over a hundred missed years to make up for.

I did answer her question. A long time later. "Since Little Piddling has helped us find each other again, it seems unfair to condemn it. Even if the name does make us laugh. Shall we make a donation so that the town can have a new stone erected? Designed so that it's impossible to add that naughty *de* at the end? Hmm?"

She chuckled at my rather pathetic joke. "Good idea. It would be a way of saying *thank you*. Though not until we are long gone, I think."

"Long gone?"

"Little Piddling is too small a town to house *two* vampires for long, Theo. We might start a panic here, and that would be unkind. Especially when Little Piddling has brought us back together." Her beautiful grey eyes were gleaming with mischief.

I could read that look. "You've got a better idea, haven't you, Lucinda?"

She nodded. "We need a big city. A place where we can explore delightful surroundings—" she grinned wickedly "—and each other. London is not nearly romantic enough for what I have in mind. Shall we begin in Paris?"

"Paris? For a new start?"

*"Oui, mon amour. À Paris, tout peut recommencer."*

**THE END**

## *About Joanna Maitland*

Joanna Maitland has published 13 Regency historicals with Harlequin Mills & Boon since 2000. She is also an independently-published author—of Regencies, timeslip, speculative fiction (as KC Abbott) and more—and one of the founding partners of Libertà Books where she blogs around twice a month. She lives in the romantic Marcher country on the Welsh border, where a large pollen-filled garden and her hay fever battle it out.
You can find out more about Joanna and her books on her website, libertabooks.com/joanna

### *Want Joanna's latest book?*
You can get Joanna's latest book, and find earlier ones you may have missed at books2read.com/JoannaMaitland
where you'll also be able to follow Joanna for her latest releases

# GRAPES AND ALE
*by Louise Allen*

# Chapter One

The view should have been soothing—the blue sea, the waves creaming on the expanse of firm sand that was not yet warm from the early morning sun, the swoop of gulls scavenging at the tideline. The same sand drew the holidaymakers to Little Piddling in droves, although not at seven o'clock on a breezy morning in May. Now the beach was deserted, which was why Jac came to the hut as soon as she had gulped down the first mug of tea.

Tranquillity was not helping, she decided, flipping over another page in the battered ledger. Her brain felt like the contents of a mash tun and she was in danger of forgetting everything she had painfully learnt about brewing.

She had put down the last penny of her savings, her legacy from an unexpectedly well-off great-aunt, plus the sale of her Brighton flat to buy Little Piddling's Bascombe Brewery and the top floor apartment in what had been the brewer's house next door. Now she was broke and coming to the painful realisation that twelve years in the hospitality industry did not necessarily give a girl the skills to rescue a business that was going down the drain—literally—for want of a decent product.

The trippers might come into the Brewery Tap, buy a pint of Prime Piddle beer just for the name and for the Instagram post of them downing a liquid that was suggestively pale yellow, but one was enough. More than enough. The locals wouldn't touch the stuff with a bargepole and did their drinking in The Jolly Mariner where they could sample an array of big brand beers, watch sports TV and scoff tastily greasy pub grub.

The firm of administrators who had organised the distress sale of the bankrupt brewery must have been ecstatic when they saw Jacintha Francis heading their way. She had thought she was buying it cheap—they couldn't believe their luck.

She made herself study the ledger again. Last night, when she had found it in the back of a dusty cupboard in the brewery office, she had been too tired to more than flick through. Now she found the recipe for Prime Piddle in the same distinctive sloping handwriting of Bertram Bascombe that she recognised from the deeds. He had founded the brewery in 1885 and vanished mysteriously in May 1899, leaving a crumbling business behind him. Somehow it had limped on with a succession of optimistic owners for one hundred and twenty years but, unless she could find a way to rescue it, this was the end of the line.

"Ouch!" Jac sucked at the paper cut as she squinted at the ledger—one sheet had been sliced out, leaving a sharp edge in the gutter. Beyond it, the final page with any writing on it simply read, *The bastard. The bastard. The bastard. This is the end.*

There was a thump, a sharp smell of the sea, a shower of water droplets on the page and beside her stood a man. A stark naked man, dripping wet. They stared at each other, then—

"You pervert! Get out of my hut! I'm calling the police."

"Madam, remove yourself from my bathing hut this instant!"

"Your *what*?" Jac's hand froze over her phone. She recognised him, which was, of course, quite impossible.

The man looked around, water spraying from his hair with the jerky movements. "What is this? What have you done with my hut?"

He was forty-ish, lanky with a little pot belly, overlong wet hair slicked back and a handsome, if bony, face decorated with flourishing, bushy sideburns. He was very familiar indeed, although Jac had never seen him wearing anything but a cutaway coat, striped trousers, a four-in-hand tie and a top hat. His portrait hung in the Brewery Tap and she had polished the glass on it only yesterday, buffing up the gilt plaque at the bottom of the frame that read: *The Founder*.

"Mr Bascombe?" Jac grabbed a towel from the hook beside her and thrust it at him. "Take this."

He snatched the towel and swathed it around himself which was, Jac considered, a considerable improvement. Her heart was pounding and it wasn't from the sight of far too much goose-pimpled male skin.

With the towel securely wound around his waist, Bascombe stabbed a finger at the ledger. "What are you doing with that? It is mine. You stole the recipe. You..." He subsided like a soufflé in a draught. "But you cannot have done. It had been cut out when I left home this morning."

"Um... Sit down, why don't you? Have another towel," Jac added as he sank onto one of the cushioned benches along the side of the hut. "I know this sounds ridiculous, but are you a ghost?"

"Certainly not." He looked affronted. "I am not dead yet!"

"You are now; this is the twenty-first century." From the way his face whitened, telling him that so abruptly had been tactless and unkind. "You must be a time-traveller," she amended, wondering at how calm she sounded. Shock, presumably. *Delirium, fever...*

"H. G. Wells," he exclaimed. "*The Time Machine.* A fascinating book, but I had never realised it was possible."

Jac reviewed what she had drunk last night. Not enough, it had seemed at the time, and certainly insufficient to account for hallucinating a naked Victorian time-traveller this morning. She pinched herself. Yes, definitely awake. "What year is it in your time?"

"Eighteen ninety-nine. The twentieth of May."

That was when he had disappeared, wasn't it? Exactly to the day. Hell, was she about to be stuck with a displaced Victorian brewer? Although he could be useful. Very useful. Which was a selfish way of looking at it, she scolded herself. The poor man must be as shocked as she was. More so.

"I'm sure you'll get back in a moment," she soothed. "Meanwhile, what has been cut out of here?"

"The recipe for Piddling Perfection." He almost moaned the name. "Franklin Outram, my brewmaster, invented it and had it refined to a pitch of perfection. He wrote down the recipe only on Saturday after we tried the first cask. It was brilliant. Nectar. The finest beer I have ever tasted. Naturally, we could make no more then, it being the Sabbath the next day, but Outram noted it all down, all the special ingredients, all the timings. Then he dropped dead coming out of church after the morning service. Then on Monday—this morning—when I opened the recipe ledger, the page had been cut out."

"And you wrote that?" Jac pointed at the furious scrawl.

"Yes," he admitted, blushing. Of course, Victorian gentlemen did not swear in front of ladies.

"Who did it? Do you know?"

"Dastard!" he cried, leaping to his feet, unfortunately scattering towels as he did so. "Dastard! But he is too..."

He vanished with a *pop* and a shower of droplets.

"Oh, bugger." Jac picked up the towels, which were damp. There were wet footprints on the nasty vinyl flooring that she couldn't afford to replace. The door was still firmly closed. Mr Bascombe had been real and, unless there was such a thing as a soggy ghost, he had travelled from the past and, presumably, had now returned there to vanish for ever more.

"Poor man. I wonder who the dastard was who robbed him. What a sweetie—even under so much stress he couldn't bring himself to say *bastard* to a woman." Jac eyed the ledger that had once contained the recipe for the finest beer Mr Bascombe had ever tasted. It might not have been that wonderful if he was used to producing Prime Piddle, but it had obviously been an improvement.

With a sigh she rolled up the damp towels, stuck the ledger in her tote and went out, locking the hut behind her with a glance up at the pole she had fixed above the door, wilting greenery twined around it. The Hop Pole, the name she had chosen for the hut which had come with the brewery, was the sign that a fresh brew was in the ale house.

All it needed was the local Trading Standards inspector to decide that Prime Piddle wasn't beer within the meaning of the Act and everything would go down the tubes before she had the new name plate painted for the hut door.

They'd come up with a replacement soon, Jac told herself as she trudged through loose sand on the boardwalk to the steps up to the Promenade. Andy Gregg, her brewmaster, might not be very experienced, but he was keen. Could she tell him about Bertram Bascombe? No. He'd think she had cracked under the strain, had been hallucinating.

*Why don't I think that myself?* she wondered, crossing the Promenade at an angle and then turning up Brewery Lane to the Square, with a wave to Pete who was cleaning the fish and chip shop windows.

It was not as though she believed in ghosts or aliens or time travel. Although that might be why, Jac reasoned as she went through the passageway at the side of Brewery House. *I'm not predisposed to believe this stuff, so it must have been totally convincing on a rational basis.* Did that make it any less weird? No, although at least she'd managed to reassure herself that she wasn't losing it entirely.

She dug out her key to the back door that had once been the kitchen entrance of the old house. The conversion had been sensitively done with the minimum of partitioning and she had her own front door right at the top of what had been the servants' stair at the back of the house. Henry Dumaine, who occupied the ground and first floors, used the original front door, but for safety reasons there were fire doors between the back stairs and the main house at each level. They were secure, soundproofed, and she was rarely aware that someone else was in the house.

And that was good, because Henry Dumaine owned Dumaine's Wine Bar right across the square.

The shiny, attractive, modern, buzzy wine bar that only made the poor old Brewery Tap look even sadder and emptier in contrast.

"Bah humbug," Jac muttered as she stood on the top stair and juggled the keyring in an attempt to find her front door key which was, of course, wedged in with the keys for the beach hut, back door and brewery.

"Hi."

Jac yelped, dropped the roll of towels and the tote. The ledger fell out on her foot, she yelped again as she turned and it slid down half a dozen stairs to land at the feet of the man who stood looking up at her.

"Sorry, didn't mean to startle you." Henry Dumaine, of course. Not a burglar, just six feet of expensively casual male with an over-assertive nose, boring mouse-brown hair and a killer pair of blue eyes. Oh yes, and a smug smile. "I brought you this." He brandished a bottle of white wine in one hand as he stooped to pick up the ledger with the other. "Your keys are on the next step down."

"Why?" Jac demanded, grabbing the towels. *At least this one has his clothes on.*

"Because that's where they landed when you dropped them, just after you screamed for the first time." He came up another step.

"I did not scream, I yelped in shock and pain. Why are you on my stairs bringing me wine? And what is wrong with the perfectly good bell on my front door?"

"I saw you come in and doing it this way saved you the walk down again." He smiled, altogether too charmingly. "The fire door creaks, I thought you'd have heard it."

"I had something on my mind." Jac scooped up the keys, decided that a passably good-looking man bearing wine was probably better than having a quiet attack of the heebie-jeebies by herself, and opened the door. "Come in. It's a bit early in the day for me, but don't let me stop you if you need it." She waved a hand towards the bottle as he passed her.

That got her a narrow-eyed look. "It's more than just something on your mind. You look as though you've had a shock."

"Yes, someone creeping up behind me on the stairs." She went into the galley kitchen that opened onto the living room and filled the kettle. "Tea or coffee, Mr Dumaine?"

"Henry, for heaven's sake. Is it decent coffee?" He took the packet she thrust at him with one hand as she reached for the cafetière with the other. "Yeah, coffee, please. Black and one. What's this?"

"Nothing."

Henry perched on a bar stool on the other side of the island and opened the book. "The old brewery ledger? This is great. What's the date?"

"Eighteen nineties." She wanted to snatch it away but poured the coffee with a steady hand instead, then slid his along to him.

"What happened here?" He'd flipped through to the cut page.

"That's the last thing that Bertram Bascombe wrote before he disappeared." Henry looked up and she found herself telling him. "Someone stole the recipe for a fabulous new beer, Piddling Perfection. The brewmaster wrote it down, then had a heart attack or something the next day. Bascombe found the recipe was gone before he had a chance to study it. Then he went for a swim and vanished."

"Drowned? Suicide?"

"No one knows. I don't think there was a note."

"Poor guy." Henry ran his fingertips over the scrawled swear words. "Strange. I wonder…" He looked up again sharply. "How do you know all this if the recipe's gone and Bascombe left no note?"

"I—er—guessed. Pieced it together." Jac gulped coffee.

"Really? Down to knowing what this fabulous beer was going to be called? And working it out left you pale and jumpy at eight o'clock in the morning?"

"If I told you, you wouldn't believe me."

"Try me."

"Do you believe in ghosts? Or time travel?"

"No and no. Nor alien invaders, nor that the earth is flat."

"Exactly what I think. But… Look, I wanted some peace and quiet to think about—about stuff. And I wanted to read this ledger. So I took it down to my beach hut early this morning. And I'd just found the cut page the hard way." She held up her paper-sliced finger, still with a blood smear. "And then Bertram turned up."

Henry opened his mouth. Shut it. Drank some more coffee. "As in, Bertram Bascombe, brewer, deceased?"

"He wasn't deceased, he was very clear about that. He was stark naked, dripping wet and very indignant that some strange woman was in his bathing hut."

"Do you often hallucinate naked men? Wet, naked men?" There was an interested glint in Henry's eye that she didn't trust.

"Not as a matter of routine, no. Not ones with a small pot belly and side-whiskers at any rate. I gave him a towel. He told me that this was May the twentieth, eighteen ninety-nine. Then he saw the ledger, forgot about me intruding in his bathing hut and went off on a rant about what had happened to the recipe for Piddling Perfection. When he got really agitated, he vanished."

"Have you ever considered writing fiction? Scripts for TV? The producers of *Doctor Who* would love you."

Jac slammed down her mug, then shifted the ledger away quickly when the coffee slopped out. "Look—look there. Do you think I'd take the trouble to drip water on the page just in case my neighbour ambushes me on my stairs and I decide to spin him a yarn?"

Henry narrowed his eyes at her, then sniffed at the page, rubbed his right index fingertip on the biggest splash, still damp. He licked it. "Salt."

"Exactly. Cunning of me to traipse down to the sea, which is a fair way given that the tide's out, just to add verisimilitude to my fantasy by sprinkling the book with salt water."

"OK. I'll buy it for now. You saw something, or you genuinely believe you did. And I like a mystery. Piddling Perfection, you say? This town's name really is the gift that goes on giving, isn't it?" He pushed the wine bottle towards her. "The first release of wine from my new vineyard. I wanted to celebrate with a neighbour."

Jac tilted the bottle to read the label. *Dandelion Vineyard. Petit Piddling Grand Reserve 2018.* It was a relief to think about something that didn't involve dead men and lousy beer. The label was elegant with a faintly Edwardian flavour to it and a stylised dandelion in the bottom left corner. "Dandelion?"

"*Pissenlit* in French," Henry said, straight-faced.

"Pis… Literally *piddle in bed*? That's truly awful."

"Couldn't resist," he admitted.

"I hadn't realised the vineyard was productive yet." She wasn't going to give him the satisfaction of smiling at his dual-language pun.

"Very productive, that south-facing slope is perfect. But it takes a while to mature the wine from that first harvest, to experiment, to get it just right. My ancestor bought the land when he came here as an émigré during the French Revolutionary Terror at the end of the eighteenth century. My grandfather planted the vines, but my father wasn't so interested. It has taken time to get it to this stage."

"But how do you know about it? What to do? I know you have the family wine business, but that's selling the stuff, not growing it. I know about selling it, serving it, but I wouldn't be able to make it."

"After uni, I studied in Alsace, then New Zealand and one of the Sussex wineries."

"All good places for cooler temperature wine-making."

"Exactly."

"Congratulations." She wanted to be pleased for him, but the smile was an effort.

"I had the vines, the tradition, the training. You haven't any of those for brewing, have you? It must be tough. You need an experienced brewmaster."

It took no effort to let the smile slip. "Thank you for mansplaining that to me. I have the one I can afford. Andy might not be experienced, but he's keen, he's creative, he knows good beer when he tastes it, and he's a friend."

"And cheap?"

"And cheap," Jac admitted. "Look, thanks for the wine and for not assuming I was out of my mind, but Andy will be arriving soon so we can work on the latest experimental brew and I want to see what I can find online about Bertram."

"I'll help." Henry stood up, stretched. "You know, the best place to start would be the local newspaper. Hard copy, though."

"What, the *Piddling Post*? That's just a 'what's on' handout, isn't it? We've got some in the bar that the Tourist Info people drop off. Adverts and vouchers and snippets about the new zebra foals at Piddling Magna zoo."

"It used to be a decent broadsheet newspaper until the seventies. I found a few old copies when we cleared my grandfather's place and it was the real thing, packed with local news. But the back issues haven't been digitised. I checked, because I wanted to see what I could find about my nineteenth-century ancestors, thought if anyone had made the headlines it might make an amusing piece to put up in the wine bar. I couldn't find anything online, went along to the office and they told me they'd got a storeroom full of the back issues." He shrugged. "I didn't have the time to wade through them, so I left it." He tapped one finger on the ledger. "We could go and look now."

"You've got time now? Being so busy." It was hard to keep the jeer out of her voice. The jealousy. He'd got a flourishing business, an exciting new winery and she was slowly sinking. Even if she and Andy came up with a decent brew, she still didn't have enough cash—or credit—to turn The Tap into an attractive pub.

"Nothing much on, it's the quietest day at Dumaine's. I can take it off; the staff can manage."

"Well… But I've got to spend at least an hour with Andy."

"Meet you at the brewery at half-ten?"

"OK. Yes. Thanks."

Jac closed the door behind him, listened to the sound of his feet as he ran down the stairs, the creak and thump of the fire door opening and closing.

Henry Dumaine was attractive, intelligent, nice enough not to fall about laughing at her story. It was ridiculous to wonder what his motives were in agreeing to help with her mystery. He probably simply enjoyed that kind of thing.

*Or he finds me attractive, intelligent…* That theory lasted as long as a confrontation with the bedroom mirror: blonde hair doing a passable imitation of a haystack thanks to a stiff sea breeze, sloppy old hoodie, just the wrong shade of blue for her eyes—eyes with nice dark shadows under them. Jac made a dive for the hairbrush.

# Chapter Two

"The summer wheat beer is coming on. Close, I think." Andy offered her a glass of rather cloudy pale-gold liquid. "Still needs tweaking," he added when Jac sipped, made a *maybe, maybe not* rocking gesture with her free hand.

"You're right. It is close. Refreshing, but needs a bit more bite, more citrus."

"The winter-warmer dark style is better this batch, I reckon." He offered another glass, this time a rich mahogany.

"Colour's good." Jac took another mouthful. "Chewy but not very… I don't know… memorable. Are we aiming for a Strong Old Ale style with this?"

"Yeah." Andy scowled at the cask he'd tapped for the sample. "Not malty enough for that yet, though. No chocolate or fruit in there, either."

"We've got time to get the heavy beer right and a month, perhaps, for the wheat beer, but what we need right now is a good Best Bitter, something to replace Prime Piddle, or I'm going to have to buy beer in, which I can barely afford at the same time as buying all the supplies to keep experimenting."

"And it's hardly the Brewery Tap if we don't serve our own beer," Andy said mournfully. "We could keep on serving Prime— the tourists like it."

"The tourists find it amusing. There's a difference. Look, I've got the ghost of a lead on something better, but it means digging in the archives at the *Post*. You OK if I go along there this morning? I'll be back for the lunchtime stampede."

The sarcasm left Andy even more hangdog. The *stampede* would be a trickle, easily manageable by Jac alone behind the bar, and they both knew it. "I'll check stocks now," he offered. "Then get back to reading up on Best Bitters." He turned to walk back to the old gleaming coppers, his shoulders straightening as he went, as though they gave him confidence.

Henry was waiting when she left through the brewery office door. He had one shoulder propped against the wall, his eyes narrowed critically on the front of his wine bar across the square. "Needs more planters," he muttered as Jac joined him. "More typically French. Bay trees in small Versailles tubs, do you think?"

"My knowledge of French gardening is restricted to the fact that they plant acres of pelargoniums and their parks have the kind of sandy gravel that gets between your toes when you're wearing sandals. Oh, and that loopy green metal stuff round the edges of the lawns." She fell into step beside him as he cut through the alleyway into the maze of small streets behind the promenade.

"How's it going with the brewery generally?" he asked. "Besides trying to find some new brews, I mean. Haven't had time to wander over to the Tap during opening hours yet."

It could just be friendly interest, one local businessperson to another.

"OK. Just some teething problems, lots to do all at once."

Or it could be a business rival snooping, because that was what Henry was and the rivalry was all one-sided. *At the moment. I'll get there.*

"You OK? You walked right past the office."

"Oh. Thinking." Jac turned and walked back, peered at the narrow shopfront. "They're open."

"I know. I checked."

"Of course you did, Mr Efficient Businessman," Jac muttered as she followed him in, trying not to think about what a truly excellent bum he'd got in those faded old blue jeans. That white linen shirt looked good, too. French? "Sorry?"

"What dates do we want to look at?" Henry asked with exaggerated patience.

The lad behind the counter, who was surely not old enough to be out without his mum, fiddled with a piercing in his upper lip that looked painfully inflamed and waited. He seemed moderately alert. Perhaps a trip into the vaults was light relief.

"Um. First of April eighteen ninety-nine to the end of May nineteen hundred, please."

"Down here." He rummaged in a drawer, took out a key and led the way through an office with three desks jammed in, each with a slightly dated PC, some filing cabinets, a sink with a stack of mugs. A woman was opening a vast brown box.

"Morning."

"They want the old stuff, Mo."

"Archives. Oldest at the back. There's a table in there somewhere." She went back to rummaging. Clearly no one was going to rush into the *Piddling Post* crying, "Hold the presses!"

"Don't smoke in there!" she shouted as the door closed behind them.

The back room was lit with fluorescent tubes and stuffed with metal industrial shelving loaded with bundles of newspapers tied up with tape. The lad wandered out again as Henry forged through to the back, clambering over some discarded office chairs and a box marked *Christmas*.

"Aagh!"

"What? Are you hurt?" Jac tried to find a way through the maze.

"No, just picked up a mouse-sized spider. This time travel thing may be spreading—it's probably from the Jurassic. Here we are. Nineteen hundred."

They finally settled opposite each other at the table, Jac working forward from the first of April eighteen ninety-nine and Henry going backwards from the end of May, a year later. The paper came out weekly on a Wednesday so, as she expected, she found something in the first edition after the twentieth of May, which had been a Monday.

Under a grainy photo of the brewery, the headline read: *Concern Grows For Respected Local Businessman.*

"May twenty-second. They say he has not been seen since the night of the nineteenth," Jac said. "The housemaid—looks as though there was a cook-housekeeper and a maid living in—found his bed slept in on the morning of the twentieth and assumed he had gone for an early-morning swim as was his habit from the beginning of May. He did not return for breakfast and Cook asked at the brewery, but no one had seen him there. When he was still not home at midday, she called for the Constable and he searched Bascombe's bathing hut, which was the one I now own. It says the PC found his clothes, his watch and his card case and some cash amounting to three pounds and seven shillings. There was no note. A tragic accident is feared."

"They'd be careful not to suggest anything else in those days," Henry said.

"What—murder?"

"Suicide, which would be far more scandalous than murder. Failing business, perhaps?"

"It wasn't failing until he disappeared," Jac protested. "And someone stole that recipe. That hardly sounds like a harmless prank."

"There is no other brewery in town. Piddling Magna doesn't have one, either. Who would have it in for him? A disgruntled Prime Piddle drinker?"

"What did...? No, never mind." She could hardly ask Henry exactly what form his ancestor's business took in those days. A wine merchant shouldn't have been in direct competition with a brewer, but what if wealthy Mr Dumaine had decided to branch out? She turned to the next week's issue.

"He's front page news now. Look." She moved the paper so Henry could see the picture of Bertram Bascombe with the headline in large type under it: *Have You Seen This Man?*

"They searched the house and the brewery and the Tap and found nothing. No note. The brewery manager is reported as saying that Bascombe had seemed a little distracted the previous week, but that there were no financial difficulties and he envisaged no problems continuing to run the business under the supervision of Mr Bascombe's solicitors until his return."

"It is beginning to sound like a straightforward accidental drowning," Henry said. "Poor devil. But he was probably alone on the beach that early in the day, and the sea is still cold at this time of year. If he got cramp or was caught in a rip, there'd be no one to help him."

"Let's keep going; we might find a report of a body being washed up."

"Here's something." Henry jabbed a finger at a column. "It is understood, with the approach of the anniversary of the tragic disappearance of Mr Bertram Bascombe, that his solicitors will announce that, although he is still missing, they will not be applying to the courts for an Assumption of Death notice and intend to keep the business running until the seven years has elapsed before death may legally be assumed. Mr Bascombe leaves only a cousin in Australia who approves of this approach and is reported to be praying for his relative's safe return."

"They couldn't continue to run the business if his assets were frozen, so they wouldn't risk that," Jac said. "The law is different now. I suppose that, without an owner at the helm, it began to go downhill and the Aussie cousin sold it after the seven years were up. I'll just see if there's anything in the next few issues."

They found nothing more about the Bascombe disappearance and advertisements for Bascombe's Beers continued to be run. Then, a month later, at the end of June, Jac spotted another name.

"Here's something about your family in the Society column. *The return of Mrs Dumaine to the town after her sojourn in the Swiss Alps has been greeted with great pleasure by all persons in Society. Mrs Dumaine's energy and leadership in all aspects of Little Piddling's social and charitable life have been sadly missed.*

Henry counted on his fingers. "I think that's my two times, no, three times great grandmother. My grandfather's grandmother. There was socking great oil painting of her in my grandparents' dining room that I inherited—all pompadour hair, fierce corseting, strings of pearls and an impressive bosom. Quite a looker in the style of the time."

"I wonder what she was doing in the Alps for a stay that was long enough for her to be missed to that extent," Jac said.

"Could just be creeping on the part of the newspaper—what an important person you are, don't forget to give us the guest list for your next dinner party, sort of thing."

"Very upper-class Edwardian, swanning off to the Alps for your hols. She wasn't one of Edward VII's mistresses, was she?"

Henry snorted. "Not unless the family's been keeping it very quiet. She didn't bring any souvenirs back from Switzerland, which is odd, now I think about it. My grandparents' house was full of everything from tiger-skin rugs to hideous Venetian glass chandeliers from various travels down the generations. We've even got an elephant's foot umbrella stand, of all the ghastly things. But no cuckoo clocks or carved wooden bears."

"You certainly can't miss a cuckoo clock," Jac said vaguely, flicking back through the newspapers, looking at the Society columns. "Here she is leaving. Middle of April. *The ladies of the Piddling sur Mer Waifs and Orphans Relief Committee wished their President, Mrs Dumaine, bon voyage for her forthcoming journey to the spa of St Moritz where it is hoped she will rapidly recover her health and bloom.* So she left because she was unwell, not because she wanted to trip through the Alpine meadows in search of lonely cowherds and a spot of yodelling."

"She may have been after some yodelling, as you put it," Henry said, with a grin that did something disturbing to the base of Jac's spine. "The word in the family is that she was a bit of a goer in her time, although I've never heard anything to substantiate it. Could just be the general Edwardian naughtiness that the Prince of Wales embodied, and all that happened was that she flirted with the Mayor or goosed the Town Clerk at some civic reception after a glass or two of wine."

They carried on working through the papers with an occasional sneeze, the discovery of some advertisements for the brewery and for Dumaine's *High Class Wines and Spirits,* and several long-dead spiders.

Jac finished her pile first and found herself watching Henry's fingers turning the crumbling pages. Long fingers, a signet ring with what looked like a bird rising out of long grass, or rushes, on his left hand.

"It's a phoenix," Henry said, flipping over the last page. "On the ring."

"Oh, sorry, didn't mean to be nosy."

He shrugged. "No problem. It's a bit bling, I admit, and my father won't wear it, so Grandfather gave it to me. Apparently my French ancestor adopted it after arriving in England to symbolize the family rising from the ashes."

They replaced the papers on the shelf, dusted themselves down and went out. Henry dropped some coins in the charity collecting box on the counter by way of payment, as none had been asked.

"Fancy having lunch at Dumaine's? On me—I want to celebrate the new wine."

"Um... Yes, thank you, I would like that. But I need to check on Andy, see if he minds manning the bar." She really ought to stop feeling so suspicious of Henry. There was no reason to and what she was experiencing was probably just good old-fashioned jealousy. Henry had a flourishing business, his winery was taking off— thanks to his hard work and studying—and she was a cow to be resentful. What on earth would he want the brewery or the Tap for? Neither was the slightest threat to him.

Andy was more than happy to polish glasses behind the bar. It was just coming up to half-twelve when Henry opened the door of his wine bar for her and already more than half the tables were occupied. He waved at the person behind the bar and made for a small table set in the angle of the wall with a Reserved label on it.

"The owner's table, best view in the house," he said, pulling out a chair for her. "What do you think?"

"I like it," Jac said honestly. The big room had pale wood floors and wood panelling painted aqua covered three quarters of the walls, with chalk white plaster above. The tables had crisp white cloths, the long, curving bar was a deeper honey tone than the floor, and the art work scattered throughout on walls and shelves was a quirky mix of semi-abstract landscapes and obviously old pieces.

The staff were very French-waiter, in black trousers and waistcoats, large white wrap-around aprons, white shirts and black ties. One, a skinny redhead, came and gave them menus and a drinks list, came back with a carafe of water, grinned at Henry and shot off to another table to clear it.

"The new late Spring menu," Henry said, frowning at the card. "What do you think of the dandelion?" he pointed to the same motif she'd seen on the wine label. "I was thinking like this: just opening, for Spring, fully open for Summer, a dandelion clock for Autumn and the rosette of leaves for winter."

"Good," Jac decided. "Really crisp and fresh line drawing; and clearly related to your wine branding. Who is the artist?"

"A designer called Rose Redmayne. She set up recently in Piddling Magna with an actual shop—she was working online up to then. All kinds of interiors stuff, upcycled furniture and so forth, alongside her design work. She's got a beach hut down here, I think.

"She did the interior here *and* your wine label? I'm impressed."

"I had a go myself first off, fancied myself a bit of an artist, but I know my limitations."

And it was becoming harder and harder to be suspicious of the man, Jac thought, studying the menu. She wasn't even sure why she had felt suspicious in the first place; it was just some niggling little instinct telling her there was more to Henry Dumaine than met the eye.

She gave herself a mental shake and made a decision, about lunch, at least. "I think I'll have the baked crab and green salad. That should go well with your new wine."

"I'll join you." Henry waved at the redhead who came over, pulling a pad and pencil from one of his waistcoat pockets. Clearly Henry was going for old-school methods.

They ordered and the waiter brought the wine over immediately.

"So where are we?" Jac asked, taking a sip. "Oh yes, this really is good. Not much further forward, really. We know Bertram's disappearance was a surprise to everyone and, unless people were being exceedingly discreet, no one suspected suicide."

"It doesn't mean it wasn't," Henry pointed out. "It's pretty scary, the number of times you hear about people who are in absolute despair and who manage to hide it."

"Don't forget I met him just before he vanished," Jac pointed out. "He was furious and jumpy but he wasn't depressed or despairing as far as I could see."

"Yes, well, he'd been dead for over a hundred years when you encountered him," Henry began.

The waiter, who was just putting their plates on the table, recoiled. He shot off and came back warily with salad, then a basket of crusty bread and some unsalted butter. "Is there anything else I can get you?" he asked with a sideways look at his boss, clearly expecting an exorcist to arrive at any moment.

"No, thanks, Jim."

Jac waited until he had retreated to a safe distance. "I can't see why that would make a difference. Anyway, he wasn't dead in his reality, nor in mine, come to that." She took a mouthful of the crab, which had been baked in the shell with cheese and breadcrumbs, and gave a whimper of pleasure. "God, that's good. I vote against it being suicide. So that leaves murder, accident, kidnap or deliberate disappearance."

"Unless we imagine the distant cousin in Australia organising his disappearance, I can't imagine who'd want him gone. And as the Australian didn't put in an appearance and claim the inheritance, then that is vanishingly unlikely."

"Rabid teetotallers?" Jac suggested. "Although I'm sure they were, and are, law-abiding and even if they weren't, surely they'd smite him with tightly rolled copies of the Pledge, or lecture him to death, rather than make him mysteriously vanish."

She grinned at Henry, inviting him to share the ludicrous idea, but he was staring back at her, with no sign of a smile. Something in his expression made her grope for the wine bottle.

It seemed he had the same impulse. Their fingers brushed, stilled, locked together.

Henry broke the silence. "Like to come up and see my family portraits?"

"Love to," Jac said lightly. "Thought for a moment you were going to mention etchings."

But Henry was already on his feet, his fingers still entwined with hers. He waved to Jim the waiter, then made for the door at a gratifyingly brisk stride.

LOUISE ALLEN

"You have been driving me insane for weeks," he remarked conversationally, as they crossed Brewery Square.

"I have?" Jac did her best not to pant. She needed to because of the pace, of course, nothing to do with lust…

"But every time I saw you, you glared."

"I did?"

"And I couldn't think of an excuse until we were packing the first consignment of the wine and I realised it would be only neighbourly to take you a sample. And then you screamed."

"Well, sort of."

They'd reached the front door of Brewery House. Henry fumbled with his keys.

"And I didn't mean to glare, I was preoccupied. I just didn't see you, I expect." *Liar.*

Henry unlocked the door with a vicious jerk of his wrist. "Right."

"But I'm seeing you now," Jac said as the door slammed behind them.

"Is that a *yes*?" Henry was already half out of his shirt.

"That's a yes."

# Chapter Three

The front door was a solid piece of Victorian carpentry and thank goodness for that, Jac thought, half an hour later. The door mat was an equally solid piece of coir matting and, between that and the panelling on the door, she suspected that her back, her bum and various other bits of her anatomy bore interesting impressions from what had just occurred.

And thank goodness for men who carried condoms in their pocket. "But we haven't…" she'd managed, with what was left of her common sense after five minutes of pressed-to-the-door kissing.

Henry had rummaged in the discarded clothing and produced a foil packet. "Been living in hope," he said.

After that, very little conversation had taken place.

She prodded him in the ribs. "Hoping to breathe here."

"Ough. Sorry." Henry rolled off and gave a faint yelp as he landed on the original, cold, red and blue floor tiles.

"Nothing to apologise for." And he really hadn't. That had been… Jac's brain failed to come up with a word and just carried on fizzing gently.

Henry hauled himself to his feet, pulled on his jeans and held out one hand. "Tea? Coffee?"

*Bed?* Jac's libido said hopefully and, given that she suspected her entire central nervous system was fused by overload, with wild optimism.

"Coffee." She took his hand and staggered up, blinked at the crumpled clothing around her feet and wondered vaguely where her underwear had ended up.

Henry reached up and removed her bra from the antler-encrusted hall stand, then pointed to where a pair of regrettably sensible white pants hung off the door knob. "I'll put the kettle on," he said and headed down the hall to the end, the rest of his clothing under one arm.

He was dressed by the time she joined him and the kettle was making encouraging noises.

"The front door mat was not where I intended making love to you," he said, apparently intent on spooning coffee into the

307

cafetière. He was clearly unimpressed by celeb endorsements for more quick and convenient methods of coffee making.

He sounded cool and casual, but Jac noticed that the tips of his ears were pink, which was endearing. She did a startled double take. *Endearing* was not a word she'd have ever imagined using about Henry. Hot, yes. Infuriatingly competent, yes. Superior, yes. Suspicious, yes.

"You had been planning this for some time?" she said, trying for cool too, distracted by the fact that he had expensive knobbly brown sugar lumps. *See, even his sugar is superior.* "I have to say, I didn't miss the bed. Didn't notice its absence, to be frank."

He looked up, his sudden smug male grin somehow endearing, too. "Since I saw you up a ladder in dungarees fixing hanging baskets a month ago."

"*Dungarees*?" Surely the least erotic garment known to woman, short of a Mr Bunnykins onesie.

"I found myself imagining taking them off," he admitted. "And then you became a challenge."

"So I'm just a notch on your bedpost—I mean, doorpost—am I?"

"No!" Henry protested, clearly aware that he had narrowly missed being disembowelled with sugar tongs.

*Sugar tongs? Who has sugar tongs? Someone who's inherited grandparents' antiques, that's who. Rich people.*

"I was hoping for something a bit less one-night-standish." He had the sense to move away and get the coffee mugs. "I thought you looked interesting. Brave, too, taking on the brewery."

He'd managed to say that without sounding patronising, Jac decided, mellowing again. *Brave* was probably a tactful substitute for *insane,* but if that was what he thought, he was probably right.

"I found myself liking you," she admitted. "Somewhere about July 1899. I admire a man who can admit he's frightened of spiders and I have to own up to admiring the rear view going into the newspaper offices. Oh, and I like the way you've decorated the wine bar. I could never fancy a guy who is all black and chrome or has bicycles hanging everywhere."

"Bicycles?" Henry dropped a third sugar lump into his coffee, apparently without realising.

"Six months in London with a hipster. I gave up when I couldn't stand the beard-trimmings in the basin every morning and the gear-oil drips."

"Ah. I promise not to grow a beard and I fall off bikes." He took a gulp of coffee, looked startled, went to pour it away and make fresh. "And I can't take much credit for the design at Dumaine's. I told you about the interior designer from Piddling Magna, didn't I? I knew what I didn't want, but couldn't explain what I did, so I kept sending her Pinterest stuff and waved my hands about a lot and she came up with that."

Jac wasn't too sure she quite believed that. Now she'd had time to look around the kitchen, she liked the way old and new, efficient and interesting, had been combined. There was a back door which must be the one next to what was now her own front door and another with an emergency crash bar and notices about fire doors and not obstructing.

"Can I see the rest of the house?"

"Sure, top up your coffee." He led the way up the two steps back to the hall. "The original formal sitting room is at the front this side and the dining room's opposite. I only really use those when I'm entertaining. The old study is my office." He opened another door behind the dining room and Jac saw a vast old desk with some very new IT on top and shelves of books and files.

"Then there's what must have been a breakfast room at the back. I use that as my snug. It's got the TV. And I had a downstairs loo put under the stairs." He nodded towards what Jac had imagined was the cellar entrance.

"Four bedrooms?"

"Yes. Originally they all had dressing rooms; I had those converted into shower rooms so everything's *en suite*."

"Flash."

"I have two sisters. When the family comes to stay, that's not flash so much as essential."

"So where's the cellar door?" Jac wondered out loud, trying to visualise the overall plan.

"You've got that, surely? I assumed it was in your share of the back garden."

"No. I thought you'd got it. So who owns it then?"

"Whoever's got the door, I guess," Henry said. "It wasn't on my deeds."

"Or mine. Perhaps there isn't one."

"Odd if there isn't, in a house of this period." He shrugged. "Come and meet Hermione, my three times great grandmother, she of the Piddling sur Mer Waifs and Orphans Relief Committee."

Hermione hung in splendour over the fireplace in the dining room. At first glance, she looked like a typical Edwardian matron, corseted to within an inch of her life, stern and upright. Jac went closer and studied her face.

"You know, I think the rumours might have been right. I think she was a bit of a party girl, Hermione. Pretty too, under it all. And look at the glint in her eye. I wonder if the artist had tight trousers."

"You are right. Those are definitely come-to-the-chaise, if not come-to-bed eyes. And that mouth has a sort of pout to it. If you want to see why she might be ogling artists in tight trousers, turn around and see her husband."

"D'A George Albert Cornelius Dumaine," Jac read. "He looks as though he'd rant about the immoral lower classes, insist on attending church three times on Sunday and pinch the parlour maids, if not worse." She went to peer more closely at him. "And I wouldn't want to get on the wrong side of him. If Hermione was off to Switzerland for some extramarital yodelling with a strapping goatherd, I wouldn't blame her in the slightest. I realise that he's your esteemed ancestor and so on, but doesn't he put people off their dinner?"

"Oddly, no. I think he has an 'eat, drink and be merry or you'll end up like me' effect. Do you want to see the bedrooms?"

"Is that an offer to admire the shower fittings or another opportunity to study your etchings?"

"The latter." Henry sent her a heavy-lidded, smouldering look.

"In that case, lead the way, Mr Dumaine."

What a difference a month makes, Jac thought, giving the bar in The Brewery Tap a quick polish after serving six pints of the new wheat beer to some earnest real ale enthusiasts who were making appreciative noises and talking about clarity and citrus top notes at the corner table.

Andy had come up trumps with the wheat beer and he was making great strides with a pale ale and an alcoholic ginger beer which were both selling well, although he was still tweaking the recipes.

At his suggestion, Jac had set up an A-sign on the pavement outside advertising "Are you a Piddler? The Notorious Prime Piddle here! We challenge you to finish a pint."

That was bringing in the punters and an art school mate of Andy's had created an end-of-the-pier-style backdrop of jolly Edwardian drinkers and buxom bathers at the back of the room for the brave Piddlers to take selfies against. By the time they had had fun with that, an encouraging number were ordering something more drinkable, plus a sandwich from the selection that Andy was knocking up in the miniscule kitchen.

Jac and Henry were no further forward with the Mystery of the Vanishing Brewer as Henry liked to call it, but whenever they got together to talk about it, a discussion of historical research turned into something else altogether.

Living so close and yet completely separately had its advantages, Jac concluded. They had less opportunity to get on each other's nerves than if they were cohabiting, the freedom to stumble about bleary-eyed and bed-haired in the morning without a man underfoot was welcome and yet there was only a fire door and a few stairs between them.

"What can I get you?" Jac smiled at the curvy brunette with the freckles who was leaning on the bar and studying the portrait of Bertram Bascombe with surprising intensity. How old was she? Eighteen or nineteen, Jac guessed, and she hardly looked the type to be fascinated by Edwardian brewers.

"What? Oh, sorry. Is that a wheat beer? I'll have a pint and some nuts please. The mixed ones." She waited until Jac had drawn the pint and yanked the packet of nuts from the card hanging behind the bar and put them both in front of her, then held out a ten pound note. "Thanks. Is that Bertram Bascombe?"

"It is."

"I thought it had to be, but I couldn't be certain because of the side-whiskers. They're quite something, aren't they?"

"They're magnificent, although you could keep squirrels in them." Jac felt a shiver run down her spine. "You know Bertram?"

"Well, not personally." The girl gave a hoot of laughter that made Jac grin back. *If only she knew…*

"But look." She pushed her phone across the bar.

The sepia photograph was of a clean-shaven man in his late forties, quite clearly Bertram, despite the absence of whiskers. "That's my—hang on, I have to do this on my fingers—my great, great, great, great grandfather Basil Bonfield."

"Then he didn't drown. I am so relieved." Jac pressed the bell for Andy and pulled herself a pint. "Let's go and get more comfortable outside."

They found a table behind a tub of flowers and sat down. "Tell me what you know about him," Jac urged. "It has been driving us distracted, but we couldn't find any more clues to follow up."

"Us?"

"Yes. Hang on, I'll just call Henry. No, there he is." She waved as Henry came out of the wine bar and straightened the stand with the menus on it. He waved back, then sauntered over when she made sweeping *come here* gestures.

"This is Henry Dumaine who owns the wine bar opposite. He knows about Bertram's disappearance. Henry, this is—sorry, I don't your name."

"Tamsin Pascoe. I'm from St Mary's on the Isles of Scilly. Bertram, or Basil, rather, is my four-times great grandfather."

"Wait, I need a drink." Henry vanished inside the Tap and came out two minutes later with a pint in his hand. "Right, go on."

"My grandmother died a month ago. It was rotten, she was only sixty-two but... Anyway, Grandpops went last year so I had to help Mum clear out the cottage. It's the family one next to our pub." She rummaged in her bag, found a tissue, blew her nose while Jac and Henry pretended great interest in the clarity of their beer.

"Sorry. The thing is, the family's always been hoarders and the place was jammed with stuff. We're keeping it on, though, the cottage I mean. I'm going to live there with my fiancé. I'm rambling, you don't need to hear all this." She took a deep breath, a gulp of her beer. "The point is, we found a locked tin box in the attic. It was thick with dust, didn't look as though it had been opened in years. We had to break the lock in the end. But the great thing is, it solved the mystery of where Basil Bonfield had come from."

"I thought we were taking about Bascombe," Henry said.

"Well, that's it. You see, in St Mary's, we all knew the story about how one of the fishing boats came in with this man they'd picked up off the coast, miles from here. He was clinging to some driftwood and they thought he was dead at first, but they hauled him in anyway and it turned out he was alive. Stark naked, no papers, said he'd forgotten where he was from or his name. So they brought him back to St Mary's and took him to the inn my ancestors ran.

"To cut a long story short, he recovered but said he had no idea of who he was, what he was. He decided to call himself Basil Bonfield, fell in love with the innkeeper's daughter, who was the man's only child, and married her. Eventually they took over the pub and that, as far as we knew, was that."

"So what was in the box?" Jac was almost on the edge of her seat.

"A letter, *To Whom It May Concern*, saying that he had never actually lost his memory. He was really a brewer called Bertram Bascombe and he came from Little Piddling and that he'd been swept out to sea while distracted because of a hopeless love and he couldn't ever go back because it was doomed and he was in fear of his life from the woman's husband. But he wanted the truth known after his death. The trouble was, he locked the box and tucked it away so safely that no one found it, or if they did, they didn't realise it was important. It had been in the loft ever since."

"Bloody hell," Jac said. "It must have happened right after I—I mean, he must have gone down for his usual swim, which explains why he was naked—men didn't always wear bathing suits in those days and Bertram certainly didn't, we have—er—proof of that."

"Have I got any relatives here, do you know?" Tamsin asked.

"Sorry, no. He wasn't married and when he disappeared his nearest relative was in Australia. They declared Bertram dead after seven years and the brewery was sold. Oh hell." She glanced at Henry, aghast. "Does that mean you own the brewery, Tamsin? If he wasn't dead—"

"Goodness, no," Tamsin protested. "No, no, I didn't come here on a property grab, honestly. If Bertram stayed missing voluntarily, then in my book he made the decision to give up everything in his old life. The brewery was inherited and then sold and bought in good faith. If he had wanted to, he could have contacted his solicitor and given him instructions, without revealing where he was.

"No, I just came because we were curious and I was hoping for some long-lost cousins. And to find out more about the mystery woman in his life."

"You mean the one with the potentially homicidal husband?" Henry said. "I feel another rummage through the newspaper archives coming on."

"How would that help?" Jac quibbled. "With Bertram gone, he'd have just gone back to brooding jealously."

"He might have murdered his wife or divorced her," Tamsin suggested. "Or the poor woman might have committed suicide."

"Divorce was pretty difficult and seriously scandalous," Henry said. "But mysterious deaths after Bertram vanished might be worth looking for."

"Parish registers," Tamsin said. "I can check those online. The nonconformist chapels as well, I've got a sub to one of the family history sites. Oh, and I can check coroners' reports, I think." She dug in her bag and came up with a tablet. "I'll have a sandwich or something for lunch and do it now."

"I spent all morning in the kitchens tasting for the new menu," Henry said. "I'm stuffed, so I'll go and try the newspaper office. Jac?"

"Er—no, sorry. I've just thought of something I absolutely must do and I'm starving, so I'll grab a sandwich, get it done and then I'll ring you to see how you're getting on. OK?"

"OK." Henry stood up, lean and distractingly sexy in the sunshine.

The thought of forgetting the sandwich, ignoring the nagging little idea and seeing what wickedness they could get up to in the newspaper vaults had its attractions. Jac told herself to be strong: they still had one of Henry's bedrooms, two of his shower rooms and all of her apartment to try out first.

"I'll tell Andy at the bar that whatever you want is on the house," she told Tamsin. "Where are you staying?"

"Thanks. I'm at the Plumtree Guest House just behind the Jubilee Gardens. I'm going up to London tomorrow to see an aunt."

"Come to dinner tonight and we'll pool our findings," Jac said. "My door's round the back of that red brick house there. Just go in and climb right to the top. Sevenish?"

She went through to the bar, told Andy about Tamsin, grabbed two cheese and pickle sandwiches and a bag of crisps and went over to Brewery House. It had an attic, a dusty, dark space that she'd never explored other than to sweep the bit nearest to the hatch to store her empty suitcases. If Bertram had hidden one important document in a box in an attic, he might have hidden others.

# Chapter Four

The company that had sold the brewery after it had run gently into the ground had owned the house too and had employed a builder to do the conversion. They'd made a good job of it, largely because they hadn't wanted to do any more than they had to. The roof had been mended, the wiring replaced, two separate heating, water and electricity supplies run in and the fire doors installed. A lick of paint and a rather basic kitchen and bathroom in the top apartment and that was it.

Henry had done a great deal more to the rest of the house, but all Jac's time and money had gone into the brewery and, even though things were now a fraction easier, clearing out the attic had been low on her list of priorities for the apartment.

Now she unhooked the hatch with the pole, hooked down the loft ladder and climbed up. The light switch just by the hatch worked, although two feeble bulbs merely produced an effect that Hammer Horror films would have appreciated. Her torch, however, was large, powerful and swept the space like a lighthouse beam, revealing piles of boxes, a large crate and a scattering of furniture.

Jac dragged the boxes to the edge of the hatch for easier unloading, opened the crate to find what looked like an entire dinner service for twenty four diners, prodded the six chairs (two broken legs, one sagging seat, one splintered back between them), admired the washstand (which she thought she'd ask Adam and Henry to give her a hand getting down again) and decided the side table was fit only for firewood.

But Bertram had stashed the Isles of Scilly box away somewhere inconspicuous, not put it in a box of other stuff. She began to prowl around the edges of the space where the roof sloped down. Henry would not appreciate the spiders, she thought vaguely, then sat and contemplated Henry for a bit, in a way that made her regret asking Tamsin for dinner.

The torch rolled off her lap and she scrambled after it, then froze as the beam of light glinted off the corner of a tin box.

By the time she'd got it out and downstairs and the hatch closed, she was filthy and the exasperating thing was locked. "Behave like an adult," Jac muttered. That involved wiping the box clean then going and showering, changing, making a cup of tea and sitting down to approach unlocking it in a calm and logical frame of mind.

She managed the first part of the programme, then dumped her tool box on the kitchen table with the intention of applying simple brute force. But in daylight the box looked very familiar, with its black japanned finish and narrow red and gold lines. There was a cash box in the brewery just like that. Andy had found it and used it for odds and ends. And it had a key. The boxes were cheap and mass produced, she was sure, which might mean...

Jac put down the hammer and chisel and ran downstairs. Yes, Andy's odds and sods box was exactly the same and, when she got the key upstairs and applied some lubricant to the keyhole, the lock clicked open.

And inside was a mass of paper. *Letters.*

Jac lifted out the topmost one and unfolded it. Good quality paper crackled and a fine shower of red sealing wax fell out as she spread it open.

*Dearest,*

*He is suspicious, I know he is. He says nothing, only grows more cold and distant by the hour. And I fear what he will do if he discovers that it is you who has my heart. Oh, Bertram, do take care. He would not harm you physically directly, I am certain of that, it is not his way—but he could afford to hire ruffians and I could not bear it if you were hurt. Or worse.*

*We cannot go on, Dearest. It breaks my heart, but this must end.*

It was signed with a squiggle: possibly an H or an M or an N, Jac wasn't sure. She held it up to the light, then looked around for the torch to try shining that through, and realised she had left it in the attic.

Cursing mildly under her breath she unhooked the hatch and brought down the ladder again and then began to climb. Damn, she had left the torch switched on, it was still glowing in the corner where she had found the box.

And then, just as she was about to climb off the ladder onto the attic floor, she put her hand on something metallic and round. Her torch.

In the far corner a man stood up, an oil lamp in his hand. "Who are you? Get away from me! Dastard! You won't get away with this, I am armed!"

Jac shot back down the ladder, shoved it back, pushed up the hatch and then sat on the floor and had a quiet meltdown for a minute. There was silence from the attic above, no voice, no footsteps, so she went on hands and knees into the kitchen where her bag hung on the back of the chair, pulled out her phone and called Henry.

"I'm just leaving," he said and she heard the sounds of traffic. "Didn't take long, couldn't find anything that looked relevant, although there was something interesting. But—"

"Can you come here? My flat, now? Quickly. There's someone in the attic."

"Get out and go to the Tap," he said urgently. "I'm coming."

Jac hauled herself to her feet, wished she hadn't eaten those sandwiches, and then flopped into the chair. Henry was right, she should get out, but she realised she knew who that was up there: Bertram. Bertram hiding his letters. Bertram thinking she was someone sent to hurt him. All he could have seen was a tallish figure in trousers—she had pulled back her hair—so he must have thought she was a man.

She heard feet pounding up the stairs and on an impulse she couldn't explain, grabbed the box and shoved it into the cupboard under the sink as the front door began to reverberate.

"Jac!"

"Coming."

She opened the door and Henry almost fell in. He was panting and clutching one of the big spanners Andy used on the brewery pipes. "You weren't in the Tap! I told you to go to the Tap. Where is he?"

"Gone, I think. It was Bertram, but I didn't realise until I rang you and got my breath back. He must have thought I was a man, with me wearing trousers and my hair looking short. I came up through the hatch and he only had an oil lamp. I frightened him; he assumed I was coming to attack him."

"Why the devil should he think that? Wait here, I'll go up and check. How do you open this thing?"

Jac found she was quite happy to be the little woman and hide behind Henry's broad shoulders. She'd been up and down that ladder quite enough for one day, thank you. She handed him the pole with the hook on the end and stood back while he advanced cautiously upwards.

"Nobody here. There's a torch by the hatch. Yours?"

"Yes. Is there an oil lamp? You'll need to switch on the torch."

Henry's legs and feet disappeared, light bounced down. "Yes."

Jac moved to the foot of the ladder and raised her voice. "There wasn't one when I first went up. I looked around, moved some boxes closer to the hatch then came down. I had a shower and got changed, realised I'd forgotten the torch, went back up and there was Bertram."

"I'll bring it— Shit!"

"What?" Jac shot up the ladder and peered over the edge.

"It's warm." Henry stood there with the lamp in one hand, the other cupped around the glass chimney. "He really was here."

He came back down the ladder with the torch, handing the oil lamp to Jac first. They closed the hatch again, then retreated to the table with a bottle of wine.

"This must have been before you saw him in the beach hut," Henry said. "We know he didn't come back from that swim. What triggered this appearance, do you think? The first time it must have been you having the ledger."

*And this time I've taken his box of love letters.* "You are convinced I did see him then? Both times?"

"Yeah." Henry poured himself another glass of wine. "That lamp being warm... But why the attic?"

"Perhaps he was hiding the love letters from the lady with the threatening husband," Jac suggested, still oddly reluctant to say that she had found them. "He might not want to risk one of the servants finding them if he kept them in the house."

"I'll go up again and have a look."

"Pass down the boxes I'd moved to the hatch while you are up there, will you?" Jac asked. "Goodness knows what's in those. The crate has a dinner service."

Henry climbed up and, as soon as she heard him moving about, Jac rescued the box of letters and flipped through, scanning as fast as she could. They seemed to cover three months of rapidly escalating attraction and then, at the beginning of April, it seemed passion had overpowered them. The note had been written on a torn scrap of notepaper.

*I never knew. I never dreamed... Oh, my darling, how can I bear even to be with D after this? How can I act so he suspects nothing?*

And again, that odd initial of a signature. Frustrated, one ear on the sounds of Henry in the attic, Jac refolded the note and realised this one had an embossed crest at the top, mostly torn away, leaving only what looked like a pair of clawed feet and a flame on the scrap of paper.

A phoenix, like Henry's signet ring. Bertram had been having an affair with a Dumaine? And the obvious candidate was his three times great grandmother, the one who had a vague reputation for being fast, the one who had spent months away in Switzerland.

"Oh hell," she said. How would Henry take that news? An amusing bit of family gossip about an ancestor was one thing, but would adultery upset him or intrigue him?

"Jac? These boxes are too heavy to pass down. Shall I unpack them up here?"

"Yes, hang on, I'll pass you some bags for the stuff." She hid the tin box more securely in her wardrobe, then came back to the foot of the ladder. "Did you find anything?"

"No, but the dust is disturbed in that corner. You are right: when Bertram appears, he's solid, not a ghost."

The boxes proved to hold a man's clothing. Judging by the style, Jac guessed it must have been Bertram's, packed away by his housekeeper and never looked at again.

"A costume museum might be interested," she said. "They aren't in bad condition." Then, "Hell, look at the time. I need to do some shopping if I'm going to cook dinner tonight."

"Shall I take these downstairs?" Henry gestured at the clothing strewn around. "I can hang them all up in one of the spare rooms, let them air, check the pockets, that sort of thing."

"Great. I'll lock the door at the bottom, don't worry about this one," she called back as she went out to the stairs.

"Everything all right?" Andy asked as she passed through the bar. He had just locked the doors and cashed up for the afternoon, ready to straighten things ready for the evening opening, when their recently-employed barmaid Angie would come in to help him. "Saw Henry rushing through earlier. He looked a bit stressed."

"False alarm. Good business?"

"Excellent." Andy shuffled his feet and Jac wondered if he was about to ask for a pay rise. She'd been working it out and was pretty sure she could manage it. He certainly deserved it.

"Do you think we can redecorate soon?" he said instead. "The takings have been really good and I reckon if you were to risk a few hundred, it might pay off with the summer season coming. We'd need to start soon though, so as to lose as little trade as possible while we're closed."

"Good idea, Andy. But a rise for you is top of my list. We'll talk about it tomorrow," she called back over her shoulder as he gaped at her, the till drawer in his hands.

A lick of paint, some tubs, new chairs and tables for outside. No, not DIY. Jac stopped, turned round and looked at the Tap, then at Dumaine's Wine Bar. No, a proper professional job. It wasn't a big space; it would do no harm to see how much a proper designer would charge.

She strode across the Square to have another look at the interior of the wine bar. Rose Redmayne, Henry had said. Jac stopped to admire the door handle, an ornate brass affair with a bar between two bunches of grapes. It was clearly old and just right. She glanced up and saw the licensee notice over the door.

*Henry James d'Astarde Dumaine. Licensed to sell all intoxicating liquor for consumption on and off the premises.*

*D'Astarde.* The realisation had her standing stock-still in the middle of the entrance and she had to step aside with an apology when a young couple with a buggy tried to come out.

That was what the initials under his several greats grandfather's portrait stood for. It must be a family name from their French heritage. And that was what Bertram had meant—not *dastard*, but d'Astarde. Hermione had been Bertram's lover and her husband had so alarmed Bertram that he had not wanted to come back to Little Piddling after his miraculous rescue.

Poor things, Jac thought, walking towards the shops. It must have seemed hopeless and Mr Dumaine had been a wealthy and powerful man from what she had read in the local history books. Bertram wouldn't have stood a chance if his rival had turned on him; he would probably have put him out of business, drummed him out of town.

It was an effort to think about what to cook for dinner with that on her mind. And what to tell Henry? Would it concern him that his ancestress had had an affair? Probably not, although you never knew how people would react to the skeletons in their family closet.

Hermione had written to Bertram of her anxieties over her husband, then Jac had loomed up in the attic like the hitman of his nightmares. No wonder the discovery that his wonderful new recipe had been stolen had made him so distracted that he'd almost lost his life.

And that was another thing, she realised as she stared blankly at the display outside the Gaol Street Greengrocer's, Bertram had clearly decided that Dastardy Dumaine was responsible for the theft, so that was a double hit for Henry.

But it was a long time ago, Jac told herself as she exited the shop with a bag full of salad and new potatoes and made for the Old Town Hall Dairy and Deli. Cheese soufflé followed by a choice of either *tarte citron* or *tarte chocolat* from Prunella's Patisserie: that would work, she decided. It would be fine if Tamsin was a vegetarian and, surely, she'd have mentioned it if she was vegan? It was also an easy meal to prepare whilst worrying—despite their rep, soufflés always behaved for Jac.

It was not until she was toiling up the stairs with her loaded bags that Jac wondered just why she was so concerned. It was pointless to feel guilty about Bertram—she had done nothing deliberate to cause him to appear. No, it was Henry she was worried about. Henry's feelings, Henry's reaction.

*Because I'm falling in love with the man*, she admitted to herself as she dumped the bags on the kitchen island. *And I feel guilty about being suspicious of him in the first place and now I don't know how he feels about me.*

Henry hadn't said anything about tricky emotional things like feelings. He'd made it clear he didn't play the field and that while this—whatever it was—lasted, they were an item, but that was it.

The sex was excellent and it would be no lie to describe them as friends, but however much she prodded and poked at her inner workings, Jac could not convince herself that this was liking or desire or friends-with-benefits. She was in love with the man.

Which was absolutely wonderful of course, provided Henry came to feel the same. If not, it was going to be damn painful living and working literally on his doorstep when this came to an end and he moved on to someone else or just decided the affair had run its course.

She could tell him.

Jac stood with a box of eggs in one hand and contemplated the idea. Just how did you do it? Shriek it in a moment of passion? Have a serious discussion about Where This Is Going? Get him drunk and tell him? Wander hand-in-hand along the beach at sunset and confess it?

*And then sink slowly through the floor with embarrassment while keeping a brave smile on your face when he says, kindly, that he doesn't feel the same way.*

The serious discussion option might be the most dignified...

Love was not supposed to make you confused and anxious. Love was supposed to be wonderful. Another illusion shattered.

# Chapter Five

Henry arrived at half past six with a selection of wine, by which time Jac had got the soufflé in the oven, the salad prepared and the potatoes were almost ready. The apartment was also tidy and she had showered, slapped on some make-up and was laying the table.

She had also, by an effort of will, talked herself into accepting that it was best to let things take their course with Henry, see how their relationship felt after another week or so.

"Don't you dare," she warned as he put down the wine and advanced purposefully around the table. "I've just beaten my hair into submission, put on some slap and Tamsin will be here any moment. And I don't want to open the door to her looking as though I've just been ravished."

"I can do smooth," Henry said, catching her, sweeping her into a dip that would have caused Rudolph Valentino to gasp in envy and kissing her. "There. Not a hair out of place and lipstick not smudged." He set her back on her feet.

"No, but you are wearing most of it," Jac pointed out and laughed when he cursed and made for the bathroom. She'd show him Hermione's love letters when Tamsin had gone, she decided. It was only fair.

"That went well." Henry came in from putting Tamsin into the taxi he'd insisted on calling for her.

Jac straightened up from the dishwasher and pressed the "On" button. "Yes, she's nice, isn't she? Pity she didn't find anything helpful with all that internet searching, but it was a long shot. And she was thrilled when you offered her whatever of Bertram's clothes she wanted. Having the top hat and the frock coat on display in their pub will be great. I'm really tempted to take her up on her offer to visit St Mary's."

"Yeah, me too. Shall we see if the town museum would like the rest of the things? I could give them a ring in the morning."

"Good idea." Jac fetched mugs while Henry filled the kettle. "What?"

The smile still lifted the corner of his mouth. "Our first dinner party was a success and we make coffee together like a couple."

"Yes." Jac managed a smile despite all the breath leaving her lungs. "Don't we?"

"It's good." Henry measured coffee into the cafetière with close attention, then looked up suddenly so he caught her staring, held her gaze. "I like this." He reached for the kettle. "There was something I wanted to ask you. A proposition." He poured the boiling water while Jac's insides seethed in unison. "Let's sit down, talk about it."

They sorted the coffee and sat and Henry said, "We've got a lot in common."

"Yes." The mouthful of coffee went down like lava.

"I wondered whether there might be some benefit in working together with the two businesses."

"Oh." Jac added an entirely unnecessary spoonful of sugar to her mug.

"Start off with some joint PR, mutual promo. Do something with a theme in both venues."

Jac pulled herself together. "Attract people into the Square. Good idea. I haven't got much of a budget for that sort of thing, though. I don't want to hang off your coat tails."

"I could have a look at your books, if you like," Henry offered. "I guess I've had a bit more experience and I spent a lot of time with my accountants when I was starting up to really get the hang of things. I might be able to make some suggestions about where you could cut some corners, shift things about." He shrugged. "It's not as though we're in competition, right? More complementary."

"Yes, why not? Great. Thanks for offering." The smile was pretty good, she reckoned, catching a glimpse of her reflection in the uncurtained window. It felt as though it had been stapled on. "We'll talk about it tomorrow, shall we? When we've got clear heads. I think that was one glass of wine too many."

"Sure. Sleep on it. Oh, yes, I didn't tell you what I found at the newspaper offices—the birth announcement for my two times great grandfather."

"Hermione's son?"

"Yes. And it was the Christmas after she got back from Switzerland, so she must have gone for her health."

"Yes. Right. Perhaps she was suffering from morning sickness or something and they thought the mountain air would do her good."

Jac did some frantic calculations in her head. Could the child have been Bertram's? D'Astarde suspects the affair, sends Hermione off to Switzerland, puts the frighteners on Bertram…

Poor Bertram must have lived with that anxiety and harassment for weeks until he was in such a state that he was careless swimming and decided not to return when he was rescued. Then Hermione came home and somehow convinced D'Astarde that the child was his. It could have been: he wasn't likely to have been very sensitive to her reluctance to sleep with him and, in those days, what the husband wanted, the husband got.

Poor Hermione, believing her lover dead, not certain who the father of her chid was, on tenterhooks as he grew up, looking for a resemblance one way or another…

Jac would make up her mind tomorrow about showing Henry the letters. She was feeling too unsettled now, what with the wine and the shock of what Henry's proposition had turned out to be.

"I think I'll go to bed in a minute," she said as the clock struck eleven.

"OK." Henry stood up, dumped his mug in the sink and leant over to kiss her. "Get some sleep. You look tired."

"Thanks, just what a girl wants to hear."

"Tired but gorgeous," he amended. "I'll check the downstairs door. Shall we discuss the PR thing tomorrow afternoon? I've got to spend the morning at the vineyard."

"Sure. Night." *Love you.*

Jac slept surprisingly well considering that she had switched off the light expecting to lie awake agonising over Henry, or listening to Bertram marching up and down in the attic overhead. She had fallen asleep almost at once and woke up before the alarm without a hangover and feeling remarkably calm.

He wanted to co-operate, that was sensible. It would bring them closer together. And she could surely swallow her pride and learn from his experience now she trusted him not to be acting as a business rival. And, after they'd had their discussion that afternoon, she'd tell him about the letters because she couldn't hide them from him.

But if they were going to be doing joint promo, then she wanted to do something about the look of the Tap. She'd go over to Piddling Magna after breakfast, have a look at Rose Redmayne's shop and, if it looked as though she might be able to afford a consultation, she'd go in and make an appointment. If she rang first, then turned up and found it was going to be wildly expensive, that would be embarrassing.

It was only fifteen minutes on the bus from the Prom to the market square in Little Piddling's inland neighbour and Rose Redmayne's shop was easy to find.

Jac browsed around the retail section for a while, checked out the prices, which seemed reasonable and the quality, which was just what she'd expected from the work at the wine bar.

"Can I help?" A young woman came out from the back.

"I wanted to discuss some design work. I haven't an appointment. But my name's Jacintha Francis and it's about the Brewery Tap in Little—"

"Oh, Henry's made up his mind, has he? That's great. Do come on through."

*What?* Jac went through into a small studio with a big MAC on one desk, a drawing table and a whole series of mood boards propped up.

"Henry?"

"Yes. I mean I was delighted with the concept when he first approached me, months ago, and I admit I did a fair bit of work on spec and then he told me he'd missed buying the brewery. So I was thrilled when he rang yesterday and said to go ahead and work it up."

Something cold was slithering down Jac's spine, but she found a smile. "It's very exciting, isn't it? I thought I'd drop in and see where you are so far. I manage the place, you see."

"Right. Of course, you are Jac. Henry mentioned you. OK, I'll just get it up. Take a seat."

Jac watched while Rose brought up not just the ground plan of the Tap, but the whole brewery.

"That's what you've got at the moment. Now, with you not needing all that space for the actual brewery—this bit at the front was originally stabling for the dray horses and the drays and so forth—we can put the dividing wall with its large clear panels all along here, then this part becomes the casual dining and audience space. There's a small stage for performers and I've got a couple of dressing rooms and a loo in the back there.

"Then the Tap gets a makeover like this, keeping the charm of the old interior as much as possible, and double doors through to the new dining area."

"Marvellous," Jac said. Her voice seemed to be coming from a very long way away. "Great concept."

"Well, I think so and I'm glad you agree. Henry wanted it to complement Dumaine's Wine Bar which would retain the rather more formal restaurant feel, while the Tap would be casual drinking and eating and performance space for musicians, stand-up, poetry and so forth."

"It would certainly unify the Square."

"Henry's a Dumaine and you know what they're like," Rose said. "My partner Daniel says the Dumaines have always been a cut-throat lot." She laughed. "Well, I exaggerate, but you know what I mean."

"Oh yes, I know." Jac echoed the laugh. It sounded hollow. "Do you have something I can take back? On paper," she added when Rose began to say something about shooting it over. "I want to pin it up, show the bar staff. It will be easier that way."

"Yes, of course." Rose touched keys and a large printer clicked into life, rolling out a big sheet with the whole ground floor plan on it. "Do you want the bar design sketches as well?"

"Not yet, thank you. This is… very informative."

There was a maddening half-hour wait for the bus, which then turned out to be the one that went all round Piddling Magna, then out to the hamlets of Station End and Starveling Acre, before finally crawling back to Little Piddling.

By the time Jac was off the bus and striding into Brewery Square on a tide of anger and hurt, she was in a mood to upend a wine bar owner into the nearest barrel of Prime Piddle and hammer the lid down tight. The sight of Henry just leaving by his own front door sent her storming across, the plans rolled tight in her fist like a light sabre.

"Henry Dumaine, I want a word with you."

He took a step back into the hallway.

*No idiot, Henry*, Jac thought. *He knows trouble when he sees it. And I'll give him trouble.*

"Jac? You look upset."

"Upset?" She followed him in, slammed the door and flourished the roll of plans. "So you want to have a look at my books, do you?

Offer some advice? Find out all the weaknesses in my finances, all the ways you can undermine my business?"

"What? Jac—"

"A bit of joint promo, you said. A joint PR strategy, you said. Nothing about taking over my brewery or extending your damned wine bar into the Tap along with your *performance space.* We could rename the area, call it Dumaine Square. Although Bertram would probably call it Dastard's Square."

Henry grabbed the end of the plan that was being jabbed at his face and let it unroll. "Oh. Bugger."

"Yes. Bugger," Jac repeated, suddenly calm. "I trusted you, against my instincts. I thought we were friends. Lovers. And all the while I was falling in love with you, you were after my business. It seems to run in the family." She marched straight through the hall into the kitchen, banged through the fire door and ran upstairs.

Behind her, she heard Henry curse, the sound of skidding feet, then she had the door shut and locked.

Jac slumped back against it, jolted as a fist thumped on the other side.

"Let me in!"

"You have to be joking."

"Jac, I had those plans drawn up when the brewery was on the market, before you bought it. Then I got distracted with problems at the vineyard and you bought it."

"And yesterday you ring up the designer and give her the go-ahead, after you've thought of a way to get into my financials. You must have found it as easy as getting into my knickers."

Henry swore again—this time it was decidedly Anglo-Saxon. There was silence, then the door shifted as though someone had slumped against it on the other side. Jac didn't move.

"Jac, did you say you'd fallen in love with me?"

"Go ahead, remind me what a complete gullible idiot I am."

"I... Jac, I wanted to surprise you."

"You certainly achieved that," she said bitterly, her cheek pressed against the door panel, her lips close to the edge. She could almost feel the heat of Henry's face pressed against the other side, the texture of his stubble. "You're a real Dumaine, aren't you, even if D'Astarde isn't your ancestor."

"What do you mean?"

"Wait."

Jac went and found the box of letters, took the one on the scrap of embossed paper and slid it under the door. "Do the maths."

There was the sound of someone sitting down with a thump on the top step. "Where did you get this?"

"There was a boxful in the attic. That's what Bertram was looking for. I was trying to work out how to tell you tactfully that he might be your ancestor and not Dumaine."

Silence. Then Jac heard footsteps going downstairs, the bang of the ground floor fire door. That was that, then. She turned to the table to replace the letters in the box; they probably belonged to Henry, after all.

There was a sound from the door and, as she looked up, a large sheet of yellowed paper slid underneath. Jac approached it cautiously, then saw what it was.

*Piddling Perfection* ran the heading in flowing copperplate and beneath it was the unfortunate brewmaster's recipe and instructions for Bertram's brilliant new beer.

"Where did you get it?" Jac found she was sitting on the floor.

"In the cellar. I couldn't sleep last night, I kept thinking about… things. Oh, damn it. About you. And I was all keyed up to discuss a partnership, a proper one, not just some co-operation, and at first light, I thought I'd get up and try and find the cellar, see who owned it, you or me, just for something to do."

"And it's yours?"

"I finally found the trapdoor under the rug under the kitchen table. Hadn't been opened for decades by the look of it. There was a big tin trunk down there. I smashed the padlock. Great great whatever D'Astarde was a nasty piece of work. There are all sorts of things in there that he collected. He liked to know people's secrets, that's obvious.

"Jac, if he's not my ancestor, all I can say is, damn good thing. Will you let me in now?"

She stood up, looked at the door, wishing she could see through it. Henry could have destroyed that recipe; she'd have never known. The key turned in the lock and she twisted the handle and braced herself for whatever was coming next.

Henry walked in looking grim, took her by the shoulders, hauled her close and kissed her; then, just as Jac found herself kissing him back, set her away.

"We've both made a right balls-up of this," he said. "I should have told you what I was planning, you should have told me about

Bertram and we both ought to have trusted each other to have a straightforward discussion about business."

"Yes. Yes, we should."

"OK. Me first." Henry went and sat down at the table. "You sit the other side, because there are things I'd rather be doing than talk.

"I told you the truth down there about the original plans I had done and why I didn't buy the brewery—a potentially nasty cashflow situation with the winery equipment that turned out to be a false alarm.

"Then I got to know you." His smile came and went in a flicker, but something inside her warmed and relaxed. "And I could see how we would work together and how the businesses would work in unison. I want a partnership, Jac, and I should have come right out with it, instead of pussyfooting about, leading up to it by talking about joint promo."

"A partnership?"

Henry was contemplating his joined hands, then he took a deep breath and looked up. "Actually, I was wondering what you'd think about getting married."

"Married? But… But you never said anything about even wanting to live together."

"We are already. It's just rather a big house."

"But you don't love me."

"How do you know?" He grinned suddenly. "Jacintha, I love you. I realised about a week ago what was wrong with me, but I thought you were the independent businesswoman type who wouldn't want to get that closely involved with a bloke. I thought if I could persuade you into a bit of a business partnership, then I could work up from there."

"I don't want to get involved with a bloke. Not with any old bloke, just with you." When he smiled back, she was seized with doubts all over again. "Henry, you're bringing so much more to the party than I am. The wine bar's established, you've got the vineyard and winery. I've got a brewery lurching out of the doldrums and a shabby little pub."

"We'll work it out," he said comfortably. "Besides, you bought cheap and the potential value is huge. You've got a winner, if the new beer is as good as Bertram thought it would be. The area inland is full of pubs that are free houses—you can sell to them once you get up to speed. You could move out of this apartment and let it out as a holiday flat and then we could buy that derelict terrace on the other side of the square, refurbish it, turn it into holiday cottages. We'll make Brewery Square the upmarket must-visit district of Little Piddling."

"We could do all that without getting married. I don't want a husband to look after me."

Henry looked mildly affronted. "And I don't want a wife to look after the house and pair up my socks. I want a partner for everything." He shifted in his chair. "I don't know how to convince you I'm not just saying *I love you* because you said it first."

"Did you believe me?"

"Yes." He looked at her, clearly puzzled. "I don't know why, though."

"And I believe you," Jac said. "And I have no idea why, either. And I think it's like me believing in Bertram when I first saw him. I didn't want to and it seemed so unlikely, but instinct told me it was true."

There was a muffled thump from overhead.

They both stood up. "Either a tile's fallen off, or there's a pigeon in the loft, or that's Bertram." Jac looked round for the torch.

"We ought to give him his letters back," Henry said. "Should we lock it again or admit we've read them?"

"Lock it," Jac said. "I don't want to upset him any more than he is already."

She lit the oil lamp and Henry hooked down the ladder, then climbed up into the darkness. When he got up, he leaned down, took the lamp from her and straightened again.

Jac saw the soft glow move away, then jerk suddenly.

"Mr Bascombe?" Henry said. "I'm afraid we inadvertently moved something of yours when we were tidying up."

Jac climbed the ladder, looked through the hole. Henry and Bertram confronted each other, then Henry held out the tin box in his hand.

"Who are you?" Bertram demanded, snatching it back, almost knocking over the lamp at his feet in the process.

"I'm Henry D— Henry. A descendant of yours. You are time-travelling again."

"It is very confusing. And upsetting," Bertram said stiffly. "But... A descendant? Not... Hermione?"

"Hermione is going to be perfectly fine, but I think you are right to be worried about Dumaine," Henry said. "And don't be concerned about your brewery, because a descendant of yours will be running it again."

"Why are you crying?" he asked Jac when he followed her back down the ladder.

"Because of his expression when you said a descendant of his would run the brewery. He was so happy." She blew her nose briskly. "I suppose I'll have to marry you now."

"I didn't mean me. I thought perhaps you ought to call it The Bascombe and Francis Brewery and then, one day, we can make it And Sons or Daughters or Family, depending."

"Children?" Jac stared at him.

"Well, they do happen. Look, I know this is a bit old school, but I've been meaning to do this properly when I finally thought the time was right." He went down on one knee and dug in the pocket of his jeans. "I've been carrying this around, waiting for the right moment and I think this might be it." He held up a ring. The diamond in the centre sparkled in the lamplight and the sapphires surrounding it glowed a deep and mysterious blue. "It was Hermione's, and Gran told me it was her mother's, not the ring D'Astarde gave her."

"Oh, Henry."

"I'd rather you said, *Yes, Henry* and saved the, *Oh, Henry* for later. Will you marry me, Jac? I do love you very much."

She took his hand, pulled him to his feet. "Yes, Henry." And when she kissed him, he took her left hand and slid the ring on her finger and it fitted perfectly.

As the Town Hall clock struck twelve—two minutes before the church clock, because, after all, this was Little Piddling—Jac and Henry wandered barefoot along the beach, hand in hand.

Jac had remembered that the beach hut had a bed, one that she'd made up ready for lazy siestas, and had never had the time to use. It had seemed the perfect place to consummate their engagement along with a bottle of wine and a picnic dinner.

"One last stroll?" Jac had suggested when Henry had been remaking the bed in case they actually managed to get some sleep.

They wandered as far as the rocks at the eastern end of the beach, then turned back. "Look," Jac murmured. "Someone else is about. See? On the boardwalk just outside my hut."

"It's them," Henry whispered back.

The man straightened up from kissing the woman and replaced a tall hat on his head, then offered his arm. There was the hiss of fine fabric sliding over sand as she turned, her long skirts dragging behind her, and they walked quietly away and vanished into the shadows. Into the past.

# THE END

## *About Louise Allen*

Louise Allen lives in a village on the North Norfolk coast and is the award-winning author of over seventy books—historical romance, timeslip romantic mystery and non-fiction. She collects Georgian prints and newspapers and is bullied by her garden. You can find out more at louiseallenregency.
She blogs about the 'long' Regency at janeaustenslondon.com and is on Twitter and BlueSky @LouiseRegency

### *Want Louise's latest book?*
You can get Louise's latest book, and find earlier ones you may have missed, at author.to/LouiseAllen
where you'll also be able to follow Louise for her latest releases

## *Dear Reader from Libertà Books*

This was our first venture into a beach reads anthology so, if you enjoyed these new stories, we'd be really grateful if you could leave a review at your local retailer or on your favourite reader website. Your review can help other readers to find and enjoy our books, too.
*Thank you!*

Libertà Books is a light-hearted website where readers and authors chat and laugh about books, films, history, costume, the craft of writing and much, much more. There's a new Libertà blog every Sunday.

The Libertà hive features four multi-published authors:
Sophie Weston
Joanna Maitland
Liz Fielding
Sarah Mallory/Melinda Hammond
And favourite authors blog as guest contributors

To sign up for Libertà's occasional newsletters, click on the Subscribe button at the top of the sidebar on the Libertà website at
https://libertabooks.com

The Libertà hive tweets @LibertaBooks
and most of us are also on BlueSky [bsky.social]
@joannamaitland
@lizfielding
@sarahmallory
@louiseregency
You can also find us on FaceBook/libertabooks